SABOTAGE

Fletcher Knebel

SABOTAGE

DOUBLEDAY & COMPANY, INC.
GARDEN CITY, NEW YORK
1986

Library of Congress Cataloging-in-Publication Data
Knebel, Fletcher.
    Sabotage.
    I. Title.
PS3561.N4S23   1986   813′.54   86-4555
ISBN: 0-385-23289-6

To Constance

SABOTAGE

1

He met her at twilight at the outdoor bar of the Royal Hawaiian Hotel, the old pink palace of the Pacific now imprisoned by the concrete towers of Waikiki like a lone rosebush in a canyon.

It was the quiet hour when the sun sank into the sea off Honolulu, muting bald daylight into the soft pastels of evening. Shadowed surfers rode their last long waves, a haze veiled the gullied flanks of Diamond Head and the glassware made small subdued sounds as if muffled for the night. The Mai Tai bar, magnet for tourists though it might be, seldom failed to soothe him and it had become his Friday custom to stop by for a drink on his way home from work.

"The usual, Mitch?" The bartender, a big Tongan with a scar on his cheekbone, already was pouring Scotch over cubes of ice and reaching for a twist of lemon with his other hand.

He debated crossing up Joey by ordering a gin and tonic, but at that moment came a scent of perfume on a curl of breeze. She slid onto the empty seat between Mitch and the next customer, denoting intent to possess regardless of neighboring wishes. Mitch took his usual inventory: neither beautiful nor plain, a touch of class, certainly attractive. She wore her brown hair pinned up. A simple white knit sheath, cut low in front, hinted that the label probably bore the name of an expensive designer.

"I'll have the usual without the twist," she said.

Joey stood before her, palms on the bar. He looked from the woman to Mitch with a quizzical grin that seemed to ask: you guys teaming up to kid me or what?

Mitch answered with a shake of his head. "She looks fresh from the mainland, Joey. She must want a mai tai."

"Definitely not." The emphatic tone surprised him. "I can't stand all that fruit. Just the usual, please, Mr. Bartender."

There was a crisp decisiveness about her that while not warring with the feminine—ruby tinted fingernails, full breasts, peach fuzz on her bare arms—compelled attention. Her height added to an aura of poise. Mitch, himself nudging six feet, guessed she measured only a few inches less. But so what? Tall or short, fat or skinny, they came by the planeload, these secretaries and waitresses and career women from the mainland, all hungering for an airline poster romance.

"One usual, no twist," Joey placed a Scotch-on-the-rocks before her with a swift you-take-it-from-here glance at his regular customer.

Don't bother, Joey, thought Mitch. He wasn't in the mood tonight for unknown females from the mainland. Truly beat this Friday. Been a bitch of a day and in the end, he lost the A.G.-Rot charter to Platou, thereby winding up zilch for the week. Tonight a short swim and dinner at the Outrigger, then maybe catch the movie at the Varsity and to bed alone before midnight.

Still, that perfume invited. Subtle yet insistent, as the wine ads put it. And a lady sharp enough to pick up on the "usual" deserved an answer. Why waste rudeness on a stranger?

He turned toward her. "Is Scotch-on-the-rocks the usual where you come from?"

"Let's see." She ran a finger lightly around the rim of the wide-mouthed glass while pretending to ponder the matter. "No, I'd say beer is more popular."

"That means you could be local. Beer's by far the big favorite in the islands." But he knew she was no kamaaina. He'd place her accent as somewhere in New England, though definitely not Boston. "Go to a baby luau over on Molokai and you'll drown in beer."

"Baby luau. What's that? A small outdoor barbecue?" She had smoky eyes, more gray than blue, that centered candidly on his for a second more than the conventional span for casual meeting.

"No. A kid's first birthday. The father throws a big feast for all his friends and neighbors. He'll spend a couple of weeks' pay on it."

"Did you have one?" She had paid no attention to the man on her left, sunburned beef in a splashy aloha shirt.

"No. I live here now, but I grew up and worked on the mainland. And you?"

"Grew up in New Hampshire."

"And now you live . . . ?"

"In Europe."

"Big place, Europe."

"Yes." Her smile, though easy and friendly, closed off that avenue. "Just your typical tourist, here for a week. Been to Maui and the Big Island. Now four nights in Waikiki."

"And your husband's up in the room showering?"

The scent of perfume arose again when she threw back her head in laughter. "Haven't had one of those in years." Mitch guessed her age at about his own, somewhere around forty. "But I had to laugh. The one I did have was always bathing and showering. A Mr. Clean."

For some reason, the blond hairs on her tanned arms gave him an erotic charge, and he became aware now of her legs, also tanned and trim. High-heeled sandals showed off toenails painted the same ruby shade as her fingernails. It wasn't fatigue he felt, after all, he decided, just a kind of pleasant letdown from a day of hard maneuvering.

The sun had vanished now and the ocean coasted in long mauve rollers toward the darkening shore and fringe of palms. Out on the beach one of the treasure hunters, headphones tuned to signals from his broom-like metal detector, swept the sand for lost coins and jewelry. "First time in Hawaii?" asked Mitch, aware that he, too, was scouting.

"No, third. I stayed a month once on account of that." She motioned with her drink toward the sea. Her voice had a full, throaty texture. "And that." She waved her glass toward Diamond Head and the lights along the shore. "Hawaii's the only state that imitates its own postcards."

"No. There's Alaska."

"Too cold," she snapped. Hunching her shoulders against imagined williwaws, she dismissed America's largest state. "This is the kind of weather I adore. If I were a flower, I'd be in perpetual bloom here." Like a cat, he noted, she had switched in an instant from arched back to a purr.

"Another?" He nodded at her glass. A dove flew in and perched on a strut supporting the bamboo-thatched roof.

"How about you? I'm buying."

"In that case . . ."

"Two more usuals," she said to Joey in a voice obviously accustomed to giving orders. "And put it on my tab, please."

Probably a buyer, women's apparel, or perhaps she owned her own shop, Mitch guessed. He pictured a display of expensive evening gowns, mannequins angled in modish ennui, in a store window on Paris's fashionable Rue de Rivoli or along Bruton Street in London. Interesting, this woman. His weariness had dropped away.

When Joey brought the refills, Mitch hoisted his for a toast. "To you, first woman to buy me a drink this year."

She clinked his glass, sipped at the Scotch, then trained the gray eyes on him. "And your wife? Is she at home, showering for dinner?"

Mitch laughed. "To steal your line, I haven't had one of those in years. Six, to be exact." He matched her candid look with an appraisal of his own. A bit of the patrician, very much the WASP, this haole from New Hampshire. A nice blend of the firm and the feminine. He'd always admired independent women. "But you look like you couldn't care less whether I was married or not."

"Not true." She turned full on her stool to face him. "I had a friend, Brenda Ueland, a wonderful woman, who died in Minneapolis at the age of ninety-three. She had three husbands and scads of lovers, and when it came to an affair with a married man she liked, she said fine, as long as he brought a note from his wife saying it was all right. I take my cue on married men from Brenda: no tickee, no washee."

"You bought a round of drinks," he said on impulse. "I'll spring for dinner—unless, of course, you're busy."

"No, I'm not busy, and yes, I accept. Here?"

"I thought you might like the Outrigger Canoe Club. Ever been there?"

"No, but I've heard of it. I'd like that. Am I dressed all right?"

"Perfect. Besides, you know in Hawaii you're always dressed all right. . . . Would you mind stopping by my apartment first for a couple of minutes? A guy is due at seven to see me. You can wait in the car."

"No problem."

They finished their drinks as night fell, blotting out the ocean save for the sound of small waves lapping the shore. Waikiki met the hour with a shower of lights, the trade winds creaked in the coconut palms, a dine-and-dance ship rose and fell on the horizon and Joey, with what in Tonga might pass as a smirk, refused Mitch's money when the haole woman from the mainland swept up both bar cards and handed him several bills.

"I've got my car here," said Mitch as they walked the long red carpetway through the Royal Hawaiian's marbled lobby. "Oh yeah, by the way, I'm Mitch Donahey."

"I'm Mona."

He waited a moment. "That's it? Just Mona?"

"Mona for now, okay." The "okay," a flat assertion, did not solicit consent.

As he drove his Mustang through Kapiolani Park, beneath the shivering ironwoods, she mentioned her trip to Maui. She had ridden a trail horse into Haleakala crater, "an awesome place where you can believe the old Hawaiian legends." But she spoke sparingly. She was not a chatterer and lapses into silence apparently did not bother her.

"I don't look forward to this chore," said Mitch as they neared his apartment. "The guy coming to see me is a jerk."

"Is it business?"

"No, he used to be my sergeant years ago in Viet Nam. Now he's second engineer on a tanker. He lives in L.A. but he vacations here a lot and he keeps pestering me. This time it's something about a sloop he's having sailed up here from Tahiti."

"If you don't like him, why don't you tell him to get lost?" In her throaty voice, banishment sounded alluring.

"I've tried. Bones Elger thrives on rejection."

His apartment occupied the top floor of a two-story frame house at the end of Kalakaua Avenue. Mitch pulled into the driveway beside a parked cream-colored sedan with two men in it, a Caucasian and a Japanese. The white man got out.

"Mitcher, you old bastard." He wore a chartreuse aloha shirt and he walked unsteadily to the side where Mona sat, leaned on the car and thrust his head inside. "How did a wimp like you luck into this beautiful stuff? Lady, you're risking your life with this character. Talks like a knee-jerk liberal, but he's really a rapist and a pillager from the Nam. Am I right, grunt?" A fetid mix of liquor and sour breath filled the interior.

Leaving the car, Mitch came around to join his visitor. "Hank, Mona. Mona, Hank." They nodded to each other. Mitch looked inquiringly toward the Japanese in the front seat of the sedan, but Hank made no move to introduce his companion who had a genial smile and the mark of affluence.

"Can't ask you in for a drink, Bones. We're due for dinner."

"Knock off that Bones crap, Mitcher. I told you that before." Intended as a threat, it came out as a whine. "Has your gorgeous friend got a last name?"

"When you're sober, Bones."

"Hank, goddam it."

"You wanted to see me. What's on your mind?"

"Like I told you, a friend is sailing my sloop up from Tahiti," said Elger. "He should arrive next weekend, so I'll fly over from L.A. to meet him. His name's Claude Bouchon."

"So?" Mitch found it difficult to be pleasant to this thin bony man in his aloha shirt, white polyester pants and white moccasins with gold buckles.

"I gave Bouchon your phone number and a map of this Diamond Head area. Maybe he can anchor out front of your place. We'll take you and your dish out for a Sunday sail."

"I don't know about the sail. But, sure, tell Bouchon to come on by. He can sleep on the lanai if he wants. He's welcome. . . . Anything else?"

"Shit, man, can't you spare five minutes and invite me in for a drink?" Elger's question seemed to exclude his friend sitting in the car.

"Can't. We're late now." He made contact with Elger's hand in what passed for a handshake and walked around to the driver's side of the Mustang.

"That's next weekend, Mitcher."

"Got it." Mitch put the car in reverse, backed into the street and drove off. He turned to Mona. "I can't stand that guy."

"You're angry." She purred it.

"Just the thought of that right-wing creep makes me angry."

"You said he was your sergeant in the Viet Nam war?"

"Yeah, I did an enlisted tour there. Hank Elger—we all called him

Bones—was one of those damn Rambo war lovers. A racist to boot. Gunned down civilians in a village once—but that's no story for tonight."

"He smelled like a saloon." She fanned the air. "And he's got a big sharp Adam's apple that bobs up and down when he talks."

At the Outrigger, the nearby beachside club on Kalakaua Avenue, their table faced the sea, banded by ivory light from the early September moon. A gentle breeze, a shade above cool, sauntered through the open-sided dining area. They both chose mahimahi, the tasty fish of Hawaiian waters, and Mona agreed to his selection of a California white wine.

"Do you have a woman here?" she asked after they exhausted some brief small talk about the weather and the day's news.

"I used to. We split up a couple of months ago. She wanted to get married but I'm not ready to try that again."

"So you play the field?" Her gray eyes studied him anew.

"Cautiously." Mitch grinned. "In fact, so cautiously, you almost couldn't call it playing. And it sure isn't a 'field.' "

"Why so careful? Doesn't fit the roving bachelor image."

"Energy. At my age, I conserve the stuff. I'm not decrepit, but the disco singles scene doesn't send me anymore."

"How about the church social scene?" She sipped at her after-dinner coffee. "I have a nephew who gets his best girls at the local Youth-For-Christ."

"I'm not a church type. Are you?"

"I'm not a believer anymore. But you know, I still go to church on Easter."

Mitch leaned forward on the table, closing the gap between them. "Let me guess which church." He looked her over in mock examination. "Okay, Mona. . . . Episcopal."

"That's right." She seemed delighted. "How'd you guess?"

"I went to Methodist Sunday School. The social-set girls all went to Trinity Episcopal. You've got that Episcopal look."

"Is it an attractive one?" Playful, she tilted her head.

"The tops. Classy too."

"What kind of work do you do, Mitch?" She still had that appraising look. He remembered the day, returning from Mexico, when a customs officer in Nogales studied him with the same quiet intensity.

"Most people ask that the first couple of minutes after meeting. It took you . . ." He glanced at his wristwatch. "Almost three hours."

"I have to care about the person before I care what he does."

"Hey, I like that. . . . Your turn to guess."

"Let's see." She gave herself to apparently serious pondering. "You're an executive, corporate type." When he shook his head, she said, "Lawyer." Flunked once more, she gave a last try: "Stockbroker."

"Half right. I'm a shipbroker, specializing in tankers."

"Oh." She studied him over her raised coffee cup.

"Yeah. If you're an oil company and you want to move your crude, you call me—or more likely one of my hard-ass competitors— and one of us will get a tanker for you."

"What's the name of your firm?"

"McCafferty & Sons, New York."

"Oh, yes. I've heard of it."

"You have?" He was surprised. "Not many people outside the trade know the names of the shipbrokers."

"Well, I have." She offered nothing further.

"And you. Do you own something or . . ."

"I work for a living," she cut in. "And frankly, on the job I work like hell." Again that abrupt switch from the softly feminine to the curtly masculine.

"At what, Mona?"

She hesitated as if weighing her answer. "Not now, please. I'm on vacation."

Sweetly compliant again, she agreed to an after-dinner drink and chose an Irish coffee to his brandy. They chatted, gently probing without appearing to, and it occurred to him that Mona was measuring him, inspecting him as she might a bracelet, a cheese or an exercise suit while shopping. He had heard women complain at a disco bar of feeling like meat in a market, and now the reversal struck him as funny. His laugh, however, came with a flick of embarrassment.

"Can you let me in on the joke?"

"It hit me that you're treating me as a body and you're trying to decide whether to go to bed with it."

"Oh, I'm sorry." She reached out and took his hand. "I wouldn't want to give that impression." Her smile danced. "Because I decided to do that some time ago—if you'll have me, that is."

"I wanted you back at the Mai Tai bar. Now I crave you."

"Terrific. It's been awfully long since a handsome man craved me. . . . And Mitch, treat me gently, won't you?"

"Trust me."

"It all comes down to trust, doesn't it?"

"Always. In my business, we do a $150,000,000 deal, including tanker and cargo, on one another's word. How about in yours?"

"Oh, no you don't." She laughed. "I told you I'm on vacation from all that."

He was signing the chit for dinner and drinks when he looked up suddenly. "Now, Mona, sweet lady, if we're going to bed together, I think the least you can tell me is your last name."

"My full name is Mona Susan Harkinson." She said it grudgingly as she might to a night desk sergeant.

"Mona Harkinson." He frowned, reflecting. "Sounds familiar. Haven't I heard that somewhere?"

"I doubt it. I'm not in the movies or any kind of celebrity thing."

"Harkinson." But the name triggered no immediate association. "So, how about my place? It's on the water, as you know."

"I'd love to see what it looks like inside." A faint flush came to her cheeks and, as she rose from her chair, he again caught the fragrance of her perfume.

The ride to the house took only a minute or two. His three rooms on the upper floor had a large lanai, cooled by steady trade breezes and overlooking such favored surfing waters as Rice Bowl, Tongg's and the Winch.

"Oh, I love it here." She hooked his arm and walked to the railing of the lanai facing the ocean. Two bandy-legged coconut palms leaned across the seawall and the narrow beach. "Look at that lane of moonlight on the water. Isn't that beautiful? All silvery and shimmering like sequined gowns at a great ball."

"I'm going to smoke some marijuana," he said. "Would you like to join me?"

She thought for a moment, studied him once more with that impersonal concentration of the Nogales customs officer. "Yes," she said, "I think I'd like that."

When he fetched a cigaret from his kitchen cache in the freezer, the familiar odor after lighting impinged on the domain of Mona's perfume. They sat down at a wicker table and each took several drags, grinning as they held in the smoke, avoiding talk. The hot acrid sensation at the back of his throat made him cough, but soon the languors of marijuana drifted through his senses, inducing that tranquil yet exhilarated mood he liked. Within minutes his world changed, the weed carrying him from the everyday sphere of work, form, rules, measurements, logic and numbers into that other realm where beings floated in a great pool of consciousness, reservoir for a kind of tribal tolerance shared by all. From the world of chop-chop, shape-up, stiff upper lip to the world of flow, bonelessness, surrender. From the world of judgment to that of acceptance.

He looked at Mona with new eyes. Where he had once seen a woman of poise and confidence, perhaps a mite too tall with an unnerving reticence about herself and a manner more direct than flexible, he now saw a beautiful woman in all ways perfect. Even the wisps of hair curling loose from her upswept coiffure looked just right, precisely in place as though shaped with meticulous care by a hairdresser of extravagant skill. Mona smelled delicious. Her presence beside him on the lanai appeared fated and he could not imagine a more delectable creature with whom to share this balmy night.

She crushed out the roach in an ashtray, tore open the paper and scraped the remnants of marijuana into a little pile. "For your next time," she said. "See what a frugal old hen I am?"

"Tsk, tsk. Self-disapproval—and from such a lovely chick."

She giggled. "Holy Jesus, at thirty-nine, I'm a chick?"

"Thirty-nine is perfect. You're ageless."

"What delightful pot!"

"The best. From the Big Island."

They were looking at each other, not appraisingly, but with a mutual absorption that soon excluded all but themselves. They drew closer. Mitch felt a rush, sensed the desire mounting in Mona.

They came together gently and their kiss had a tentative, savoring quality. When he held her, Mona's touch was feathery, her arms as soft as fleece, her breasts pressed but lightly against him. But soon a fire lit somewhere within her and she kissed him fervently, her tongue questing against his, her eyes closed, her body arching. He hardened at once and her lips crushed his, moving slowly back and forth as though feasting on a delicacy long-desired. Their embrace lasted for long minutes, two bodies clinging together while waves broke against the seawall, receded across the sand and surged back in rhythmic flood.

"I'd like to go to your bed now," she said when they parted at last.

Pleased by her simple candor, he took her hand and led her through the sliding doors, through the living room where he had left a floor lamp burning and into his bedroom. The moon's ivory light powdered the open louvers of the window and sketched pale designs on the spare Scandinavian pieces in the room, a dresser, two chairs, the sheeted bed without a coverlet.

They undressed wordlessly. He admired her as she stood in the nude, her long limbs and firm full breasts brushed by the splintered moonlight. The nest of pubic hair matched the soft brown of her upswept hairdo which now seemed quite formal and regal. As if reading his thoughts, Mona pulled out several combs, letting her hair cascade over her shoulders.

Desire seized him, but as they embraced and her long smooth body molded to his, he became tentative again. They were, after all, strangers, and this sudden physical intimacy with a woman he had known but a few hours gave him pause. It was as if they were guests in each other's homes and so must observe a certain etiquette, honor the amenities, before bursting into the earthy confidences and self-revelations that had lured them there in the first place. There was a shyness in her touch that he found beguiling, and he treated her as though she bore a label: Handle With Care.

They kissed, fondled and caressed each other in this preliminary tour of tactile discovery, but then a gust of passion blew in, seemingly out of nowhere, and shook them both. He swiveled against her, holding her fast, and soon she dropped to her knees, closed her lips about his hardened penis and massaged it with mouth and tongue. The sensation cut through him like knives of satin.

Now he felt a rush of intensity, a centering, a narrowing of focus that shut out everything save this splendid woman, these two uncovered bodies, this act of love of the moment, this room, this night, this hour. And though he could not know, he sensed in her every movement that Mona felt the same flight from the world of many to the world of two.

Soon he picked her up and laid her on the bed. Her hair flowed over the pillows and she lay with her eyes closed and her limbs extended. He bent his head and began kissing her body. Elation overwhelmed him, left him mindless, blocked out all but this erotic mission, a driving passion to pleasure this woman, a communion at the altar of sex.

He kissed her arms, face, throat, shoulders, spent so many tender minutes feeding open-mouthed at her breasts that she whispered a protest even as she pressed his head hard against her bosom. His fluttering massage of kisses covered her body, lingered at her toes and feet, then moved slowly up her inner thighs until his tongue plunged deep inside her. He lavished kisses on the entire sensual province, sucking, mouthing, nuzzling, darting within to thrust against her clitoris. A kind of carnal madness seized him, sending him into paroxysms. He covered her flesh with kisses, sank his face into her wide wet vagina and grabbed her rump with both hands. He fell into sexual frenzy, thirsting for her juices, thrusting his head into her as if to burrow back to the womb.

Later she moved away, swung around and took his penis in her mouth once more. Now they lay side by side, each feasting on the other, a slow torment of the senses. They went from lazy caresses to urgent mouthings, from coma-like bliss to wild hungering.

She got on top of him and pumped with her back arched, her hair flung back over her shoulders and a fevered, faraway look in her eyes. For a time she fondled her own breasts, then leaned forward to suck at his nipples. Mona, like Mitch, seemed possessed. She spoke not a word, her only sounds the cries and moans of passion.

At last he mounted her and they swept into an embattled rhythm, almost machine-like in its regularity and insistence, ever accelerating. Having nearly spent themselves in the long urgencies of love, from rapture to lust, they now must end it all swiftly or be consumed by nameless furies.

"Oh, yes, harder." Her first words in more than an hour. "Don't stop. We'll come together."

A typhoon of the senses flooded him. "Now!"

And when Mitch collapsed on Mona, they lay welded fast in sweat while their hearts beat in tandem and their breath came in staggered columns of near exhaustion. After a time she eased from beneath him, then lay close, her cheek pressed against his arm.

He wondered, as he did occasionally, at this storm that had inundated his mind and body and raged away, leaving him drained and numb. Was this strange journey into the recesses of another person the culmination of mere animal stimulus-and-response, no different from the copulation of coyotes, lizards or butterfish? Or was it a vehicle of deep awareness, a way of knowing another human being through a sharing of ancient longings and a ravaging hunger for union that transcended the loneliness of self? Had he and Mona touched, however fleetingly, a higher realm of the spirit?

"Mona, you're another Madam Pele, the volcano goddess." He felt clean, purged, fresh.

"It had been building up." She kissed his forehead. "I wanted you, maybe not the moment we met, but soon after. And it had been building for weeks—for a loving man like you." Mona snuggled against him. "Holy Jesus, it feels wonderful to be taken. I love to surrender, absolutely adore it. It's like something snaps in me and the defenses, the tight little knots, those steel bands, they all get vaporized, blown away, leaving me feeling very, very female."

"Very female is putting it mildly." Lovemaking, he noted, had loosened her tongue as well. "I love you that way."

"I know you do. But surrender scares me. I want it terribly and yet I'm repelled by it too. Do you know what I mean?"

"No, I don't. If two people trust each other, surrendering is no big deal."

"But it's so different from life out there. If I ever started giving in at work, whew, I'd be finished. You have to keep your guard up every minute, stay in charge."

To Mitch, still afloat on marijuana, the idea of guarded command seemed quite alien, even ludicrous. Why was this sweet-scented, abundant woman worrying her head about remaining in charge? Who was she, anyway?

"It seems weird to me that with all that beautiful lovemaking, being as close as we are, I still know nothing about you except your name."

"Fibber." She tapped his lips. "You know I grew up in New Hampshire, live in Europe, that I used to be married, but am now single. What else do you want to know?"

"Oh, all the mundane stuff you know about me." He yawned. "Occupation, home address, etc., etc."

"Well, let's see." She sat upright, pulled the sheet over her breasts. "Like you, I don't smoke tobacco. . . . I have one child, a daughter named Chris. She's sixteen and in school in Switzerland. Do you have kids?"

"Nope."

"I play good tennis, swim, ride horses when I get the chance, travel a lot, work my ass off and go to church Easters like I told you, stay fairly sane and happy, but wish to God I had a steady lover who'd send me the way you do."

"And your work is what?" He leaned on an elbow looking up at her. Her face was in shadow, but moonlight dappled her shoulders and already he felt desire mounting again. This woman had a strange new appeal for him.

"Would you believe cocktail waitress at the Frankfurt Hilton?"

"No, I would not. Try again."

"How about airline stewardess?"

"No. Not the type."

"There's a type?" Her hand drifted to his head and she began running her fingers through his hair. "Oh, I like that wiry feel. Very man stuff."

He would not be diverted. "I think you own an exclusive women's dress shop on a fashionable street in some European city."

Her laugh, rich and genuine, sank into him and he thought how easy it would be to fall in love with her. "Oh dear, no," she said. "You have me all wrong. Try some work 180 degrees from running a women's shop."

"Okay. You're a foreman in a Welsh coal mine."

Again her deep laugh captured the room. Like her throaty voice, it gave him pleasure, so far removed from those thin screechy cries that pierced the din at cocktail parties.

"You're lots closer, Mitch. Oh, much the same atmosphere. A coal miner! If you just put that mine shaft on. . . ." She halted. "No, that's enough. No more job talk."

He resented the rebuff. Was Mona into something illegal, drugs, a financial scam? Afraid of being traced? Had she given her right name? He felt used and was about to tell her so when she began nuzzling his neck and once more rumpling his hair. Soon she planted kisses on his chest as her long hair brushed his skin like feathers. He seized her, kissed her harshly, felt a new powerful urge and a desire to overwhelm her.

She responded with a strength that surprised him and soon they had surged into another round of lovemaking like combatants of sex, rough, demanding and commanding, insistent, heady with power. They tugged, fought, slapped, rolled about, nipped, crushed kisses. They loved on the very edge of violence, yet always drew back from the brink, becoming suddenly tender and vulnerable in a kind of kinesthetic apology before unpenning a new stampede of passion.

At the end, after an hour or more, the climax engulfed them together and within minutes they fell into sleep, that dark canyon where once again they followed separate trails.

They awoke with the first light of dawn, made love once more in the gray husk of the vanishing night, again fell asleep, then repeated the pattern in early morning after the sun climbed above Diamond Head and showered its rays over land and ocean. Glutted with sex and intimacy, heavy with fatigue, they ate breakfast on the breezy lanai, drinking coffee and eating papaya, soft-boiled eggs and toast as they watched the surfers catch their five-second rides on the green curls of Tongg's and the Winch.

Later Mitch would remember the next three days as one long sweet nerveless blur, the female scent of Mona, her lazing voluptuously about his apartment in the nude, several marijuana cigarets, her rich laughter and throaty voice, the overpowering odor of sex in the bedroom, the damp, crumpled sheets, Mona's shying again from more particulars about herself, the boom of surf against the seawall, the bright afternoons. He took Monday off from work and that evening they watched a massive orange sunset climaxed by the green flash as the top rim of the sun sank into the Pacific.

In bed an hour later, she suddenly wrenched free of his arms and ran for the bathroom. "Holy Jesus, it's after eight," she called. "I have to go. My plane leaves at eleven for San Francisco."

"I thought you said you had to leave Tuesday night."

"No, no. Monday night." Back in the bedroom, she rattled the hangers in the closet, searching for her dress. "I have to get back to the hotel and pack." Although she had spent only a few minutes in her hotel room, she had never checked out.

She hurried into her clothes, applied swift makeup before his dresser mirror, gathered up her handbag and then retrieved her shoes at the front door. Only then did she turn to him, her face sad with departure.

"Will you drive me to the hotel, please, Mitch?"

"Of course." He would, for that matter, put the car on ferries and drive her to Nepal if she asked.

"Oh, one thing." She centered those gray eyes on his. "Please don't tell anyone ever that I smoked grass. I'd be fired. Promise?"

"Not ever. It's a promise. And Mona, take it easy, after you pack your things at the hotel, I'll drive you to the airport."

But under the portico of the Royal Hawaiian, when he beckoned to a parking attendant, she shook her head. "No, this is it." She threw her arms around him, mashed his lips with a frantic kiss and then swung around to leave the car. He caught her arm.

"You can't leave like this, Mona. I've got to know where and how to reach you." He knew his voice had an imploring sound. God, he couldn't lose this woman. "Please, write down some kind of address for me."

"American Express, London. It'll get to me eventually." Then seeing his stricken look, she took his hands. "Listen, my sweet man. You have given me the most beautiful days and nights of my life. Now I must have time to absorb it all. My life isn't simple. I must leave it like this: sometime I'll get in touch with you."

"Sometime! Mona, please. Sometime could be ten years from now."

"I mean sometime before long, sometime this fall for sure." She kissed him quickly but tenderly. "I'm leaving now, Mitch, and God how I loathe it."

She stepped from the car and without looking back she walked swiftly to the hotel's wide entrance and disappeared into the ornate, red-ceilinged lobby.

He waited, dismayed and bruised, for several minutes, thought briefly of turning the car over to the valet parkers and waiting under the great banyan tree until she reappeared. He could follow her to the airport, then see her once more before her flight. No, he would not stoop to spying on her and tagging after her like some lovesick kid.

He drove off slowly, returning through Waikiki with its jarring lights, restless crowds, pedicabs and leafleteers. Back at his place, he walked across the wide lanai and into his apartment without stopping to watch the ocean, jeweled by moonlight, rolling toward the shore. In the bedroom, where he undressed slowly, her scent lingered like the dusk of summer.

Never had he felt so empty and lonely.

2

The moment he saw it, Mitch Donahey thought of Bones Elger.

Still yawning, he had padded out to the wide lanai of his apartment, coffee mug in one hand and the *Advertiser* in the other, prepared for his Saturday morning ritual: coffee and headlines at the wicker table and gazing out to sea while the trade breezes blew away the cobwebs of sleep.

It had been almost a week, five nights, count 'em, since Mona had swept in and out of his life, leaving him restless, perturbed, lonelier than he had ever been and yes, resentful. He had begun wondering whether she were a shady lady of some kind, maybe even a hooker on vacation, who needed to get laid and picked a decent-looking body out of the pack to do the job. Yet night prowler or not, she fascinated him. He could not put her out of mind. She stuck like glue.

Leaning back in the wicker chair, he took a sip of coffee and looked out to sea. There, not far from shore, he saw a bare-masted sloop, deck tilted sharply and bow thrust skyward as if cresting a wave. Of elegant lines, though old and scarred, the vessel lurched sideways with each rise and fall of the ocean. Caught on the reef?

Mitch went indoors to fetch his binoculars, then returned to focus on the sailboat. It had driven high and hard on the reef and was in danger of smashing itself beyond repair unless soon freed by means not immediately apparent. The wooden mermaid at the bow had lost her nose and several scales as well.

Halfway between boat and land a dinghy moved toward shore, sculled by a lean unshaven man wearing a ragged blue shirt and a tasseled stocking cap, long faded. He had loaded a mound of gear aboard and was heading his tub-like craft toward Mitch's place. Morning surfers, neglecting their sport, floated on their boards as they watched the stranger and his stranded vessel. The sun climbed higher over Honolulu and Diamond Head, showering its clean white rays over Kapiolani Park and the far end of Kalakaua Avenue.

The apparent master of the shipwreck beached his dinghy and lifted his bundles of belongings over the seawall. Some of the gear was wet, so he spread all of it out beneath a coconut palm in the yard: clothes, radio, stereo set, sheath knife, sleeping bag, rifle, a carton of papers, some books. When Mitch pointed to a spiral iron stairway, the stranger climbed the steps to the second floor.

The weathered boatman had pale blue eyes and a roguish air that his look of embarrassment did not quite dispel. The frayed woolen stocking cap, tassel dangling, seemed curious headgear in the tropical trade breezes skipping across the spacious lanai.

Mitch put out his hand. "Mitch Donahey."

"I thought this was your house. I'm Claude Bouchon." The Claude rhymed with "ode" and the Bouchon had the French nasal intonation. He shook hands firmly, his own calloused hand deeply tanned. "First time in my life I hit a reef, but I make a grand slam when I do it." He shrugged in the fatalistic Gallic salute to human folly.

"Yeah, you got a mess out there, Claude. You better have a wide ass because Henry Elger's going to have a piece of it. What the hell happened?"

"I came up from Tahiti okay and put into Waikiki yacht basin late last night. Then I went out and got drunk at one of those Korean hostess bars." He tapped a cigaret from a blue pack of Gauloises. "This morning I pull out the map Hank gave me and sail down here to anchor." He lit the cigaret and took a deep drag. "I came in too far. *Zut, alors.* Never sail with a bad hangover."

"How long did it take you from Tahiti?"

"I make it alone in twenty-eight days. Then the reef." Bouchon tried to appear contrite, but came off looking mischievous, a puzzling mien for a man apparently in his forties.

Mitch brought out another cup of coffee from the kitchen, Bouchon accepted gratefully, but waved off a suggested shot of whisky.

"Too much to do this morning." He looked at his gold-banded wristwatch, took a swallow of the hot coffee and wiped his mouth on the back of his hand. Then he lit another Gauloise. "Two big phone calls to make. . . ."

"Tell me first how you got hooked up with Elger and his boat," Mitch broke in.

"Okay." Swiftly the sailor ran through the gist of his story while he smoked and gazed sadly at the sloop which heaved with a shudder of mast at each wave breaking against her hull.

A transplanted Frenchman, he made his living in Tahiti, he said, running day charters of his own snappy ketch for the Japanese and American tourists who swarmed over the island. The ketch rode snugly in her berth in a Tahitian cove at the moment, thanks. One boozing night in Papeete he met a skinny tanker engineer who bought drinks for all comers. It turned out that the tanker officer, an American named Henry Elger, had come into a lot of money and recently had purchased an old but seaworthy thirty-eight-foot sloop named *Buffy.*

"There she sits." Bouchon nodded toward the wrecked boat. *"La Buffy."*

Couldn't have happened to a nicer guy, thought Mitch with gratifying malice. Now just keep quiet and listen, he counseled himself, and you might learn something new about the man who plagues so many of your nights.

Elger, Bouchon related, wanted his new possession sailed to Los Angeles, but did not relish the long ocean voyage when he spent so much time at sea anyway. More boozy talk led to a deal: Bouchon would sail the *Buffy* to Los Angeles via Hawaii for $2,000 and expenses, including return air fare. After they sobered up, the tanker engineer accompanied him several times while Bouchon sailed the sloop to nearby Mooréa and farther northwest to Bora-Bora. Satisfied with Bouchon's seamanship, Elger stocked the sailboat with food stores and wished him good luck. Bouchon urged him to insure the craft, but Elger refused, claiming the high premium wasn't worth it for a craft that cost him but $35,000. Bouchon sailed north alone after a friend, a good hand around boats, bugged out at the last minute.

Save for one brief storm, the voyage proved uneventful, even dull. He sighted the big island of Hawaii two evenings ago off his starboard bow, thus confirming his navigation, and set course for Honolulu harbor, arriving last night. This morning he sailed back to Diamond Head, looking for the house where Mitch lived. His head, which was growing another Eiffel Tower inside it, damn near exploded when he struck the reef two hours ago and tore the hull open.

He had spent the time since then assessing the damage and gathering ship's papers and personal belongings. The reef had holed the sloop just below the waterline. He tried to plug the break with sailcloth, rags and bunk sheets, but seawater poured in, widening the rupture and washing the fabric away. Now instruments, fittings, bunks and appliances were all under water while foodstuffs and cushions floated around the cabin.

Bouchon rose wearily from the table. "Must phone for salvage. An estimate for Elger, eh?"

Mitch fetched the yellow pages of the Oahu telephone directory and he and the Frenchman together went through the short list of salvage companies. The first number Bouchon called had been disconnected and at the second a recorded voice asked people to leave word. On the third try, however, the boss of Gus's Marine Salvage—"We Never Close"—after listening to Bouchon's predicament offered to start operations at once for half the sum realized upon sale of boat parts and equipment. Bouchon said he'd relay the proposition to the owner.

Mitch closed the glass sliding door, giving the Frenchman privacy in the living room while he called Elger in Los Angeles, but Bouchon soon emerged fretting. The number did not answer.

"I must order the salvage soon," he said, frowning, "while the boat still has some value. But I need permission."

"How big a deal is this either way?" asked Mitch. "You say Hank is well-heeled, huh?"

"Yeah, he's got plenty. He makes good money at sea, but like I told you he came into a lot too."

"What do you mean? Did he inherit it?"

"I don't know." Bouchon lit another Gauloise. He wasn't a chain-smoker. Every few minutes he skipped a link. "He just has money." He preferred to drop the subject.

Bones Elger recently rich? It was news to Mitch. Could the money be linked to those old suspicions about the *Gunnison Bay?*

"How long has Bones been around Tahiti?" Mitch decided to lead the Frenchman gently.

"Bones? Oh, Hank. He's been in and out of Papeete for a few years."

"On tankers? I'd guess only an occasional small one puts in there."

Bouchon sucked at his Gauloise. "The first time they brought him to Papeete." He grinned. "Now he comes back for the women and the good times."

"Brought him? Oh, yes, that rescue ship. After his tanker went down."

"Exactly, *mon vieux*. He was an engineer aboard."

"Yeah, third engineer on the *Gunnison Bay* when she exploded and sank west of the Galápagos." And, thought Mitch, set off a train of suspicion.

"Did Hank tell you about it?" Bouchon's shortened cigaret hung from his lower lip like a scab.

"Mostly I know about it because I'm a shipbroker. I match up oil cargoes with available tankers." Out from the house a surfer caught a long wave and rode the curl until his board upended in a geyser of surf.

"You lost money when the tanker went down?" Bouchon, who seemed mildly interested, fussed with his stocking cap. The rakish angle was not a random tilt.

"None. But in the trade we brokers keep track of things involving tankers . . . sales, overhaul, scrapping the big mothers, collisions, spills, sinkings, all that."

What Mitch Donahey did not tell the Frenchman was that his firm, McCafferty & Sons, fixed the charter for the *Gunnison Bay*'s last voyage, a deal between Pacific Triad Oil, shippers of the crude, and Petrolift Shipping which owned the tanker. Mitch in Honolulu had helped on aspects of the fixture made by other McCafferty brokers in New York. A further untold item: when suspicion focused on the crew, Mitch first learned that Henry Squires (Bones) Elger, his former sergeant, had been third engineer on the vanished tanker.

"Who did lose the money?" Now Bouchon's curiosity was aroused.

"The people who dropped a potful were the insurance companies that insured the ship and cargo."

"How much?"

"Hell, the oil was worth more than the ship." Mitch toyed with his second cup of coffee as he weighed just how far to go with Bouchon. "The *Gunnison Bay* was carrying about 105,000 tons of crude from Esmeraldas, Ecuador, to Japan. The oil was worth $22,000,000, more or less—oil was much higher then—and the tanker about twenty million. The *Bay* went down west of the Galápagos Islands and the ship that picked up the crew from lifeboats was headed for Tahiti, so it put the men ashore in Papeete."

Bouchon slouched in his chair, bathing his fatigue in the cool breeze. "When did the *Gunnison Bay* sink?"

"Three years ago." The sinking still rankled. Pacific Triad Oil, once disposed to favor McCafferty & Sons as their brokers when chartering tankers, had been cool ever since the loss of the *Gunnison Bay* stirred rumors and speculation throughout the trade. "Petrolift collected on the tanker and a Lloyd's group finally paid off the cargo owners, Pacific Triad, last spring. There was some talk of double dealing—insurance inspectors found that a lot of crude suddenly showed up at bargain prices in ports along the west coast of South America. But nothing was ever substantiated. And where the tanker sank, the bottom of the Pacific lies three miles down."

"You never heard anything like that from Hank?" Bouchon became wary.

"No, no. Just talk in the trade. Did you hear the story?"

"We don't hear much in Tahiti."

But the crew had come ashore there. Mitch decided to bore straight in. "When did Elger come into that money you talked about?"

"Look, I never got that from Hank." Bouchon shied away. He righted his tasseled stocking cap once more. "The only thing I heard, I got from a friend of Hank's, a deckhand from the tanker."

"What did he tell you?"

"No more questions, eh." The Frenchman said it sharply. His look of mischief had vanished. "You want to know Hank's business, you ask him. You're supposed to be his friend."

"A friend, I'm not." Mitch took a new tack. "Fact is, I can't stand the guy. You like him?"

"Eh *bien.*" Bouchon hunched his shoulders once more. "He was going to pay me $2,000, no?"

"You know you won't get a penny now, don't you?"

"At least I got my plane ticket home." He tapped a side pocket of his dungarees.

Mitch studied the transplanted Frenchman, seriocomic in his rakish stocking cap and torn blue shirt. How to ease his alarms and pry loose more information? Mitch reflected.

"Excuse me a sec." Mitch went into his living room, opened the top desk drawer and pulled out the emergency cash that he kept beneath an old hockey puck from college days. He counted out three fifties and four twenties. Damn, Bouchon, he guessed, would need more priming than $230. And this was Saturday.

He stepped to the extension phone in the bedroom and dialed his office where Bert Takahara, a University of Hawaii graduate student, manned the phones for him on weekends.

"Bert," he said in a low voice after the amenities, "do me a favor and look in the cash box." They kept the office petty cash fund in a box in a file cabinet. "See how much we got."

"Lotta coins here, brah," said Takahara when he returned to the phone.

"The hell with the coins. Just count the bills."

"Okay." In a moment he said, "I make it a hundred and ninety-three."

"Not enough. You got a Bank of Hawaii money card, right?"

"Right."

"You got enough in your account to draw out the $200 max from the machine?"

"Just."

"Okay. Two hundred today brings you two-fifty Monday. We pay the kind of interest the *yakuza* charges, brah." The yakuza, Japanese criminal gangs, fascinated Takahara almost as much as tankers and life on the high seas. "Look, bring the money from the cash box and I'll meet you in twenty minutes by the Bank of Hawaii machine at Bishop and King. Then we'll each hit the money-spitter for $200. That just might do it."

"Got it." Takahara reveled in mystery. "Twenty minutes."

Mitch sauntered back to the lanai. "I have to bug out for an hour." He rolled his eyes upward. "You know women. Always something." The detour around an outright lie buoyed his spirits. "Make yourself at home, Claude. Beer in the fridge. Plenty of food." Bouchon sighed wearily. "No thanks. But I'll use your phone to try Hank again."

"Anytime." Mitch trotted down the front stairs, revved up the Mustang and drove through Kapiolani Park, along the Ala Wai canal and over to Ala Moana Boulevard for the ride to downtown Honolulu. It was almost noon and the sun showered down on tourists thronging toward the beach with their mats, beach bags and floppy hats. In his quick survey of the bikinis, Mitch counted bare-ass cleavage on seven women, one short of his Saturday morning record.

The city's commercial center, cool gullies of shadow between the high mirrored fortresses of finance, was all but deserted. Bert Takahara, waiting by the Bankoh machine, wore his weekend working clothes, aloha shirt, Stubbies and battered running shoes that had carried him through two Honolulu marathons.

"Already hit it." Bert counted $393 into Mitch's hand, then waited while Mitch put in his card and punched his code—CHIMT. The machine, creaking electronic laments for loss of its life's blood, coughed out ten twenties, then popped out Mitch's card as if sticking its tongue out at him.

"So what's the story, brah?" Wide black eyes matching his hair and moustache, Takahara awaited enlightenment.

"Haven't got time now, Bert." Mitch turned back toward his car, illegally parked on King Street. "Heavy business. Tell you tomorrow. A check for $250 will be in the mail to you tonight. Thanks."

Back at his apartment, he found Bouchon on the lanai, drinking the beer he said he didn't want, with his feet up on the wicker table. "Elger still doesn't answer in Los Angeles," he said.

Mitch fetched himself a beer and sat down across from the Frenchman. After some obfuscatory chitchat about the non-existent woman and her problems, he asked: "Claude, how you fixed for money?"

"I thought I'd have $2,000." A smile intended to be insouciant came out rueful. "Instead I have six dollars."

Mitch inclined his head toward the wicker table. "I'll pay $750 for some confidential information." He arranged the currency on the table like a green fan, placed a seashell ashtray and beer can on the money to keep fitful breezes from blowing it away. "You have my word that I'll never reveal the source. You never told me a thing."

"What kind of information?" Bouchon's eyes flicked over the money fan. He was counting.

"Just tell me how Elger got a lot of money. . . . And listen, I've got more reason than you have to keep this discussion secret from Elger."

"How do I know you're not a lawman?"

"My only connection with the police is paying traffic fines." Mitch opened his wallet, showed the McCafferty card with his picture that identified him as a shipbroker.

"I never heard a thing from Elger." A look of fear swept Bouchon's face. "He don't like to be crossed, that one."

"But somebody must have told you how he came into money." Mitch fingered the currency. "I don't care who told you. Just tell me and take the seven-fifty."

Bouchon's eyes, hinting at his quandary, went from the money to Mitch and back again. "I did hear one story about the sinking from Elger's tanker friend, a Greek, I think he was."

"Fine." Mitch tried not to appear overly eager. "What did he tell you?"

"He said the crew of the *Gunnyday* . . ."

"The *Gunnison Bay?*"

"*Oui, oui*. They sold off the oil at cut rates in South America. Then they sank the ship in the deep ocean and claimed there had been an explosion in the engine room."

Bouchon reached for the money, but Mitch covered his hand. "Hold it, Claude. How much did he say they got out of it?"

"The lowest cut was $500,000." The Frenchman looked as if he had betrayed his own mother. "Some, he said, got more than a million."

"What was his name?"

Bouchon shook his head vigorously. "He never said. He was drunk, *alors*. He didn't know the next day that he'd told me."

"The whole crew was in on it?"

"That's what he said."

"And the captain?"

"He didn't say."

When further questions failed to yield more information, Mitch gathered up the bills and handed them to Bouchon. "We're even. And don't worry. You never mentioned oil or tanker to me."

Bouchon stuffed the bills in his pants pocket, took a last swallow of beer and rose to his feet. "Right now I got to get the boat off that reef." He looked harried. "I'll make one last try at Hank."

When Mitch told him to help himself, Bouchon went to the living room, closing the glass door behind him.

So, thought Mitch, Bones had scammed himself a young fortune. As third engineer, he probably netted a million or more from the split. Mitch was not surprised. After that night in Viet Nam, he could believe anything of his war-sotted sergeant who slaughtered defenseless civilians, kept a shell-case collection of ears hacked off Viet Cong bodies, spouted racist vitriol despite the black troops around him and spent endless hours polishing his combat boots to a high sheen. He hated Elger, not for his scoffing savagery alone but for the crime of luring Mitch himself to the brink of murder, for poisoning so many of his nights with that long-ago scene of blood lust and self-revulsion. He knew what a psychiatrist would tell him— that he despised Elger less for the man himself than for the evil that the foppish sergeant had awakened in Pvt. Donahey. Time after time, while his anger smoldered, he had evaded a confrontation with Elger, but he knew that sooner or later he had to face the man as well as his own guilt.

He had relived the night so many times. His squad had been ordered to scout the friendly village, only a mile from base, because of reports of Viet Cong infiltration. American soldiers counted numerous people in the hamlet as their friends, especially the grinning twelve-year-old they'd nicknamed Sammy, the happy kid who ran errands for them and hung around their bunkhouse, and his grandfather, the sweet old guy with the wispy beard and the sad, sad eyes.

Once again the night passed through his mind like a ghost: Sergeant Bones leading Jimmy, Calvin, Stacks and himself through the fringe of woods along the rice paddy, the night moonless and slimy hot. Near the hooches they flop to the ground, fan out and crawl forward. A few yards out, Calvin gives a low one-note whistle. Back comes a two-note whistle, meaning no VC on the premises. They crawl some more, Mitch scared and sweating up a river in the damp heat. He can smell his own stink. Calvin and Stacks, two blacks from Newark, get up and walk into the village at a crouch. The three others on the ground start to rise when they hear drupp, drupp, two blasts. Stacks and Calvin fall, Stacks with a wild screech of surprise. Twenty years later, Mitch can still hear the eerie falsetto.

They see a bunch of VC, maybe four or five, running out of the village toward a branch of the Ho Chi Minh trail to the west.

Sergeant Bones, the war addict from Fort Worth, goes ape. He howls, waves the others forward and runs into the village shooting. Jimmy throws up a flare and at that moment Sammy runs out of a hooch with that kid's silly grin on his face. Bones gives the boy a blast. The slugs lift Sammy off his feet, practically tear his head off. The old man, Sammy's grandfather, follows the kid out, gets another round from Bones. One shot hits him in the heart and he sinks in a spout of blood like a sad rag doll thrown into a colored fountain.

Calvin is moaning on the ground. "No, Bones, no," he pleads. "Don't, don't." But Elger is standing there, looking like a maniac, wheeling his weapon right and left, craving to waste the whole God-lost village. And who's standing beside him, swiveling his M-16, panting and snarling, ready like Bones to shoot anything that moves? Why, that nice young man from the Methodist Sunday School in Evanston, Mitchell Donahey. He has a powerful compulsive urge he has never felt before, an urge to kill, kill—anybody with a flat yellow face. He yells to Calvin, bleeding into the dirt but still beseeching Bones to hold it: "Shut up, Cal! They asked for it!" Mitch's own voice sounds demented, hoarse, strangely detached.

Bones yells, "We're goin' in," and starts for one of the huts, Mitch right behind him. Suddenly Jimmy, a big solid guy from Kentucky, decks Bones with a flying tackle, knocking the M-16 out of his hands and tripping Mitch who goes down on top of Bones, losing his weapon too.

"You son-of-a-bitch," Bones yells at Jimmy, "whose side are you on? The fuckers been hiding VC."

Jimmy stands over them, breathing hard. Mitch knows that he'll tolerate no more shooting of civilians. And as Mitch lies there tangled with Elger, sweating in that swampy heat, it comes over him what he almost did. He starts to cry and soon he's shaking with fear or shock or God-knows-what and then he pisses his pants like a baby.

"I'm sorry, Jimmy," Mitch says. "I don't know, oh Christ, it just came over me." Jimmy helps Mitch to his feet and shoves the M-16 back into his hands. "Forget it," he says. "We got to get Cal and Stacks out of here fast."

Bones never says boo to Jimmy, just gets up, takes his gun and starts giving orders. They carry Calvin and Stacks back, but Cal is bleeding from the mouth and dies on the way. Stacks has one foot almost blown away, but he makes it. Before they reach base, Jimmy primes them for the debriefing. "Listen, guys. The VC shot up the hooches when they hauled ass. That's the fact and we all saw it."

No one challenges the story. The captain, in fact, admires Bones and calls him the best soldier in the company, even though he knows that Bones keeps those human ears, several dozen of them, in an old shell case under his bunk. Ears and shoes, Elger's hobbies.

And the recurrent memory, again speeding through Mitch's mind as he sat there in Honolulu at the wicker table looking out to sea at surfers and a sailboat wreck, faded away as it usually did: a picture of Bones bent over his combat boots with a shoe rag, shining the torn crinkled leather to a mirror-like gloss.

Bouchon, another cigaret hanging from his lips, came out of the living room shaking his head. "Elger's phone still doesn't answer, so I ordered the salvage. Only thing to do."

The salvage crew arrived an hour later. Three brawny young men in swim trunks took orders from Gus Suafoa, a sweaty beer-guzzling operator who wore a dirty fishing cap and sported a coiled snake tattooed on his chest. Setting to work promptly, they dismantled the mast and floated it ashore, then loaded a pair of rowboats with loose items from the sloop. As the skiffs shuttled between wreck and shore, the heap of goods in the ocean-front yard grew higher.

The occupants of the first-floor apartment, an elderly couple who, like Mitch Donahey, rented their quarters for an unconscionable sum, voiced mild protests over the mounting pile of what they took to be debris. Gus, a can of beer in hand, overwhelmed them. Not to worry, he boomed, every last scrap would be trucked away by nightfall. But when the sun sank over the rolling Pacific, veiling Honolulu in rose and gold and spilling scarlet streams through rain clouds hovering over Manoa valley, the remains of *La Buffy* lay strewn over half the yard.

After the mast and such loose articles as sails, anchor, bedding, medical kit and canned goods, had come fittings and appliances that had to be detached from the bulkheads. Because of high water inside the boat, salvaging of the motor and navigational and depth-sounding equipment took time. Gus and his crew never lagged, worked steadily into the night after laughing and cursing their way through a lantern-lit outdoor dinner of *saimin,* chili dogs and six-packs.

Mid-evening Saturday Bouchon finally reached Elger who said he would fly over to Honolulu the next day, arriving late afternoon Sunday.

"He wants to talk to you." Bouchon came away from the phone with a deep frown. "Please, Mitch, nothing about what his tanker pal told me."

"Quit worrying. I gave my word."

"Hey, Mitcher, old buddy," greeted the familiar voice. Mitch could envision the Adam's apple bobbing. "How they hangin'? It's a gas, right, that Claude winds up on the reef in front of your place? I thought I'd be buying drinks tomorrow at the Waikiki Yacht Club. Now I'm coming by your house to strangle the bastard. You know that shithead cost me thirty-five grand."

"He said he wasn't drinking this morning." Mitch had an urge to defend Bouchon.

"You can bet your ass he was last night. . . . I'll get there about five. How about dinner after I finish with the salvage people?"

"I'll make us a sandwich or something here." Mitch braced himself. It was hard to do this. "I want to talk with you. It's been due for a long time, Bones."

"Henry, please. Okay, I don't know what there is to talk about outside that goddam boat, but whatever you want."

Buffy, stripped down to her bare deck and plucked as clean as a supermarket turkey, came off the reef in mid-afternoon Sunday after Gus and his men attached air-filled pontoons to the hull, enabling what was left of the craft to float free. Crewmen, swimming and pulling, propelled *Buffy*'s carcas out to deep water where Gus, waiting on a power boat, threw out a towline. One of the crew made the line fast to the noseless mermaid still adorning the bow and hauled the pontoons aboard. With spray drenching Gus, his beer can and the wrathful cobra on his hairy chest, the power boat headed up the coast, dragging the last bones of *Buffy* to a potter's field of salvagedom.

Elger arrived on a late afternoon flight, conferred with Bouchon and Suafoa at the salvage yard, then came to Mitch's apartment with Bouchon. The Frenchman, eager for some comfort to balance the long voyage and hours on the reef, departed early for the Hyatt Regency in Waikiki, leaving most of his gear in Mitch's garage stall. In a whispered aside, he again implored Mitch not to mention what Elger's tanker friend had told him about the lost *Gunnison Bay*.

Mitch broiled hamburgers and he and Elger sat down at the wicker table on the lanai with the sandwiches and a few cans of beer. Mitch merely nibbled at the food. His stomach felt queasy, reflecting the tension. This talk, so long postponed like unwanted surgery, would not come easily. Elger rattled on about the wreck of the *Buffy*, cursing Bouchon and lamenting his bad luck.

"All right, what's this serious talk you're busting to have?" Elger pushed away his plate and stretched out his legs. He had the same lean figure, scrawny neck and jutting Adam's apple of Viet Nam days as well as the old alley fighter's truculence. But now he catered to his yen for the foppish, the corn-silk hair obviously coiffed by a hair stylist, thin gold necklace, monogrammed polo shirt, spotless white trousers and the white moccasins with gold buckles. The fragrance of an understated male cologne eddied about him, so that he even smelled expensive. "Mitcher the bitcher," he said with a shake of his head. "Looking good these days, mate."

"And you're not a bad middle-aged model for Pierre Cardin."

"Same old sharp tongue, hey Mitcher? So what's to talk about?"

"That night in Viet Nam." God, he had to force himself to do this.

"What night in Viet Nam?" Elger's laugh had a scoffing edge. "I had more nights over there than a cunt has hairs. I wasn't one of your one-year duck-and-run war heroes."

"Come on, Bones. You know the night I mean."

"Hank, please. Nobody's called me Bones since the Nam."

"You proud of Sergeant Henry Elger's record there?"

"Fuckin' A. I don't regret a day of that war. We did a job. With some guts back in Washington, we could have chased the gooks back to Hanoi."

"How about that night at the village near base? The kid, Sammy? His grandfather with the wispy beard?"

"Yeah, well, that was ugly." Elger shook his head. "The goddam

VC wasting those poor guys. Nice kid, Sammy. I just pray to God I got one of the VC when I blasted them hauling ass out of there."

Mitch gazed at Elger in amazement. In all his conjectures of what Elger might say when they finally talked of that tormented night, he had not imagined this.

"I liked the old man too, you know," Elger continued. "I remember that one joke he told us about . . ."

"Bones!" He yelled it.

"What's up?" Elger looked perplexed.

"You know what happened. Why are you trying to shit me?"

"What do you mean? Sure, I know what happened."

"The Cong didn't kill them. You did. You creamed Sammy with your M-16 and then shot his granddaddy through the heart."

"Whoa, buddy. Just a goddam fuckin' minute. Are you hallucinating or what? How about the report that you and I and Jimmy and the nigger Stacks made that night? Straight eye-witness stuff right after the VC shot up the hooches."

Mitch stared at him in disbelief. Elger returned the stare in a frowning querulous way and they sat silently for a time.

"What about Calvin yelling at you to stop? Jimmy tackling you and spilling me on top of you?" Now Mitch's voice had a chill in it.

Elger seemed to reflect. He shook his head slowly. "I don't remember anything like that. Of them two black boys, Calvin was dying and Stacks had part of his foot shot away. As soon as we chased the VC, we started carrying them back."

"You never called Jimmy a son-of-a-bitch after he sacked you? Never asked him whose side he was on?"

"Just where are you getting this shit, Donahey?" Elger's voice rose angrily. "Hell, Jimmy and I carried Calvin out of there, but he'd had it. Died in our arms."

"I know." Again silence, this time prolonged.

"Listen, Bones." Mitch arose and walked to the lanai railing, then sat down facing Elger. The trade winds had died, leaving a damp calm and evoking that thick swampy night near Hue. "You can deny what you did if you like. That's between you and your conscience. . . ."

"What kind of crap . . ."

"Don't interrupt me, Bones." Mitch said it slowly and distinctly as he leveled a finger at the former sergeant. "I've been waiting twenty years to have this out with you. I don't give a shit about you turning the facts of that night inside out, but I don't intend to. You blasted Sammy when the kid came running out of his hut with that sweet silly-ass grin of his and then you shot his grandpa through the heart. . . ."

"Mitcher, you lyin' bas . . ."

"Shut up!" His anger turned to rage, ballooned, threatened to engulf him. Had Bones made the least move toward him at that moment, Mitch might have knocked him off the lanai. "I'm talking and by Christ, you're going to sit there and listen. You stood there, waving your weapon back and forth, and me, me . . ." He hesitated. "I stood right beside you, M-16 ready to blast the first head that showed from a hooch, woman, kid, old man, made no difference. I was full to choking with that madness to kill, ready to murder every living thing in that village, waste it all, burn it down over the bloody bodies. You yelled, 'We're goin' in!' and if Jimmy hadn't tackled you then, spilling me on top, you and I would have wiped out half that village and wound up court-martialed like Lieutenant Calley. Those are the facts, Sergeant Bones, and if you haven't got the guts to face them, so be it. Me, I can't live a lie."

Elger, who had followed him as he might a performer on a stage, reached for a new can of beer, slowly snapped the metal tab and took a long swallow. A light rain began to patter on the roof.

"You mind if I ask a question?" He was cool, controlled, his initial anger dissipated.

"Go ahead." Mitch still seethed.

"Did you ever tell that sorry excuse for the truth to anybody?"

"I mentioned it to that woman you saw the other night. No details."

"Have you ever been to a psychiatrist. V.A. or private?"

"No, and what the hell's that supposed to mean?"

"Well, you've obviously been traumatized about that night and I thought you might have tried to get some medical help."

"Horse shit, Bones. Try that load on somebody else. I know what you did and I know what I almost did."

"It's mighty strange that you're the only man in the world who has that twisted slant on events that night. You sure won't find that version in the official report of action."

"I guess not. We all agreed to lie. You want the truth, look up Jimmy." Mitch was cooling down now.

"Some kind of look that would be." Elger glanced upward. "Jimmy got killed a couple of months after your tour was up. Night fire fight. Didn't you know that?"

"No, I didn't."

"And Stacks died of cancer two years ago in Newark."

"I didn't know that either. I liked the guy."

"I've seen worse niggers. . . . So, of the five in the squad who went out on recon that night, only you and I are left, Mitcher."

"Oh." He felt older.

"Yeah, they're all gone." Elger leaned back in his chair, took another swallow of beer. "I think of that kid Sammy and his granddad now and then. If they hadn't made friends with us, the VC never would have killed them. But shit, that's the way it was in that God-crapped country."

Mitch found his eyes fixed hypnotically on Elger's rising and falling Adam's apple. A kind of torpor settled over him, snuffing out any will to contest further this blatant revision of a shared lust for slaughter. Was the fabrication a shell to shield the skinny war-hound from odium? Or had Bones absorbed the story into his bloodstream, rendering himself immune to tortured dreams and the lash of self-contempt? Either way, Mitch took some small comfort in the fact that Bones too had felt the need to distance himself from those dungeons of the soul. If Elger craved the reassurance of civility, desired to be called decent and ranked among the blameless, then perhaps after all these years he should be allowed to pass without further challenge.

The reawakened *Gunnison Bay* case, however, was another story. Mitch had a strong urge to sail into that scene too but he sensed that he'd accomplish little save alerting Bones to the fact one of his fellow crew members had talked.

Bones, anxious to end a session that had ripped the scar from old wounds, pushed back from the table and rose to leave.

"Got to get going," he said. "Bouchon and I still have a lot of talking to do tonight. The ass-hole loses me thirty-five grand and he acts like he's done me a favor."

Mitch led Elger through the living room to the front entrance. At the door, Elger put his hand on Mitch's shoulder. "No hard feelings, man," he said. "You've got plenty of company. That war fucked up the memories of lots of good men."

Instantly angry again, Mitch shook off Elger's hand. "Goddam it, don't patronize me, Bones. We both know that you shot down a kid and his granddad and if Jimmy hadn't stopped us, you and I would have wasted the village."

Elger looked at him as he might at someone mentally retarded. "Drop it, Mitch, drop it. You're only hurting yourself." Glancing downward, he frowned, took a handkerchief from his hip pocket, leaned over and wiped a spot of some kind from his gleaming white moccasins.

The incident, seeming to dismiss Mitch's memory as no more significant than a speck of dirt, further enraged him. "Say, Bones," he asked, "where do you keep your collection of ears these days?"

Elger's quick glance held venom, but his tone was bland enough. "Ears? What ears?"

"The ones you used to cut off the VC and NVA guys you killed."

"Jesus, Donahey, you sure got a weird memory. It was Jimmy kept that stinkin' ear collection, not me. I never cut off an ear in my life." He glared at Mitch, then turned away. "Thanks for the burger. See yah."

Mitch closed the door with relief. He felt emotionally drained. Would this confrontation at long last exorcise those stunted demons of the night? Perhaps. But whether or not his guilt now withered, he sensed that he was far from through with Henry Squires Elger.

3

Mitch clamped the phone between jaw and shoulder, crossed his canvas loafers beneath the desk and settled in for a schmoose. Light action this Monday morning—damn it, the prolonged depression in the tanker game was gnawing at everybody—so plenty of time to explore the new lead on the old *Gunnison Bay* sinking. Also to cosset a few heavy egos around the circuit. Heavy egos? He marked the unfocused hostility behind the thought and reminded himself to proceed with caution. The old anger, fanned anew by the head-to-head with Bones Elger, threatened to burst out again.

The phone rang in Los Angeles, home of Pacific Triad Oil, a company that had steered but few charter requests to McCafferty & Sons since the costly loss of the tanker and its cargo of oil.

"Hi. Mitch Donahey. What's new, Don?" He punched three keys summoning a profile from the biographical index and stringing it across his desk-top computer screen in pulsing green letters: **Donald R. Kelleher, chartering dept., Pacific Triad Oil. Charter average: 1/2 mill. tons month. Birthday June 11. Sails 40-ft. ketch, Green Flash. Dodger fan. Drinking binges. Wife, Ethel.**

"I'm calling you," said Mitch, "before you head out this afternoon for Marina del Rey and the *Green Flash.*" Best to ease into the *Gunnison Bay* story. Kelleher had joined the chartering department just a year ago, knew only by hearsay of the skirmishing and strained relations between Pac-Tri officers and McCafferty brokers after the tanker settled to the floor of the Pacific.

"You're two weeks behind the news, Mitch." The voice coasted lazily over the channel from Los Angeles. Although the oil man had given McCafferty scant business since taking charge of chartering, Mitch knew he liked to gossip with all tanker brokers. "I sold the *Flash* before she sailed me into bankruptcy. I've got a small cat' now, the *Ina May*. How's the weather out there in Aloha land?"

"Another shitty day in paradise. Eighty degrees. Blue skies. Soft trades." Mitch tapped noiseless keys, vaporizing the *Green Flash* and installing the *Ina May* in its place. "How's it in Smogville?"

"Poisonous. One of those days when the eyeballs bleed pebbles." The leisurely cadence, echoing on the satellite channel, signaled a desire for chitchat. "Say, can you hold a minute? They're buzzing me from upstairs on the other line."

"Take your time." Through the window of this branch office of McCafferty & Sons, shipbrokers, Mitch could see the sun gripping Honolulu's commercial harbor in hard possessive light, hands on the Aloha Tower clock pointing upward in late morning, two tugs waddling toward Sand Island and in the distance, crawling on the surface like a sea reptile, a submarine heading for Pearl Harbor.

From this high window of the mirrored PRI Tower, he also could look far down on the tiled roof of the Dillingham Transportation Building, nostalgic remnant of downtown Honolulu in bygone days when no layered office piles split the sky, strollers along Bishop Street had an indolent gait and the Big Five ran the islands as their fiefdom.

Still, working here for the last five years at his trade of broking tanker charters, Mitchell Paul Donahey had grown fond of Honolulu's modern commercial and financial center, a mix of tall office hives and old ground-hugging landmarks such as the mansion-like headquarters of C. Brewer & Co. and the pillared home of Alexander & Baldwin. Trade winds sailed through cool shaded streets. The Fort Street Mall teemed with sleek Asian clerical workers, Bible-hammering evangelists, messenger boys padding along in zoris and shorts, haole executives in their flowered aloha shirts and bosomy part-Hawaiian women engulfed in ankle-length muumuus, legacy of the New England missionaries who recoiled at the sight of bare brown flesh. Withered little Filipino men, as neat and brittle as whisk brooms, sat on sidewalk benches talking of cockfights or the old days on the sugar and pineapple plantations. A good place to work, downtown Honolulu, casual, friendly, never hectic. If it was also about as stimulating as tofu, well, whoever said heaven had brash combative angels?

The idea of a feisty angel made prompt connection with that other thought that had crowded out so many others recently. Mona Harkinson had swooped into his life like a parachutist, entangling them both in spangled shrouds that swept them through those days and nights of fevered lovemaking. And it was just a week ago tonight that she rushed off again, this strangely compelling woman of no fixed address, leaving him with a unfamiliar but insistent ache, the pain of emptiness.

"Okay, Mitch." Kelleher came back on the line. "Where were we?"

"Hung up on the weather." He took another item from the screen's biographical display. "I see your Dodgers are only two games off the lead. Can they make it?"

"They're hot this month." The voice from Los Angeles, however, was cool as a lazing cat. "I saw them win last night."

"Birdbrains!" Roving the clutter on his desk, Mitch's eyes had fallen on a Page One headline in the previous evening's *Star-Bulletin:* MILITARY DOLLAR GETS MORE MILEAGE. A Bank of Hawaii economist opined that the Pentagon's tax money flooding Pearl Harbor, Hickam Air Force Base, Schofield Barracks and Kaneohe Bay Marine Air Station churned the state's economy at a faster pace and with less "leakage" than did tourist spending from the mainland and Japan.

"What do you mean, birdbrains? L.A. plays the smartest baseball in the league."

"No, no, not the Dodgers." Mitch explained. "It burns me, Don. The establishment out here treats Tomahawk missiles and F-14 fighters like they were uptown food stamps. A new Hyatt hotel, a new McDonald's, a new battleship group, a new MIRV ten-megaton nuke, what's the difference? If you can sleep in it, eat it, shoot it or kill a million people a second with it, okay, what the hell, it's all good for business."

The oil man yawned. "We need a strong defense, Mitch," he cautioned. "It's a jungle out there."

"Yeah, and we helped make the jungle." The word enveloped him like sudden miasma, swarming dankly with the old images. He saw Bones screaming and swiveling his weapon, the old man with the wispy beard spurting blood like a fountain, his own rage to kill and finally the clot of horror in his throat. But the scene vanished swiftly, no more than a flash, and he wondered if the long-delayed facing of Bones might have defanged his ghosts.

Mitch fastened his attention once more on the phone channel to Los Angeles. "I keep forgetting that people make money out of government terrorism, slaughtering a whole city with one bomb. Just so you call it war or defense, terrorism's okay, right?" The anger still simmered. He would have to watch himself.

"Heavy stuff on an empty stomach, man." Kelleher wanted gossipy tidbits, not a lecture on humanity's self-inflicted atrocities. "You're a Viet Nam vet, aren't you?" He mentioned the status as he might a disease.

"Yeah." Time to cut back to business. Sometimes, if uncurbed, the anger swelled into rage. He'd once lost a fixture of a Hong Kong-owned tanker because of chaotic fury that blew up over images evoked by an idle remark. Steadying himself now, he glanced up at the old ship's bell that hung near his map of the world. Given him by Jim McCafferty of the fourth generation of owners, the brass bell duplicated the original which hung in New York headquarters where a broker rang it to hail each new fixture. As the lone McCafferty broker in Honolulu, Mitch sounded his bell every time he sealed a charter even though no ears but his own heard it. He liked the private ceremony, one of the few traditions that appealed to him.

"Say, Don." He felt relaxed now. "Remember the *Gunnison Bay?*"

"Who around here could forget her? We took a loss on that oil."

"How much?"

"I don't recall, but insurance didn't cover it all. Worse, Dakoi in Japan never got the 105,000 tons of crude and they blamed us. Used to be a good customer. Now they're off and on."

Like Pacific Triad and McCafferty, thought Mitch. "Did you ever hear rumors of a scam in that sinking?"

"Yeah, some. One story had the crew selling the oil off and then sinking the ship. It was a fact that a lot of crude, unaccounted for, showed up in South American ports for sale cheap. But hell, insurance investigators never pinned anything down. And the crew all told the same story. Why are you asking?"

"I had a weird weekend, Don. It started off with a sloop from Tahiti cracking up on the reef right in front of my place." He related the story, stressing what Elger's fellow crew member reportedly admitted to Claude Bouchon while drunk.

"One thing about all that," Mitch concluded. "Whether or not it happened that way, I'm damn sure that my old sergeant, Bones, is perfectly capable of participating in that kind of scam, maybe even running it. Believe me, he's an ugly one. Without going into all the gory details, let's just say he's the kind of guy who used to hack the ears off Viet Cong bodies, then keep the ears in a shell case under his bunk."

"What did Elger say when you brought up what Bouchon told you?"

"I never mentioned it, Don. I didn't want to tip him off that I knew. Also it wasn't the time. We got hot enough over an old scene from Viet Nam. I had to hold the bastard to the fire."

"Well, if one of the crew talked while drunk," said Kelleher, "a sharp investigator ought to be able to loosen him up again."

"That's what I've been thinking."

"Any description of the guy who talked to Bouchon?"

"No. I couldn't press him. Bouchon was getting skittish. But he did say he was on deck, not down below. He used the word 'deckhand,' so he probably wasn't an officer. Also he thought he was Greek. A Greek seaman ought to offer a fair lead."

"Mitch, I'll call you right back. I'll have my secretary get our file on the crew. We have a whole cabinet full of stuff on the *Gunnison Bay* case."

Kelleher called back several minutes later. "Mitch, apparently there were two Greek nationals aboard at the time the crew claims there was an engine-room explosion. Both named Miaoulis, Saul and Nikos, brothers. Saul worked in the engine room. Nikos was a deckhand."

"I gathered Bouchon's talk with the Greek seaman occurred fairly recently," said Mitch. "Maybe the man's still in Papeete. A good place to start asking, anyway."

"You know, our people are still very interested in this case.

They're convinced it was barratry. Do you mind, Mitch, if I go topside with this story?"

"Of course not. That's why I told you."

"One good tip deserves another," said Kelleher in his easy drawl. "I hear there's a good chartering job opening up, in case you're interested. Top bucks, they say."

"What outfit?" Excepting one flare-up, he had not thought to leave McCafferty.

"Lorikeet Tankers, head office in Copenhagen. An Arab named Wasif Zabib is expanding his fleet. Rare thing, these days, what?"

"You said it. Wasif Zabib? I've heard the name some recently. What do you know about him?"

"Only that he's buying tankers when most people are selling."

"Oh, I'm satisfied where I am. McCaffertys are good people to work for." Mitch steered the talk to current business. "My trusty guesstimator says you'll need a 200,000-tonner in the A.G. along about the end of next week."

"Could be. Nothing solid from upstairs yet." The chartering man of Pacific Triad Oil reverted to his measured drawl.

"Discharging Tokyo Bay?"

"Possible. Your guess is as good as mine."

"But Tokyo Bay figures, right? Probably Chiba." Was Kelleher playing dumb on purpose? Lately, instead of coming on the market where any broker could grab at a fixture, Kelleher had favored Poten & Partners in New York.

"Quite possible."

"Can we call it probable?" Mitch persisted. He knew the Pacific Triad official didn't mind aggressive tactics. In fact, Kelleher rather liked heavy pushers and sometimes rewarded them. Always better, Mitch kept reminding himself, to show keen, if sometimes fraudulent, interest in a past and future client than to wait passively for a charterer to throw his shipment on the open market.

"I wouldn't quarrel with the word, Mitch." Now Kelleher was enjoying the game.

"And two hundred is likely?"

"That's been routine lately."

"Right." Mitch tapped several keys, erasing the oil officer's profile and calling up a chart of Pacific Triad shipments in the past year. "You haven't asked for a big one in a long time." The list showed

only one charter over 220,000 tons, the *Fjord Duchess,* a Norwegian
behemoth of 430,000 deadweight tons. She stretched as long as four
football fields and if a ship's officer inspecting an empty bow tank
started to climb out and go aft for breakfast, so the story went, he'd
arrive in time for lunch—if his bicycle didn't have a flat.

Mitch shifted back to personals. "I'd like a sail on your new cat'
someday, Don." He had his tip now. Pacific Triad Oil most likely
would ship 200,000 tons of Arab light crude from the Arabian Gulf
to Japan within ten days. He chatted with Kelleher in deceptively
casual vein for several minutes before signing off.

The instant he replaced the phone, Mitch tapped out the code that
brought the Estermann Noon Position Report to his screen. For an
extravagant fee, Estermann Marine of Hamburg, a rival of Mardata
and other computerized ship-movement services, provided its customers with sophisticated graphics showing the daily position of all
cargo vessels of 10,000 deadweight tons or more as of noon Green-
wich time. Another tap on the keyboard narrowed Estermann's
global charts to oil tankers and a further refinement called up graphics that focused on tankers of more than 150,000 tons. Mitch sought
a carrier of about 200,000 tons either in the Arabian Gulf or within a
few days' sailing time of the world's greatest pool of petroleum. In
the domain of tankers, men almost never spoke or thought of the
Persian Gulf. With a bow to the immense oil reserves beneath the
sands of the Arabian Peninsula, it was the Arabian Gulf or simply
"the Gulf."

Mitch rummaged through the big tankers on his screen until he
found one that might fit: *Monteporo,* 217,000 DWT, moored off
Aden near the Strait of Bab al Mandab between the Red Sea and the
Gulf of Aden.

Hadn't the *Monteporo* lain idle for a month or more? At least it
seemed that every time recently he'd called up data on this leg of the
great tankerways, he noted the *Monteporo* off Aden, apparently swel-
tering at anchor in the heat waves pouring off the long shimmering
sands of the Arabian peninsula. With costs averaging $20,000 a day
for idle tankers of that size, owners despaired when their giant crude
carriers went unemployed for long. Let's see, who did own the ship?

Mitch switched to the program carrying *Lloyd's Register* and ran
his eye down the M's until he found it: *Monteporo,* Liberian flag,
owner Lorikeet Tankers, Copenhagen. Well, well, coincidence, small-

world department. No sooner does Kelleher mention Wasif Zabib and his Lorikeet Tankers than one of Zabib's ships shows up on the screen.

And where had he heard that name earlier, some years ago? A wheel of his memory began clicking insistently. Zabib, Zabib. He switched to the biographical index of the shipping industry, but the computer replied: NOT IN FILE. Walking to his bookcase of shipping reference books, Mitch searched through several recent Lloyd's volumes that listed shipowners. Ah, right. Three years ago Zabib had been chief executive officer of Petrolift Shipping, owner of the vanished *Gunnison Bay*. Now, according to the shipping lists, Petrolift no longer existed, apparently dismantled and replaced by Lorikeet.

And just who was Wasif Zabib whose tanker had sunk under suspicious circumstances? He scratched around in memory. What had he heard? Let's see, trade gossip pinned Zabib as a relative newcomer to the patchwork peerage of tanker owners. Wasn't he the wealthy Jordanian who preferred to live in London, Paris or Copenhagen? Either owned several tankers outright or fronted for a group of Arab investors, according to trade speculation?

Well, no combination would surprise Mitch Donahey. In the tangled skein of tankerdom, one of the monster carriers might be designed in New York, built in Korea, financed by Swiss bank loans, pronounced seaworthy by a West German classification society, sold to Hong Kong operators, registered in Panama, insured by British underwriters, chartered to Dutch oil traders by Norwegian brokers, crewed by Turks, Portuguese and Yugoslavs under a Swedish captain, loaded with Arabian oil and sailed on a hundred voyages to ports of oil-thirsty Japan before being sold for scrap to Taiwan breaker yards.

As for Zabib's Lorikeet Tankers, the chartering manager was Henri Picot, a Frenchman who operated from his office in Marseille. Mitch had never met Picot on his semiannual trips to contact the trade, but as with many unseen chartering men with whom he negotiated by phone, he had formed a distinct impression. Mitch pictured a stout soft-muscled self-indulgent man who wore expensive rings and preferred the sybaritic life to the work that made it possible.

Donahey tapped the code that brought Picot's biographical sketch to the screen, refreshed his recollection on the Frenchman's dominant interests—women, soccer, women, Mediterranean landscapes, women, chemin de fer, women. Since it was after nine o'clock at night in Marseille, Mitch dialed the home number. In this business that made hash of time zones, an alert broker kept a file of many numbers: office, home, club, occasionally even a mistress.

The phone rang several times before Picot answered in a muffled voice as if speaking through vapors of a hot bath. As they traded amenities in slow tortuous fashion, Mitch surmised that Picot might be drinking, sleepy, distracted or in the act of love, perhaps all four.

"I see the *Monteporo* is off Aden." Mitch spoke in English, worldwide tongue of the international tanker industry. "I may have a cargo coming up next week at 200,000, loading A.G., discharging Japan. You interested, Henri?"

The Frenchman sighed a negative. "We're not chartering the VLCC for a while." Like most charter and tanker men, he used the initials for the industry category, Very Large Crude Carrier. "Repairs, Monsieur." Also he disliked the American habit of using the first names of mere phone acquaintances.

"Off Aden?" Mitch registered shock. "You got to be kidding. Unless you're a Soviet destroyer needing overhaul at the Russians' naval base there, you'd be lucky to find parts for a four-horse outboard anywhere around Yemen."

"*Monteporo* has plenty spare parts on board." Picot sounded lax, uninterested. Mitch concluded that the Frenchman was in bed with one of his women, a scene that promptly evoked thoughts of Mona. God, where was she? He had nourished a thin hope that she might get in touch with him. Seven days had passed since she had run up the front steps of the Royal Hawaiian and out of his life. He would write care of American Express, London, tomorrow. He had to reach her.

"The ship's main job is cleaning." Picot could have been swimming through glue. "All tanks. Major scrub down."

"In that heat? Her master must be mad. I'll bet the crew loves him. . . . Hey, wait a sec. There's no cleaning or mucking gear near Aden. What do you mean?"

"All I know is what they tell me."

"Henri, that tanker's been sitting there for a month."

"I know, I know." Picot said something in French in a soft aside. "I'm losing plenty money myself, Monsieur. Don't remind me, please."

"It's not the only idle tanker, of course. Things are still slow, but some owners manage to keep their fleets sailing most of the time." Mitch edged toward his new target. "I thought your boss, Wasif Zabib, was supposed to be such a smart operator."

"He is, he is." The charter manager rushed to the ramparts. Shedding the lassitude of dalliance? "He's a shrewd one, believe me."

"What's he like? I don't know much about him."

"Would you believe I've never seen him?" Picot's inquiry had a plaintive note. "He hired me on the phone. But he pays well and insists on good work. He's got a wife and family in Jordan, I hear, but he lives alone in Copenhagen. Likes women. You know the Arabs."

"Didn't he used to own an outfit called Petrolift Shipping?" Mitch paused. "You know, the one that owned the *Gunnison Bay* when she went down."

"Could be, but I doubt it." The Frenchman backed off. "I don't think he had anything to do with the *Gunnison Bay.*" Like the corpse in an unsolved murder, the sunken tanker was thought to taint all those who knew the victim.

"I think he ran Petrolift and I'm certain that Petrolift Shipping owned the *Gunnison Bay.*"

"I never heard it mentioned." Picot wanted no more of the doomed ship.

Ending the exchange after a few pleasantries, social bank account for future deals, Mitch marked his memory with an asterisk before *Monteporo*. Something a bit off here. Maybe Zabib intended to sell her for scrap. The tanker had been afloat thirteen years, the danger age for a VLCC, especially one holed by an Iraqi missile in the splurge of attacks on Arabian Gulf shipping.

Well, cross out *Monteporo* for any probable Pacific Triad Oil shipment. Mitch switched his screen back to the Estermann charts showing locations of tankers of more than 150,000 tons. He picked about in the computer's listings until he found a suitable ship: *Channel Cliffs II*, 204,000 DWT, currently in ballast, heading to the Arabian Gulf after a voyage to Bonair in the Caribbean where supertankers transferred oil to smaller vessels for delivery to North American ports.

Tapping back to *Lloyd's Register*, he confirmed his memory. *Channel Cliffs II*, three years old, Panamanian flag, was owned by

the Michaelson & Lygdamis Syndicate, Montreal, a company meld-
ing Canadian and American money, the Michaelson family of Montreal and the Lygdamis family of New York. Mitch had known
M & L's chartering manager, George Littleton, for several years, but
playing it safe, he punched up Littleton's profile and plotted his
opening before phoning.

Eleven in the morning in Hawaii, 5 P.M. in Montreal this time of
year when Hawaii had no daylight saving.

"Mitch Donahey, George." He recognized the voice that answered. Like most players in the fast-breaking game of tanker chartering, Littleton manned his own phones. "I lucked out. I figured
there might be a couple of minutes yet before you hit Guy's joint for
the evening drink."

"Guy's? Oh, we quit Guy's, you know. They demanded decorum,
if you know what I mean." The voice from Montreal plodded with
heavy tread like ski boots in a tiled lobby. "We're taking our evening
grog now at the Chantilly. I think I took you there last spring."

Mitch did remember the Chantilly, smoked timbers, long bar of
pitted wood, an odor of cheese and ale, rear booths lighted by hanging lanterns. On his last trip to show the flag and polish contacts, a
McCafferty & Sons must for all its brokers, he had made Montreal
on his swing through the Americas, Asia and Australia. Next time
Europe and the Middle East. Many shipbrokers made regular visits
to the major cities where chartering people of both oil companies and
independent tanker fleets tended to concentrate. Most traveled with
liberal entertainment accounts. In the lucrative business of fixing the
thick black liquid cargoes that fueled the world, pinchpennies wound
up losers.

Mitch jousted briefly with Littleton, a man who often sorted heavy
lumber in his attic before replying. While he talked, Mitch substi-
tuted the Chantilly for Guy's in his computer-stored sketch of Littleton.

"Is the *Channel Cliffs II* open?" asked Mitch when he switched
the talk to business.

"Nothing definite, if you know what I mean."

"I may have a cargo loading in the Gulf for her."

"What discharge?"

"Japan. . . . I'd guess we could get World Scale thirty-four,
maybe thirty-five. Basis 200,000 tons."

"Did something just come on the market?" Littleton trudged from word to word as if selecting dry spots while crossing a muddy road.

"No, this comes from one of my sources, George. They'll probably work next week late."

"Is this by any chance Pacific Triad? Lifting 200,000 from the Gulf to Japan?"

Goddam, so Don Kelleher had leaked to another broker. He'd been had. "Yeah, you guessed it. Triad may come open. How'd you hear?"

"A Platou man in Oslo called me a few minutes ago." Littleton paused. "My hunch is you're both speculating."

"I admit I am." Disarm them with candor. It had been one of the mottoes of the first J. P. McCafferty. "If you deal with McCafferty, you get it straight. . . . But the odds are good that Pacific Triad will need a 200,000-tonner in a few days. Same question, George. Are you interested?"

"You know we listen to all proposals, Mitch. Bring me the cargo firm and you'll have the business."

A nothing answer. Littleton was not his type. Stuffy, clumsy at banter, mannered even at play as Mitch had noted the evening George took him to his favorite retreat, the Royal Montreal Curling Club, to see a match on the ice lanes. Still, he needed the Canadian.

He offered trade chitchat to feed the conversation. "George, do you know anything about an owner named Wasif Zabib?"

Shipbrokers, like all professionals, relished trade talk. It played to the human propensity to dwell on the familiar, created the illusion of membership in an exclusive club, enabled a gossiper to show off his jargon and inside knowledge and not infrequently led by circuitous routes to a profitable deal. In the small world of tanker chartering, most of the four hundred or so brokers knew one another and shared friendship with many of the oil company and shipowners' chartering managers. Friendship counted in the heavily personal business and its cultivation in the Pacific had brought Mitch to Honolulu in the first place. Although computers and telephones permitted tanker brokers to live and work anywhere, McCafferty, as well as Platou and other shipbroker firms, believed that men located in the Pacific basin could make valuable contacts not readily accessible to New York, London or Oslo officers.

But East or West, shipbrokers thrived on insider talk. Behind their

shell of brusque, often cynical professionalism, many preened themselves on participation in vast global affairs and thus doted on gossip
of fellow movers and shakers. Scattered in many of the world's major
cities, the brokers took part in a truly international industry, one
heavily politicized and involving exchange of large sums of money.
While governments and cartels regulated the production of oil, the
shipment of crude and refined oil products remained wildly speculative, one of the last great free markets unfettered by the decrees of
bureaucrats.

"Zabib," said Littleton, "is one of those highly sensitive Iraqis, if
you know what I mean. So devout a Moslem, they say, he won't even
take a drink in Europe."

"I heard he was Jordanian."

"Might be. I heard Iraqi, but they're all alike in that bloody desert." Littleton cleared his throat. "Whatever, he taps big money. I
heard the other day that the Zabib group is dickering to buy the
D'Artagnan from the French."

"Any offers to your people?" Mitch asked less out of curiosity
than to edge his way gracefully toward an exit. Nothing to be gained
from Littleton today.

"Yes, actually. Zabib made an approach the other day for our
Channel Treasure. They turned him down."

"Well, I'll let you take off for the Chantilly." Mitch, suppressing a
yawn, prepared to hang up. "Oh, by the way, are you the guy that
Marvin Crouch of our New York office dealt with on a fixture for the
Yandoon Princesss?"

"No, that was Stu Leppart, our man in New York. You know I
don't like to handle our big tankers when they get that old. We
agreed on that, remember?"

"Right, so we did. Crouch wanted me to call you last week to help
on the *Princess* deal, but I told him no way. No aging mothers for
me. The *Princess* has turned sixteen. My cutoff date is a tanker's
fifteenth birthday."

"Same here. Remember? We talked about this before."

"That's right. Also the *Princess* goes to drydock only once in
thirty months. Two years is my outside limit. Personally, I'd scrap
the old lady."

"The *Yandoon Princess* isn't the only one I'd scrap." Littleton
lowered his voice. "That's between us, if you know what I mean. But

maybe the brass is persuaded on the *Princess*. I hear they may scrap her after another trip or two."

"Okay, George. I'll get back to you on the *Channel Cliffs* when Pacific Triad breaks."

Decent guy, thought Mitch as he replaced the phone. Maybe he'd been too hard on him. Well, no problem about the *Channel Cliffs II*. She was only three years old, stuffed with the latest safety gear, pride of the M & L tanker fleet.

Mitch's mind wandered. He saw Mona standing nude in the tiled bath of his apartment, beckoning to him to join her under the streaming shower. He saw her sitting at the wicker table on his lanai, the breeze teasing at her pinned-up hair. He could hear her throaty voice talking about her love of surrendering, "absolutely adore it," and the way she gave herself completely in love. And then he could see the contrasting Mona, quite in command, sweeping up his bar tab and paying both bills as if that were the custom. Unique, she was, and she intrigued and stirred him like no other woman since his divorce from Fran. Yes, he would write Mona tomorrow. He had to make contact again.

His phone rang, breaking the reverie. "Hello, Mitch." It was Kelleher in Los Angeles. "I just got word from upstairs. We're shipping 185,000 tons Kuwait crude next week. We want to load Wednesday at Mina al Ahmadi."

"Where discharging, Don?" Mitch went on the alert, his mind fully engaged, already sorting through possible tankers in or near the Arabian Gulf. "Japan?"

"Right. Chiba."

"You putting this on the market, Don?"

"No, this one's all for you, sweetie." The voice that had coasted along in neutral now had a crisp business-like set.

"God, to what do I owe the favor? McCafferty's unblemished reputation for fair dealing or my own saintly character?"

Kelleher laughed. "Neither, chum. We appreciated your tip on the *Gunnison Bay*. If that master and crew stole our oil, we're going to nail them."

"You going to re-open your investigation?"

"I think so. There's talk upstairs of hiring Moses & Fabian, best in the field of marine accident investigation."

"Thanks for the business. I thought lately you were in bed with Poten & Partners."

"No, but they're live ones. Dick Innis called me twice from New York yesterday."

"But not today, lucky for me."

"No. Today a bunch of you other bandits were after me, starting with a Fearnleys guy in Oslo who caught me at breakfast."

Mitch got down to business. "Don, you know the *Channel Cliffs II?* She's 204,000 tons, an M & L carrier."

"Yeah, a fairly new ship."

"Any problems with her?"

"None that I know of." He paused. "You know our requirements, Mitch. The usual. No heat needed. One grade Kuwait crude. We'd like to load on the sixteenth and need lay days, sixteenth canceling the eighteenth."

"The Mina al Ahmadi terminal loads 15,000 tons an hour. No trouble there. Rate?"

"Our ideas are World Scale Thirty-two."

"The last done in London this morning was thirty-five to Texaco." Mitch let the figure float a moment. "You adamant on thirty-two?"

"We have some flexibility, not much." Kelleher draped the final phrase in sober tones.

"Okay, Don. I'll get back to you soonest."

Mitch caught George Littleton on his second martini at the Chantilly in Montreal. The Canadian's ponderous manner failed to disguise his surprise at the news from Pacific Triad.

"All right, then," he said after listening to Mitch's proposal. "Let me go back to the office and see what we can work out. It'll be a while, what with the martinis, if you know what I mean."

Littleton called back a half-hour later with a tentative offer. *Channel Cliffs II* could reach Mina al Ahmadi Wednesday afternoon, September 15. She would load 185,000 tons of crude on Thursday and would sail early Friday, September 17, for Chiba. Average speed 11 knots, 25 days sailing time. Cost: World Scale Thirty-four. Translating that international method of calculating sea transport prices for oil into dollars, it would cost Pacific Triad Oil $1,061,000 to ship the cargo some 6,700 miles. As its brokerage fee, McCafferty & Sons would gross $13,150.

"Okay, let me put it up to the Pac-Tri people." Mitch deliberately avoided calculating his own commission of fifteen percent. Bad luck in the trade to start counting before locking up a deal. "I'll phone you at home."

"Only one problem," said Littleton. "We need a full cargo. The Pac-Tri order falls 19,000 tons short of *Channel Cliffs* capacity."

"Let me handle that. I'll see if they won't increase the cargo a few tons."

Working swiftly, Mitchell canceled his practice session with Wong's Auto softball team on which he played third base and begged off a Sierra Club committee meeting later.

What seemed at first to be a simple mating of shipper and ship-owner after a bit of haggling over price turned out to be an abrasive frustrating negotiation that ran on for hours. Kelleher declined to pay World Scale Thirty-four, or $5.73 a ton to ship the oil to Japan, offering only World Scale Thirty and refusing to budge above his last offer of 32.5. Littleton at last agreed to WS 32.5, or $5.48 a ton, but insisted that Pacific Triad had to ship 204,000 tons of crude, filling the tanker to capacity. Kelleher threw down a flat refusal, declaring that for storage reasons Mitsui could receive no more than 185,000 tons at the Chiba terminal.

With both Kelleher and Littleton threatening to break off negotiations, Mitch stalled for time. Then, in one of those fortuitous twitches of memory, he recalled that Tsuno Oil Co. in Yokohama, across Tokyo Bay from Chiba, often bought odd lots of crude for its refinery if the price and grade were right. It was the next day in Japan and Mitch's phone call found Tsuno's purchasing agent snacking at his desk. After prolonged if routine haggling, the officer agreed to buy 19,000 tons of Kuwait crude from Pacific Triad at a figure below the prevailing spot market. In Los Angeles a weary Kelleher consented at last to Mitch's proposal: Pac-Tri to add 19,000 tons to its Kuwait order and then resell the additional oil to Tsuno at a slight profit, the crude to be lightered across Tokyo Bay by barge from Chiba.

Mitch concluded the deal with a phone to each ear, one tuned to the assent from Los Angeles, the other to Littleton's "it's confirmed" from Montreal. By the time he had transmitted a recapitulation of the fixture details to each principal by Telex, the clock had ticked past 6 P.M. in Honolulu, past nine in Los Angeles and past midnight in Montreal.

Sighing with fatigue, Mitch switched off his computer and tilted back in the swivel chair. He watched the sun sink into the Pacific horizon, tinting foamy clouds a hot pink. Below he could hear the hum of traffic on Ala Moana Boulevard. Past Sand Island a dine-and-dance motorship, loaded with tourists below its bogus sails, cruised toward Waikiki. The mellow afterglow of sunset settled over Honolulu harbor, coating the wharves in amber, rich shade of nostalgia.

As he often did, Mitch Donahey ended his work day, a routine one withal, in a mood tinged with sadness. The bright daylight hours, geared to the rush of business, the global phone calls, the sudden hunches and quick decisions, possessed him, stamped the day with purpose and kept at bay the long night with its emptiness, its random moods and its gargoyles of despair. How he would love to see Mona tonight. No woman in years had made him feel so alive in the dark hours. If only he could phone her.

When his own phone rang once more, Mitch ignored it. He was tired. Time to wrap it up, go home and shower, nap, catch a late supper at Romeo's and climb into bed with a book. He reached for the button that would switch his four phone lines to tape recorders.

Oh, what the hell. One more call wouldn't kill him. Might be Littleton or Kelleher wanting to clear up some detail. Picking up the phone, he delivered his standard line: "Hello. McCafferty & Sons. Donahey."

"Mitchell Donahey, this is Wasif Zabib calling from Copenhagen."

Zabib? Was this someone fooling him?

"Good morning or rather good evening." The voice came across smooth, urbane, British accent. "I'm here with my first coffee. You undoubtedly are ready for your evening drink."

"Good morning is right, Mr. Zabib." Mitch knew his time zones as he knew the spelling of his own name. Copenhagen stood twelve hours ahead of Honolulu at this time of year. "Are you always up by six-thirty?"

"I never fail, Mr. Donahey. I arise at six, perform my obligations for Allah and have my first coffee, as I am now doing, at six-thirty."

When Zabib said nothing further, Mitch let silence occupy the phone channel. Wordlessness often had tactical advantages and he was not sure that this voice actually belonged to the Arab tanker owner.

A clink of china. Cup on saucer? "I understand from my man Picot in Marseille that you've been asking questions about one of our VLCCs, the *Monteporo.*"

"That's right." Mitch's doubts faded. Had Picot also spoken of Mitch's inquiries about Zabib's ownership of the lost *Gunnison Bay?* "I had a possible charter, but Henri says the *Monteporo* is under repair."

"Yes, unfortunately for our P & L statement." Another sound of china on china. "You know, Mr. Donahey, that our Lorikeet Tankers is in an expansion stage?"

"I hear you've bought some tankers. Hard to miss in this slack market. Not many buyers for VLCCs right now."

"Good time for bargains. Of course, with more ships comes necessary expansion of executive personnel." While Zabib's accent was standard British castle, club and hounds, his precise articulation would have put that of Prince Charles to shame. "I talked at some length about you with Monsieur Picot and I've done some checking elsewhere. Of course, I've known you by reputation for some time."

"My name's hardly a household word, Mr. Zabib."

"But you enjoy a reputation for smart fair dealing in the trade. To come to the point, Mr. Donahey, I'm prepared to offer you an important position at Lorikeet Tankers and I'd like you to fly over here to Copenhagen and discuss it."

"Right out of the blue like that?" Work in Copenhagen? All that cold harsh weather?

"Yes, right now." A sound over the line of a piece of paper being unfolded. "I'm ready to offer you $175,000 to start or considerably more than I understand you're making there annually."

The figure surprised Mitch. Below the family ownership level, even veteran brokers at McCafferty failed to make that much. "That's a good chunk of money, Mr. Zabib."

"No one goes hungry at Lorikeet."

"Just what kind of job did you have in mind? I heard today that you were looking for a chartering manager." The only thought of leaving McCafferty had occurred during a fit of anger over an act of seeming sabotage by Marvin Crouch in the New York office. He swore he'd quit, but a night's sleep unstitched that rash vow. The truth was that he felt at home in the old firm where a broker's single word linked continents, ships and fortunes. Actually, in tanker broking, it wasn't the money alone, but the international cast of characters, the often hectic pace and the need for utter concentration that held him.

"Yes, I am. Same thing you're doing, but on the owner's end," said Zabib. "I'm looking for a vice-president for chartering."

"How soon?"

"By next month. I'd like you to fly over here this coming weekend so we could discuss the matter in detail."

"Well . . ."

"I never ask twice, Mr. Donahey." Zabib's tone sharpened. "Either you're interested or you're not. Are you?"

"Yes, of course." A man couldn't automatically reject an offer that would double his income. "I think I could come this weekend, but I'll have to see. I man this office alone."

"Fine. Call me before noon tomorrow, your time." Zabib gave the number. "And then I'll expect you for dinner Saturday night. Agreed?"

"Okay. I'll let you know tomorrow."

Mitch's thoughts churned as he tidied his desk, locked the file cabinet, stowed the computer software and turned down the air-conditioning control. Now what was that all about? Just who was Zabib? Did Abu Dhabi money back him? Or Kuwait? The Kingdom perhaps? And how did this Moslem stranger happen to settle on Mitch Donahey? Had talk of the *Gunnison Bay* triggered this? One thing was sure. When Claude Bouchon, the Frenchman with the rakish stocking cap, rammed a sloop on a Diamond Head reef, the shock tumbled more than one person into unknown waters.

Leaving the office, Mitch had reached the door before he remembered. Smiling at the oversight, he retraced his steps and reached for the rope that hung from the bell that once did service on a McCafferty yacht.

He tugged. The clapper struck the brass with a solid satisfying clang. He rang it twice more in this marine salute to another fixture, his forty-ninth of the year and one in which his trade savvy had helped win the day.

As the echo died, Mitch Donahey thought of Wasif Zabib's offer and rang the bell once more. This time for luck.

4

Far below the Scandinavian Airlines jet on which Mitchell Donahey flew from Hawaii to Denmark, two seamen sat over mugs of coffee in the crew's lounge of the *Yandoon Princess*, a supertanker bound for Delaware Bay from the west coast of Africa with a capacity cargo of 1,700,000 barrels of Nigerian crude oil.

Situated on the fifth deck down from the bridge in the seven-deck superstructure, or "house" as mariners called it, the lounge served as library, card room, sitting room and video cassette movie theater for the twenty seamen, pumpmen, enginemen, cooks and mess stewards who sailed the tanker under the orders of nine licensed officers.

The great steel ship, stretching longer than three football fields, had begun to roll and heave as dirty weather, hung on the ribs of strong easterly winds, came flapping across the wide Atlantic.

With the throb of engines below, the echo of clanging doors within and the rush of wind and sea outside, the lounge was a noisy place, but the two off-watch tankermen nevertheless spoke in low voices as they leaned toward each other across a card table. They did not wish their private business to be overheard. Also, they were gnawing on that ever-juicy conversational bone of seamen since the dawn of sail: the captain.

"They planned it this way," said Nikos Miaoulis, a Greek able seaman who had spent more than twenty years on tankers. "Lots easier to blame this captain."

"I suppose so." Jerry Artwick, an Englishman from Bristol, had worked in the clamoring engine rooms of a dozen tankers. "When the fuck will we get paid for the job?"

"Like I told you, this one takes patience." Miaoulis looked over his shoulder, making sure they were still alone. "It'll be a year or so, after Tiggemann collects the arbitration award. Quit worrying, Jerry. You stand to rake in two hundred grand minimum. . . . When's it going to blow?"

"Anytime soon. Should have by now." Artwick had thinning red hair and skin as white as eggshells. "The switch of captains made the job possible, okay, but Christ, that don't mean I have to like it. Those shirt-and-tie geniuses in Montreal got to be out of their stupid minds. What kind of captain is it has to give a bloody speech before shoving off?" He tilted his head as if wincing with pain.

"All began in the galley." Miaoulis was a brooding dark-visaged man with a drooping moustache. "First they started hiring 'em for the mess, then next thing you know, they're letting officers take turns bringing a wife along on a trip."

"I seen one turn up as third mate on the old *Skagway Dolphin.* Lasted one voyage, no more. Wanted it both ways, like they all do, and the crew wouldn't put up with it."

"It gives me a royal pain in the ass." Miaoulis scowled down at his coffee. "Christ, what with Gertie serving mess, that bitch Kathleen in the galley and the first engineer's wife, they got enough for a fuckin' table of bridge."

Artwick nodded in sad assent. "I liked the old man we had. Just what the hell did we do to deserve an old lady?"

"I've taken crap from a lot of masters in my day," said Miaoulis morosely. "Now I gotta take it from a goddam missy."

At that moment the cause of their distress stood on the enclosed bridge, five decks above, resting elbows on a window ledge and gazing ahead at the rising seas and darkening clouds. An occasional wave broke over the bulbous bow and now and then the forward part of the ship reared up as though on a hinge. Seas washed over the gray deck and its network of pipes that looked like an abstraction wrung from metal and flung out flat by some demented sculptor.

The bridge, often the scene of meandering chitchat, had grown quieter as the weather worsened and the captain came up to check conditions. A weather report from the radio officer, showing a gale-force storm rapidly approaching from the east, had propelled the captain from cabin to bridge where the four-to-eight watch included the second mate, a seaman at the wheel and another serving as look-out on the starboard wing. In the last few minutes a switch had been made from autopilot to manual steering.

"Bring her to three zero four, please, Fuqua." The captain, dressed in gray turtleneck sweater, jeans and rubber-soled shoes, still peered ahead past the heaving bow.

"Three zero four, ma'am," repeated the helmsman. Michael Fuqua, a young man who wore a tiny diamond in one earlobe and trimmed his hair like a scrub brush, turned the wheel slightly to the left.

"You can knock off the 'ma'am,' Fuqua."

"Yes ma'am. . . . Oops, I'm sorry. Captain Kirk insisted I call him sir and I got used to talking like that."

Fuqua, shrugging, glanced helplessly behind the captain's back at Second Mate Stjepan Pasic, a burly Yugoslav, who returned a small grin of sympathy before burying his head in the leather hood covering the radar.

"No big deal either way, Fuqua," said the captain quietly. "I like to keep things simple."

"Yes, ma'am. Oh, shi . . . it's just that . . ."

The captain turned around toward Fuqua. Pasic raised his head from the radar hood and at the same instant, like musicians striking an opening note, all three people burst into laughter.

"That's tonight's story for the crew's lounge, Fuqua."

"Yes . . . Captain . . . If you don't mind."

"Mind it or not," she said, keeping it light, "the story will be all over the ship by midnight."

The tanker lurched as a large wave smashed against the bow and the three occupants of the bridge stowed the banter while they tended to business. The master and the mate paced the bridge, stared out the windows, now spotted with the coming storm's first rain, put their heads in the hoods of the two radar sets and occasionally glanced at the screen displaying the digital recording of the ship's speed, 12.7 knots.

No captain enjoys scruffy weather, but Captain M. S. Harkinson especially had no stomach for it on this trip. For one thing, the *Yandoon Princess,* a VLCC of 240,000 deadweight tons, was much too old by her reckoning and had taken the pounding seas for many years. For another, the *Princess* had not been drydocked for major repairs in more than two years, a matter of contention between the master, or as Nikos Miaoulis would have it, mistress, and the Michaelson & Lygdamis executives in Montreal. Thirdly, this was her initial voyage—the snickering crew called it "virgin" or "maiden"— as captain of a supertanker. She had worked tankers nine years as an officer, rising from third to second to chief mate, before obtaining her master's license. Then she had held the command of two small M & L tankers in the Mediterranean before being selected as one of the two rotating captains of the *Yandoon Princess.* She would have preferred a younger ship for her first large tanker, but no captain, especially not a female, could pick and choose in these days of laid-up crude carriers.

So gladly she went off to Port Revel Lake near Grenoble, France, for special training on simulated supertankers that sailed themselves into a variety of engineering and navigational crises. Then a vacation in Hawaii where she almost lost her bearings during the last three days with a strangely compelling man named Mitch Donahey—she had sniffled and mooned and dreamed through the long flight from Honolulu to Montreal and even now the thought of the man could raise goose bumps. And then at last, after a brief session with the Montreal brass, she flew off to Nigeria where she boarded the *Princess* as it loaded oil in the steamy delta of the Niger River.

Coming aboard with the knowledge that a good part of the crew would detest the idea of a female captain, believing it an insult to their manhood and an invasion of a province historically male, she gave a brief talk to the assembled crew the first day. Gist: I intend to run this ship like any other professional captain, with firmness, with fairness and, I hope, with some humor. If we all do our job to the best of our ability, this can be a happy ship.

Right now, with the seas mounting higher by the minute, Captain Harkinson did not like the feel of the ship's shudder. The tanker was taking too many big waves broadside.

"A new heading, Fuqua. Two eight five," she ordered. "Two eight five."

"Two eight five." Fuqua turned the small wheel, looked up and frowned. The angle indicator above his helm showed that the rudder had not moved despite electronic linkage affording instant response.

He was about to give the wheel another turn when an alarm bell drilled the silence of the bridge. Two red lights flashed on a control panel behind the radar scopes.

"Steering lost." Mike Fuqua spoke in a flat stoic tone, unwilling to let his voice betray his twinge of fear.

The old tanker yawed to starboard, rolled into a trough, sluggishly righted herself, then bulled ahead. Now the rudder indicator moved erratically.

Mona Harkinson did not need Fuqua's footnote. The second the alarm clanged, she turned and strode to the emergency phone connecting to the engine room far below.

The second engineer, Yukio Osagawa, answered the phone on his control platform where the alarm had also rung. Yes, he said, the chief already was on his way to the steering room with two enginemen. "Good," said Harkinson. Chief Engineer Mario Didati, an Italian, commanded the captain's respect as the most competent officer aboard, not excluding herself.

The aging tanker wallowed like a sick whale while the engineer's men set to work to repair the steering system. Several bolts, it turned out, had ground free of their threads, springing a steel plate. Though the plate played but a small part in the intricate hydraulic mechanism that moved the giant rudder, Didati faced a troublesome task in trying to rebolt it. Oil flowed out steadily and fluid in the gravity tank had to be replenished by hand, crewmen carrying buckets of hydraulic oil from a nearby drum. Others sought to purge air from the system's ram cylinders.

Didati briefed Mona Harkinson when the captain, scrambling down the steep yellow ladder, came below to check on progress of repairs. Didati's prognosis was mixed. The good news, he said, was that he believed he could get the rudder operating again. The bad news: he could not promise that the repaired mechanism would withstand heavy seas.

On Didati's word that the mending would take several hours, Captain Harkinson phoned up to her young radio officer Arno Joahannes, and ordered him to send out a VHF advisory, notifying any shipping in the vicinity that a fully loaded tanker had lost steering and would remain out of control until the fault could be corrected.

In her own cabin Mona Harkinson placed a call on the ship-to-shore satellite telephone to M & L headquarters in Montreal, using one of the special numbers that connected her to the vice-president for operations. Homer deL. Richert, an executive with stooped shoulders, an icy smile and a fancy for subdued silk ties, had come up through purchasing and accounting segments of the industry. Since he had sailed the oceans only as a passenger, Mona viewed him as an untrustworthy alien.

The captain reported on the trouble and said it might be some time before the *Yandoon Princess* got under way again. Richert fretted about delivery schedules, urged all possible speed in repairs, then remarked that "on the face of it, we appear to have a case of negligence in maintenance by your engineering department."

"Absolutely not," said Mona with some asperity. "Mario Didati pays careful attention to every piece of machinery aboard." She moved to score points in the dispute that had started weeks ago in Montreal. "Yearly drydocking most certainly would have caught this weakness in the steering gear." Three times Mona had urged annual drydocking as recommended by the Korean builders, or at most every two years, and three times M & L officers had instructed her in company policy—drydocking every thirty months.

"You know the position here," Richert reminded her yet again. "President Michaelson has made that quite clear."

"He's 180 degrees wrong." Mona's throaty voice grew raspy in irritation. "I just hope I can make the Delaware capes before this foul weather blows in."

"Do your best, Captain, and let's not lose any more time than we have to." Richert focused not on rudders and possible storms, but on the M & L fleet's reputation for delivery on schedule.

Mona hung up with a sigh of frustration. As a junior captain, and a female at that, she had no clout to compare with some of the veteran masters who actually could force changes in company policy from time to time.

Fortunately the wind did not pick up while Didati and his men toiled below decks, but the *Yandoon Princess* wallowed in heavy seas and the threatened storm continued barreling westward toward the ship, according to the marine weather bulletins from America's Atlantic Coast.

Returning to the bridge, Mona Harkinson thought about her

jumbo tanker as she paced back and forth, stopping briefly to peer at the radar scopes to make sure no other ships had entered the area. She thought first of the vessel's age. An old lady by the standards of tanker crews who knew how swiftly the elongated superships aged under constant hammering of the seas, the *Yandoon Princess* had plowed the tanker roadways for sixteen years, lugging 230,000 tons of crude oil across oceans and returning to the loading pipes high in the water and as empty as a wind sock.

The very large crude carrier had been built in Korea under recognized rules of ship design and construction at a cost of $36,000,000, rated sound and seaworthy by a British classification society, sold several times before the purchase by M & L. Actually, if ownership could be apportioned by compartment, all but the great bulbous bow would belong to the West German bank that loaned M & L the money to buy the vessel.

Like all supertankers in the range from 200,000 deadweight tons up to the 564,000-ton *Seawise Giant,* world champion of monster carriers, the *Yandoon Princess* challenged outer limits of marine technology and the craft of navigation. The state-of-the-art in construction and sailing of these new behemoths trembled for a decade, vacillating between advance into the unknown of further gigantism and retreat to safer waters. At the moment a kind of cautious holding psychology prevailed in the shipping industry with only a few VLCCs on order and plans for the gargantuan 1,000,000-tonners shelved indefinitely. Most new construction centered on tankers of less than 75,000 tons.

Reasons for the new prudence, Mona knew, were two-fold. One was economic. With lowered oil consumption, reopening of the Suez Canal and steady growth of pipelines such as that across the Isthmus of Panama, the demand for supertankers had declined from the mid-seventies' peak.

The other reason, strewn over the rocks, reefs, harbors, channels and record books of the world, had a more personal impact. Since 1967 when the *Torrey Canyon* ushered in an era of pestilential ocean oil spills by cracking open on the rocky English coast, hundreds of major accidents—collisions, founderings, explosions and broken hull plates—accompanied the reign of the supertanker. Millions of tons of oil had seeped over the oceans from these shattered hulls, killing fish, embalming crabs and oysters, coating seabirds in lethal black mantles, fouling beaches, poisoning delta wetlands and clotting rocky shorelines with a vile oozing pox.

One trouble was that in the not infrequent emergencies of the high seas, the long lumbering supertankers and their massive loads could not respond with sufficient speed and flexibility. The *Yandoon Princess* needed almost three miles to come to a halt from her cruising gait and in bad weather in congested waterways like the English Channel captains of nearby vessels breathed easier when she had passed.

The business of hauling large amounts of oil over long ocean spans with reasonable speed and safety produced tankers with interior mechanisms of incredible complexity. Officers of the *Yandoon Princess* had to monitor, maintain and repair more than ninety complicated systems, including no less than fifteen alarm networks, thirteen navigation aids and five propulsion control layouts. Hundreds of thousands of connections held the pipes, lines and wires of these systems in working partnership. Damage to a bolt here, a flange there or a valve over there could put the mighty ship at risk. Actually, some important piece of machinery frequently failed to function and only the principle of dual works, one of them in reserve, kept the supertanker going. So sophisticated were many of the systems that no man aboard, not even the highly skilled veteran engineer, knew how to repair all of them.

Stormy seas subjected the tanker's lengthy hull to weird unforeseen stresses that still eluded full understanding. Also troubling was her tendency, like other large tankers, to "squat" when maneuvering in shallow waters, a phenomenon that acted as if the marine floor were sucking the hull downward.

Partially monitored by small computers that sent millions of electronic signals coursing through automatic valves, sprockets, gears, pumps and engines at the speed of light, the *Yandoon Princess* resembled nothing so much as a sluggish whale being adjusted constantly by clever fleas under the wary eyes of the chief engineer and the captain.

For all their training on simulated tankers at Port Revel, masters of the new scale of VLCCs viewed their charges with a kind of chilly respect often mingled with some awe and apprehension. The great steel hulks did, after all, break apart in roaring wintry seas or explode off the southern coasts of Africa and they did run aground from sea-lanes seldom regarded as perilous by the captains of ordinary tankers.

Captain Mona Harkinson regarded the object of her command with a special ambivalence. She had signed on with M & L Syndicate to conduct handy-sized tankers on predictable voyages along well-known, thickly traveled tanker lanes. Give her anything less than 70,000 tons, she once told Homer Richert, and she'd sail it through the queen's bosom. Yet she could not refuse command of one of the huge tankers and retain respect in the industry. Men could and did, but a female captain who shied from handling a VLCC might as well hit the beach and stay there.

Her schooling period at Port Revel convinced her that the whole idea of the big-bellied steel ships threading constricted waterways had fatal flaws somewhat like a scheme to train Sumo wrestlers for water polo. In short, she saw the *Yandoon Princess* as a potential menace and she would cheer the day when the owners sold her for scrap and sailed the ship off to Taiwan or Korea where hordes of sweating workers would disembowel the old lady and rip her apart.

This was not only Mona Harkinson's first voyage in charge of a VLCC, it was also a special trip for the *Yandoon Princess*. Since U.S. Atlantic ports were not equipped to handle the big supertankers, they ordinarily sailed their cargos to Bonaire in the Caribbean or to a Gulf of Mexico anchorage south of Galveston and there transferred the crude to smaller tankers. But a few 250,000-tonners had entered Delaware Bay and lightered their cargo to barges for the trip upriver to refineries near Philadelphia. M & L executives were anxious to follow suit, perhaps establishing a pattern of routine deliveries.

Mona could sense, through the motion of the seas and the new insistent lament of the wind, that the predicted storm was drawing closer, and she was just about to make another trip to the steering gear room when Didati called. The plate had been repaired and the tanker could resume normal cruising speed. Captain Harkinson gave the orders and soon the *Yandoon Princess* again headed toward the American east coast, propelled at 13 knots by her powerful diesel engine.

A few minutes later Didati, a lean intense man who wore a religious medal around his neck, appeared on the bridge, still wiping grime from his hands and forearms with a swatch of cotton waste.

"What's the latest on the weather?" he asked.

"Heavy rain and strong easterly winds due in an hour or so," replied Mona. "Gale-force storm by morning."

"I'm not sure that plate will take rough water." The rag that Didati had crammed in a hip pocket trailed like a spotted tail. The engineer described in some detail the nature of the repairs. "But with the plate buckling like that," he concluded, "there's no guarantee the new bolts will hold. . . . How far out are we?"

"We should pass into Delaware Bay tomorrow morning. What odds of the rudder holding until then, Mario?"

"In fair weather, fifty-fifty." He was beginning to like this captain. When she came below, she knew in detail how the steering mechanism functioned. Not many masters could say as much. "In a storm, eighty-twenty against us."

"In that case," said Mona, "I want a man stationed in the steering gear room at all hours."

"Already done, Captain. I've assigned men there for all watches." He took a steel bolt from his pants pocket and showed it to Mona. "That's one of the six from the plate that came off."

"Six came loose all at once?" She was skeptical.

"No. My guess is that a couple of them worked free and then the oil pressure blew the rest." He turned the bolt several times. "Innocent-looking bugger, isn't it? But see where the threads had worn."

She inspected the bolt, then asked, "Anything further we can do, Mario?" Worry lines about her eyes reflected Mona's concern.

"Yeah." Grinning, Didati slipped the bolt in a pocket and pulled from beneath his soiled shirt the medal that hung from his neck. "If you've got a St. Francis of Paola like me, pray for his help."

The chief engineer kissed the emblem of the patron saint of Italian seamen. The captain forced a smile.

Engineman Jerry Artwick, his hands newly scoured but his shirt daubed with muck, met Seaman Nikos Miaoulis in the passageway of the house where their rooms were located.

"Didati suspect anything?" asked Miaoulis in a voice just above a whisper.

"Not a thing." Artwick shook his head. "He blames it all on age and no drydocking."

"Any chance of it holding into the bay?"

"Doubt it. We're lucky if the fucker holds through the heavy weather they say is coming."

"Cross your fingers that it holds through the night." Miaoulis waited until a seaman, leaving his quarters, disappeared around a corner of the passageway. "The best spot for Tiggemann would be five or ten miles out."

"What if it breaks sooner? Shit, I can't time the bloody thing."

"Oh, the Tiggemann guys can come way out. They got a 14,000-horse job, a big bastard. It's just that everything will work better close in."

"I still don't like laying this whole thing on Tiggemann." If worrying were a profession, the British engineman would have his Ph.D. "How do we know the old lady won't pick some other outfit for the tow?"

Miaoulis shot him an annoyed ye-of-little-faith look. "Like I told you, Elger's got it all worked out. Tiggemann'll be flooding the approaches to the bay with three tugs. They'll be ready. No one else will."

"If this Elger's so fuckin' smart, how come he didn't figure the weather?" Artwick fingered his few strands of red hair as if to make sure they were still there. "Sparks says there's one helluva'n easterly coming across at us."

"The weather, that we gotta risk. Quit worrying, Jerry. We got it made. . . . Is it true the old lady went down to steering?"

"Yeah, she put on her act." Artwick's tone was that of the skilled artisan at the mercy of a dilettante.

"God Almighty, twenty-four years at sea and here I am limping across the Atlantic with two old ladies." Miaoulis put a hand on the Englishman's shoulder. "Which, Jerry, come to think of it, ain't a bad way to go to the bank."

5

The scant Danish summer, an imposter of a season, had come and gone this September afternoon as Mitchell Donahey rode the airport bus into Copenhagen.

A sickly sun peered through overcast skies at ragged intervals and a chill wind off the Oresund whistled about the old seaport city with the soprano moan of winds that scour the plains of Kansas. Danes in heavy Scandinavian sweaters and down-filled jackets bent to the wind along great broad avenues. Pedestrians seemed reduced to scurrying insects, overwhelmed by the ancient gray monuments, museums, castles and ponderous public buildings, many with stone walls a yard thick, that lent such a melancholy aspect to the city.

Actually, as Mitch knew from a previous visit, inhabitants of little Denmark's capital liked roistering good times and managed via fork and bottle to add a festive touch to the most ordinary of days.

Mitch had flown from Hawaii after notifying his New York headquarters that Bert Takahara, the University of Hawaii grad student, would cover for him during a three-day absence while he conferred with Wasif Zabib, a tanker owner of perhaps growing value to shipbrokers, at the operator's behest.

Only two passengers, Mitch and a man whose tan raincoat betrayed his pessimism about Danish weather, remained on the bus when the vehicle reached its terminal. The building also served as the station for hydrofoil vessels that sprinted to Sweden across the sound, an arm of the Baltic. His hotel, 71 Nyhavn, lay just a few meters away on the other side of Nyhavn Canal, a bridged waterway crammed with high-masted sailing ships and bordered by narrow gabled buildings dating back three centuries and more.

A bellboy who met the bus trundled Mitch's overnight bag along the cobblestone lane to the hotel where a blond reception clerk, beaming and convivial, handed him an envelope.

"Delighted your plane landed on schedule," read the message. "You have time for a jet-lag nap. My car will call for you at 6:30. W.Z."

The attentive welcome flattered Mitch and added a droplet to his thimble of information about Zabib, obviously a man with an eye for detail.

The appearance of his room, overlooking an arm of Copenhagen's thriving harbor, widened the pleasant vacation feeling that had settled on him as he read, drowsed and chatted with fellow passengers on the long flights from Hawaii. The hotel room reminded him of home. The furniture had the same spare design and economy of line that marked the Scandinavian pieces in his Honolulu apartment.

His nap became the heavy sleep of the drugged for several hours, but he felt refreshed and reasonably alert when he awoke in time to dress before Zabib's BMW sedan rolled into the hotel driveway. The chauffeur turned out to be a weathered talkative Dane with a slanted grin who, like many of his countrymen, spoke good English.

Zabib occupied a three-story town house on fashionable Amaliegade not far from the offices of Lorikeet Tankers. Built like its neighbors of heavy stone blocks, the town house and its thick wooden door, brass fittings gleaming, bespoke solidity, age, respectability. Mitch was surprised then to have the door opened by a woman who looked as if she had stepped off a fashion-show runway. A svelte blonde with an attentive smile, she wore a modish dress of black wool flecked with red, gathered at the waist by a red belt and flaring at the shoulders into wide sleeves.

"Mr. Donahey?" She held out her hand. "Do come in. I'm Grethe Knudsen."

She chatted brightly of the weather and clucked sympathetically over Mitch's long plane rides as she led him up a curving stairway carpeted in a deep burgundy pile and enclosed by handsome wooden railings hand-carved in intricate patterns.

The tall man who waited at the head of the stairs looked more Gallic than Semitic. Black hair parted on the side, dark eyes, pale skin that might have belonged to an Irishman or Frenchman, he had wide shoulders and a trim waistline. He wore a blue pinstripe suit of conservative cut and a jeweled ring and he gave off disquieting vibrations, fretfulness perhaps, certainly impatience.

"Wasif Zabib." He gripped with authority, then ushered Mitch toward wide leather armchairs ranged along a coffee table apparently fashioned from a ship's deck planking. Two small brightly colored parrots perched in a nearby brass cage. "My lorikeets," said Zabib.

The room and its furnishings, splashily modern with an auxiliary marine theme, included a corner wet bar with high stools, bright throw rugs of Mexican design and vivid abstract paintings, one of which looked like a Jasper Johns. The photograph of a tanker monopolized one wall. Looming through mist, the huge ship's bulbous bow threw curtains of spray as it plunged forward like some implacable primeval beast of the sea. Beneath the picture stood a magazine rack featuring petroleum and shipping journals. Through wide front windows could be seen several cargo ships docked in a branch of Copenhagen's harbor.

Another woman, also slim, attractive and stylishly dressed, appeared at Grethe Knudsen's side.

"Hanne Thorvald, may I present Mitchell Donahey." Zabib bowed toward the woman. She had cropped black hair and wore an orange blouse of decided cleavage. A small veiled smile gave her an appearance at once shy yet flirtatious and she looked at Mitch as if she were uncomfortable in his presence. He had a quick first impression of a woman sending conflicting messages. And did Hanne's glance, in the customary initial appraisal, linger for an instant at his crotch?

Sudden airs of ambivalent sensuality fluttered in the room, an odd social climate for Mitch who had flown across two oceans under a summons to urgent business.

"I thought the ladies might join us for cocktails," said Zabib as they seated themselves. "You and I can do our business privately over dinner and then perhaps later . . ." He let the unfinished sentence float. "Does that suit you, Mr. Donahey?"

"Fine." As always he adjusted swiftly to new ground rules. "And call me Mitch."

"Thanks, I will. I'm known as Zab to my friends and colleagues." Whether that would include Mitchell Donahey, his manner implied, was a matter for further examination.

The settled domestic air with which Grethe Knudsen took drink orders marked her as the woman of the house. Mitch had no firm idea of Zabib's personal arrangements, although Henri Picot had said the shipowner had a wife and family back in Jordan.

Zabib noted Mitch's puzzled expression when Grethe placed what looked like a martini-on-the-rocks in front of the tanker owner. "Yes, I hold the faith of Islam and of course the Koran admonishes us to abstain. But one must exercise personal judgment and look to the sources of the Prophet's teachings. Scholars tell us that Muhammed one day visited a friend's house and saw many guests drinking wine and enjoying one another. He thought the intoxicant a pleasurable thing. But he changed his mind when he returned the next morning and found blood and gore and severed limbs around the premises. Maddened by too much drink, the guests had run amok and tried to kill one another." He paused, eyeing his martini. "For me, that story says plainly: 'Drink in moderation.' I do. And I honor the pledge to my father that I would never let the first drop of intoxicating liquor touch my lips."

Zabib tilted the heavy glass, poured a drop on his forefinger, then wiped the finger dry on a cocktail napkin. The shipowner raised the glass in a toast "to the ladies" and favored the little group with a benignly triumphant smile. In that moment, Mitch formed his first impression of Zabib. He rather liked the man—and he did not trust him.

They chatted of Copenhagen's weather (too chilly too early), the lorikeets (Zabib had fetched them from Kuala Lumpur and liked the Malaysian birds so much that he named a tanker company after them), fashions (Grethe thought black would be the color again this season), and Queen Margrethe's recent visit to the high cliffs and peat turf of the Faeroe Islands (the women regarded the queen with affection). Grethe addressed the host as Zab while Hanne managed to avoid use of his name.

They conversed in lively fashion, Zabib inclined to broad judgments, Grethe Knudsen warming to gossip and Hanne Thorvald making remarks that seemed either tart or coy. Mitch concluded that Zabib and Grethe were lovers. He didn't know quite what to make of Hanne. At one point she dropped her cocktail napkin. Retrieving it from the floor, she brushed Mitch's knee, letting her hand linger for an intimate moment. The evening had taken an unexpected turn.

The women excused themselves after the first drink, just in time, they said, to catch another episode of "Matador," a popular Danish television serial.

Zabib escorted Mitch to a formal dining room where crystal sparkled on the chandelier, venerable sterling ware graced the table and a serving maid, dressed in a gray uniform trimmed with white lace at cuffs and collar, stood by.

"Through this window you can see the queen's four palaces of Amalienborg." Zabib pointed to another window. "And through there you often see the passenger-cargo vessel to Oslo. Fine overnight voyage. I often make it. Easy way to arrive for business with the shipping people up there."

Zabib continued as they seated themselves and began the first course, a delicious asparagus soup. "You might wonder why I brought Lorikeet Tankers to Copenhagen. No major oil or tanker business here. True. But I've always been fond of this city. I have blood ties, you know. But also Copenhagen is tolerant, mature, urbane, a city filled with excellent restaurants and fine music. The Danes like a good time and they have a libertine streak despite the stolid Lutheran religion that people still adhere to."

He paused, soup spoon in air. "My life-style is a liberal one, Mitch. Did you know there are good Moslems who don't follow the old rigorous ways? I'm one of them. I believe we only go around once on this earth and I don't intend to spend the whole trip praying to Mecca. I do my duty by Allah, never fear, but I don't fall into the trap of overdoing."

"I take it you're not a Shi'ite Moslem?"

"No, no. They're our noisy minority. Something like your rightwing Protestant evangelicals."

An endive salad with tangy dressing followed the soup. "Why is my English so good?" Zabib obviously enjoyed answering his own questions. "As a young man, my father left Amman for schooling in London. There he met my mother, a woman of smashing looks, half

Irish and half Danish. I always spoke English with my mother. As for Copenhagen, I spent several summers here as a boy."

"You said Amman," Mitch interrupted. "Are you a citizen of Jordan?"

"Yes, but I spend very little time there."

"I wondered. Some people in the trade think that you're an Iraqi."

"Allah forbid." Zabib's laugh was hearty. "The most suspicious chauvinists in the world, the Iraqis, forever accusing foreigners of slighting or insulting them over trivial incidents. Tremendously insecure, those people."

By the time they had finished the main course, a pinkish leg of lamb with roast potatoes and chard, the tanker owner had laid out multiple reasons for choosing Copenhagen as his headquarters. Thanks to the computer and telephone, a man could now manage a business from any place. He sometimes ran Lorikeet Tankers from such sunny resorts as Agadir, Cannes and Acapulco. As for personal contacts in shipping, half the world's tonnage was owned, managed, brokered and insured within pre-breakfast flying time of the Danish capital.

Zabib spent nearly an hour talking about the business of transporting oil from its sources to the industrial centers, Europe, America, Japan, where vast industries, institutions and peoples craved oil as an addict craves heroin. Here they needed their daily fix, millions of barrels of injections, to run their cars, heat and cool their homes, power their factories, fuel their utilities and light their streets and playing fields. They could no more do without oil than they could breathe without oxygen. And although all thinking people knew that petroleum was a finite resource swiftly being exhausted, they stuck their heads in the sand like ostriches and refused to envision the day when the last oil well ran dry. Instead they slurped up the viscous black fluid like hogs at a trough, swilling ten gallons for every one they conserved by turning down thermostats, mounting solar panels or driving fewer miles.

"So there's money to be made on the world's fuel addiction even at today's low oil prices," said Zabib. "Lorikeet will make big money in the days to come. I'm neither altruistic nor reformist. I take the world as it is."

They finished the dessert, a strawberry mousse, and the maid fetched a silver tray of liqueurs. At Zabib's urging, Mitch selected a brandy and swished it around the balloon-like snifter.

"Some people wonder why I'm buying up tankers at a time when a number of carriers are unemployed, some big tankers are being hurried to the breaker yards and others are being used as floating storage bins." Zabib sipped a crème de menthe. "Because I'm getting terrific bargains, that's why. Because within a couple of years, at most, there'll be a shortage of tankers and we'll cash in millions, that's why. Because we don't need a big cash flow today and can afford to wait, that's why." He said it with an edge of truculence as if Mitch had challenged his business judgment.

"Everyone in the industry has the same facts." He leaned on the table toward Mitch. "They all know today's oversupply of tankers will turn into tomorrow's undersupply. The difference is that I'm willing to bet a lot of money on it."

Zabib set his cordial aside. "And now to the point. Lorikeet is expanding. We have nine tankers now, including four VLCCs, and we expect to have twenty by this time next year. To earn as much as we can while waiting for the payoff day of tanker shortages, I want to charter to the maximum. Right now I have only one charter man, Henri Picot in Marseille, and as you know, Picot isn't the most energetic man alive. Location made no difference when we had only a couple of ships, but now I need my charter man here in Copenhagen and I need a good one."

He pointed a finger at Mitch. "So I want you. Salary, as I said, $175,000 a year, payable monthly, $25,000 in advance the moment you'll say you'll come aboard. What do you say?"

Mitch toyed with his brandy snifter before replying. "An attractive offer, Mr. Zabib. Naturally I have questions."

"Fire away." That air of impatience clung to him.

"Okay. First, why me, a guy mostly out of sight way off in Honolulu? You know hardly anything about me."

"Oh, but I do." Zabib, smiling broadly, took a paper from his jacket's inner breast pocket. "Here's the file on you, compiled by my research people. You see, I've looked at a number of brokers, including you, in recent weeks. Then, when Henri mentioned your name, I quizzed him about you and got a good report. Since I'd already been impressed by your record, I decided to go ahead and call you."

While plausible, this seemed short of persuasive. For one thing, Henry Picot knew him only casually, had never met him.

"I know a lot about you." Zabib looked down at the paper. "You're forty-one and single. Five feet eleven, 165 pounds. You grew up in Chicago mostly, played high-school football and enlisted in your army the summer after graduation. They shipped you to Viet Nam where you fought a full year and earned a decoration for bravery . . ."

"For survival," Mitch cut in sourly.

"Your army says bravery. After Viet Nam, you went to Cornell, made good grades and then took a master's in business at Stanford. You worked for an oil outfit and a couple of shipping companies on your West Coast. Then you became a shipbroker, went to Tankship Operation School and concentrated on tankers. You've been with McCafferty & Sons seven years, the last five in Honolulu. You were married, but have been divorced for about six years. No children."

Zabib flipped to another page. "A sampling of opinion among charter people in the tanker trade finds you reliable, hard worker, trustworthy, competitive, aggressive and especially adept at anticipating shipments of oil. One charter manager says, 'He'd be a good man to steal horses with.' " Zabib smiled. "Another says, 'I've committed us to millions on Mitch's word.' "

"Anybody tell you I've been known to wake up screaming at night?" Mitch felt a flick of anger. "How about my telling off some of those ass-hole patriots at home who want to send in the Marines whenever some little country thumbs its nose at the U.S.? And do you know that I think about a third of the adults on this planet are morons, one third are insane and that the rest of us must be too sleepy to tell a fart from a sneeze because we let the crazies run the fucking world?"

Wasif Zabib, patently taken aback, cleared his throat before asking, "Why do you tell me this?" He spoke in a low voice as though to defuse Mitch.

"Because, damn it, you're telling me what a lot of people think I'm like. So I'm telling you, right from the mouth of the guy who knows, what I'm really like." Mitch took a swallow of brandy. "Look, I'm not your corporate type. I'm a free speech freak. I don't trust any institution, Army, Catholic Church, General Motors, political parties, B'nai B'rith, the Danish government, you name it."

"Interesting." Zabib rose from the table, took a silver cigar box from the sideboard and held it out to Mitch. "Try one. They're Cuban."

Mitch shook his head. "No thanks. The only thing I smoke is grass and not a whole lot of that."

Zabib busied himself lighting a cigar before taking his chair again. He puffed, savoring the smoke and eyeing the panatela as though it had valuable information to impart. "Your file contains a number of comments from the trade about your outbursts. I just didn't bother to read them to you."

"Outbursts!" Mitch snorted. "I'd call them 'snatches of wisdom generated by passion.' "

"They don't seem to interfere with your charter fixtures. You're rated tops as a broker."

"Yeah, well, when there's business, I tend to it."

The cigar appeared to act on Zabib as a pacifier. His restlessness, a seeming dissatisfaction with the current moment, wafted away on eddies of smoke. He sat studying Mitch. "Viet Nam, I would guess, had a big impact on your life."

"I like the way you put that." Mitch smiled. "Some people claim the war left me a psycho." When Zabib made no response, Mitch continued. "Yeah, I do blow off when the anger gets to me. But Viet Nam did me one favor. I can't tolerate bullshitters and I'm wary of hype. Also, short of a gun in my face, nothing scares me. I don't run from threats."

Zabib smoked quietly for a few moments, then said, "I suspect that people trust you because you do blow your top now and then. They figure you're being yourself. It's the rigidly self-disciplined types that raise questions about what they're hiding." He eyed the long ash on his cigar. "Anything else you'd like to bring up?"

"Yes." Mitch did not hesitate. "I refuse to handle charter fixes on VLCCs more than fifteen years old. Also I don't like to handle tankers that haven't been drydocked in more than two years."

"Even if rated in satisfactory condition by a classification society?"

"Most of the tankers that break up in heavy weather have been approved in class."

"So you want us to set our own standards?" Zabib had the critical tone of an examiner.

"Only way to go to gain a good reputation with the majors. Look at Exxon. They have their own screening department that checks out every tanker they charter. How about your policy here?"

"I don't like the old ladies. I plan to scrap or sell my VLCCs before the fifteenth year. There may be exceptions to that policy, special situations involving megabucks, but if that occurs, I'll take over. I won't expect you to charter out any vessel you think is too old. As for drydocking, I follow the builder's recommendation. If he says every year, every year it is."

"Fair enough." Mitch liked what he heard. "What about registry? I notice your *Monteporo* flies the Liberian flag. What about the others?"

"All Liberian registry."

"I don't like that."

"Unless you go to a flag of convenience, you can't make money. You must know that."

"Yeah, I do. It's a fact of life. I've lived with it up to now, so I guess I can keep on keeping on." Mitch moved to a prime concern. "Who bankrolls Lorikeet?"

"I can't tell you unless you come to work for me. If you do, you'll get the full facts the first day on the job."

"Can I get your assurance there's no trouble money involved?"

"Trouble money?"

"Yeah. Mafia, say, or some Shi'ite Moslem group that backs Arab terrorists. Or maybe just crooks who order their masters to sell paid-for-oil to third parties on the sly and then scuttle the tanker to collect the insurance." Watching Zabib closely, Mitch observed no unusual reaction to this last remark.

Zabib merely shook his head. "The principals are law-abiding people with no criminal record and no intent to violate the laws or customs of the sea."

"And I'd get their names and background the day I came to work?"

"You have my word on it." Zabib blew a smoke ring that skidded toward the window overlooking Amalienborg palace.

Mitch attempted to channel the conversation back to Zabib himself, but the half-Arab adroitly deflected some questions and smothered others under extraneous anecdotal chitchat. Zabib did offer that he had inherited money, spent a year at the London School of Economics and had a wife back in Jordan and three grown children in as many countries. Along with these scattered biographical bones, Mitch picked up but little meat. Zabib had been "in and around tankers for years," he said, but he volunteered no names, companies or places. Apparently a man in his fifties, he gave only the vaguest clues to self and business during the last two decades.

"You headed Petrolift Shipping, didn't you?" asked Mitch.

"Ah, you've done some research yourself, I see." He seemed not displeased as he examined his lengthening cigar ash.

"What happened to Petrolift?" Mitch put the question when Zabib appeared indisposed to speak further about the corporation.

"We dissolved it after the *Gunnison Bay* loss." He glanced at Mitch. "You know about that, of course?" When Mitch nodded, Zabib said, "We took a loss, only partially offset by the insurance, when she sank in the Pacific with a cargo of oil. She went down, as you may recall, after an explosion in the engine room, one never fully understood." He studied the cigar ash as if estimating its life expectancy. Apparently deciding that it might fall on his jacket at any moment, he tapped off the ash on a copper ashtray. "You know how such a loss taints the owners, no matter how blameless."

"Yeah, McCafferty fixed that charter and I had a piece of the action. It hurt us some, no doubt about it." Mitch hoped the mutual setback would loosen Zabib's tongue.

"Ah, yes, McCafferty & Sons did make the fixture. . . . Well, there were a few ugly stories, all completely false. I trusted that master as I would my own brother. At any rate, we thought it best just to erase the Petrolift name and start fresh." He smiled. " 'Clean sweep down, fore and aft,' to use your Navy's expression."

When Zabib said nothing further on the lost tanker, Mitch reverted to personal history, attempting to explore the Jordanian's student years, but Zabib would have none of it. He turned aside several inquiries, used another to expatiate on his ideas about education in general.

"You're a hard man to pin down," said Mitch at last.

"All belongs to the past." Zabib waved his shortened cigar, consigning personal data to the trash bins of history. "What matters right now is how I run this company. Believe me, Lorikeet Tankers will succeed. A man who comes aboard now can make himself a fortune."

"A man who comes aboard now also has to take you on faith."

Zabib deposited the last of his cigar in the copper ashtray. "To that I would respond in a word." He looked Mitch in the eye, then asked tartly, "What do you have to lose?"

The shipowner tossed his napkin on the table. "That's it, Mitchell. I know you'll need time to think this over. Let's see, you're flying back tomorrow. I'll want my answer by 9 A.M. Tuesday, Danish time. A plain yes or no will do it."

"Okay, I'll phone you."

"Good." Zabib stood up. "So let's adjourn to the living room."

Mitch was intrigued, if not unduly surprised, to find the women waiting for them. Grethe Knudsen lounged in one of the leather armchairs, thumbing through that day's edition of the *Ekstrabladet*. Hanne Thorvald placed records on the turntable of a stereo set near the window. Ship and harbor lights winked on as the late Danish twilight faded into darkness. A record dropped and Diana Ross, candidly sexual, sang "Upside Down" to a driving disco beat.

"I love your black women singers." Hanne Thorvald came toward him as if to a long-planned meeting. Again he had the distinct impression that her glance of welcome swept his crotch. "Dance?" She kicked a Mexican throw rug aside.

"Sure, but how about food? Don't Danish women eat?"

She laughed. "We went out to a nice restaurant. Grethe treated me. . . . I like this beat."

They danced apart, disco style, quickly finding a mutual rhythm. Hanne took small swift steps, let her hips and shoulders shake and roll. Zabib and Grethe joined them and Zabib, although still quite proper in his pinstripe suit and closely knotted tie, danced with verve. He grinned a wordless message at Mitch that seemed to say: "A Lorikeet Tankers bonus. Enjoy."

But at the end of the record's second number, Zabib said his goodnights. "Long day, Mitchell. I'm tired." They shook hands and Zabib, Grethe at his side, left by a rear door. That restless perturbed air still marked him.

Mitch picked up the beat with Hanne. "I guess he means to leave us alone."

"That's bad?" She took his hand and swung herself in a circle.

They danced, sat on the planked coffee table to chat, danced again. When another record dropped, he looked at his wristwatch. "I have a flight home soon after breakfast. Much as I dislike breaking this off, I'd better leave now."

"Oh, no. You mustn't do that." She seemed overly distressed.

"No? Why not? I have to get home and home's 10,000 miles away."

"But you're supposed to come to my apartment." Hanne was quite agitated now.

"I am? Just who is expecting us . . . Oh, I get it." Suddenly he realized. Zabib had hired her, probably from one of Copenhagen's many "escort or massage" services, to entertain him for the night. "Let's talk a bit." He led her to one of the leather armchairs and sat down on the edge of the coffee table facing her.

"I didn't understand," he said. "Mr. Zabib is employing you to show me a good time, isn't he?"

"No. I never met him before. It's Grethe Knudsen I know. She used to work in the shipping office where I do." Again her troubled look took in his crotch.

"But you are getting paid for tonight, right?" Mitch felt somehow remiss for not managing an erection.

"Only if you go home with me." She had a look at once perturbed and relieved. "Otherwise I get just the gift."

"Gift?"

"Yes, Grethe gave me this for coming." She opened a small beaded handbag and withdrew a silver cigaret lighter. "I hated to tell her that I quit smoking last month."

"How much extra would you be paid if we went to bed together?"

"Let me see." She thought for a moment. "In American money, it would be about $400."

"Well, Hanne, I don't like to deprive you of the 400 bucks, but I honestly don't feel in a mood for sex and/or romance tonight."

To his amazement, she sprang from her chair, embraced him and planted a large kiss on his cheek. "Oh, I'm so glad. Neither do I." She quickly grew serious. "But I hate to lose the money. It's worth two weeks' wages."

"Why don't we pretend that we did go to bed? You collect your fee, Zabib figures I've been properly entertained, I get a good night's sleep and everybody's happy."

"Oh, I couldn't do that." She evinced genuine disapproval. "You see, I'm just starting out in this night work and I want people to trust me."

"I was to be your first customer?"

Her smile was shy, vulnerable. "No, second. I went out with a man last week. You're much more attractive."

"Thanks. It's too bad you lost a night's pay. Better luck next time. Now could you call us each a cab?"

When the taxis arrived a few minutes later, they descended the carpeted stairway together and said their good-byes on the sidewalk. As they parted, she slipped a card into his hand. "My number," she said, "just in case you come back sometime and want company."

In his hotel bed, he had trouble dropping off to sleep, but even more trouble fixing his mind on Zabib and the job offer. Each time his mind centered on a thought, Mona Harkinson intruded. Just where in Europe, he wondered, was she? He had written to her last week, care of American Express, London, had told her that he missed her sorely, that he wanted to see her as soon as possible and that he would fly anywhere on short notice to meet her. He had urged her, if she missed him at all, to write or call. "Given our spectacular start," he had written, "it would be a sad waste of talent to close the show after opening night."

His mind's last picture, as he finally fell asleep, framed Mona beside him in bed in his Honolulu apartment as she whispered of her deep joy in giving herself to him. "The tight little knots all get blown away, leaving me feeling very, very female." He could hear her husky voice and smell her fragrance and he wanted her more than he had wanted any woman in many years.

In the lobby of Kastrup Airport, a Scandinavian offering to the jet age, high, airy, bright, neat, Mitch stopped at the newsstand to buy a *London Times* and a *Lloyd's List.* As he pawed his pocket for change, he saw the man sitting on a nearby bench. He wore a snap brim felt hat and a tan raincoat and his eyes were lowered to a newspaper. Hadn't he seen the same man on the airport bus yesterday? And again last night outside his hotel when Zabib's BMW called for him?

Mitch tried to get a look at the man's face, but the head remained lowered and the hat brim obstructed the line of vision so that his glimpse took in little more than an impression. Later when his flight was called, Mitch looked back. The man in the tan raincoat was walking rapidly toward the exit.

6

Not long after Mitchell Donahey began his return flight across the Atlantic, alarm bells once again hammered a tense silence on the bridge of the *Yandoon Princess* and for the second time in as many days Helmsman Mike Fuqua saw that the angle indicator above him recorded no movement despite a sharp turn of the wheel.

The supertanker, laboring through heavy seas, had shuddered as an enormous wave struck the starboard quarter, hurling spray as high as the bridge seven decks above the waterline. Fuqua had swung the wheel to bring the lumbering vessel back on course.

"Steering gone," he called.

But again Captain Mona Harkinson, brushing past the second mate, already had reached the phone to the engine room.

"The chief's on his way to steering," reported Second Engineer Osagawa. He had picked up his end of the line on the engine room control platform at the same moment as the captain far above him.

"Get word to Didati that I need his report as soon as he can manage." Mona cursed softly. It made for raw nerves for a captain to lose control of a ship at any time, but to have steering fail her during a storm like this was the stuff of nightmares. Holy Jesus, what a day! For an hour she had tried in vain to see her heaving bow, some three hundred yards farther west, through violent draperies of rain sweeping across the long deck's webwork of pipes, winches, valves and hatches.

Not that the steering failure surprised her. Mario Didati had given the mechanism but a twenty percent chance of holding in stormy seas and the anticipated foul weather had arrived with unpredicted fury. The tanker had been scheduled to reach Delaware Bay soon after dawn, pick up a river pilot and transfer most of her cargo, 230,000 tons of Bonny light crude from Nigeria, to barges that would deliver it to one of many holding tanks along a hundred miles of the Delaware River's dense concentration of petroleum facilities. Lightened to 75,000 tons in the haven of the bay, the *Yandoon Princess* would crawl upriver to a New Jersey refinery.

Now, after the initial repair of her steering gear, the tanker ran three hours late in seas lashed into massive walls of water by easterly winds shrieking across the Atlantic. The waves, mounting ever higher, left deep swirling troughs in which the *Yandoon Princess* plunged and rolled. Black clouds heaved westward under a solid overcast that battened down the horizon tight to the sea. The first rains had come as a splattering prelude, quickly swelling to a slashing storm that drilled the tanker's long deck and made walking there a lethal hazard. The wind flung wave crests into sculptures of spray, howled past struts, wires and railings and beat against the covered bridge where Mona stood with two mates, the helmsman and another seaman.

The chief mate, Bill Muldoon, a gregarious Irish American from Philadelphia, stood by the chart table, keeping a continuous watch on the tanker's position, for the ship was not many miles from the Delaware coast. He swung from the automatic satellite navigation display screen to the LORAN recorder to the radar scopes, plotting the ship's location on the rolling ocean every ten minutes. The second mate, the Yugoslav Stjepan Pasic, kept his head buried in the leather cones that covered the two radar scopes during daylight. Thus far only one other vessel had shown on the screen about seventeen miles to the east, but Pasic knew they were not far from the Delaware capes and that moderate to heavy coastwise traffic could be expected. A loaded supertanker out of control posed an ominous threat to all shipping.

Five minutes after the alarm had sounded, Yukio Osagawa phoned back to the bridge. "Chief says the buckled plate broke loose again.

The repair party's having trouble. The chief says you should know there's not much hope this time."

"Tell Mario to do his best." Long windshield wipers swept back and forth over the bridge's streaming windows with a precision that belied the chaos of rain and wind outside.

Mona Harkinson, ordinarily not given to swift decision, now volleyed a series of appropriate commands that surprised the other mariners on the bridge. In response to seemingly simultaneous orders delivered in her full-throated voice, subordinates in addition to Didati took these prompt actions:

Chief Mate Muldoon used his navigation aids to produce a special fix of position, locating the unguided tanker near Cape Henlopen, the southern point of land at the entrance to Delaware Bay. He also noted that the ship stood almost due east of Rehoboth Beach, a Delaware resort popular in summer with federal bureaucrats from Washington, D.C.

Arno Joahannes, the young radio officer, taking the position from Muldoon, sent out a VHF advisory, notifying all ships and the U.S. Coast Guard that a fully loaded tanker had gone out of control seven nautical miles southeast of Cape Henlopen and was drifting under strong easterly winds, gusting to gale force, toward the Delaware coast. The radioman repeated the warning every minute.

A deckhand switched on two red lights, vertically aligned, and hoisted two black balls, one above the other. Both signals gave notice that the *Yandoon Princess* was not under control, a futile gesture since the raging storm limited visibility to a dingy rain-swept gray bowl not more than a quarter mile in diameter.

Another deckhand started the foghorn that began bawling like a wounded bull. It sounded one long and two short blasts—signal for a vessel out of control—and would continue to do so every two minutes.

Although his duties normally kept him landlocked, the ship's manager, a combination treasurer, purchasing agent, ship chandler and chambermaid to the *Princess,* happened to be aboard for this voyage from Nigeria. Captain Harkinson impressed him for work on the ship's log with orders to note down in chronological fashion, exact to the minute, every step taken during the emergency.

Mona's thoroughness and precision of command stemmed directly from the odds quoted her the previous day by Mario Didati. If the tanker had only one chance in five of keeping its weakened steering apparatus intact during a storm, then it behooved the captain to prepare herself for emergencies. Actually, awe of the great ship had inspired Mona to undertake a number of mental drills some days earlier. Since from the start she had regarded her huge aging tanker as a potential menace to the sane conduct of ocean transport, the New England saltwater sailor had assumed that sooner or later, if the owners persisted in their noodleheaded plan to keep the *Yandoon Princess* slaving away in ocean commerce, the old lady would come to grief. The way she had imagined it, the *Princess* would just burst her seams one night like some overfed diabetic dowager and would sink beneath the waves with a snort and a gurgle, leaving Mona to go through the ludicrous ritual of being the last person, at dire risk to her skin, to quit the cadaver and climb into a lifeboat.

With this debacle in mind, Mona often had practiced the command routine she would follow should the old woman lose some of her parts and become a drifting invalid. And now, in the last few hours, she had swung several times through a specific emergency drill in the event that the tanker lost steering power again.

Like other masters, Mona had been conscious of rudderless tankers ever since 1978 when the *Amoco Cadiz,* a 230,000-ton vessel, lost her steering system in French waters during bad weather and crashed on the rocky coast of Brittany, spewing crude oil over 400 square miles of the Atlantic, swamping the French shoreline in a funereal black tide, suffocating marine life and entangling her owners in the most costly litigation in maritime history.

The *Amoco Cadiz* and the *Yandoon Princess,* along with hundreds of other big tankers, shared what Mona rated as a severe defect. They both had but a single propeller. Shoving several city blocks of petroleum through heaving oceans in all kinds of weather with no propeller in reserve seemed to her an act of folly.

After firing off her commands and turning over the bridge to her chief mate, who had roused from a sorely needed sleep at the sound of the alarms, Mona hurried aft and down the steep metal ladders to the steering gear compartment. There was always the chance that Didati, by some miracle, might save the steering mechanism once more.

Her first glimpse inside the room destroyed all hope. The place looked as though it had been struck by shellfire. Oil gushed from a broken pipe, splattering the freshly painted bulkhead. Pieces of metal were strewn over the deck. The top of the rudder shaft slammed back and forth, crashing into metal supports of the steering rams. Just as Mona entered, chunks of steel broken off by the rudder shot about the room like bullets. Five men, trying to dodge the missiles, slipped and slid on the rolling oil-slick deck. One of them dropped, felled by a flying slug that gashed his forehead. Blood dripped over his eyes as two crewmen helped him to his feet.

Didati waved his work party out of the room. The men retreated to the safety of the passageway as metal chunks continued to bang against the bulkheads.

Mona's eyes shot Didati a wordless query.

"No way this time. We can't fix it," said the chief engineer. He gave a swift diagnosis of the failure and a summation of their repair efforts.

After urging the injured seaman to obtain immediate first aid from the clinic-in-a-box maintained by the second mate, Mona hurried to the nearest emergency telephone, part of the intricate communications system that laced the tanker's interior, and called the radio room. She ordered Joahannes to send an SOS distress signal at once, dispatch a "rudder gone" message to the Coast Guard and broadcast an appeal for help to any salvage tugs in the area. Mona checked herself on each command as she gave it. Should the *Yandoon Princess* not survive the perils confronting her, the captain wanted a spotless record of timely action for the hordes of insurance inspectors, owners' experts, lawmen, marine authorities and admiralty lawyers to pore over.

By the time she reached the bridge again, the storm had worsened. Waves as big as three-story houses came rushing out of the east, the driving rain obscured the whole forward half of the tanker, winds keened past the bridge and the vessel lurched and rolled. Mona experienced that familiar sinking sensation, slightly nauseous, that afflicts seamen aboard a ship that has gone out of control in a storm only a few miles off a coast. Here wallowed her ungainly charge, swollen to bursting with 230,000 tons of oil, as helpless as a pregnant elephant on a ski slope.

Bill Muldoon's plot on the charting table showed the *Yandoon Princess* to be six miles southeast of the channel entrance to Delaware Bay, but less than four miles off the beaches of Delaware. In the bare half hour since the tanker lost steering and the engine was shut down, the winds careening across the Atlantic had driven her much nearer to shore.

Having done her best on behalf of her ship, Mona went down a deck to her cabin and placed a phone call via satellite to M & L Syndicate headquarters in Montreal. On her plea of emergency, Homer Richert's secretary connected her at once to the frosty operations vice-president whom Mona thought belonged in the accounting department.

The captain put the glum news succinctly.

"No chance of repairing the damage this time, Mona?" asked Richert.

"I already told you that," she replied with a drip of acid.

"I still think you have a severe problem in your engineering department."

Mona, ordinarily cool under stress, felt her temper rise. "Damn it, I told you yesterday, the fault's not with Mario Didati, but company policy on drydocking."

Richert lowered his voice. "I trust you're not going to make a point of that again today, Captain."

Mona ignored the remark. Obviously a breath of disaster had touched Richert, prompting him to think of possible marine inquiries ahead. Time pressed. The captain cut to her prime concern.

"I request permission," she said, "to hire the first salvage tug or tugs that show up. I need authority to accept LOF no-cure-no-pay terms." Lloyd's Open Form was a standard contract vehicle between salvage firms and disabled vessels at sea, affording later arbitration of the fee.

"We prefer a simple towage contract," said Richert. "It would save us a bundle." Arbitration awards usually took a solid percentage of the value of the ship and cargo.

"We have about as much chance of getting a towing deal out here as finding a winning lottery ticket on top of a wave." Mona could not conceal her scorn. How ridiculous could dry-land people get? "Listen, Mr. Richert, I'm out here in an ugly gale-force blow that's shoving me toward the Delaware coast faster than I care to think. No salvage captain in his right mind would accept a mere towing contract. He knows we'll be aground by late afternoon or sooner if we're not pulled out of here. And he'll want a piece of this ship, mister. You better believe it."

"Company policy stipulates that towing contracts be tried first." Someone knocked at the door. "Come in!" Mona shouted. It was Arno Joahannes, the young radio officer. She held up a hand. "Just a second, Arno." When she spoke into the phone again, Mona's husky voice sprang to a tenor register. "The hell with company policy on trying towing contracts first. We're liable to dump more than a million and a half barrels of crude all over the U.S. Atlantic Coast. The suers will wind up owning your damn company. Don't you realize that?" She turned to Joahannes. "Okay, Arno. What is it?"

"Captain, I've got the *Molly J.* calling." The radio officer's infectious grin unfortunately bared bad teeth. "Says she's a big tug with heavy towing gear. Tiggemann Brothers, owners. She's coming out of the bay at top speed and she wants an LOF no-cure-no-pay."

Mona relayed the news to Richert who said, "Damn it, this should wait until we can reach President Michaelson. We understand he's due any minute at his club. We'll . . ."

"This can't wait for Michaelson or the stockholders or anyone else," Mona cut in. "I need permission to hire this tug on LOF terms. Right now. Yes or no?"

"Do what you think best, Captain."

Mona refused to accept equivocal surrender. "Is that yes or no?"

"Yes—if you insist it's necessary."

"Holy Jesus!" Mona hung up with a look of exasperation. "Okay, Arno," she said to the radio officer, "tell the tug we accept. LOF terms."

"Oh, Sparks," she called as he reached the door, "one second. Do me a favor and try to remember what you just heard me say to Richert in Montreal. Do you think you could?"

"Every word, ma'am." He grinned again.

"If we don't make it, there'll be hearings and inquiries from here to the Azores."

"I know it. Don't worry. I remember everything."

As soon as the door closed, Mona telephoned Houston headquarters of Octagon Oil Corporation, owner of the *Princess*'s cargo, and told the director of operations that the company's crude, valued at $20,000,000, rode at risk off the Delaware capes in the tanks of a rudderless ship being buffeted by high winds and tall seas. Mona could only guess at the prompt flowering of calls that would fan out from Octagon officers to insurance agents, attorneys, government bureaus and traveling Octagon executives. As for the coming exchange between Octagon officers and M & L chiefs, she'd give a week's salary to be plugged into that conversation.

A half hour went by before the *Molly J.,* a large yellow-and-green tug grossing over 1,000 tons, churned into sight, breasting hill-high waves to enter the small world of a stricken ship rolling drunkenly under mutilated skies that limited visibility to less than the length of the tanker itself. The storm's fury had abated only fractionally. Rain, driven by strong winds, still came down in long slanting sheets. The weather reports handed Mona forecast continued high easterly winds, heavy rain and seas throughout the day.

Two other Tiggemann Brothers tugs were steaming toward the *Yandoon Princess.* The *Kathy J.,* which had been off Barnegat Light almost one hundred miles north, estimated that it could not arrive until mid-afternoon, but the *Thelma J.,* coming from some miles inside the Bay, signaled arrival on the scene in less than two hours.

Mona quickly assented to the general plan proposed over voice radio by Captain Steve Pattimore of the *Molly J.,* who did not seem surprised at finding the supertanker under command of a woman. The tug would attempt to haul the tanker straight east into the teeth of the storm, seeking to pull the crippled ship as far from the coast and shallow water as possible. Then when the storm had passed and the sea returned to normal conditions, he would tow the *Yandoon Princess* into Delaware Bay where the cargo of oil could be lightered to barges and an empty *Princess* towed upriver for repairs.

The two captains also agreed after some discussion that the tanker should be towed by the stern rather than the bow. They both knew and mentioned that an effort some years earlier to pull the *Amoco Cadiz* by the bow, history's first attempt to tow a disabled and loaded supertanker into the wind in heavy weather, proved unfeasible. Pattimore said that a powerful tug, like the sister *Thelma J.,* boasting a 14,000 horsepower engine, could pull the *Princess* by the bow, but that the *Molly J.* probably could not manage it. His engine, he said, produced but 8,500 horsepower, approximately the same as that of the West German tug that failed to pull the *Amoco Cadiz* in the normal manner. Yes, Mona agreed, VLCCs with the heavy superstructure aft tend to put their sterns into wind and seas. Also, she knew from trials at supertanker training at Port Revel in France that only powerful tugs could be relied on to tow large loaded tankers by the bow.

Bill Muldoon, making rapid calculations as the *Molly J.* maneuvered for position, predicted for his captain that at the current rate of drift the big tanker would go aground on the shelf of the coast in about three hours, possibly less. A turn to an outgoing tide, further lowering the shallow shelf waters, complicated matters. Fully loaded, the *Yandoon Princess* needed at least sixty feet of water. Mona gave the numbers to Pattimore of the *Molly J.* in a hurried radio exchange. Both captains realized that the salvage mission had become a race against the clock.

"This would be a piece of cake if the *Thelma J.* were here too," said Pattimore. "Usually she watches the bay entrance, but she was down for engine repairs and just came out this morning."

"It figures," said Mona. "This is my bad-luck day. Okay, let's get at it, captain."

Valuable minutes passed before the tug could position itself behind the tanker which was rolling on a north-south axis, her port side parallel to the coast. Bursts of seawater washed over the deck of the *Molly J.* each time she crawled up a towering wave. Tug hands, already drenched in the pelting rain, fought for footing on the slippery steel deck that flooded anew every few seconds.

One of the tug's seamen aimed a line-throwing shoulder gun at the afterdeck of the tanker. Twice rubber bullets failed to hit the tanker's deck as both vessels rolled perversely. The third shot succeeded. Crewmen on the tanker deck far above the tug hauled in the attached hemp line that became progressively thicker, then changed to wire that brought aboard a heavy stud link chain via a deck winch. Captain Pattimore on the tug began paying out the long towing wire attached to the chain.

While the tanker's foghorn bleated as if in mourning, the tow got under way a few minutes later, the *Molly J.* heading east in its effort to pull the tanker's stern into the wind. At first no movement could be ascertained. Pattimore had to make delicate judgments. If he put on full power, he feared the towline might part. If he ordered too little power, the stern could not be moved. He settled at about seventy-five percent of the tug's full muscle. Ever so slowly the stern of the mammoth ship began to swing toward the east.

A Coast Guard helicopter, clattering out of solid overcast against high winds, hovered over the two vessels. As seen from the air, a green-and-yellow water bug struggled up great walls of water, skidded down the slopes and by a seeming thread pulled an immobilized sea monster in a slow arc. Visibility improved slightly at times, but then a new onslaught of wind and rain would race across the seas, collapsing the rescue arena into a grotto of knifing winds and heaving waters. It took almost an hour to bring the stern of the *Yandoon Princess* into the wind.

Now the supertanker lay at right angles to the coast and the two captains agreed that the tow by the *Molly J.* out into the Atlantic would be aided by operating the tanker's engine in reverse. This helped—but only briefly. Throughout the enterprise the ship's crippled rudder had been swinging erratically, smashing the rudder brakes, banging against the stops and threatening to disintegrate. Now an unusually powerful wave ruptured it and sent a chunk crashing against the propeller. The projectile, weighing several tons, sheared off a blade of the screw and twisted the shaft, rendering the propeller useless. Now the *Yandoon Princess* lay at the complete mercy of the elements, no more in command of its fate than driftwood.

No sooner did the two captains absorb the portent of a powerless ship than they had to swallow more bad news. The high-powered *Thelma J.,* the sister tug racing from inside Delaware Bay to assist in salvage, radioed that she had developed renewed engine trouble upon encountering the heavy open seas and was limping back to port under half power. The second sister, the *Kathy J.,* would not arrive from Barnegat Light until mid-afternoon.

Mona ordered Arno Joahannes to broadcast another appeal for salvage aid, but the nearest ocean-going tug could not reach the scene before the *Kathy J.* Pattimore's tug would have to fight the battle alone, striving to haul the wallowing tanker windward or at least prevent her from drifting farther toward the Delaware coast.

Pattimore soon found that seventy-five percent power would not do the job. With the great seas pounding the stern of the *Princess* and with no propeller churning in reverse, the long gray tanker drifted inexorably toward shore. The tug skipper slowly increased throttle, but still the dangerous drift toward shallow water continued. At last, deciding that he had to take the risk or lose the ship, Pattimore eased the *Molly J.* up to full power.

The drift seemed unchecked at first, but then Pattimore and crew noticed that the rugged little craft began to make a bit of headway. Her prow nosing up house-high waves, her 8,500-horsepower diesel engine shaking with maximum effort, her hull shuddering, the chunky *Molly J.* gained inches, then feet, then yards. The crew cheered. Soon the men watching on the tanker's bridge saw the movement. Arms waved from the bridge wings of the *Princess* and Mona used voice radio for terse congratulations. "Nice work, Captain." Slowly the tanker moved toward deeper water.

Jerry Artwick, the red-haired British engineman, came up to the crew's lounge in the tanker's house to "take five." Like the rest of the crew he had been working steadily since the steering alarms sounded. His friend, Nikos Miaoulis, the veteran deckhand, joined him for a cup of coffee at a table removed from the others.

"If this tow don't work," said Artwick, "we've had it. No-cure-no-pay, so no salvage award."

"It's got to work." Miaoulis said it belligerently as though might made right.

"I don't know." Pessimism put downward lines in the Englishman's face. "Didn't you hear that the big tug had to put back into the bay? Engine trouble. And I'm not sure the *Molly J.* has the horses for the job."

"That's one bitch of a sea, no question," Miaoulis conceded.

Artwick leaned far across the table. "Be just my fuckin' luck to have us go aground with no salvage. After all the chances I took!"

"You and me both. Well, we gotta hope the old lady and the tug will bring it off."

Artwick shrugged in disgust. "So now I have to bet on a skirt to save me two hundred big ones."

Ten minutes after this conversation a freak acceleration of the storm slammed the two vessels with winds of hurricane force. The burst lasted only a few seconds, but during that snip of time the *Molly J.* lurched at the crest of a wave and the towing line, coming under extraordinary pressure, snapped off at the chain that had been made fast to the *Yandoon Princess.* Once again the rudderless power-less ship, submissive to the forces of the sea, wind and tide began drifting toward the Delaware shore while the storm hammered her stern.

The two captains swore almost simultaneously, Pattimore blaming fate and Mona Harkinson excoriating the pinchpenny noodleheads at M & L's headquarters who had denied her the annual drydocking that surely would have prevented this whole agonizing scene.

The log of the *Yandoon Princess,* as kept by the impressed ship's manager, told the rest of the tale:

1040: *Yandoon Princess* drops anchor to slow shoreward drift.

1050: *Kathy J.* radios that she will arrive at 1545 to assist the *Molly J.*

1053: First Coast Guard helicopter leaves scene as replacement arrives to monitor salvage effort.

1135: Third Mate Muldoon estimates drift has increased. Coast lies two miles off at 272 degrees.

1151: Captain Pattimore reports that towline has been repaired and that he will make new attempt at tow.

1209: Rifle line from *Molly J.* fired to port afterdeck, but falls short.

1220: Second rifle line lands on tanker's starboard afterdeck and is made fast.

1228: Anchor hoisted.

1233: Second tow begins.

1304: Stern now on heading of 91 degrees.

1306: Captain Pattimore reports he has increased power to 90 percent maximum.

1322: Tanker holds steady under tow, halting westward drift.

1326: Captains Harkinson and Pattimore confer. Pattimore says he fears to increase to maximum power, prefers to hold tanker in place until the *Kathy J.* arrives at 1545 when the two tugs should be able to tow the tanker eastward.

1337: Weather report predicts storm will pass this position around mid-afternoon.

1340: Captain Harkinson informs Montreal office of holding action.

1342: Towing wire parts, snapping off unexpectedly at tanker stern. *Molly J.* again reels in.

1358: *Molly J.* crewman M. Isaacs breaks leg. Hurled against metal stowage box by sudden pitch. Carried below.

1401: Captain Pattimore reports he will make new attempt at secure tow.

1402: Captain Harkinson informs Montreal of conditions.

1405: Last piece of rudder breaks off.

1448: Captain Pattimore completes repair of towline.

1503: *Molly J.* maneuvers aft of tanker for third shot of towline's rubber bullet.

1512: Third towline made fast at tanker stern.

1515: *Yandoon Princess* strikes bottom on port side amidships.

1517: *Molly J.* begins tow to dislodge tanker from shelf bank.

1525: Captain Pattimore increases to 100-percent power. Tanker fails to move.

1536: No. 3 port tank springs plate. Oil emission.

1540: Plate gives way at No. 4 port tank. Oil emission.

1544: New thrust of heavier seas drives tanker farther aground. More port plates give way. Oil flows from two more ruptured tanks.

1548: *Kathy J.* arrives. Second Coast Guard helicopter joins overhead patrol. Storm slacking off.

1553: Large oil flow from all six port tanks.

1609: *Kathy J.* gets lines to tanker afterdeck. Made fast.

1628: Both tugs tow on 90-degree heading at 85-percent power. Searchlights switched on.

1634: No discernible movement of *Yandoon Princess.*

1637: Both tugs increase to 90-percent power. No movement of tanker.

1643: Port plates near stern give way.

1655: Captain Harkinson reports to Montreal that salvage has failed. *Yandoon Princess* has 40-degree list and is slowly breaking up with widening oil slick. Storm has passed. Rain ceases. Winds down to 15 knots.

1716: Captain Harkinson orders officers and crew to get personal belongings and gather on deck forward of bridge.

1740: Coast Guard helicopters begin lifting crew and officers off tanker.

Eight minutes later, as the tanker began breaking apart in the still heavy seas, a third Coast Guard helicopter, arriving on the scene, warned Mona Harkinson that she must evacuate the ship at once.

At 6:10 P.M. the chopper plucked the captain off the deck of the collapsing tanker. Ironically, the storm that prevented the tug from pulling the *Yandoon Princess* to safety had passed so far to the west that a sinking sun in a cloudless sky emblazoned the wreck of the tanker like a sculpture commemorating some great maritime triumph.

As she whirled off under theatrical skies with the ship's log and papers tucked in her briefcase, Mona Harkinson noted the darker hue of the water near her smashed vessel. Oil poured from the shattered hull and she knew that the lethal slick soon would spread over a vast extent of ocean as it poisoned marine life, clotted Delaware beaches and blackened her career, perhaps beyond repair.

As the steel cadaver faded from view, she fought back tears of frustration and wished, not for the first time in this awful day, that she had the strong lean body of Mitchell Donahey beside her tonight.

But beside her at this moment the young Coast Guard public-relations officer was talking. "You'd better get your thoughts in order. There'll be a mob of press waiting for you when we land in Philly."

Oh my God, she thought, the first that Mitch would learn of her full identity would be on the day of her worst defeat.

7

First the crescent of Hanauma Bay below him, the floating specks actually Japanese bridal couples scouting the shallow reef waters with flippers, snorkels and masks, then the shoreline communities of Hawaii Kai, Niu Valley and Aina Haina funneling into the deep green valleys of the island of Oahu. Now the jumbo jet turned right around Diamond Head, its high tiara still brown and parched from the long dry season.

Then came the concrete spikes of Waikiki anchored like guardian lances around the Royal Hawaiian Hotel, that candy-castle remnant of a bygone era. The sight of the old pink hotel evoked once again the image of Mona hurrying up the portico steps and out of his life. Would his letter reach her? If so, would she answer?

Like all returning residents with a yen for a scenic welcome, Mitch Donahey occupied a window seat on the plane's right side. After Waikiki, as the plane lowered, came Ala Moana Beach Park, the ocean between sand and breakwater as calm as a pond, then the shining office buildings of downtown Honolulu, the Aloha Tower and the commercial harbor. Beyond the airport lay Pearl Harbor, submarines, frigates and destroyers snug to its piers, and the sinking sun glinting on the three distinct bays of the naval base ravaged by Japanese carrier bombers almost a half century ago.

Out in the warm air of evening after eighteen hours in the cocoon of plane travel, Mitch promptly shed his jacket and rolled back his shirt sleeves. It was good to be home again under blue skies and floating pillows of clouds, good to see palm fronds trembling in the trade breezes that grazed the skin like silk. Cold drafty Copenhagen lay two continents away and the prospect of working there seemed to melt with the setting tropic sun.

A headline in the afternoon *Star-Bulletin* broke the homecoming reverie: TANKER OIL SPILL SMEARS EAST COAST. When he bought a copy and stood reading the story while waiting for his luggage, pictures and two names jumped off the page at him—Capt. Mona Harkinson and *Yandoon Princess*. Incredible. But yes, the picture from a Philadelphia press conference showed the Mona he knew, tall, upswept hair, air of class, but now a drawn tight look. She wore a gray turtleneck sweater, jeans. Good Lord, of all of the identities he'd imagined for her in his conjectures, merchant-marine master had never occurred to him. Mona, captain of a supertanker? But then, as his mind ticked off scenes from those three days, he realized that she did give off occasional emanations of one accustomed to authority. And oh yes, now he remembered why her name sounded vaguely familiar when she first used it. He had read in a marine journal of a woman named Harkinson who captained a small tanker in the Mediterranean.

The front page carried two aerial shots of the *Yandoon Princess*, one showing the tanker in younger happier days and another, taken only hours ago, of the carcass protruding from a sea of oil off the Delaware coast. Bad news for McCafferty & Sons. Marvin Crouch of the New York office had made the fixture for this voyage of the *Yandoon Princess*. Thank God, Mitch had refused to help. And if Jim McCafferty ever had doubted the validity of Mitch's stand against aging VLCCs, this grounding ought to set him straight.

Standing by a baggage carousel, Mitch completely forgot about his bag as his eyes planed swiftly through the story of the tanker's demise.

"Worst U.S. oil spill . . . Tide of oil to blacken beaches and resorts of four states . . . Governors urge White House declare national emergency . . . Long litigation threatens . . . Octagon Oil loses $20,000,000 petroleum cargo . . .

"A day of anguish for Captain Mona Harkinson, one of the first female graduates of California Maritime Academy and a seagoing

tanker officer for eleven years . . . Her maiden voyage as captain of
a supertanker . . . Fought to keep her ship afloat . . . Last person
off the smashed vessel . . . The captain is mother of sixteen-year-
old daughter . . . One of only three women worldwide to captain
large merchant ships . . . Describes two-day ordeal of ruptured
steering system . . .

"At headquarters of Michaelson & Lygdamis, tanker owners,
Montreal, executive source says had no reason to doubt Harkinson's
competence . . . Industry expert says disaster will set female
marine officers back twenty years . . . *Yandoon Princess* crew di-
vided on their captain's skills . . . Majority dislike female in command, but several praise her talents and cool head in emergency
. . . 'Knew her tanker's complex systems better than most masters,'
said Mario Didati, chief engineer. 'In no way was she at fault.' . . .
'A tanker's no place for a woman captain,' said Able Seaman Nikos
Miaoulis. 'The ship was jinxed the minute she walked on board.' "

Mitch marked the seaman's name. Wasn't that the Greek from the
lost *Gunnison Bay?* Probably. Same name.

Not until he had devoured every detail in the long story did Mitch
finally stuff the paper in his hip pocket and pluck his bag from
among only three remaining on the carousel. He abruptly changed
plans. Instead of going home, he retrieved his Mustang from the
parking lot and drove directly to the office garage in downtown Honolulu.

Bert Takahara, caretaker of the phones and files during Mitch's
absence, greeted him. "Aloha, world traveler. The phone's been ringing off the hook." The communications graduate student grinned.
Intrigued by the romance of the seas, he could think of nothing more
engrossing than a noble marine disaster.

"*Yandoon Princess?*"

"That's right, Boss." The genial assistant with the shiny black hair
wore his customary running shoes. "Jim McCafferty's been calling.
He's still at the office."

"Bert, I want you to get on the horn and find that *Yandoon Princess* captain, Mona Harkinson." He spelled the name. "Try the major
Philadelphia hotels. Try Michaelson & Lygdamis in Montreal. They
ought to know where she is. Try the Coast Guard. Whatever, try it.
This is an emergency. We've got to find the woman."

"Will do." Takahara turned at once to a phone. He reveled in crises.

It was after midnight in New York, but McCafferty was indeed still at his desk, according to his secretary, who put Donahey on hold until the president of McCafferty & Sons finished another call. Mitch enjoyed an easy relationship with the man who hired him seven years ago. They were of a similar age, had both gone to Ivy League schools and shared a zest for ship brokerage. They bantered and gossiped and Mitch always had drinks, and occasionally dinner, with this fourth-generation McCafferty when he paid his regular calls on the home office. Jim had lauded him publicly at a recent company banquet. For his part, Mitch liked and trusted Jim and rated him high on executive talent.

"I guess you know the kind of flak I've been getting from Octagon Oil." McCafferty, skipping salutations, got right to business. "Of course, Octagon has to take the heat. They wanted the bargain they got because of the *Yandoon Princess*'s age. Still, you know the Octagon crowd. Losing a shipload of oil, especially this cargo with all the publicity about pollution, they hold it against us for making the fixture."

"The old story, Jim." Mitch wondered at the frost in McCafferty's voice. "They always blame the broker."

"Right. You know this is only our second loss in more than a decade. We fixed the last trip of the *Gunnison Bay*—and by the way, Mitch, thanks for that tip on the engineer and the seaman. If that story's true, I want to see the whole crew in jail. And now it's the *Yandoon Princess,* a bigger loss. This last one's going to hurt our reputation, no question."

Since all that went without saying, Mitch speculated as to where McCafferty was heading at his usual fast clip. Was there some undetected Pacific Basin angle that Mitch could handle in Honolulu?

"Now how to get out of this the best we can?" McCafferty continued. "On that basic question, I need input from the two men primarily involved with the fixture, you and Marvin."

"Me?" Mitch was astounded.

"Why, yes. Your advice to Marvin that the *Yandoon Princess* would make a good charter for Octagon on the haul between . . ."

"Whoa, slow down, Jim. Just a goddam minute. Where did you get the idea that I recommended to fix that creaking old bitch?"

"Are you saying you did not?"

"You bet your ass I am." Mitch's temper flared. "Hell, Jim, I did just the opposite. I advised against us fixing that dog."

"Well . . ." McCafferty fell silent a moment. "That's certainly contrary to the information I have here."

"Who'd you get your info from?" He could feel the anger rising. "Crouch?"

"Yes. . . . Mitch, I'm surprised at your reaction. It's my understanding from Crouch that he called you last month to solicit your help on a charter for the *Yandoon Princess* to carry 240,000 tons Bonny light for Octagon from Nigeria to the Delaware."

"That's right. He did. So?"

"And that you were busy on another fix, but that you advised him that the *Princess* would fill the bill nicely."

"He's a liar." The anger flamed now.

"You say that you . . ."

"I'm saying that Crouch is a fuckin' liar. I told him just the opposite. I said I wouldn't have anything to do with chartering the *Yandoon Princess.*"

"Did you give reasons?"

"Sure did. I never mess with charters on any VLCC more than fifteen years old and she's turned sixteen. Also I don't handle big tankers that don't drydock at least every two years. The *Princess* had gone about thirty months since her last overhaul."

"You told that to Crouch?"

"Exactly. I tell it to everybody, including you, Jim. You know my stand on those issues. And by the way, one of M & L's own men agrees with me. He also told me that M & L planned to scrap the *Yandoon Princess* after 'another trip or two' as he put it."

"Did you tell that to Marvin?"

"No. I just heard it last week from one of the M & L people."

"Was that Stu Leppart of their New York office?"

"No, it was not." Mitch's anger veered in another direction. "Christ, Jim, what's with you? You're quizzing me like a damn prosecutor."

"Well, frankly, I'm confronted with two versions of a conversation that are 180 degrees apart." McCafferty spoke slowly, judiciously.

"Crouch is a flat-out liar and if you have to have that proved to you, then put him on an extension there. We'll go through who said what to whom and you can judge for yourself."

"Sorry. I wish we could, but he went over to Octagon's New York office to talk to Stedman. Our effort at damage control. They've since adjourned to a bar somewhere. The Octagon people already have started the insurance fight. That cargo was worth more than $20,000,000, Mitch."

"Yeah, I know." Was McCafferty pitching him the value of the polluting crude as a reprimand? The implied blame fired his indignation anew. "Look, Jim, you're treating me like I'm under investigation for some kind of crime. I had nothing to do with the *Yandoon Princess* charter. I was against it and I said so loud and clear to Marvin Crouch."

"That's not Marvin's story."

"I'll bet not. Marvin Crouch is a busybody office politician who's been strung out over me ever since you gave me the Honolulu job instead of him. Crouch is a liar and in this business where millions change hands on a guy's word, I wouldn't trust him with the price of a hamburger."

"He's a good broker," said McCafferty quietly. "Mitch, you're beginning to sound a bit paranoid."

"Is it paranoid to get mad when your word is doubted?" He bit off the sentence. "If you're playing interrogator, Jim, how about quizzing Crouch as to precisely what he claims I told him?"

"I have two radically different stories from two brokers I have no reason to distrust." McCafferty seemed to be pleading for understanding now. "In light of what's involved, both inside and outside the firm, I want this cleared up at once." He paused. "So, you better fly over here tomorrow. Then you and I and Marvin can sit down together and thrash this thing out."

"To put that in other words, you refuse to believe what I've told you. You think I may be lying."

"I'm trying not to do anyone an injustice." McCafferty, obviously nettled, spoke with deliberate coolness. "When the three of us sit down, it will be evident if anyone is misstating the facts."

"I'm not flying to New York, Jim." Mitch made the decision in a split second as rage swept him. "If you think I may be lying, then you don't trust me and if you don't trust me, well fuck it, I'm of no further use to you."

"What does that mean?"

"It means you can take this job and shove it."

"Hey, Mitch, hold it, man. This is no time for quickie resignations. We're in a jam here and I need help. That means your help too. We've been friends for a lot of years and you've done a fine job for this firm. I'm sure we can work out what's an obvious misunderstanding."

"Misunderstanding, my ass." Mitch could feel his own body heat. The anger seethed. "Crouch lied to you and you're putting me down on his level. I've always been dead straight with you, Jim, and damn it, if you don't recognize that, there's no sense going on."

"I don't think you appreciate my position in this." Again McCafferty had a pleading note in his voice.

"Could be, but you refuse to take my word, which is worse. We can't do business when you don't trust me. It's that simple. So I quit. . . . Frankly, I had a good offer during the days I took off. I had about decided to turn it down, but now I'm leaving McCafferty & Sons for the new job."

"You'd make a major blunder leaving under these circumstances. Think of your reputation, Mitch. If you decline to go face-to-face with Marvin, there'll be a presumption that you're afraid to."

"The only thing I fear is that I might crack the bastard's jaw. You miss the point entirely. I quit because you don't trust me."

"I suggest that you hold off any decision until tomorrow. Let's let things cool overnight."

"Nothing will change at this end."

"Perhaps, but do me the favor of honoring our good years of working together." McCafferty mingled appeal with command. "Nothing final until tomorrow. Call me late tomorrow morning, your time. Okay?"

"All right." But when he hung up, still seething, Mitch Donahey knew that a chapter in his life was ending.

Bert Takahara stood at his elbow with a slip of paper. "Captain Harkinson's at the Bellevue Stratford in Philadelphia. Here's the number."

"Thanks, Bert." Mitch glanced at his watch. "Oh, it's almost 1 A.M. there. After her day, the woman's probably sound asleep."

Mitch called the Philadelphia number and spoke to a hotel operator. "I assume Captain Harkinson has a stack of messages. Please add this request and see that she gets it when she wakes up. Quote. 'Dearest Mona. Right now you need support. I'll fly anywhere at once to provide it. Please call me soonest in Honolulu.' " He gave his home and office numbers. " 'I miss you every hour. Love, Mitch.' Unquote."

"What a sweet message!" The operator giggled.

"Honey, make sure she gets that, will you?" he said. "And what's your name? I'll mail you a box of candy."

"Don't worry. My pleasure. This is one message I'll make sure she gets. She's some woman. I saw her in the lobby." Another excited laugh. "Nice dreams, Mr. Mitch."

Takahara stood leaning against the water cooler. "Hey, Boss, what's with the lovebug talk to the tanker lady?" He grinned. "You didn't tell me you knew her."

"My secret private life, Bert. She was out here for a vacation just before her voyage from Nigeria. I'll tell you more about it someday. . . . Did you hear my end of the talk with McCafferty?"

"Some. You sounded teed off."

"Plenty. In fact, I quit."

"Quit!" The news at once astonished and galvanized Takahara. While he preferred his drama on the high seas, dry-land variations delighted him as well.

Mitch spent a half hour telling the story to his part-time assistant before picking through his mail—no letter from Mona—and locking up the office for the night. He drove home with his mind so flooded with thoughts of Mona that he realized that only a smidgeon of anger remained from the exchange with McCafferty. Indeed he gave himself to the amber mood of dusk as sailboats glided back into the yacht harbor, a knot of small boys stood gawking at the huge building mural of playful whales and couples began their evening strolls on Ala Moana Boulevard. Farther along, beneath the concrete towers of Waikiki, tourists straggled from the beach laden with mats and tote bags, their limbs parboiled a lobster red. In Kapiolani Park trade breezes shaped feathery designs among the long needles of the Australian pines. Ordinarily Mitch would have slowed to watch the kite flyers or the tennis players under lights, but this evening, tired from his long trip, he drove directly home.

After only a snack from the refrigerator, he undressed and went to bed. He intended to nap until the ten o'clock television news, when he hoped to see some of Mona's press conference. As he waited for sleep, he wondered about the nature of the rage that had overwhelmed him. What exactly caused the anger to seize him like some mugger bursting through a shadowed doorway? The fact that Jim McCafferty did not trust him completely? Mitch knew that he himself placed utter trust in no one. Why then expect McCafferty to take his every word as if it had been sanctified in heaven and borne to earth on the breath of saints? He realized that his initial indignation arose as much from Jim's underestimation of his intelligence as from lack of trust. For only a stupid man would try to deceive his boss with a major lie so easily negated. Stupid like Crouch, for instance. On another level, Mitch knew that he tended to clothe McCafferty in vestments of "the establishment," that amorphous yet powerful body of men and women who controlled the nation, shaped its culture and its myths and sent young men off to foreign lands to be blown apart, like Calvin and Stacks, in the endless lethal chess games of ideology.

Yet beneath all this, he sensed, was a deep hurt that Jim McCafferty would give as much weight to Marvin Crouch's word as to his own. The incident showed that Jim knew him only superficially despite their occasional good times together and despite the friendship that Jim symbolized in the gift of the ship's bell from an old family racing yacht. Jim just did not comprehend that Mitch scorned the lie as a tool for self-advancement or as a shield for cowardice. The bloody memories of Viet Nam that tortured so many of his nights also liberated his days. Since no terror could surpass that already experienced, why lie to avoid imaged perils to person, purse or psyche?

Then, as drowsiness set in, his thoughts drifted to Mona and a montage of images—Mona holding him in a vice-like grip of passion, facing newspaper questioners in her jeans and sweater, sweeping up their checks at the Mai Tai bar, lounging in one of his bathrobes on the lanai while soft breezes fingered her hair—escorted him past the portals of sleep.

A heavy drill chewed up concrete only a foot from his ear and not until he awoke did the sound become the insistent ringing of his bedside telephone. The small digital clock showed 4:17 in green—the A.M. color. Obviously some maniac from the mainland on the line.

"This is Mitch Donahey—I think." He shook his head to clear it of sleep, a maneuver he had tried for years without the least evidence that it worked.

"Mitch, darling, I adored your message." The deep rich tone resonated in the receiver. "Did you mean it?"

"Every word." What had he said? It didn't matter. At the sound of her voice, he soared.

"I slept, zonked out, for ten hours, then started pawing through a bunch of messages. I had to answer yours first. I loved it. Are you angry with me?"

"Hell no, but for what?"

"Not telling you what I did, about my job, who I was, all that biz-buzz."

"I was hurt when you left so frantically, but the minute I got the news, I realized you must have had good reasons."

"They seemed terribly important at the time. I might have told you, but when I found out you were a shipbroker, I was afraid you'd either be disdainful of me, like a lot of tanker people, or you'd patronize me. I so wanted you to accept and value me for myself."

"Understood. In your place . . ."

"And especially during those three marvelous days, Mitch, I wanted to have the whole woman bit, perfume, romance, high heels, surrender, you know, positively wallow in all of it. If I'd said I was a tanker captain, you might have dropped me—or so I thought."

"Are you kidding?" A dozen images of her raced through his mind. "I should drop a gorgeous woman who's a horny sea captain to boot!"

"If I'd only known." Her laugh had a gay lilt. "There was still another thing. I was facing my first trip as a master of a VLCC and I thought a big affair, with you knowing all about me, would divide my energies."

"I understand, Mona. I miss you much more than I thought I would."

"Oh Mitch, and I miss you. Holy Jesus, do I miss you!"

"How about my offer of support?" He sat up in bed, peering out at the black moonless night. "Can you use it?"

"Oh, yes, yes. All you can offer."

"Okay, I'm ready. Where do you want me to come—Philadelphia?"

"But your job?"

"I just quit." He gave a quick summary of the exchange with McCafferty. "So you see, the *Yandoon Princess* did us both in. I'll fly there today, Mona."

"I'd love it. And I need you awfully. But let's wait a few hours. I'm not sure what comes first. The brass in Montreal? A Coast Guard hearing around here somewhere? The insurance people in New York maybe? Let me call you this afternoon your time, okay?"

"Sure. If I'm not at the office number, I'll be here. . . . Keep your chin up, babe."

"Easier said than done. I'm afraid I'm finished as a captain, Mitch. And it's so cruel. That steering would have failed the most senior captain in anybody's fleet."

"Of course it would. The *Princess* was overage and under dry-docked, Mona. Even my friend at M & L knew that." He related his conversation with George Littleton, the chartering officer at Michaelson & Lygdamis. "So there's a long way to go yet. Just hold firm, honey, and you'll come out of this looking good."

"I wish I could believe that. Anyway, Mitch, I'm thrilled you called. I feel I can face anything now. Not for one hour have those days and nights with you been out of my mind."

"So, see how I can haunt you? We need lots more time very soon."

"Oh yes, very soon. And now to my other important call—my daughter Chris in Switzerland."

She called me first, even before her daughter, he thought as he hung up. She did need loving support right now and probably some advice as well. All ideas of going back to bed had fled. He was fully and nervously awake now, buoyed by elation, his mind churning. Suddenly the vista of a new life opened. He pulled on a pair of shorts, brewed coffee and sat on the lanai sipping at the hot liquid. Only the pulsing lights of a plane approaching from the south broke the solid black of the sky, the overcast blotting out stars and the new moon. The first glimmers of daylight would not come for another hour yet.

Later the morning news shows and the columns of the *Advertiser* told of the bleak aftermath of the U.S. Atlantic Coast's worst oil spill. The sunken *Yandoon Princess* had generated an oil slick that would soon stretch, the experts forecast, from Atlantic City on the north to Cape Charles at the mouth of Chesapeake Bay on the south. Already the sands at Rehoboth and Bethany beaches in Delaware and Ocean City, Maryland, had taken their first petroleum bath with gumballs of grit and oil strewn about like big black marbles. Mousse, an emulsion of one part oil to three parts seawater, washed ashore along a wide front, would soon become heavy and viscous, clogging pumps and turning the cleansing job into hard labor.

The White House declared the coastlines of four states, New Jersey, Delaware, Maryland and Virginia, disaster areas eligible for emergency federal aid. Oil-spill contractors, beginning the lengthy task of scrubbing oil from rock, sand, turf, wharf and wetlands, estimated the removal would take months and cost millions. British insurance adjusters went into conference with executives of Michaelson & Lygdamis, the shipowners, in Montreal, and Octagon Oil Co., owner of the cargo, in Houston. Lawyers mobilized in platoon strength as threatened litigation promptly surfaced in the coastal communities, at Octagon Oil, at M & L syndicate and from three injured crewmen of the *Princess* and the *Molly J.* Attorneys foresaw interwoven lawsuits dragging on for years, perhaps rivaling the hoary legal snarls concocted by Charles Dickens.

Self-appointed commanders in the endless warfare between the sexes rushed into print and onto television screens with heady pronouncements. Feminists, shy of facts but long on rhetoric, said the supertanker was doomed regardless of the gender of the captain on the bridge. Several declared that Mona Harkinson had conducted herself with a remarkable clarity and sangfroid that blustering male captains might well emulate. Female students at the U.S. Merchant Marine Academy at Kings Point, N.Y., launched a Mona Harkinson Fan Club and at the California Maritime Academy where she had graduated, two professors praised her scholastic abilities. From officers of the anti-Equal Rights forces came the predictable homilies —woman's place was in the home, not on the bridge of a tanker; instead of shelving her daughter in a fashionable Swiss boarding school and sailing around the world, the divorced mother should be at home cooking for the child. A fundamentalist evangelist, renowned for raising millions of dollars a month for godly missions among the literate heathen, saw the hand of Satan at work on the bridge of the *Yandoon Princess* and that of divine retribution in the supertanker's engine room.

At the office that morning, the case of the foundered tanker monopolized the phone lines. Everyone in the chartering business had either a sprig of news or an opinion, angle or prejudice to vent, and when Mitch finally called the New York office, Jim McCafferty spent much time elaborating on the psychological damage suffered by the firm because of its fixture of the lost tanker's last voyage.

"So I'm hoping," McCafferty concluded, "that you'll stay aboard and help us clear the decks for a fight to regain our old reputation. Any fair-minded person knows that we can't be blamed for any part of that oil spill."

"The firm no, but Crouch has to share some blame. He's the guy who offered the old lady to Octagon. Has he got a new version today since I called his first one a lie?"

"Marvin says it's entirely possible he may have misunderstood you." McCafferty spoke slowly, choosing his words with caution. "Shall I put him on an extension?"

"Nope. Jim, I refuse to get into a pissing contest with a skunk. I told Crouch flat out that I'd have nothing to do with fixing the *Yandoon Princess*. Now he's lying about it and he's half persuaded you."

"You're being obstinate. You make it very difficult for us."

"My word's all I've got in this business. You won't accept it fully. I can't operate with you when you don't. As I told you last night, I resign." He paused, but McCafferty made no rejoinder. "No hard feelings, Jim. I understand your predicament. I hope you can value my position. . . . Too bad we didn't have a company policy against fixes on old ladies that stay away from drydock too long. All this could have been avoided. I blame myself for not going to the mat with you on policy."

"I would not want any hard-and-fast stand on age and repairs. Too many variables in this game. But I respect your viewpoint. . . . Well, I hate to have you go, Mitch. You've been good for us." McCafferty's tone turned brisk. Business pressed. "Any chance of your changing your mind?"

"None."

"I regret that. Sincerely. Well, when do you want to wind it up?"

They hurried through the details of departure. McCafferty would have a replacement broker on hand within a week. Mitch had to fly to the mainland for a spell, but he promised to return and spend a few days laying out the local angles for his successor. When they hung up after brief good-byes, Mitch realized with a start that for the first time in seven years he was unemployed.

He cured that at 6:30 P.M. when he called Copenhagen and reached Wasif Zabib at the next morning's breakfast, undoubtedly with Grethe Knudsen. Mitch accepted the post of vice-president for chartering of Lorikeet Tankers and agreed to be on the job in Copenhagen by mid-October, three weeks hence.

"That's an awful mess on your East Coast," said Zabib after they finished the business at hand.

"Overage tanker," said Mitch. "She should have been scrapped."

"I got the same message. Too bad about the captain. I liked what I saw of her on television. She handled herself well at the press conference."

"Yeah, sure can't blame her." Every favorable mention of Mona gave him a lift.

He realized as he hung up that his Honolulu era had ended. Bert Takahara wanted his to end as well. "How about getting me a job over there with that outfit?" he asked when Mitch informed him of his new post. "Tanker fleets need electronic experts—all those fancy marine computers and satellite communications they have now."

Mitch promised to do his best. In truth, he would like having a Honolulu friend in Copenhagen. He knew he would miss Hawaii, especially during those long cold Scandinavian winters.

He waited in vain for Mona's call at the office, but soon after he reached home, the phone rang and her low rich voice warmed him like wine.

"Can you come to Philadelphia? Most of the action seems to be here. The Coast Guard has lots of questions and several M & L people are coming down from Montreal tomorrow."

"On the first plane that'll take me there. Do you know you have a sexy voice?"

"That's not what they call it aboard ship. . . . I'll book you a single here at the Bellevue, but we can stay in my room. It's nice and big and has a delicious king-size bed."

"Sold. I've got a compliment for you." He told her of accepting the Lorikeet job and what Zabib had said about her.

"Oh, thanks. I can use that right now. But believe me, he hasn't much company."

"You haven't been watching the news. You've even got a fan club at Kings Point. By the way, how you holding up?"

"Before our talk this morning, barely. Ever since, terrific."

Though they somewhat self-consciously avoided terms of endearment, their voices echoed with love over the satellite channel and ten minutes after they hung up, Mitchell Donahey obtained a seat on a midnight plane that would fetch him to Philadelphia by nightfall the next day. He felt light-headed, eager as a teenager.

8

The plane landed two hours late in Philadelphia and by the time Mitch had reached the hotel near the old sooty city hall, checked into his room overlooking Broad Street, tipped the bellman and splashed some water on his face, it was after nine o'clock. He called Mona at once.

"Captain Harkinson's room." It was a male voice.

"May I speak to her, please? This is Mitchell Donahey."

She came on within moments. "Mitch!" Her voice rang bells. "Are you in town?"

"Yep. Three doors down the hall. I've got the ice if you've got a bottle."

"Damn, we're busy . . . No, wait a sec." He could tell that she had palmed the mouthpiece. A minute went by. "I'm with my chief engineer. I'd like you to hear what he's telling me. If you're decent, come join us."

The instant he saw her, he wanted to wrap her in his arms. She wore black slacks and a yellow blouse and her smoky eyes, filled with delight, signaled him a private greeting. Curiously, he felt as if he had come home, although he had known this woman but a few days and had no connections whatever with Philadelphia. It was a rare feeling, comfortable yet heady.

Mario Didati, not at all comfortable, shook hands somewhat

fiercely after the introduction. He was a hard lean man with an intense manner who seemed ill at ease in jacket and tie.

"I told Mario that you're here to help me," said Mona. "He's brought something to show me. . . . Could you explain it again, Mario?" She motioned the two men to seats on a beige sofa and drew up a chair near them.

"This is a bolt from the steel plate that broke loose on our steering gear." Didati picked up a thick piece of metal from the end table by the divan and turned it in his hand so that Mitch could inspect it. "Do you notice anything about it?"

Mitch scrutinized the bolt for some time. "Well, a lot of the thread has been worn away."

"Anything else?"

Mitch, still inspecting, shook his head.

"Look, here's the worn thread." Didati pointed to one place on the bolt, then turned it slightly. "Now, look here. Does that look the same to you?"

Mitch squinted at the new section. "Well, yeah, kind of. Or maybe. Oh hell, I don't know."

"If you'd worked shops and ships' engine rooms as long as I have, you'd see the difference." Didati, tapping the bolt in the palm of his hand, launched into a description of the late supertanker's steering system. Rams, cylinders, gravity tanks, gear pumps, valves and pipe loops clattered off his tongue. While Mona followed intently, Mitch found his mind wandering. He had but scant idea what Didati was talking about.

"So when the bolts came loose, the plate came off and we lost the hydraulic pressure," the engineer concluded.

"And why did the bolts come loose, Mario?" Mona prompted.

"Because somebody filed away a lot of the threads." Didati made it a formal pronouncement, not without theatrics. He had a sense of timing. "At least somebody filed this bolt." He held it up as a lawyer might Exhibit One. "And my guess is that the same guy or guys filed some other bolts of the plate so's they'd give way too." He ended on a note of prideful gloom.

"How did you get it?" asked Mitch. "I thought the steering practically exploded and drove you out of there."

"No, this was from the first repair." Didati brandished the steel object once more. "I brought it up to the bridge to show the captain what we had replaced. I didn't notice a thing at the time, but this afternoon I started to look closely at the bolt."

Mario, a natural storyteller, recounted the circumstances at some length. To a local television progran, where he had consented to be interviewed about the sinking and oil disaster, he had brought the bolt and showed it as the only piece of the *Yandoon Princess* remaining above water. Riding back to his hotel in a cab, he idly turned the metal cylinder around in his hand. All at once, maybe because of the way the light came through the taxi window, he noticed the two differing areas, one part showing merely badly worn threads, the other shiny and clean from filing.

"There's no question that someone has been at this with a file, probably a number eight Zudkern. We had a couple number eights in the engine room." He again held out the bolt for Mitch's inspection. "Can't you see where I mean?"

"Yes, I guess I see that now." Mitch frowned. "But I don't think I would have without help. How about you, Mona?"

"Oh yes. I think it's quite clear." She tapped one side. "This is decidedly different from the other side. But Mario, couldn't that have happened when the bolt worked loose?"

"Not a chance. Those are definite file marks there."

She fingered a slim silver bracelet. "So, the next question, Mario. Do you suspect anyone?"

"No, I don't." Didati, ignoring Mitch now, addressed himself to his captain. "I've gone over the four enginemen in my mind. Nothing out of line about any of them that I can recall."

"What about your three officers?" asked Mona.

"None of them." Mario shook his head. "You know I've had blow-ups with the third, Captain, but I trust all three licensed engineers."

"Could any deck people have done it?" Mitch failed to see why Didati confined his conjectures to the engine specialists.

"Not possible." Didati shook off the inquiry. "To get to steering, you have to come down to the engine room, pass the control platform and climb down four levels of ladders. Nobody from deck went down there the last trip excepting Captain Harkinson and the chief mate—and I was with both of them. Besides, even if some seaman snuck down there, he'd have to know what to do. Whoever went after those bolts knew the weak points in the steering system."

Mona and Didati discussed the apparent act of sabotage for another half hour while Mitch sat by mute for the most part. It was decided that Didati would make it a point to talk casually but at length with each of the four enginemen within the next few days. Members of the crew were quartered in the Warwick during the preliminary investigation by the U.S. Coast Guard and pending the setting of a date for a formal hearing.

"Mario, while you're doing that, I'm going to talk to each of your three engineers," said Mona. "We're all here at the Bellevue, so that will be handy and each of them will be expecting me to fire a lot of questions anyway."

When Didati left, the bolt in his jacket pocket, the door had no sooner closed than Mitch and Mona rushed into each other's arms. They kissed hungrily, held each other in a passionate clinch, alternately lost their breath and sense of balance. Then, glowing with the certainty of the other's desire, they stood apart, holding hands while they admired each other. They stood silently, aware of the tension between them, each charged with the other, each heated by the other's sensual warmth and both certain and exhilarated about the harmonics to follow this prelude.

There come those rare times between a man and a woman when all seems perfect, right, so beautifully in balance that the seconds dance by like pearls on a string. Nothing can mar the sheen of place and person, and the lovers, filled to overflowing with themselves, speak chiefly with their eyes and limbs.

This was one of those times. Mona had suffered defeat in the first major trial of her career, and Mitch, asking no questions, had flown to her side. The act itself, its meaning as plain as sunrise, rendered words superfluous for now. Later might come the explanations, the whereases, the bits and pieces of reason and logic that would put clothes on a body already deeply known. It was as if sexual union had been created to celebrate moments like these. Anything less would seem to trivialize the occasion, like whistling pop tunes in a cathedral.

When they parted, Mona stepped to the telephone and told the operator to put no more calls through to the room until nine in the morning. A bottle of Scotch and bucket of ice stood on a table by the window and she mixed them each a drink.

"I'd like it now if you'd undress me," she said after they took long swallows.

"Aye, aye, Captain."

She put down her drink and came close to him, fixing her eyes on his. "Mitch, could we get one thing straight, please? When we're alone, I am never, never, never the captain. I am your lover, your bed partner, your friend, maybe your inamorata—doesn't that sound romantic?—anything but captain. Okay?"

"Sold forever." He understood. There was so much about her that he sensed intuitively. "Out there, you battle and you win or you lose. Here with me, you battle and you surrender—and you always win."

She laughed, threw her arms around him and kissed him roughly. "You put it just right. Now please, undress me—and hurry, huh?"

In bed they clasped each other with a kind of feral joy, felt the luxury of skin touching skin, trembled in anticipation of the covey of pleasures that lay ahead. Then they quickly fell away to a slow teasing, the nibbles of love, kissing, nuzzling, caressing. They soon found that they remembered each nook and curve of the other's body and how to please, arouse and cherish it. The long days and nights since Honolulu dropped away now and their lovemaking flowed like a river, seemingly an endless stream that carried them like floating gossamers.

They mingled in love in slowly spiraling passion while a tepid breeze from the air-conditioning machine slipped over their moist bodies and the rumble of traffic on Broad Street below came through as a distant hum. Their first lovemaking in Honolulu had been unexpectedly rich, possessing them and carrying them into other worlds on urgent wings, but tonight they soared into rhythmic union, locking together so powerfully, yet so tenderly, that Mitch felt that they had become one body. It was as if they had passed through one another in the white heat of lust, then swept back on surges of love to fuse into a single person.

Mona peaked in passion several times, but their rhythm continued, her small cries of ecstasy goading him to more powerful exertions and a craving to bring her the ultimate in pleasure. As sweet as honey, as mindless as the wind, as painful as combat and as precious as breath, the loving went on and on, up and up. And when at last they fell to earth, spent and limp, Mitch sensed that this was as close as he would ever come to exaltation. Mitchell Donahey, the infidel, had been purified and hallowed by this act of physical union with a woman about whom he knew very little on the surface, yet felt that he knew deep to the marrow.

My God, he thought, at this moment I love this woman as I have never loved before. He wanted to tell her at once, to shout it and then crush his mouth to hers, surrendering to her and demanding full surrender in return. But then caution blew in like an autumn wind and he lay quietly, holding her close and listening to her breathe in great swelling inhalations as she came back from the world of one to the world of many. They did not speak for long minutes.

"It's so weird," she said at last, "but I knew all day exactly how we would be together."

"Never in my life have I had such powerful feelings." He struggled to find the words. "Like this is the way it's supposed to be, but never was until now."

"You know, I believe you, probably because I felt the same way. No, more than that. I could feel it in your whole body."

"Thanks. If you'd said, 'Oh, I'll bet you tell that to all your women,' it would have hurt."

"Oh, I couldn't have said that." She nuzzled his shoulder. "Your body talks, you know."

"I love your voice, Mona. It gets me down here." He patted her flat belly. "It's kind of a silky growl. Lots of animal in it, but flutes and flowers too."

"Good grief, all that? . . . Mitch, there's lots I have to tell you. First, I want to get straight on why I didn't tell you in Honolulu all about my self and my job."

"I thought you told me on the phone yesterday."

She rubbed her head on his shoulder. "Holy Jesus, I've been talking so much, I've forgotten. What did I say?"

"Among other things, you said that in Honolulu you had been facing your first trip as master of a supertanker and that you couldn't divide your energies. That seemed terribly important at the time, but meant nothing now. Well, hell, I understand that."

"You do, honestly? Don't fib to me now."

"Of course." He caressed her forehead. "If I were a woman in the same spot, I'd feel the same way. Hell, Mona, that's a big-league challenge, running one of those giant mothers."

She rolled her eyes upward, mocking the situation. "Don't tell me I've finally found a man who understands me."

"Maybe. Tell me about it. You know, when and how you learned you wanted to be a tanker captain?"

"I'd love to." She snuggled against his shoulder. "I grew up in Keene, New Hampshire, a spacious old town—do you know it?— that has a fine wide main drag. I was a tomboy, played softball, climbed trees, went fishing, stuff like that. Dad was a banker, but an armchair sea rover. He read all kinds of marine adventure stuff from *Mutiny on the Bounty* to the battles of Captain Horatio Hornblower.

"Fascination with the sea must be contagious because I came down with it too. In high school, most of my girl friends wanted to get married, but I decided I was going to be different—a seafaring woman. My folks wanted me to go to Wellesley where mother went. So with a lot of reluctance, I put my sailor ideas in moth balls and went off to college. But I dropped out after two years, married a young investment banker named Clay Floberg—sweet, selfish, immature Clay—and after a time we had Christine.

"I adored being a mother and I stayed glued to house and Chrissy for a while. But then one day, when she was becoming her own little person, I said, 'Hey, Mona, what you gonna do with the rest of your sappy life?' Also, about that time, Clay took up with another woman and I found out that, jealous on the surface, deep down I really didn't give a damn. So when he took off, it was with my private blessing. My sister Ruth had three kids with whom Chrissy was thick as thieves, so I persuaded Ruth, as a trial, to take Chrissy while I tried going to a marine school of some kind.

"So I applied and got accepted at California Maritime Academy soon after they started taking women. The Academy's at Vallejo on San Pablo Bay not far from San Francisco. I made good grades, worked hard, trained two summers on the school's converted troop transport, *Golden Bear,* and graduated with a B.S. in marine transportation. But the only job I could get was as a mess steward even though I had my third mate's license. It was three years before I got the chance to work as a third mate aboard a reefer that brought bananas up from Guatemala."

"Was the crew rough on you?"

"That crew and every other one I've sailed with. But you know, there's always a minority of guys, six or seven on every ship, who like to look out for a woman. So I've had lots of good advice and help and some men have been especially kind to me. . . . Is this boring you?"

"No, no. I want to learn all about you."

She laughed. "When you do, tell me. I'd like to know myself. Anyway, I still managed to be a pretty fair mother to Chris because you get so much time off in the merchant marine, usually a couple of months at sea and then a couple at home. I built an extension on Ruth's house in Keene and I lived there with Chrissy when I was not at sea. That went on for seven, eight years while I worked as third, then second mate on tankers, mostly running from the Gulf of Mexico to East Coast ports. I moved to London several years ago because I was working M & L tankers in the Med.

"I put Chrissy in a girls' boarding school in Switzerland and now I juggle my time off to coincide with her vacations. She's happy at Mademoiselle Jupon's school near Zurich, goes skiing and horseback riding and learns things like ballet. Oh, very very fawncy at Jupon's. If you don't believe me, look at my check stubs.

"Then I made chief mate and finally master of a small M & L tanker in the Med. . . . So, there you have my life story, more or less."

"Did your folks approve of your seagoing career?"

"Let's say they didn't disapprove, out loud anyway. My dad, well, I've always had trouble with my father. He's always pushed me hard, thinks I should be Number One at whatever I try. So when I went to sea, he just assumed I'd be a captain before long. He has no appreciation of the barriers women face."

"Have you talked to him since the sinking?"

"We talked last night." Mona's voice faltered. "It was not a success. While he didn't say it outright, I knew he felt the captain was to blame for whatever happened. Dad and I—well, he's not a demonstrative man. Starchy. Not a toucher. . . . Mother? Well, mother's very social, you know, and I think she's embarrassed to talk about her daughter, the tanker woman."

He could tell she felt uncomfortable discussing her parents. "How about men since Clay?"

"You mean you want numbers?"

"However you want to tell it, just so it's in that sexy contralto of yours."

"Several affairs, one ran a couple of years, and some, not many, quickie weekends, one of which I'm ashamed of because I got drunk and maudlin and sentimental and sloppy, just a God-awful mess."

"Am I an affair or a weekend?"

"You just graduated into an affair." Mona nipped at his shoulder, pushed him away and scrambled out of bed. She went to the bathroom and returned with a long white towel wrapped around her hips. She mixed two more Scotch-and-waters, handed him one, then sat cross-legged on the bed beside him. "Hey, see I'm in the lotus position. I took up yoga on ships for days when the weather's too foul for deck exercise."

"You have beautiful breasts, Mona." He could feel another lovemaking mood enveloping him like warm spring rain.

"Thanks. I guess they're not bad for an old doll." She held up her glass and eyed him judiciously over the rim. "Yes, you definitely have graduated, my love."

"My love." He tested the phrase. "Sounds great. Do you know that's the first term of endearment to pass between us?"

"I know—and it just slipped out. God, Mitch, I'm so happy when right at this hour I should feel horrible. My career, you know, is probably shot—or lying in ruins as they'd say on the soaps."

"I'm not at all sure you've had it. For one thing, there's this upcoming Coast Guard hearing which will probably exonerate you of any negligence. When does it start, by the way?"

"To be announced. My guess is next week."

"Then there's this sabotage angle. What did you think of Didati's story?"

"I'm sure he believes it and maybe it's true. Seems wild, though. Where's the motive?"

"Yeah, well, you had one guy on board I'd sure check out. His name's Nikos Miaoulis, a Greek deckhand."

"Oh, yes. Nikos, able seaman. He didn't like me and stayed out of my way, but once in a passageway I heard him parrot the crack made by our erudite cook, something about working for a 'menopause mistress.' Untrue, by the way, as you'll find out if you're still here next week."

"Do you know much about the *Gunnison Bay?*" Mitch sat up in bed, the better to sip at his drink.

"Only that she sank in the Pacific after an engine room explosion and that there were some bad rumors about it, I've forgotten just what."

"Well, your man Miaoulis and his brother were on that tanker and so was Bones Elger, the skinny super-patriot you met in my driveway that night in Honolulu." He told the story as he'd heard it from Claude Bouchon after the Frenchman had driven Elger's sloop on the reef, the apparent enrichment of Elger, Miaoulis and other crew members through illegal prior sale of the lost tanker's oil. He noted that Pacific Triad Oil had reopened the investigation of the case. "And, as I told you, I'm going to work in Copenhagen for Wasif Zabib, who was, incidentally, the owner of the *Gunnison Bay,* though I have no reason to believe he was involved in the scam."

Mitch gestured with his glass for emphasis. "The point is, your engineer, Didati, ought to check out his enginemen closely to see whether any of them were especially friendly with Nikos Miaoulis."

"Oh!" Mona came to attention. "I know one is. Miaoulis is tight with Jerry Artwick, an Englishman who's down below." She told of an incident when the crew's mess steward complained that Miaoulis and Artwick several times came late for chow and insisted on being served. "That blew over quickly, but I did see Artwick and Miaoulis talking together. . . . What time is it?" She was keyed up now.

Mitch shifted around in order to see the digital clock on the dresser. "Ten after twelve."

"Too late to call Didati." Instead she called the operator and asked that a message be tucked under the engineer's door, requesting that he call Captain Harkinson at 9 A.M.

"And now I want to hear all about you. You're a shipbroker, until just now with McCafferty & Sons . . ."

"I wondered why you knew that name when I mentioned it in Honolulu. Okay, I'll give you the quarter-hour version of my life story." And while Mona sat cross-legged, sipping at her drink, he began at birth and hauled himself through boyhood, schools, loves, war, marriage and jobs. Describing his year in Viet Nam, he told briefly of the night when he and four others flushed the Viet Cong from the nearby village and Elger killed the boy Sammy and his grandfather.

"I was no beaut myself that night," he said. "I didn't kill any civilians, but I damn sure wanted to and would have if Jimmy hadn't sacked me along with Bones. Sometime I might tell you more about it. The memory still haunts my nights." But, he realized, the emotional charge had diminished ever since his long-delayed confrontation with Elger.

"There you have it," Mitch concluded, "my autobiography, condensed version."

"You're a sweet man and sometime I want the complete story, but right now I'd like to go to sleep snuggled beside you—after we make love again." And Mona reached beneath the sheet to caress him.

A half hour later, when they undid two happily tangled bodies, Mona, surfeited and bone-tired from the trauma and aftermath of losing her first supertanker beneath her, fell asleep at once. Mitch, cradling her on his arm while his ear tuned to the cadence of her gentle snoring, fell to wondering as he waited for sleep. Why did he feel so quickly comfortable with Mona and what made her so remarkable? Was this the woman for whom he longed in the wastelands of his dreams?

Somewhere in the distant city, a siren wailed. Mona stirred, turned on her side and nestled against him as if in a cocoon. He savored her fragrance, so mingled with the pungencies of love, and as sleep overtook him, he sighed with nostalgia for precious moments already fled.

9

Seven o'clock the next evening became seven-thirty, became eight and still no Mario Didati. The chief engineer had agreed to meet his captain and Mitchell Donahey for a seafood dinner at Bookbinder's downtown Philadelphia restaurant, located a block behind the Bellevue Stratford.

Didati had phoned Mona in her room, where she was having predinner cocktails with Mitch, to report on his day-long interviews with his enginemen at the Warwick Hotel and to tell her that his suspicion of sabotage had become a conviction.

"No question that Jerry Artwick was involved," Mario told her. "Naturally, he won't admit anything, but he's a poor liar. That pale skin starts coloring up like his red hair when he lies. I doubt he did it alone, but I'm convinced he had a hand in it."

"Did you show him the bolt?"

"Oh, yeah. That was my first tip-off. When he saw me pull it out of my pocket, he was surprised and scared. Never would touch the thing either. Eyed it like it might explode or something. Claimed he didn't think the bolt had been filed, but I could tell he was lying again."

"Any other leads, Mario?"

"Yes, Artwick and Miaoulis, the seaman, are good friends, like you thought, so I'm going to talk to Nikos tomorrow. Oh yeah,

Artwick says that the second, Yukio Osagawa, can corroborate everything he says, so naturally I'm wondering now about Yukio."

"I want all the details." Mona proposed that Didati meet her and Mitch at Bookbinder's at seven.

"I'll be there at seven."

But now the clock showed eight-twenty. Mitch and Mona had finished shrimp cocktails and several handfuls of oyster crackers while they waited.

It had been a long grinding day for Mona. She had spent the morning questioning the three assistant engineering officers, became wary of Yukio Osagawa because of his bland yet evasive answers. She did not mention the suspect bolt to any of the officers, preferring to wait for Didati's report. An abrasive luncheon conference extended through most of the afternoon with M & L executives Arthur Michaelson and Homer Richert, officers of Octagon Oil, owner of the cargo of crude now blackening the mid-Atlantic shoreline, West German bankers who held the mortgage on the lost tanker and two sets of insurance agents. Then came more quizzing by Coast Guard marine safety officers. Between sessions Mona had to skirmish with a growing band of reporters. Mitch had spent the day taking a deluge of phone calls for Mona from half a dozen countries. Although most could be ignored, his list of those warranting a reply filled a page of hotel stationery by nightfall.

Now while they waited for Didati at Bookbinder's, they went over and over the circumstances surrounding the crippled steering gear of the *Yandoon Princess.*

"What irritates me about this apparent sabotage," said Mona, "is that it lets Michaelson & Lygdamis off the hook. Three or four systems aboard the *Princess* failed this trip because of the tanker's age and the lack of sufficient drydock time. She was a ship looking for an accident to happen."

"Suspecting that somebody wrecked the steering gear is a long way from proving it. Still, I'll bet Didati will bird-dog this until he finds out for sure."

Mitch made a third trip to the phone and this time informed the hotel operator where he and Mona could be reached. On two previous tries, Didati's room had failed to answer.

"He's hung up somewhere," said Mitch when he returned to the table. "Let's order. I'm hungry and if I get snappish, I'll forget to tell you how great you look in that outfit."

Mona, who preferred a business-like tailored jacket and matching skirt by day, had changed to a dress of purple linen that hugged her body and offered a hint of cleavage.

"I love your flattery." She had a radiance despite her trying day.

"It's not flattery, just factual comment."

They were halfway through the stone crab and Mitch's account of his dispute with Jim McCafferty when the waitress informed Mona that she was wanted on the telephone at the reception counter. Patrons of the restaurant watched as she walked across the crowded room. She was a celebrity now, no heroine, but a newly famous person in public difficulties, and eyes followed her wherever she went.

She spoke only briefly at the counter phone before returning to the table, again the target of most eyes. She remained standing, her posture tense.

"Mario's been killed," she said in a low voice. She beckoned to the waitress. "We need the check at once, please."

"Killed?" Mitch could not absorb the news. "How?"

"Knifed by a mugger, apparently while walking here from the Warwick. The police are waiting for me back at the hotel."

The seafood restaurant stood only a short distance from the Bellevue Stratford and as they hurried along the sidewalk, arms enlaced, Mitch attempted to envision Didati as a lifeless body, but try as he might, he could see the Italian chief engineer only in action, taut with energy, studded with resolve. He explained to Mona, "I have a hard time coping with death, which is strange, considering how much of it I saw in Viet Nam."

"I suppose your unconscious blocks it out." She spoke carefully, aware that they were engaged in the important business of self-revelation and exploring each other. "I'm different. I face death okay, I guess." She moved closer to him as they walked. "In many ways, Mitch, I'm very practical."

And good in crises, he thought. She gave no evidence of coming unstuck over the news despite her recent traumas. "I liked what I saw of the guy," he said. "He gave out a sense of integrity. You could feel it. . . . Are you sure they have the right person?"

"The assistant manager says there appears to be no doubt." She tugged on his arm. "God, I'm glad you're here with me, Mitch. Alone, I'm not sure I'd hold up."

"Oh yes, you would. The way you handled that sinking, you can handle anything."

"Thanks." She brushed his cheek with a kiss that made up in affection what it lacked in duration. "Well, then, let's say that your presence gives me extra strength."

Two policemen, a number of reporters and a knot of curious by-standers awaited them in the hotel lobby. A young woman with a halo of bushy hair pushed forward, pad and pencil at the ready. "How do you feel about the murder, Captain Harkinson?" she asked.

"I feel like hell. Mario Didati was a splendid officer. Now, no more questions until I talk to the police. I don't know all the facts yet."

The two uniformed men led the way to the assistant manager's office and one of them tried to close the door against Donahey.

"No, no," said Mona. "He comes with me. He's my man."

Her man? Mitch aimed a wide grin her way, saluting his new status.

Sergeant Will Oliver, a large, easy-mannered black man, and Patrolman Kevin Smock introduced themselves and Oliver, in a slow disarming drawl, related what was known of the lethal assault on Didati. It appeared that the *Yandoon Princess* chief engineer was collared and stabbed from behind in the doorway of a storefront on Walnut Street near Sixteenth, about halfway between the Warwick and Bookbinder's. A knife blade apparently sliced between his ribs and pierced the heart from the rear, Didati dying within a minute or two.

Since the assailant had stripped Mario's wallet and left it lying a few feet from the body, police tended to believe the motive was money. They tentatively identified the victim from cards in the wallet and a Bellevue Stratford room key in a jacket pocket led them to the hotel office where they established Didati as an officer from the ill-fated tanker.

Two witnesses had come forward, according to Oliver. A middle-aged white male, walking toward Didati, had seen a man leap from the shadows, hook an arm around Didati's throat from behind and pull him into a recessed area between two doors. When the witness heard an anguished cry, he stopped, afraid to go past the doorway.

In a few moments, a white male, indeterminate age, blurred features, wearing a windbreaker and black gloves, bolted from the doorway and ran at top speed to Sixteenth Street where he raced around the corner. The witness then called police from a nearby cigar and magazine store. Police put the call at 7:10 P.M. An elderly black woman saw the scene from across the street. Her story corroborated that of the male witness with the addition that she saw the assailant search the pockets of the prone victim and withdraw an object of some kind that the killer slipped into his own pocket. He then snatched the billfold which he tossed away after fishing out the contents. She said the mugger ran off while still stuffing the currency into a pocket.

The body was now at the city morgue and Sergeant Oliver would have to trouble Captain Harkinson to accompany him there in a few minutes to identify the corpse.

Mona agreed, then asked, "Was anything found on him aside from his clothes and the room key?"

"Like what?" Oliver's down-home manner failed to conceal his quickened interest.

"Oh, nothing special. I just wondered. His watch, maybe papers. He wore a St. Francis of Paola religious medal around his neck aboard ship."

"Kevin," ordered Oliver, "call in and get a list of the items found on the deceased excepting his clothes."

While Patrolman Smock, a tubby officer with a drooping blond moustache, used the assistant manager's phone, Oliver wrote down names, permanent residences, occupations and Philadelphia address and phone number of Mona and Mitch.

"Now," he asked, "can you offer anything that might help us in our investigation of this homicide? You knew Mr. Didati, didn't you, Captain Harkinson?"

"Yes, he was chief engineer on the tanker I was the master of, the one that sank off the Delaware coast three nights ago." She told of Didati's going from the Bellevue to the Warwick to question his enginemen about the sinking, preparatory to a Coast Guard hearing, and his seven-o'clock date at the restaurant. "So I assume he was walking from the Warwick to Bookbinder's when it happened. It's only a few blocks."

"Did he have any enemies among the crew?"

"Not that I know of."

"Any reason anyone would want him killed?"

"He was a very popular officer."

"That's not quite responsive to my question, Captain." Behind Oliver's sleepy smile the mind was clicking.

"I didn't mean to dodge."

But wasn't she? Mitch asked himself.

"No," Mona added. "I don't know why anyone would want him killed."

Oliver took down names of the officers and crew. Mona could not help him on Didati's next of kin until she consulted the personnel sheet among the ship's papers she held in her room. She agreed to phone the information to the police number supplied by Oliver.

When Patrolman Smock finished his call and handed his sergeant a sheet of paper, Oliver said, "They did find the religious medal around the neck of the deceased. He also carried a ballpoint fountain pen, the room key, a wristwatch, a small tin of aspirin and ninety-six cents in coins. That's all. . . . Now, was there anything else that he might normally carry on his person?"

"Not that I know of."

The sergeant pursued the matter for only a few more minutes. "This is just a preliminary report," he said as they wound it up. "You'll be hearing from the detectives in homicide who'll want to go into the case more thoroughly. Now if you'll accompany me to the morgue."

The press contingent had grown. Some twenty newsmen and women and a scattering of television technicians, carrying shoulder-braced cameras, awaited them outside the door. The huge oil spill had drawn representatives of TV and radio networks, news magazines and the nation's leading newspapers to swell the resident Philadelphia press corps. The hotel-lobby scene attracted spectators and a sizable crowd had gathered to watch and listen as newsmen pressed about Sergeant Oliver. After the police officer gave the gist of the discussion in the assistant manager's office, media attention centered on the captain and her escort.

"Captain Harkinson, what's your reaction to the killing?" It was the aggressive young woman with the bushy hair. "Wasn't the victim the chief engineer on your tanker that sank?"

"May I have the identity, please, when you put a question?" Mona was polite but firm.

"Sure. Maggie Josephs, *Washington Post.*"

"I'm terribly shaken. Mario Didati was not only an excellent officer, but I considered him a friend. Yes, he was my chief engineer. The press questioned him three nights ago when we all arrived from the *Yandoon Princess.*"

"Watkins, Associated Press. When was the last time you saw Didati?"

"Let's see." Mona reflected. "It was last night in my room here at the Bellevue. He and I were explaining aspects of the sinking to Mr. Donahey."

Several reporters shouted at once. "Sue Yasco, *Philadelphia Inquirer.* Who's Donahey?"

When Mona nodded to him, Mitch answered. "My name is Mitchell P. Donahey." He spelled it. "I'm a shipbroker in Honolulu and I'm here to lend Captain Harkinson what support I can. We're good friends."

"Just friends?" It was Maggie Josephs again.

"We are good friends," repeated Mitch.

"Even if we ourselves knew what our precise relationship was," said Mona with a smile, "it would not be germane to the death of Chief Didati or to the loss of the *Princess,* for that matter. . . . And by the way, how times have changed. I can't imagine that question being asked fifteen years ago."

The crowd of onlookers stirred in sympathetic response. Some people laughed and a few applauded. Mitch was amazed at Mona's aplomb and her cool deft handling of the press. He had yet to see a replay of her televised press conference immediately after the sinking, but he knew that Wasif Zabib was not the only person impressed by her performance.

"Davidow, National Public Radio. What's a shipbroker?"

Mitch explained the nature of his job. "But I did not get to know Captain Harkinson in the business of fixing tanker charters. We met socially in Honolulu."

"Crosser, *New York Times.* The obvious point here, Captain Harkinson, is whether you see any connection between the sinking of the *Yandoon Princess,* the oil spill and the murder of Mr. Didati?"

"No, I don't. Mario Didati did his best at sea to repair the steering system under abominable conditions. Then he came ashore and got mugged and knifed on city streets."

"Kelsey, Channel Two, Philadelphia. Then you think it's just happenstance that the mugger struck at Didati instead of someone else?"

"I think it was terribly bad luck for Mario. His St. Francis medal was good to him at sea, but not on land." She explained about the chief engineer's necklace.

"Lowenstein, *Newsweek.* Estimates on cleaning up the oil spill are now around $70,000,000. Do you think your tanker company, Michaelson & Lygdamis, should be made to pay the bill?"

"Fleet owners belong to a pool which helps pay cleanup costs in event damages are assessed," Mona replied. "But no more questions now about the sinking. We had a long press conference on that. The Coast Guard is convening a formal Marine Board of Investigation and you'll just have to wait for my testimony there."

"Kelsey again. Several editorials contend that as unfair as it might be, seamen refuse to work as hard for a female captain as for a man and that that fact probably contributed to the grounding of your tanker. What's your reaction?"

"Horse sh . . . feathers! Which is the same answer I gave in different words at the original press conference. Now look, I don't intend to go over the same old ground again. So if you'll let us through now, we have an unpleasant task to perform at Sergeant Oliver's request."

"The morgue?" someone shouted.

"That's right," said Oliver. He began carving a path through the crowd.

With some of the press in pursuit, they rode in a police squad car through downtown Philadelphia and across the Schuylkill to the dowdy fringe of the University of Pennsylvania campus. The morgue was located on University Drive down a hill from the massive Veterans Administration Hospital. Philadelphia collected its testaments of death in a mousey brown-yellow brick structure that resembled a college dormitory of the 1960s.

They entered along a cement ramp, past an abandoned guard shack with smashed windows and a huge abstract sculpture that looked like a pile of fused dinosaur bones. This was the Joseph W. Spelman Medical Examiners Building, according to an aluminum legend near the entrance, and the interior might have been that of a shabby motel lobby, complete with orange vinyl couch, cheap table lamp and a greeting card-type picture of an orange sun setting over misty mountains.

An assistant city medical examiner, a spare young man with rimless spectacles and bookish air, ordered the press held back while he led Mona, Mitch and the two policemen into a back office. Dr. Benjamin Weintraub explained the procedure. The bodies, he said, were. kept on stainless steel trollies in a refrigerated room at forty degrees Fahrenheit.

"But we're not going to put you through the ordeal of walking through the morgue," he said. "For a couple of decades now we've had closed-circuit TV viewing." He pointed to a television set resting on a tabletop. "So if you're ready . . ."

Dr. Weintraub picked up a phone on the cluttered desk. "Okay, Phil, we're set here. Let's have Number 83 on the monitor, please."

A sheeted figure lying on a hospital-like carriage appeared in black and white on the television screen. The camera closed in for full-screen shot of the head and shoulders.

"Is that the man you knew as Mario Didati, the chief engineer of your tanker?" asked Sergeant Oliver.

"It is." Mona, staring at video-encapsulated death, reached out for Mitch's hand.

Death had frozen the body into a caricature of Mario Didati. The engineer's intensity had become marbled truculence and the vitality that had given the Italian a kind of springy warmth now fastened on the countenance as a glower. Didati had departed under protest. If every person, at the brink of certain extinction, rails at the colossal injustice being visited on him, Didati appeared to regard the perpetrator of the indignity with contempt.

"Is that the man you knew as Mario Didati?" Sergeant Oliver asked Mitch.

They signed papers formalizing the identification and Mona promised further data from Didati's personnel folder when she returned to the hotel. Then they pushed through the crowd of newsmen waiting in the corridor. "We identified the body of Mario Didati," said Mona as she elbowed toward the exit. "Captain, captain," came the shouts, but Mona and Mitch forced their way to the sidewalk where Sergeant Oliver, ever considerate, held open the door of the squad car.

Back in the quiet of Mona's hotel room, she poured a Scotch and water for each of them, then began fingering through the *Yandoon*

Princess files in her bulky worn briefcase. Didati's folder disclosed that the Italian listed his permanent residence as Milan and his next of kin two sons, one in Milan, the other in Rome. For the rest, the chief engineer was fifty-one, a Catholic, owner of two parcels of real estate in Milan and had entrusted his will to a Milan attorney. Mona phoned in the data to the police number Oliver had supplied.

Kicking off their shoes, Mona and Mitch sank back to relax in large brocaded armchairs. She had a contented air, despite the harrowing hours.

"Are you thinking what I am?" asked Mitch. "The bolt?"

"Yes. Where is that bolt? Is that the object the old woman across the street saw the killer take from Mario?"

"The key question." Mitch leaned forward, elbows on his knees. "Ever since Sergeant Oliver briefed us, I've been wondering about that bolt. We know Mario took it to the Warwick and that the engineman—what's his name?—Jerry, Jerry Artwick, got all agitated when Mario produced it and asked him about the threads being filed."

"Would Artwick and Nikos Miaoulis kill Mario to get their hands on that piece of steel?" Mona frowned. "That's what we face, isn't it?"

"I think so. Although, of course, there's always the possibility that the killer was a street punk and the crime a routine—if you'll pardon the expression—robbery that turned into murder."

Mona sipped at her Scotch. "But if so, what was the object that the old lady saw the killer take from Mario and slip into his own pocket?"

"Could have been jewelry of some kind."

"Loose in Mario's pocket?" Mona shook her head. "And remember, the woman mentioned that the killer searched Didati's pockets. That missing bolt bugged me. I was afraid to mention it to the police or the press."

"I noticed that you didn't quite tell the truth, but I understand. We might be dealing with a sabotage conspiracy of some kind."

"If the object the killer searched for and took was that bolt, then it was definitely a planned killing."

"Right." Mitch swished the ice about in his glass while he pondered. "And if that's true, it's almost certain that Artwick and

Miaoulis were in on it. Maybe one of them actually did the stabbing. Whatever, we better damn well proceed with caution."

"That's why I avoided mentioning the bolt. This whole thing's sticky."

"Make that dangerous," said Mitch. "If they killed to steal the only existing evidence of sabotage aboard the *Yandoon Princess,* they sure wouldn't mind roughing up a tanker captain if that became necessary. . . . Another thing. What tack do we take now at the Coast Guard hearing? Do we describe the scene with Mario last night, when he showed us the filed bolt? With no bolt to put in evidence, no third person to corroborate our story, nothing in fact to show we aren't making up a yarn."

"I've thought of that too." Mona reflected a moment. "And the natural question at the hearing would be: so what does a pair of tanker hands have to gain by crippling a ship loaded with oil? Make a female captain look bad? Nobody would risk a prison sentence just for that. Dirty work by some competitor? Doesn't make sense. Too many tankers and too much competition for that to be effective. So that brings us to the only logical explanation. . . ."

"Collusion with the salvage people," Mitch broke in.

"Sure. You knock out the steering, the tanker has to be towed into port under LOF terms by salvors, so then the sabotage gang splits the big arbitration award—millions in this case—with the salvage firm."

"Who were the salvage people the other day?"

"Tiggemann Brothers. It's a fairly new outfit. As it turned out, they didn't have the horses for the job because their 14,000-horsepower tug broke down with engine trouble. But they were ready for us, so who knows, there could have been collusion."

"But you hint at that in an open hearing," said Mitch, "and you open yourself to one hell of a civil slander suit in case your theory is all wet."

"I know. And Mitch, I'm wondering about another angle. Remember that Mario, when he phoned me, said Artwick claimed Yukio Osagawa, the second engineer, would corroborate everything he said. That makes me suspicious as the devil of Osagawa."

"What do you know about him?"

"Not much. Quiet and reserved man like many Japanese. Did his job well. Polite to me, but very evasive this morning. . . . It just seems that there are lots of bits and pieces that are beyond us, that some authority ought to be investigating."

"Including," Mitch added, "the most troubling angle of all, the fact that Nikos Miaoulis, who undoubtedly got big money when the crew sold off the *Gunnison Bay* oil, was aboard your ship and is cozy with Jerry Artwick."

"You said Pacific Triad Oil was reopening the *Gunnison Bay* case. Who's doing the investigating?"

"Moses & Fabian of London, I think. Too bad they couldn't bring in the FBI, but the *Gunnison Bay* was foreign-owned. Has to be at least part American ownership of the ship for the FBI to have jurisdiction."

Mona arose, walked to the window and stood looking down on Broad Street traffic. "The *Princess* is partly American-owned. The Lygdamis family came from Greece, but they've been U.S. citizens for a long time now." She turned back to Mitch. "I think we should go to the local FBI office first thing in the morning."

"How about the Coast Guard?"

"The FBI can contact them. The Coast Guard handles marine safety matters, but we're dealing with a crime at sea."

So it was agreed and soon their thoughts switched from lawmen and death and lost tankers to themselves. Mona, preparing for bed, put aside her persona of captain, her role of authority, quite as easily as she shed her clothes. Within minutes she had become a woman open to love, less assertive than receptive, more compliant than dominant, a woman anxious to be wooed.

While the swift change fascinated Mitch, it took time for him to adjust, to banish the captain and welcome the lover. Mona, sensing his hesitation, coaxed with her eyes and her limbs and soon they were giving themselves to each other. They made love quietly and longingly, with few of the previous night's bursts of passion, yet with a continuing insistence that led to mutual surrender and climax that Mitch found deeply satisfying.

Mona's smile and smoky eyes signaled a sweet tenderness that captivated him. The proud captain, so swiftly vulnerable, had become the eternal female who paid homage to his manhood. It was as if she credited him alone for the splendor of their lovemaking.

"I'm becoming so dependent on your love, Mitch," she said when the time for words had come. "I don't know how I'll get along after you leave."

"I'm the guy who could become the addict, needing his sexual fix every day from his woman."

She trembled in his arms. "Your woman! Is that a possibility?"

"Why not? Tonight you told the sergeant I was your man."

"I did, didn't I? That popped out without my thinking." She traced a finger about his lips. "Mitch, look out. I may be falling in love."

"Tell me about it." He felt elated, yet edgy too.

"Could this be what I've wanted all my life?" She moved about as she talked. "Holy Jesus, I can't believe it. I pick you up at a bar, or get picked up, whatever, for a night of fun and games, and here we are, only the fifth night together and I feel like I've known, loved and depended on you for years."

"I feel that too, Mona." The wariness vanished, spun away by her buoyant mood. "When you called me your man tonight, it gave me a charge." He laughed. "You suppose I'm your Mr. Right and you're my Lady Truelove?"

"Oh, sweet God, I hope so." Suddenly tears welled into her eyes. "I'm so tired of going it alone. The days are okay, but the nights can be awful, simply unbearable sometimes."

They talked for another hour and Mona wept twice again, once for Mario Didati and once for being alive. When they finally fell silent, worn out by the demands of death and love, they had each said, "I love you." They had gone to bed as man and woman, but when they slipped into the cotton of sleep, they were a couple.

10

The face, remotely familiar, evoking other contexts, bothered him. Mitch, with Mona at his side, seated himself across a desk from the special agent in charge of the Federal Bureau of Investigation's Philadelphia office. The nameplate on the desk read: Thomas W. Jardine.

"So, Captain," said Jardine after the introductions and an exchange on the weather, unseasonably warm for late September, "what's the urgent business that brings you and Mr. Donahey here?"

Mona Harkinson pointed to the morning *Philadelphia Inquirer* that lay on the agent's desk. A headline read: OIL SPILL ENGINEER STABBED TO DEATH.

"To give you the kernel of the story first," said Mona, "we think Mario Didati was murdered and robbed of evidence that would have shown that someone deliberately put the steering gear of the *Yandoon Princess* out of commission. Someone wrecked the steering many miles out from shore, a crime on the high seas which, as I understand it, comes within the FBI's jurisdiction."

"Depends." A large, wide-shouldered man with closely trimmed brown hair, Jardine had a prominent scar along his right jawline, but otherwise partook of those sturdy good looks associated with American astronauts. "Only in event the vessel is fully or partially owned by U.S. citizens."

Mona nodded. "I realize that. The tanker is owned by Michaelson

& Lygdamis of Montreal, but the Lygdamises, who own about half the company, are Greek-Americans who live in New York and have been U.S. citizens for a generation or more."

"Then you've come to the right store." Jardine readied a pen and a legal-sized yellow pad on his desk. "Tell me all you know about it. Take your time and spell any names as you go, please. I'll be taking notes."

"I've got it!" Mitch aimed a finger at the FBI man. "Linebacker for the Minnesota Vikings. I was watching the day you intercepted John Brodie and then took that shot near the goal line."

Jardine grinned. "You've got a good memory. That's fifteen years ago next month. Some shot too." He pointed to the scar. "Knocked me out of the NFL."

The two men managed a five-minute detour through professional and college football—Jardine had gone to Oklahoma State—while Mona sat quietly listening. "I took law in the off-season while I played with the Vikings," the agent concluded, "so I came to the Bureau with a law degree. All right, Captain, back to the *Princess.*"

Mona talked for half an hour, naming Jerry Artwick and Nikos Miaoulis as prime suspects and Second Engineer Yukio Osagawa as a man who'd bear scrutiny. Jardine took notes, interrupted occasionally with questions and then had a secretary make copies of the tanker's personnel files that Mona brought in her well-traveled briefcase.

Through the office window Mitch could see the morning sun burning into the Delaware River several blocks away. The FBI had its Philadelphia quarters in the Federal Building next to the Federal Courthouse and a block from the U.S. Mint. From the sanctuary of air conditioning, the day outside looked like a scorcher. Men on the street carried suit coats over their arms, a woman doused two small children from a squirting hose and customers lined up at a white-panel truck selling ice cream at a nearby corner.

When Mona finished, Jardine glanced at Mitch. "Do you have anything to add, Mr. Donahey?"

"Yeah, plenty. You see Mona and I think this might be a conspiracy that includes at least two sinkings." He told of the sloop cracking up on the reef before his Honolulu apartment and Claude Bouchon's story that linked Henry Elger and Nikos Miaoulis to the apparent scuttling of the *Gunnison Bay* after the crew supposedly sold off the cargo of oil for many millions of dollars. He described Elger at some length.

"The owner of the *Gunnison Bay,* a Jordanian who lives in Copenhagen now," said Mitch, "was Wasif Zabib. He told me a few days ago that he trusted the master of the tanker as he would his own brother. So that brings Zabib into suspicion because the master almost had to be involved. How could a crew sell off stolen oil over a period of days without the captain knowing about it? If you think about that a minute, it's damn near impossible."

Jardine looked at Mona. "How about that, Captain? Do you agree?"

"Absolutely. It's ridiculous even to suggest that an operation of that magnitude could be carried out without the captain's knowledge —unless, of course, somebody killed or kidnapped him."

"Or her?"

"Yes, or her." Mona mirrored Jardine's wry smile. "And in the *Gunnison Bay* case, the master—I believe his name was Alexandros Nicias, a Greek—stayed with the ship until the last and was picked up in one of the lifeboats. Isn't that right, Mitch?"

"Yep. The captain was put ashore in Tahiti with the rest of the crew and gave statements to the French authorities and to insurance investigators too."

"What is known about Zabib?" Jardine looked up from his note-taking.

"I was coming to that. To complicate matters, for myself at least, I'm going to work for Wasif Zabib in Copenhagen." Mitch's tight smile was one of embarrassment. "The pay is excellent and besides I quit my old job in Honolulu after a fight with the boss." He told what little he knew about Zabib, then described the circumstances that led to his departure from McCafferty & Sons.

"Whoa, slow down," said Jardine. "First we have these allegations of sabotage and now you tell me that the *Yandoon Princess* was dangerously old and didn't go to drydock often enough."

Mona broke in. "Both things apply. In fact, my guess is that the men who crippled my steering picked the *Yandoon Princess* specifically because she was nearing her end, so that any kind of major failure would look quite natural."

"And not because the captain was a woman?" Jardine watched for Mona's reaction.

"Yes, that too. 'One old lady trying to run another' is the way one of my seamen put it to the press."

"I see." Jardine tapped his pen on the yellow pad while he reflected. "When does the Coast Guard's hearing take place?"

"No announcement yet, but we think next week," said Mitch. "That's one of the things we wanted to talk to you about. If we testify to what we heard from Didati, we scare off the culprits. On the other hand, with no bolt to put in evidence, who'll credit us?"

"Couldn't divers find the other filed bolts?" asked Jardine. "The tanker's in fairly shallow water."

Mona shook her head. "The hull broke wide open by the engine room and a couple of small explosions scattered stuff helter-skelter. Those bolts could be anywhere within a mile by this time, maybe buried in mud."

"What do you think?" asked Mitch. "Can Mona testify without mentioning the bolt? What can she say, for instance, in case an officer on the board asks her if she has reason to suspect sabotage? If she says no, she's committing perjury."

"There are several ways to go," said Jardine, "assuming, of course, that your story proves to have enough substance for us to continue. Now let me get some data on you two." He spent a half hour taking down general biographical background from Mona and then Mitch.

"What are those 'several ways to go'?" asked Mitch when the agent finished his questioning on personal data.

"Well, you can testify straight out at the Coast Guard inquiry as to everything you know. Or you could delete any reference to sabotage after taking the hearing officers into your confidence. Or, third, you could persuade the Coast Guard brass to postpone the hearing several months while investigation goes forward of people under suspicion."

"Which route would you favor?" asked Mona.

"I couldn't say right off." The agent pondered in silence for a time. "Much would depend on what's already known in Washington. A name check on Elger, Miaoulis, Artwick and . . ." He consulted his pad. ". . . and Osagawa might turn up some interesting stuff. Maybe we know something already about the *Gunnison Bay* case although we clearly have no jurisdiction there—foreign owner, foreign bottom, oil sold off in foreign ports."

"We have another problem," said Mona. "The Philadelphia police.

Detectives will be after us today, I suppose. I told you why I didn't feel free to mention that bolt or our murder theory to the police or the press, but I can't continue hiding the facts."

"You leave the police to me," said Jardine. "We have a good rapport with them. As long as you leveled with us, you're in no trouble. As soon as you leave, I'll have a chat with Bill Zelke, head of the homicide squad over there."

"What's our next step then?" asked Mona.

"Hang loose there at the hotel for a day or two. I'll put this up to Washington and let you know as soon as possible. Don't worry. With all the public clamor over the oil spill, this will get top priority." He stood up and reached out to shake Mona's hand, then Mitch's. "And thanks for your cooperation. You've done just right in coming here."

Riding back to the Bellevue Stratford in a taxi, Mona leaned on Mitch's shoulder. "Suddenly, it's all getting to me. I'm awfully tired, Mitch, really beat. I didn't sleep well last night after the first few hours."

"Are you frightened?" He put his arm around her.

"Not that. I feel crummy and depressed and useless. Here I am going through all these captain-in-charge motions when I know damn well my career is down the tube. No matter how this comes out, no owner is going to hire a woman captain who lost a tanker and twenty million dollars' worth of oil that smeared a hundred miles of American coastline."

"None of that, babe." He shook her lightly. "You did everything a master should and no man could have done better. What's more, you're going to come out of this completely exonerated."

"I doubt it." She was not to be cheered. "But right now, I don't want to talk to a single soul but you and my daughter. I wish we could just hide out for twenty-four hours."

But that was not to be. As they walked into the lobby of the Bellevue Stratford, they were surrounded by reporters and someone thrust a microphone at Mona.

"Captain, can you confirm your radio officer's statement?"

"What statement?" Mona was testy this time. "I don't know what you're talking about."

Several newsmen shouted. "He says . . ." . . . "He claims . . ." ". . . dispute with company officials."

"Here's the AP copy." A shirt-sleeved man whom Mona recognized as Watkins of the Associated Press handed her a sheet of Teletype copy.

Philadelphia, (AP)—Capt. M. S. Harkinson of the doomed supertanker that spewed oil over the coastline of four mid-Atlantic states warned owners at the height of the storm that litigants might wind up owning the company.

Arno Joahannes, 26, radio officer of the *Yandoon Princess,* said today that he heard Mona Harkinson, first woman to captain a supertanker, tell a Michaelson & Lygdamis executive in Montreal by satellite marine phone that she had no time to bargain with a salvage tug in hopes of obtaining a simple towing contract as per company policy.

"The hell with company policy," Joahannes quoted his captain as saying. Instead she demanded that Homer Richert, operations vice-president, give her immediate authorization to accept the salvage tug's demand for an "LOF no-cure-no-pay" contract.

By marine custom a Lloyd's Open Form contract provides for automatic arbitration of the salvage fee in event the vessel is saved. Had the Tiggemann Bros. tug been able to tow the *Yandoon Princess* safely to port, the arbitration award to Tiggemann might have run into many millions of dollars.

"Richert wanted to defer a decision until he could contact President Arthur G. Michaelson," said the radio officer, "but the old lady said she couldn't wait. She had to know right that instant. That's when she warned him that an oil spill could cost the company plenty bucks."

Joahannes overheard Harkinson's end of the conversation because he had gone to the captain's cabin to report receipt of the LOF demand from the *Molly J.,* the Tiggemann Bros. tug that tried but failed to save the 240,000-ton tanker.

The communications officer said Captain Harkinson asked him to remember what he had heard her tell the Montreal executive because "if we don't make it," as he quoted her, "there'll be hearings and inquiries from here to the Azores."

"Sorry." Mona handed the copy back to the Associated Press reporter. "I have no comment."

"That implies that Joahannes quoted you accurately." It was Maggie Josephs of the *Washington Post.*

"I imply nothing." Mona appealed with open palms. "Look, I'm sure you all recognize that I can't talk in advance of the Coast Guard marine board of investigation. I will testify in full there. It'll be an open hearing where all of you can write as much as you like about anything we witnesses say. But until then, no comment."

"How much longer will you stay here, Mr. Donahey?" asked Sue Yasco of the *Philadelphia Inquirer.*

"Not long. I'm due to go to work soon on a new job in Copenhagen and I have to clean up matters back in Honolulu."

More questions rattled through the air, but Mona brushed them off and Mitch shouldered a pathway for her through the reporters and the fringe of spectators. But at the bank of elevators, Maggie Josephs, a slip of a woman under her wilderness of hair, showed up at Mona's side.

"I'd like to interview you on your life pre-*Yandoon Princess,*" she said. "They want a big Sunday take-out on you."

"No, Maggie. I admire your persistence, but no talking before the Coast Guard hearing."

Josephs refused to yield ground. "The *National Revealer* is going Sunday with a story on your secret sex life. If you don't sit still for a decent interview, you're going to end up looking like some dumb broad who wrestled her way to the top bed by bed."

"I doubt that, but even if it's true, I can't help it. Nothing more now. If you're still interested four months from now, call me and I'll talk all day. That's a promise."

In the elevator, Mona leaned into a corner. "Holy Jesus, my sex life yet! And what do you suppose got into Sparks that made him start blabbing to the press?" Before Mitch could answer, the third passenger, a demi-mountain of female flesh, shoved an envelope at Mona.

"Could I have your autograph, Captain, for my daughter Arlene. She's thirteen and she thinks you're super."

Mona signed with a wan smile, then explained to Mitch when they got off at their floor. "The thirteen-year-old daughter got me. I have to call Chris again. . . . Mitch, you suppose it's going on like this day after day?"

"Longer. Unless you quit tankers and settle down ashore."

She turned on him. "I'm no quitter." She said it with a burst of ferocity that took him by surprise.

A red light flashing on Mona's phone prompted her to call the message operator. Apparently a flock of calls had come in during her absence and a few minutes later a bellman delivered a stack of slips to the door. She sorted through them swiftly. . . . NBC, New York . . . *London Times* . . . Homer Richert, Montreal . . . *Der Tagesspiegel,* West Berlin . . . a Belgrade, Yugoslavia, TV station . . . the BBC . . . Mike Wallace, CBS "Sixty Minutes" . . . *People Magazine* . . . *Sea Trade,* London . . . Octagon Oil Co., Houston . . . Commander, U.S. Coast Guard Base, Gloucester City, N.J. . . . Televisa, Mexico City . . . Joffers Marine Steering Systems, Baltimore . . . *Paris-Match* . . . In all, more than fifty callers were trying to reach her.

Mona kicked off her shoes, bunched pillows against the headboard of the king-size bed, lay down and put in a call to Michaelson & Lygdamis in Montreal. Both President Michaelson and Vice-President Richert had flown back to Montreal the previous evening.

She handed the stack of messages to Mitch. "Here, pick out the ones I should answer." It was a curt command, delivered without looking at him.

"Yes, *sir,* Captain!"

At once she melted like ice in August. "Oh, no. Mitch, Mitch, I didn't mean that." She hung up the phone, sprang off the bed, threw her arms around his neck and kissed him feverishly. "I'll never do that again. And if I should, belt me one, will you?"

"With this kind of postscript, you can order me around any time."

"No, never. I won't be like that with you, Mitch. I promise. That was uncaring and hateful of me."

"Forget it. If I were under your kind of pressure, I'd be climbing the walls by now."

She nestled her head on his shoulder. "I never want to be that way with you, love. I want to be your woman." Then she stood back and looked him in the eyes. "But the bossy bit is part of me. That's the way I am aboard ship. It's in me—and you have to know that."

"I understand, Mona."

"I think you do." She kissed him tenderly, then stood regarding him with wonder. "Incredible, a man who understands me."

Once again she lay down against the pillows and replaced the call to Montreal. "Ten to one Richert's in a fit over the AP story."

Homer Richert, the chilly accountant turned fleet operations officer, confirmed her prediction. While he made a few inquiries, more formal than compassionate, about the murder of Mario Didati and the subsequent fallout, his prime concern centered on Arno Joahannes. "Will you please tell me, Captain," he asked, "why you permitted your radio officer to make that reckless, irresponsible statement to the press?"

"I'm as amazed and troubled by that as you are. I warned everyone from the ship about talking further after that first press conference. But you must realize that I have no control over the officers or crew here on land."

"No legal control, but certainly a captain of stature has great influence with his—with the men at all times."

Mona made no reply to this implication of her failure to measure up to proper standards of charisma.

"That one story could cause us tremendous damage in a law suit. And what about Joahannes' claim that you asked him to remember your end of our conversation because if the ship went down, there'd be hearings and inquiries from 'here to the Azores'?"

"That's true." Mona chewed at her lower lip. "I did tell him that."

"I think you can imagine what kind of reception that reminder is getting around here." Richert's voice came cased in frost. "President Michaelson, who takes great pride in the loyalty of M & L masters to the company, is particularly offended."

"I deplore Sparks' talking to the press as much as you do, but you must realize that it would have come out eventually anyway at the Coast Guard marine board hearing."

"I fail to see why."

"Because the officers on the board will question everyone from the ship about the age of the *Princess* and the frequency of drydockings. The object is marine safety, after all."

"Captain Harkinson, I want you to get word to every officer and man there in Philadelphia." Richert gave his order the rhythm and texture of a theologian preaching from a cathedral pulpit. "The company strongly disapproves of individual statements to the press. Any man who makes one will have that fact placed in his personnel jacket where it will be evaluated whenever his continued employment is reviewed."

"I'll do that, but you ought to know that if the press gets hold of your warning, it will be headlined as a 'company gag order.' "

"We'll take that risk." Richert obviously discounted the chance. "And Captain, when you find Joahannes, tell him to call me at once. I can't raise him in his hotel room."

When she hung up, Mona looked questioningly at Mitch who was sitting on the lounge, scanning the *Philadelphia Inquirer*. It had become a habit, this business of seeking his reaction to every development.

"You didn't say a word to him about the whole sabotage angle," said Mitch. "They still don't know about that at M & L headquarters."

"Right. That was intentional. I want the bastard to sweat for a while. He and Michaelson think M & L's going to be crucified at the marine board and in the press for chartering out a tanker that should be on its way to the breaker yards."

"But Mona, you've got to tell the owners their ship may have had its steering knocked out on purpose."

"I know. But I can tell them my first duty was to inform the FBI." She picked up the phone. "Actually, I'm not sure we should tell anyone else yet."

Mona placed a call to Tom Jardine, waited on hold for several minutes, then told him of her predicament. Should she or should she not inform the owners about the suspicions of sabotage? She listened while the special agent talked, then clued in Mitch after she hung up.

"Jardine says to hold everything, tell no one, until the Bureau makes a decision on how to proceed. Well, that settles that. . . . Now for Chrissy."

Mona reached her daughter in Switzerland on the third try. It was just before the dinner hour at Mlle. Jupon's exclusive school for girls near Zurich and Christine Harkinson Floberg was in her room gossiping with her roommate. The first words of greeting transformed Mona from a wary, pressured tanker captain to an excited, doting mother. She curled up on the bed with the phone at her ear like a teenager, tossed out happy questions, listened totally absorbed as if to her first date and punctuated her own recent story with laughter and cheerful, if acidic, quips. As she described events since the sinking, the stress-ribbed days became a kind of carnival peopled by carefree clowns and pompous buffoons.

"They called him what?" she shouted. Laughing, she twisted about on the bed and turned toward Mitch. "Darling, Swiss television called you my paramour. . . . Chrissy, what in heaven's name is a paramour? . . . I see. . . . Oh, they do? Your friends all think he's handsome? Well, I do too. We've gotten to the point, honey, where I call him my man and he calls me his woman. Yes, yes, I feel wonderful even though my ship's on the ocean floor. Will you talk to him? Great." She held out the phone to Mitch. "Be a love and talk to Chrissy, will you?"

"Hi, Chrissy, I'm Mitchell Donahey, the man who flew in from Honolulu to protect your mother from all the bad guys."

"T'riffic. We know all about you, Mr. Donahey." It was a strong voice with a touch of huskiness not unlike her mother's. "You're a shipbroker and you're a looker and you've got a thing for mom."

"And you're into horses and skiing and what else?"

"Well, I wish I could say boys, but we only see them on Saturday nights at these prissy little dances that Mademoiselle puts on." She laughed and giggling could be heard in the background. "That's Riva, my roommate from Venezuela. She's silly, but she's awful cute."

"Say hello for me. Chris, I'm going to be working in Copenhagen soon. I'd like to see you some weekend, get acquainted, maybe with your mother if she isn't in a courtroom somewhere. Would you like that?"

"T'riffic. Could we eat some place fancy? The food gets boring here."

"That's a deal. See you soon. Here's your mother again."

Mona chatted on for several minutes and when she finished, she was a changed woman, her gray irritable mood swept away by the playful breezes from Zurich. "Isn't she a doll? Just in the last year, she's begun to trust me so that we can swap confidences. . . . Now, let's see."

For the next several hours, she handled the pressing business at hand. She reached Chief Mate Bill Muldoon at his home in south Philadelphia, directed him to relay Vice-President Richert's warning against press interviews to all officers and crew. Muldoon agreed to come by the hotel in late afternoon for a discussion of what needed doing while they waited for the Coast Guard inquiry.

She returned the call of Octagon Oil in Houston. A member of the legal staff wanted to know which tank had ruptured first on grounding. No. 3 port, she replied after checking her copy of the ship's log. But when he inquired about her first order after the second loss of steering, she bluntly declined to answer. Follow her testimony at the Coast Guard marine board of investigation, she said. "Not until after the hearing" became a stock phrase. She used it to fend off an investigator for the Lloyd's underwriting group that had insured the tanker, the Texas company that had insured the cargo of oil and the Frankfurt bank in West Germany that held the mortgage on the *Yandoon Princess.*

"They ought to know they're wasting time trying to get you to talk before the hearing," said Mitch.

She nodded. "Only a moron would start yakking to them at this stage, but they insist on trying. Maybe they think a woman's an easy mark."

Her quick shifts of personality amused Mitch as he helped winnow the messages and recommend responses. On the phone she was all business, crisp, controlled and controlling, a firm voice of authority. The moment she hung up and turned to him, Mona stripped off her captain's rank as she might foul-weather gear and lapsed into the role of courted woman. She softened noticeably, her smile frequently shy, and the sandy voice took on a gentle tender note. At first he thought she made a studied effort to erase his memory of the recent moment when she barked an order at him, but as time went on, he sensed that she swung quite unconsciously from one stance to the other and that both Monas, the captain and the woman wooed, were valid residents of the same house.

Once, after a harsh rebuff of an importuning manager of a lecture bureau, Mona looked over at Mitch and said, "Say, sweet guy, did I tell you that I play the guitar?"

"No, not that I remember."

"Well, I do. I never take it aboard ship. My image, you know. But I keep the guitar in my London apartment. I've played since high school. Chrissy picks too and on my recent visits to Mademoiselle Jupon's, Chrissy taught me some pretty French ballads. I'd love to play and sing for you sometime."

"Can't wait." He stared at her in wonderment. What a charmer. These sudden wide swings, from tough authority to spring-like innocence, captivated him. How different from himself. Except for his fits of temper, he saw his own behavior as fluctuating within a narrow arc, a single octave perhaps, whereas Mona's moods, roles and tempers raced across an entire keyboard, hammering the bass keys like thunder, then swirling off to tap a ballet on the treble keys.

The afternoon slipped by amid the round of phone calls and when Chief Mate Muldoon called from the lobby, Mitch excused himself. "I'll take a walk around town while you two talk. I can use the exercise."

He walked down Broad Street and around City Hall, an elderly structure topped by a statue of William Penn and seeming to approach old age with all the complaints of a dyspeptic ward leader. The blistering day had cooled somewhat with the approach of evening, but the sidewalks still threw off heat stored from the midday hours. He cooled off at an air-conditioned bar in the Hershey Philadelphia, then sauntered down Locust Street, window-gazing as he went.

A display of drums, clarinets, keyboards and guitars caught his eye. The music store was about to close, but Mitch prevailed on a salesman to show him his best guitars. Ten minutes later he had used a credit card to purchase a $775 guitar on condition that the clerk deliver it personally at once to the room of Mona Harkinson at the Bellevue Stratford. A call to Mona yielded the assurance that Bill Muldoon had left.

Mitch followed the clerk at a discreet distance, managed to ease by a knot of reporters in the hotel lobby without being recognized and arrived on the fifth floor just as the man from the music store was entering a down elevator.

Mona's greeting surprised him. Expecting an ebullient welcome, arms thrown about his neck, he met instead a subdued woman who walked to the coffee table and stood gazing down at the guitar that lay in its case atop a scatter of crumpled wrapping paper. She looked at him, smoky eyes quite sober, down at the instrument, then back again at him.

"That's a lovely gift, Mitch. I don't think I've ever received such a thoughtful present." But she spoke as if the guitar had just perished in some disaster. "You picked up so fast on what I told you."

"Do you like it?" He pumped cheer to fill the void.

"Oh, yes. It's a top make." She pinged a finger against the wood. "None better." She made no move to pick up the guitar, but stood frowning down at it.

"Is something wrong?"

"No, it's just, well, I'm awful about presents. I can give them okay, but the receiving . . . I guess it's something from childhood. Outside of Christmas and my birthday, my father never gave me a gift except as a reward for achieving some goal he'd set for me. So when I get a present now when I haven't done anything, maybe failed like this God-awful tanker thing, then . . . well, I feel shitty."

He put his arms around her. "I'm sorry, babe. I didn't know."

"Of course, how could you know?" She sniffed, forestalling tears. "Isn't that ridiculous? And you were so sweet to think of me on your walk." She pushed him away, brushed at an eye. "Oh, hey, look, I'll be okay as soon as I start playing."

She sat down with the guitar, inspected it, tuned it carefully, struck a few chords. "Here's one I made up. If I'd known I'd meet you, it would have had your name on it."

Plucking at the guitar, Mona sang low and sweet in the throaty voice that touched something deep within him. Was that too a childhood echo?

> Strange in the misty morning
> Rider on the plain.
> Soft in the misty morning
> Dawning out of rain.
> > I knew you'd come someday, you see,
> > A love so dear and strong and free.
> > With arms to hold and cares to fling,
> > With laughing eyes and songs to sing.
> Oh, strange that misty morning
> Shadow on the plain.
> So soft that misty morning
> Sunlight out of rain.

"Beautiful." Her singing and the strumming of the strings put him in a mellow mood.

"I'm going to give that a title—Mitchell D." She had brightened again. Thumbing the keys, she struck a few chords. "Oh, here's one that Chrissy taught me this summer."

> Il est cocu, le chef de gare
> Il est cocu, le chef de gare
> S'il est cocu, c'est parce que
> Sa femme la voulu.

"The station master is cuckolded because his wife wished it so." She glanced upward in mock dismay. "Which shows what weighs on the mind of a sixteen-year-old."

"Sure, at sixteen I was trying to lay my algebra teacher."

Mona swung through a motley series, country, French, Spanish, western, folk and rock. She played and sang with fervor, a flush of roses on her cheeks, her hair thrown back, surges of power in her voice. She sang of Mount McKinley, the Pont d'Avignon and Old Smoky. She mimicked Willie Nelson and Julio Yglesias in "All the Girls We Loved," sang like Donovan of the "velvet jungle night," did several of Joan Baez's anti-war songs of the sixties and Bruce Springsteen's "Born in the U.S.A.," sank to a low growling register in imitation of Mexico's Chavela Vargas lamenting a lost love and dipped back a century for the ballads of Stephen Foster.

Mitch had all phone calls held by the operator after several jarring interruptions. When it grew dark outside, they ordered dinner sent to the room, vichyssoise, filet mignon and a salad. They ate by dim lights and then Mona played again, this time singing some of her own compositions, fragile haunting melodies of love.

When at last she put the guitar away, she snapped the case and said, "Not a bad way to leave a shipwreck, is it?"

They made love like bawdy angels, a sublime rutting that tore away their breath, put fantasy to shame and left them clinging together as if glued. They fell asleep entangled in love, hope and sweat.

Tom Jardine phoned while they were eating breakfast in Mona's room.

"You'll get a call soon from the Coast Guard. The marine board of investigation on the *Yandoon Princess* has been postponed until January."

"That means you're investigating suspected sabotage?" asked Mitch.

"It means that you two have stirred up something big. I can't go into details, but the implications are much wider than any of us thought when we talked yesterday morning."

"Now what?"

"You're free to go about your business, but first they want to see you in Washington. I'd like you two to come by my office within the hour. I'll give you the word."

This time, instead of sparring with reporters in the hotel lobby, Mitch and Mona slipped out a side door.

11

The six men gathered around the long koa coffee table might have been vacationing executives of some multinational corporation. They had the sleek, self-satisfied look of the affluent, most of them carried more weight than they needed and all of them wore either custom-tailored resort clothes or the kind that came off the high-priced racks. They also had the unmistakable stamp of hierarchy. No one could glance at them without noting the pecking order.

The living room in which they sat had one side open to the southwest and commanded a panoramic view of Honolulu from Pearl Harbor on the right to Diamond Head on the left. Beyond stretched the Pacific, the morning sun etching varying water depths in a medley of marine colors, green, jade, turquoise, azure, navy blue. Here and there a cuff of shimmering white revealed the presence of reefs. Off Diamond Head a clutter of sailboats, spinnakers bellied by the trade winds, raced toward a far buoy.

The room had an understated elegance in the tropical style, bamboo furniture with sea colors woven into the upholstery, a floor of cool Mexican tile, koa wood trim at the doorways and a quiet fountain embossed with ferns where water tumbled into a small pool inhabited by bright darting fish. The walls held several Picasso prints and the paintings of two island artists, a vivid horse in the spare lines of John Young and one of Pegge Hopper's voluptuous Hawaiian women flowing into abstraction.

Located on a curving street in Makiki Heights several hundred feet above the city, the fashionable house, complete with Japanese rock garden, bamboo grove and an oval swimming pool decked by flagstones, rented for more money than most nations pay their chief executives.

Three of the men grouped about the coffee table were Japanese and three Caucasian. The white men wore freshly laundered aloha shirts and a variety of trousers and shoes, but the Japanese all wore white polo shirts, white linen pants and highly polished white shoes. The Japanese had their hair trimmed short, but obviously waved by machine. The oldest, a man of perhaps sixty who seemed wrapped in quiet amusement, had a discreet platinum emblem pinned to his shirt. The youngest Japanese, a dour man of about thirty-five, wore a similar pin, but his was made of silver as was that of the third Japanese, a plump genial middle-aged type. The two older men shared a common disfigurement. The tip of the little finger on the left hand had been cut off, leaving a nailless stub.

When the group had taken a pre-breakfast swim in the pool several hours earlier, the Caucasians had seen a profusion of tattoos on the three Japanese. One had a Buddha and a web of religious symbols encircling his torso, another displayed Mount Fuji on his back while the middle-aged man's entire body from ankles to shoulders carried a blue jungle of plants, trees and flowers, including an enormous lotus bloom. He looked like a frog man, wearing some bizarre new wet suit, who was about to put on flippers and diving helmet.

Clothing, tattoos and missing tips of the left little finger marked the Japanese as *yakuza,* members of one of the large criminal gangs that flourish in Japan, often with the tolerance of politicians and businessmen. They had managed to slip undetected into Honolulu past the screening net erected by federal law officers who feared that yakuza could melt away easily into the islands' dominant population of Asian descent. These three men would have held particular interest for federal and Honolulu police officers because they belonged to the *Yamaguchi-gumi,* largest and wealthiest of Japan's crime organizations. A well-disciplined army of several thousand men, it was headquartered in the seaport city of Kobe and ran a huge illegal enterprise embracing drugs, smuggling, usury, prostitution, entertainment, murder-for-hire and various fraudulent business and industrial schemes.

For many years the Yamaguchi-gumi had pursued illegal waterfront and marine activities in Japan, but recently as the island nation grew into the world's foremost economic power, the Yamaguchi-gumi raised its sights and aspired to mold an international organization exerting dominion over criminal endeavors on the high seas.

To the planning conference at the stylish Makiki Heights home in Honolulu had come the vice-commander of the Kobe-based yakuza, Toru Higashiyama, the elderly gentleman with the platinum pin, a truncated little finger and the look of quiet amusement; Takeo Kirihara, the plump middle-aged type with the silver pin and severed little finger, director of the new international marine division; Yukio Osagawa, youngest of the three, also rating a silver pin, most recently second engineer on the ill-fated tanker *Yandoon Princess*.

Facing them across the polished koa coffee table were the three non-Japanese, Nikos Miaoulis, a Greek seaman who had worked on both the *Gunnison Bay* and the *Yandoon Princess*, Henry (Bones) Elger, the American tanker engineer who had served aboard the lost *Gunnison Bay*, and Alexandros Nicias, once captain of the *Gunnison Bay* and now master of the *King Misura*, a tanker in the Lorikeet fleet owned by Wasif Zabib and associates of Copenhagen.

"To review briefly the agreement between myself and Mr. Henry Elger." Yukio Osagawa, the tanker engineer, was interpreting for Vice-Commander Toru Higashiyama. Of the three Japanese, only Osagawa spoke fluent English. Kirihara could make himself understood in a stumbling way, but Higashiyama spoke only Japanese. "Profits of all joint ventures are being split equally between the Yamaguchi-gumi and Elger's group. All reasonable expenses will be paid by Yamaguchi in light of its superior financial resources. In return, Elger's group will supply bail and legal services should any of our *kobun*—soldiers—be apprehended in these operations.

"Our alliance is a provisional one, a test, so to speak. We Yamaguchi have been in business a long time. Our American and Greek friends have carried out only two jobs so far and one of these was botched. So whether this alliance becomes permanent depends on results in the near future. Anyone who does not understand this, please speak out."

The silence that ensued appeared to please Higashiyama for the high officer from Kobe smiled benignly before his next volley of Japanese.

"Our first joint project was an ill-planned disaster for which all participants must share blame. I want our American and Greek friends to know that if they'd been kobun in our army, they would have sent their apologies bottled in alcohol." Yukio Osagawa felt compelled to explain. "The vice-commander means that you'd have to chop off the end of your left little finger with a sword and send it to him in a preservative."

Higashiyama beamed benevolently and held up his left hand. "Kirihara and I both made mistakes in our youth. One learns to court perfection."

Nikos Miaoulis, the darkly brooding deckhand, was not to be intimidated. "No way could we figure a storm that bad was comin'. And we couldn't know that Tiggemann's big tug would lose its engine."

Higashiyama, after the translation, stared at Miaoulis as he might at a perverse child. He said nothing, merely continued to center Miaoulis in his benign yet unnerving gaze. At last, with a sigh, he spoke and the interpreter put it this way: "Yamaguchi officers and soldiers always assume that the worst may happen and take precautions accordingly. Had a code been devised, Tiggemann could have sent a message to you on the tanker, warning that the big tug was in repair. Then you could have aborted the operation."

"But," protested Miaoulis, "in any ordinary weather, the *Molly J.* could have towed us into the bay with no sweat. The odds were about a hundred to one against getting hit by a storm that bad."

Whatever had amused Higashiyama suddenly ceased to do so. Hard eyes fastened on the Greek seaman and held him like prey. In a prolonged human silence, only the liquid voice of the fountain could be heard. Takeo Kirihara inspected his nails. Bones Elger flicked a speck of dust from his gleaming white moccasins which, along with his white trousers and strawberry aloha shirt, seemed to place him midway sartorially between the yakuza and the western contingent.

Miaoulis glowered back at the senior Yamaguchi officer. "You can't plan for every . . ."

"Shut up!" Elger threw up his hand in a halt signal. After a moment, he turned to Higashiyama. "We blew it. We have no excuse. We are paying careful attention to your words. We will not fail a second time."

"Good," replied the yakuza commander according to Osagawa's translation. "Punishment seldom fathers failure. Osagawa-kun is being fined two million yen for his part in the *Yandoon Princess* fiasco. This in default of sacrificing his finger. It would not do to have a key tanker man marked as yakuza." Osagawa translated his own punishment without expression.

Higashiyama asked about the killing of Mario Didati. Why was that done? Because, explained Elger, it was mandatory that the bolt be taken at once before Didati could go to the authorities with it. He could have been robbed without physical harm by a masked man, but it was impossible to wear a mask in downtown Philadelphia in daylight. Therefore to prevent identification . . . Bones shook his head sadly as if to lament the necessity for bloody expedients. Higashiyama nodded. How had they disposed of the bolt, the commander wanted to know.

"I got it from Jerry Artwick, the Brit, when I arrived in Philly that night," said Elger. "Then I hired a rental car and tossed the bolt off a bridge into the Schuylkill."

"The car rental was billed to us as an operations expense?" Higashiyama's snip of a smile patronized.

Taking no chances, Elger responded to the words, not to the twitting attitude, "No, sir. I paid that out of my own pocket." His Adam's apple, bobbing up and down, might have been a small animal imprisoned in his throat.

Why had the U.S. Coast Guard postponed its hearing on the tanker sinking? Higashiyama fired the question in Japanese, then looked from one westerner to the other during the translation.

"I'm not sure." Elger frowned. "I worried about that some. My best guess is that Michaelson & Lygdamis, fearing they'd be blamed because of the tanker's age and lack of drydocking, put the heat on some congressman who got to the Coast Guard."

Higashiyama spoke rapidly in a firm voice. "In Japan we do not guess. We know exactly through our political sources."

Elger exchanged glances of frustration with Alexandros Nicias, the Greek captain. Were these rebukes to be the coin of partnership? "We hope to strike a deal soon for a good Washington contact man," said Elger. He had, in fact, just that moment formulated the hope.

Higashiyama, stating curtly that a Washington power connection was a priority need, asked if there were any chance that Mario Didati had revealed the story of the bolt to his captain or another officer.

Both *Yandoon Princess* men, Miaoulis and Osagawa, thought not. Osagawa spoke to his superior at some length, then turned to the three foreigners. "I told him I had sailed with Didati on three voyages. Didati was a perfectionist, wanted everything tagged and specified. He was not the kind of man who would spread suspicion until he had done a lot of checking. That's why he interviewed the enginemen and was to talk to you, Nikos, the next day."

But Yamaguchi's number two man was not satisfied. "From all reports, our own and the media, I judge this man Mitchell Donahey to be a threat to us. To help his woman, he's surely investigating the *Yandoon Princess* sinking right now. He's very smart. He could make bad trouble for us." He looked at Nicias. "Isn't he joining your Lorikeet company, Captain?"

"Yes," said Nicias after the translation. "He'll be working under Zabib in Copenhagen."

Higashiyama conferred with his two yakuza colleagues at some length and after they apparently signaled their agreement, Osagawa said, "The vice-commander has decided that the man Donahey should be watched closely. If it appears that he might expose our pitiful *Yandoon Princess* operation, he should be dealt with promptly."

"Dealt with?" asked Elger.

"Eliminated," said Osagawa in a flat voice. "And if that becomes necessary, it should be made to appear an accident."

"Christ," protested Miaoulis with a scowl, "we already killed one guy."

The three yakuza stared at him.

"We'll handle it," said Elger. "No problem."

"Good," said Higashiyama. "Now let us turn to the future." The main objective of this Honolulu conference, he stated, was to discuss ideas for profitable joint ventures in the vast marine market. Fortunately international maritime law was cumbersome, erratic and poorly enforced. This opened golden opportunities on the high seas, heretofore seized only by random individuals and crews. Deep water cried out for exploitation by an extensive well-disciplined organization with the abundant resources, financial and otherwise, of Yamaguchi-gumi.

"I am glad," he said, "that Elger and Kirihara laid the groundwork for this conference at their sessions in Honolulu last month. They had a meeting of the minds, as the Americans say."

"Little did we know," said Elger, "that we also got a look at the next master of the tanker on which we almost scored our first hit."

"When was that?" asked Kirihara. He was puzzled.

"Remember when we went to Donahey's house near Diamond Head and waited for him in the driveway?"

Yes, the head of Yamaguchi's new international marine division acknowledged, he did remember the driveway scene that night.

"Well, the woman with him," said Elger, "turns out to have been Captain Mona Harkinson of the *Yandoon Princess.*"

"Ah, yes, the woman master." Kirihara, an easy-humored man, came to attention. "I think we should follow that woman close. Where she goes, we have opening for business."

"Right, except that her chances of getting another ship are almost nil."

"Our immediate priority is guns," said Higashiyama through the interpreter. "The pistol that you pay one hundred dollars for in America can bring fifteen hundred dollars in Japan where sale of handguns is illegal. But also we need the guns for our own use. Our arsenal is low. The commander orders us to bring in as many as possible as soon as possible."

Alexandros Nicias, the Lorikeet Tankers captain, said he could guarantee delivery of several thousand handguns to Japan provided he could bid a voyage from Nigeria, Indonesia or Mexico, easiest oil-exporting countries from which to smuggle guns aboard a tanker. Swarthy with long sideburns and a ferocious garlic breath, Nicias had the build of a wrestler.

A long discussion of tactics followed. Where could the guns be purchased easiest, soonest and cheapest? How to smuggle them out of the country of purchase and into the country of tanker embarkation? Elger knew a gun broker in Marseille who sold in bulk at prices not much above those prevailing on the U.S. market.

From guns the talk ran to the smuggling of narcotics, jewelry and people, then to the grand crimes at sea, hijacking, scuttling of vessels, stealing the cargo and sinking the ship à la *Gunnison Bay,* crippling a ship in collusion with a salvage outfit à la *Yandoon Princess.* Captain Nicias, who had spent time around the Piraeus waterfront in Greece, urged that they establish several laboratories to forge documents and licenses for merchant marine seamen and officers.

"There's a fortune in it." His breath laid wrathful stress on the rosy vision. "A man who needs to ship out will pay a couple of thousand dollars for the right papers."

The idea intrigued Higashiyama who made notes in meticulous Japanese characters as he questioned the thick-chested Nicias. Elger also stirred the interest of the Yamaguchi officer when he proposed that the combine set up a special container division.

"The big boxes are being lost or misdirected all the time." Elger fussed at his expensively styled cornsilk hair. "Two major companies make big bucks just tracing lost containers. It's a cinch in a lot of ports to steal them or bribe them off the docks. You can change bills of lading, ship boxes to the wrong place, fake theft and collect on insurance, work a foreign exchange deal with the exporter. Lots of cheap crooks are in the racket now, but not many big pros. We could have a lock on container loot within a year."

Again Higashiyama questioned as he took notes. Outside, the sky turned pale blue as the sun rose past the midday mark, the racing sailboats tacked back toward Waikiki and passenger jets, flashing in the sunlight, lowered toward the Honolulu airport.

During a break a striking Eurasian girl, long legs accentuated by a brief tennis skirt, fetched drinks from the kitchen. For $5,000 a day, the yakuza, noted as big spenders, had hired six hostesses to serve food and drinks and cater to the sexual wishes of the Japanese men and their guests. Bones Elger, many times a visitor to Hawaii, had made the arrangements through an escort bureau so strict in confidentiality that it was known as the "silent service."

Higashiyama pressed the discussion until the lunch hour when saimin and a fruit salad were served beside the pool. Then the talk continued through the afternoon. The men aired all manner of marine and waterfront scams, including proposals to infiltrate the classification societies that certified vessels as seaworthy, set up their own marine insurance agency that would dodge national insurance laws and establish a bogus shipping company in Hong Kong that could be quickly dismantled after collecting on fake invoices and consignments.

Higashiyama showed most interest in a suggestion by his own man, Yukio Osagawa, that the combine make a deal with a small island nation to establish its own ship registry system to compete with such flags of convenience as Liberia, Panama and Cyprus. By shaving minimum standards and cutting registration fees, he said, the new shipping nation could attract business away from other marine countries. A small weak nation would be satisfied with a minor split, say 25 percent, and the combine could grow fat on the profits. The vice-commander took copious notes.

The yakuza chief broke off the meeting in late afternoon and announced that the three Yamaguchi men would adjourn to a shooting gallery in downtown Honolulu. He named a gun "club" that was highly popular with Japanese tourists who fired off bullets from rifles and handguns at $1 a shot. Higashiyama invited the westerners to be his guests.

"I would advise against that." Elger, all bones and angles, looked worried. "The Honolulu police and sometimes the feds keep an eye on the place." He pointed to the commander's mutilated little finger. "They spot a finger like that and they'll haul you in for questioning."

"I need to practice." Higashiyama was unperturbed. "I shoot with my right hand. So does Kirihara."

Elger appealed to Osagawa. "Listen, Yukio, warn him, will you? This isn't Japan where the police take you guys for granted. If he gets picked up now, this meeting could go down the drain."

"I never warn my superiors." The mere suggestion appalled the tanker engineer. "If he were not wiser than I, he would not have risen to the position he holds."

"Ah, fer crisssake, what kind of stinkin' logic is that, Yukio?"

Elger's Adam's apple bobbed indignantly. "If the cops nab him down there, you know he'll blame us. Then it's your ass and mine."

"We have been ordered to go. We will go." Osagawa rose from his chair as his commander prepared to leave.

Elger and his fellow westerners begged off from the gun excursion and Osagawa phoned down for the rental limousine waiting in the garage. The three Japanese drove off in the chauffeured vehicle, its windows tinted to conceal those riding inside.

As it turned out, no one bothered the yakuza as they fired off .38's and .45's until they tired of the sport and rode back to Makiki Heights in stylish obscurity.

The outdoor dinner that night on the flagstone deck, safely screened behind flowering plumeria trees, turned rowdy early. All six men drank heavily and the Japanese, while preserving the nuances of hierarchy, grew as boisterous as the American and Greek seamen. The hostesses serving the six-course dinner, from the *igagori* shrimp balls to the filet chateaubriand to the chocolate soufflé, were fondled, caressed and pawed as they went about their chores with customary professional coquetry.

A rivalry developed between Captain Nicias and Takeo Kirihara for the favors of a slim effervescent brown-skinned girl named Pua who told spicy stories, boasted of Portuguese, Hawaiian and Korean ancestry, danced informal hulas at the edge of the pool and promised to do a nude hula later inside the house. At last Kirihara challenged the heavy muscled Nicias to a wrestling match, winner take Pua. They squared off good-naturedly, but as they rolled about the flagstone deck, they grew increasingly hostile and several times swatted at each other like alley fighters. Finally, when Kirihara snarled at the Greek and Nicias clouted back with a right to the jaw, Higashiyama gave some kind of silent signal to Osagawa who shoved both men, fully clothed, into the pool.

This brought the dinner to a raucous close. While the women snuffed out the candles and cleared the table, the men went indoors and milled about, liqueurs in hand, waiting for Kirihara and Nicias to emerge from their rooms in dry clothes. When both men and women had assembled, Pua, clad in a flowered sarong with a creamy lei falling over bare breasts, began a slow sensuous hula to the chant of another woman. Soon the sarong fell away and she danced in the nude. The men ogled and cheered.

When she finished, the yakuza chief spoke rapidly to Osagawa who said: "Commander Higashiyama says that it is up to the woman who she spends the night with, Kirihara-san or Nicias." Pua smiled her thanks for this opportunity to choose, kissed Nicias on the cheek, then took Kirihara by the hand and walked with him down the corridor to the bedrooms. Whether the choice rested on the attraction of Kirihara or the virulence of Nicias's breath, no one knew.

Higashiyama shouted after the couple in Japanese and Osagawa promptly announced, "We convene again at nine o'clock tomorrow morning." Five minutes later not a person remained in the living room.

Breakfast beside the pool the next morning was a subdued affair. Surfeited and still sleepy, the men held conversation to a minimum. Pua caused a mild stir by trying to coax Takeo Kirihara to accompany her to the kitchen and show off the floral splendor of his all-body tattoos to the other women. Kirihara, obviously smitten with his partner of the night, got up from his chair only to be ordered back down again by his superior.

"The soft night is behind us. Today we work," was the burden of Higashiyama's admonition.

In fact, the pioneers of institutionalized maritime crime spent two more hard days in conference, their work broken only by another night of dalliance with the Waikiki call girls. The yakuza commander, serene but insistent, pressed them steadily forward. The old American folk maxim erred, said Higashiyama. Not only did crime pay, it paid handsomely if one laid detailed plans, anticipated all possible reverses and worked harder than the guardians of the law. Most practitioners of crime, observed the Yamaguchi chief, were lazy characters, slovenly on the job, who fully deserved the prison sentences they invited by their sloth and incompetence.

In the end, the Elger-Yamaguchi combine ratified Higashiyama's decision to launch one project immediately, another as soon as the facilities and technicians could be assembled and two others if a study by Kobe headquarters proved them feasible. The pair of enterprises to be scrutinized by the experts: (1.) Going into partnership with a graft-amenable island nation to establish a shipping registry to rival the flags-of-convenience states such as Liberia and Panama. (2.) Establishing an international network to prey on the lucrative container traffic.

Workshops, one in Europe and one in Asia, would be established as soon as tools and technicians were procured to produce spurious licenses and other documents needed by seamen and officers seeking work in the depressed merchant marines of the world. Higashiyama said he would put a skilled Yamaguchi forger in command of the venture with Alexandros Nicias as the chief consultant.

"This enterprise meets the high standards of Yamaguchi-gumi," said Higashiyama gravely. "A grievous need exists in the world. Deserving seamen cannot get work because they do not hold a piece of paper. We supply the paper. A need fulfilled."

Bones Elger agreed to serve as chief of the priority project, procuring handguns and assorted other weapons and selecting the vessels on which they would be shipped to Japan, where Takeo Kirihara, chief of international marine operations, would command the yakuza soldiers who would smuggle them into the country.

It was further agreed, under Higashiyama's urging, that Elger and Kirihara would meet in Hong Kong to complete arrangements as soon as Elger had lined up his gun supply sources.

"I like the .357 Magnum Smith & Wesson revolver," said Higashiyama. "Buy us lots of them. For the safety and protection of the brotherhood."

The conference ended in a flurry of handshakes, bows and protestations of eternal friendship at a brief drinking session on the evening of the third day. The westerners had night planes to catch to the mainland while the three Japanese intended to stay on an extra day to take advantage of Hawaii's beguiling climate and companionship.

The yakuza and the six hostesses lined the driveway as Elger and his friends prepared to climb into the tinted Cadillac limousine for their ride to the airport. More handshakes and bows and then the women draped leis about the necks of the three tankermen and kissed them good-bye.

Along with his *sayonara*, Toru Higashiyama, gracious and benign in farewell, gave his departing guests some fuel for their moral engines. "Do not try to leap mountains, strive devoutly for the brotherhood and let five fingers forever salute your successes."

As the three yakuza strolled back into the house in advance of the women, Yukio Osagawa, who had first introduced Elger and the other tankermen to his Yamaguchi superiors, probed discreetly for their reaction to the departing business partners.

"I hope," he said, "the westerners will perform up to our own high standards."

"I was not impressed with their caliber," said Higashiyama promptly. "Elger is shrewd and ambitious, but I do not trust Nicias. As for the seaman, Miaoulis, he lacks intelligence and he does not know his place. . . . We'll give the alliance a fair test. If it does not work, there are many smart men on the high seas who would be honored to cooperate with us." The vice-commander's smile was that of a man accustomed to success. "One way or another, the brotherhood's venture into the international maritime industry will fly the banners of triumph."

Henry Elger and Nikos Miaoulis sat together as their jet swung around Diamond Head and climbed to cruising altitude for their flight to Los Angeles. Earlier they had bid good-bye to Alexandros Nicias who was flying to Copenhagen via New York. Through the window at his elbow Elger could see brilliant stars and silvery spatial dust scattered about the black tropic sky. Elger felt content. The meeting had gone well.

"The yakuza know their business," he said. "It looks like good times ahead."

"I ain't so damn sure." A steady brooder, Miaoulis seemed to bask in gloom. "That old bastard Higash is a slave driver. Shit, he'd have us working harder than they did in the engine room under Didati."

"Their methods produce. You ride along with Yamaguchi-gumi and you'll be rich, Nikos."

"I got plenty now from the *Bay* job. So do you. How much fuckin' money do you want?"

"More." Elger grinned. "Besides, with Higashiyama and his mob we'll have a ball getting it."

"Aw, you watch, Hank." Miaoulis scowled. "We white guys will be flunkies for the Yamaguchis. They'll wind up with all the green. And I don't like starting off with another murder."

"You don't have to worry about Donahey. I'll take care of that job." Elger gazed out the plane window at the night sky. "In fact, it'll be a pleasure."

"A bunch of weirdos." Miaoulis shook his head. "Chopping off their own fingers and covered with all that tattoo shit like circus freaks."

"You've got it wrong, Nikos. They're smart as hell. Going along with them, we'll own the world someday." A man who wore blinders, thought Elger as they lapsed into silence. Couldn't see the big picture. Okay as a working stiff, Nikos, but lacked the class to run with the yakuza. Time to pick a new lieutenant. Elger settled deep into his seat preparatory to sleeping. The first job, Donahey, then guns for Japan. Ought to be a piece of cake. He sighed as he closed his eyes. With the Yamaguchi and a man like Higashiyama, the future looked golden.

12

His overcoat over his arm, Mitch paced about the large pillared lobby while he waited for his contact to appear and escort him past the rope barrier where uniformed guards corked the entry bottleneck of the Central Intelligence Agency in Langley, Virginia. People streamed past him over the terrazzo floor and its embedded great seal of the agency for it was past quitting time in America's warehouse of secrets, global and parochial, factual and gossipy, significant and trivial.

He had come to the spy headquarters by a circuitous if swift route since leaving the hotel in Philadelphia the previous morning. He and Mona had conferred with Tom Jardine, who briefed them on the inter-agency consultations that resulted in the postponement of the Coast Guard inquiry. The FBI agent also warned them against telling anyone of the suspected intentional crippling of the *Yandoon Princess* lest premature disclosure ruin chances of trapping the culprits.

Mitch and Mona parted in Philadelphia, Mona flying to Montreal for conferences at Michaelson & Lygdamis offices, Mitch taking the train to Washington, D.C., where officials at FBI headquarters wished to talk further with him. Mona and Mitch, reluctant to leave each other, planned to meet within a week in Montreal where Mitch would stop en route to Copenhagen after winding up his affairs in Honolulu.

At the FBI's Washington headquarters, Mitch learned that a decision had been made at "the highest levels," as Washington jargon had it, to transfer the main investigation of marine crimes to the Central Intelligence Agency. The Federal Bureau of Investigation, primarily a domestic law enforcement agency, had only a few liaison agents abroad while the CIA had thousands. Also officials speculated that the combined *Yandoon Princess* and *Gunnison Bay* cases might lead into sensitive international political areas, terrorist groups, for instance, or perhaps well-connected citizens of friendly nations. So in a bureaucratic pact, the CIA would handle the actual investigation abroad while the FBI pursued the case within the United States.

Mitch, after meeting briefly with an associate director of the FBI, had been sent across the Potomac River to brief the man who would head the CIA's endeavors in the marine case. As he waited in the CIA lobby for his contact, Mitch was not at all sure that he wanted to be in this cavern of espionage. The Central Intelligence Agency, he had long suspected, had done more harm than good in its forty years of existence. Or did foreknowledge of the demise of China's cultural revolution cancel out the Bay of Pigs fiasco? Did American spymasters rate the failure to assassinate Fidel Castro as an A plus or a D minus on their report card? Could the CIA come within a year of forecasting the end of white rule in South Africa?

Such thoughts in mind, Mitch stood with folded arms and read the inscription chiseled into the marble wall of the lobby: **"And ye shall know the truth, and the truth shall make you free." John VIII, XXXII.**

"Not necessarily," drawled a voice at his elbow. "Sometimes if you know the truth, you can get your balls sliced off and that's hardly my idea of freedom."

Thin and haggard with dark pouches under his eyes denoting dissipation and/or liver trouble, the man wore black-rimmed glasses, an old herringbone jacket and mismatched trousers. He smoked a stubby pipe and smelled like a crowded barbershop on a rainy morning.

"Mr. Russell?"

"Well, Russell anyway." The drawl had a weary sardonic cast.

"So, unless our signals are fouled up once again, that makes you Mitchell Donahey."

"You have it."

"Of Lorikeet Tankers of Copenhagen, late of McCafferty & Sons, shipbrokers." The voice fit his appearance, that of a patient awaiting surgery. "And late, late of Cornell, that armpit of the Ivy League."

"I went to Cornell, right, but Dartmouth's the armpit."

"Oh, perhaps so. I tend to confuse these mighty seats of learning." The tone mocked the speaker along with the rest of the world. "So let's get you dog-tagged." Russell himself wore a laminated plastic badge carrying his picture and bordered by tiny boxes some of which had red spots.

Mitch signed in at the reception desk while Russell went through the routine of vouching for him with the air of a man suffering the work of fools. Mitch pinned the visitor's badge above his heart while his escort led him into the building proper and down a corridor flanked by office doors painted in bright colors—crimson, emerald, yellow, white, sky blue—like a nursery school.

Russell noted his interest. "You'll find every color but lavender. We claim we have no homosexuals on the payroll, but you know it wouldn't surprise me . . ." He stopped, nodded to a homeward-bound colleague, then tapped Mitch on the lapel with the stem of his pipe. "Wouldn't surprise me to learn that we have a whole elite gay division trained to turn Communist fags and dykes into bonny spies for our side. Amazing place, this, Mr. Donahey."

"Mitch is okay." Although he might well change his mind, he had taken a quick liking to this scoffer with the funereal look. "What do I call you?"

"Russell. Or Russ if you wish." He led the way to an elevator. "We're going to talk over dinner in the director's private dining room. Which gives you some clue as to the interest in your story."

The executive suites of the CIA director and his deputy were located on the seventh floor of the building fronting on wooded parkland above the Potomac River. At once Mitch was conscious of the atmosphere of an exclusive men's club. Deep carpeting and fine wood established a tone far removed from the bleak institutional look of most government offices.

A young woman of striking looks, including the championship teeth of a dentist's daughter, presided at the reception desk. She flashed a special smile for each man as if his mere presence crowned her superlative day. She pressed a button behind a nest of telephones.

A broad-shouldered man with the profile of an early patriot without the wig strode from an office and extended his hand. "Mr. Donahey, Perry Ireland." Mitch shook hands with the man whose recent transfer from the Pentagon had made the evening news shows, Lieutenant General Perry F. Ireland, deputy director of the Central Intelligence Agency.

"I wanted to hear some of your story firsthand," he said, "but I can't. I'm invited to Senator Dole's this evening and that, as you might suspect, is a command. . . . But we do appreciate your cooperation, sir. We need more concerned businessmen like you." He yanked his overcoat off the halltree and hurried off.

The director's private dining room, designed for no more than eight people, had walls covered with woven grass paper of muted blues and grays. Wide windows overlooked a grove of rain-splashed hardwoods, their leaves beginning to turn to the colors of autumn, on the hill that stood between spy headquarters and the Potomac. In the distance the lights of Washington continued to wink on as night began to swallow the damp dusk of September. Within the room, dimmed lights from the overhead chandelier stroked silverware at place settings for two on crisp gray table linen.

"Name your poison." Russell stood beside a bar cart fashioned of natural polished wood, perhaps cherry. The aura here was discreet, in good taste, bespeaking genteel authority, a world removed from the squalid wars, raids, thefts, bribes and sometimes murder that often resulted from decisions made in this dining nook or the nearby throne room of American secret missions.

With a Scotch and water in hand, Mitch settled into one of the high-backed dining chairs. Russell, seating himself across the table, deplored his own lack of a drink. "Doctor's orders, damn it. Well, let's get acquainted. I've been around this pit of ambition and foul play for several lifetimes, at least. Earned a doctorate in economics—dissertation on the petroleum industry—before they lured me down here. Still slaving away on oil and allied topics. Now how about you? In a little more depth, please."

Mitch took a few minutes to sketch his life from birth to the McCafferty job, then related in some detail events since the sloop from Tahiti piled up on the reef within shouting distance of his

Honolulu shorefront apartment. He wound up telling of Mario Didati's discussion of the filed bolt and his subsequent murder. "By the way," he asked when he finished, "what are the ground rules here? I assume that anything said should not be repeated."

"Never. You were never here, you never met any of us and all you know about the Agency is what you read in the papers. Any problems with that?"

"Nope. I figured as much."

"All right then, let's hear everything you know about Henry Elger and Captain Harkinson. I gather that, aside from your one meeting with Mario Didati, you know nothing firsthand about the others you've named." Russell touched a match to the pipe he had been stuffing, then sucked and puffed to fire the tobacco. "Take your time. We've got all night."

Mitch talked at length about soldiering with Elger in Viet Nam. He found description of the night at the village, when he almost joined Elger in shooting down civilians, to be a painful process, yet not as emotionally frightening as in his old dreams. Confronting Bones in Honolulu had drained off much of the memory's toxic power. Tonight he told the simple truth, neither concealing his urge to kill nor turning the scene into a vehicle of self-purging confession. When a buzzer sounded, the intelligence officer touched a finger to his lips.

"Hold it," he said. "They're bringing in the soup. The cook and waiter are under the usual Agency security, but in this outfit nobody hears what he doesn't need to know to do his job."

A white-coated waiter, wearing the inevitable plastic security badge, nodded a silent greeting as he placed a bowl at each setting. Tall, lean and young, he could have been a college tennis player. When he withdrew through the same paneled door he had entered, Russell knocked out his pipe in an ashtray and motioned to Mitch to begin.

"Tasty, what?" asked Russell as they spooned the soup. Mitch agreed. The hot leek, potato and herb dish, contrasting with the chill rainy wind beating against the window panes, warmed the spirit as well as the stomach.

"Okay," said the intelligence officer. "Let's continue."

Mitch talked about Elger for a few more minutes, then told everything he knew about Mona Harkinson. He finished by describing the course of their brief affair. "So we are in love and we intend to see each other whenever we can, probably live together when our careers make that possible—although, frankly, I'm just assuming the living together. We haven't actually discussed it."

"I take it the way your face lights up that this relationship with Captain Harkinson is a major thing in your life?"

"Major's an understatement. I've never felt so strongly about any woman before."

"Then it may be hard for you to understand what I'm about to say." Russell paused, leaned back in his chair. "The fact is, Mitchell, we have to regard your captain as one of the suspects."

"Why, that's crazy, man. Mona in on a conspiracy to cripple her own ship? No way."

"Sorry, but we have to consider that possibility. Remember, you told me that it would be impossible for the crew of the *Gunnison Bay* to sell off the oil without the captain's knowledge?"

"Sure, but the two cases are completely different." Mitch was astounded. Mona ruining her first supertanker command? Ridiculous. "To sabotage that steering gear, one guy alone at night deep in the guts of the tanker is sufficient. But to sell off oil, you've got to pump the stuff out of the tanks either ashore or onto barges. Either way, it's right in front of the captain's eyes. And detouring off the scheduled route by hundreds of miles to sell the oil. How do you do that unless the captain's in on the scam? No, no. The two cases can't be compared. Not at all."

"Nevertheless, as head of this job, I can't rule out Captain Harkinson. In fact, I can't rule out anybody aboard *Yandoon Princess.* That's just a fact of life."

"You proceed any way you like." Mitch was indignant. "I know positively that Mona had nothing to do with damaging the steering."

Again the buzzer sounded and this time the varsity tennis ace in disguise brought in a tray containing filet mignon, shoestring potatoes and Brussels sprouts together with lettuce and avocado salads. Mitch attacked at once with knife and fork. The food neared gourmet quality.

"Delicate, that salad dressing, what?" But Russell merely picked at his food. "Bad colon," he explained. "Too many years of colas and hamburgers at the desk."

The intelligence officer questioned as they went through the main course and finished off demitasses of coffee, both men skipping dessert. Making an occasional note, he asked about Wasif Zabib and his woman companion, Grethe Knudsen. He wanted to know about Zabib's connection with Alexandros Nicias, the captain of the *Gunnison Bay,* and the background of officers and crew of the *Yandoon Princess.* He returned again to Bones Elger and to Mona. Mitch drew a blank on most questions since he knew very little about Nicias, Miaoulis, Jerry Artwick or Yukio Osagawa. Nevertheless, Russell persisted and the clock ticked past ten o'clock by the time Russell finished his inquiries.

"So now we come to Phase Two of our tête-à-tête." Russell pressed a buzzer, summoning the all-American tennis profile who cleared the table in less time than it would take him to serve, rush the net and smash a winner. The intelligence officer pushed back from the table and refilled his stubby pipe. Outside the rain came down harder, streaking the windows and blurring the lights of Washington across the river. "Just what are your plans now, Mitch?"

"I'm flying to Honolulu where I'll close out my job and apartment and pack my stuff. Then I'll spend a couple of days in Montreal with Mona before continuing on to Copenhagen where I'll start my new job with Lorikeet Tankers."

Russell studied Mitch while he puffed on his pipe. "Some of our investigation, maybe the most important part, will center on Lorikeet Tankers in Copenhagen, what with Zabib being there and no doubt Alexandros Nicias reporting there from time to time after his voyages on the *Queen Misura.*"

"King Misura," corrected Mitch.

"King Misura. Also, if Zabib's in on some organized marine crime, it's probable that some of Lorikeet's other executives are too. In short, we'll have a big job ahead of us in Copenhagen."

Mitch stretched, ready to call it a night. "Well, good luck. I've told you all I know. The rest is up to you people."

Russell smoked quietly, then stuffed his notes in his jacket pocket as if the session were ended. Instead, he asked, "What if we asked you to work for us over there?"

"What do you mean?"

"Go report for work at Lorikeet and do your job." The intelligence man's tone of voice, no longer world weary and scoffing, had quickened. "But also become our eyes and ears there, give us regular reports on anything pertinent to this case."

"You mean spy for the CIA?" Mitch said it with an edge of distaste.

"Not in a professional sense, no. We don't want you skulking about trash cans, tapping phones, bugging offices or tailing people down country roads." A wave of his pipe banished all such ungentlemanly behavior. "You're not trained for that kind of game and besides it wouldn't suit you as a vice-president of Lorikeet. What we need from you is much more prosaic, keeping track of Zabib and his associates and their tanker business."

"What would that entail? What would I have to do that I'm not doing now?"

"Two ways to go. One way is to become a CIA employee." Russell's whole manner had changed. It was obvious that for all his sardonic outlook, when it came to the core of the game, he played it deftly, his radar finely tuned. "In that case we'd put you on the payroll, test you on the box—lie detector—give you a crash course in tradecraft and send you back to work under Agency discipline."

"Never," said Mitch promptly. "Forget it. No more government jobs for me. One in Viet Nam was enough."

"I don't blame you. If it weren't for my failing, I'd have left this idiot's playground years ago."

"What's the failing?" It was obvious the intelligence operator wanted to be asked.

"Puzzles. I'm a puzzle addict. So I'm hooked." Russell shrugged. "The other way for you to go is to become our informant. In that case, you'd report regularly to an Agency man over in Denmark and alert us in event of some unexpected or significant development. We'd give you a bare minimum of tradecraft—how to contact your case officer or me without arousing suspicion, make your secret reports, that kind of thing. No big deal. About the only difference in your life would be that you'd put a strong focus on what you'll probably be doing anyway—trying to find out if Zabib's involved. Your business and social life would go on as usual."

"I'm not your man. I'm no friend of the CIA. Hell, that's putting it mildly." Mitch could feel his temper rising. "Some of the stuff you guys pull is as bad as the KGB. Paramilitary goons, secret wars, assassinations, fingering insurgents for torture by local military police. Man, it's a fuckin' outrage what you get away with. You put that kind of thuggery to an open vote in the U.S. and you wouldn't get one American out of five to okay it."

"I don't agree with you for a moment," said Russell with some heat, his first show of emotion, "but even if I did, that has nothing to do with taking part in a criminal investigation. You're obviously talking about the Clandestine Service. That's a whole other ball of wax."

"So you say now, but it would be a different story once you got me involved." Mitch got up and went to the rain-streaked window. Water streamed down the trunks of the hardwoods outside. The wind, accelerating, began to sigh at the building's eaves. "You'd get me compromised in some way, then ask me to do something crummy."

"You've been reading too many lurid spy novels," said Russell tartly.

"Nope. That comes from reading the blasts of your own agents who got fed up with the Agency's scummy work."

"You'd be dealing with me and I'm straight intelligence." Russell busied himself tamping down a new load of tobacco in his pipe. "Look, Mitch, this criminal case is really out of our line. We do very little of it, only when one of the federal law-enforcement agencies finds that it needs a lot of work done abroad. So I need all the help I can get on this one."

"I can appreciate that, but I've done my duty. I reported what I knew. Now it's your job."

"True enough. But in this case, you're the ideal man. You'll be perfectly positioned at Lorikeet. It would take us months to infiltrate the corporation and by that time this marine gang could have pulled off a couple more big operations. You see, your information dovetailed with some we already had that points toward a major international criminal group."

"What group?"

"Sorry, I can't reveal that. You know our need-to-know rule. But wouldn't you like a hand in busting a big international combine?"

Mitch, returning to the table, sat down again, but did not reply.

"Come on, face it. You're a man who craves new challenges." Russell laid aside his pipe and hunched forward. Like a basketball coach in a close game, he looked poised to spring. "You're concentrating on the negatives. How about the positives? Outside a good lay, what beats the thrill of discovery? You'd be learning, out-smarting a bunch of creeps, helping to keep the industry honest. And you'd feel that adrenalin pump. Believe me, Mitch, you'd have a ball."

"No matter how you cut it, I'd still be spying on my boss and I'm not comfortable with the idea. Not at all." Yet he could see the shimmer of the lure that Russell dangled.

The intelligence man veered to another tack. "Tell me what you want most in life right now, Mitch?" When he saw his man grin, Russell added: "I mean it. Seriously."

Mitch thought for a moment. "To keep this love affair with Mona going, make her happy, stay together."

"And how do you think she's going to feel if we never flush these *Yandoon Princess* thugs and she has to share the blame for the sinking and the oil spill with her tanker company?"

"Unhappy as hell."

"Right. And suppose the Coast Guard marine board, after its hearing next year, comes out with a report saying the captain should have refused to sail on the *Yandoon Princess?*"

"Nobody would hire her after that kind of finding."

"Right again. And what if you hadn't done your best to get her name cleared by turning up the guys that crippled her ship?"

"I guess I'd feel shitty."

"So?" Russell fell silent. A minute went by while he smoked qui-etly. Then he said, "If you want to help the woman you love, you don't have much choice, Mitch."

Mitch hesitated, sighed, then said: "All right, I'll do it—on one condition."

"Which is?"

"That I can tell Mona that Washington officials list her as one of the suspects."

"You can't be serious. That could blow the whole investigation."

"Only if Mona were involved. And that's not remotely possible. She's as clean in this thing as you and I are."

Russell, frowning, shook his head. "That's love and hope talking, not fact."

"Whatever, I can't take on the assignment unless I can tell Mona." Mitch leaned forward. "Use your head, man. Trust is everything between lovers. I can't betray her."

"Not revealing everything hardly constitutes betrayal."

"I don't care what words you put on it. I refuse to sneak around behind her back." Mitch raised his palms. "So forget it. No deal."

Russell sat smoking for a time, then pushed back from the table. "Please excuse me. I'll be back in a few minutes. Pour yourself a brandy, if you like." He disappeared through the door of the dining room.

Mitch remained seated, watching the rain lash the windows and cloak the lights of Washington across the river. He thought of Mona, alone in Montreal amid a circle of hostile male executives and he wondered how she was faring. He glanced at his wristwatch. 10:45. He would call her as soon as he returned to his hotel in downtown Washington. He missed her sorely. In those brief days and nights in Philadelphia, his infatuation had ripened into love and he wanted her with him, in the same city, the same room. He fell to musing about her, recalling her strumming the guitar, talking happily to her daughter, her poise as she faced the press.

Russell returned. "Your condition is accepted." His smile was a wry one. "The upper levels agree that the chances of Captain Harkinson's being involved are remote. To land you as an informant at Lorikeet, they're willing to take the risk."

They sealed the deal with a handshake.

"Now that I'm working for you," said Mitch, "what's your full name, please?"

"Persistent cuss, aren't you? My name is Russell Upchurch, but in all our dealings, I'm plain Russell."

Once agreed upon, YANTANK, as the operation became known in Agency files, moved swiftly. Mitch spent the next day at Langley, cramming on procedures, signing papers, skimming through several lessons in elementary tradecraft and lunching with Upchurch at his desk beside the plastic basket with the red BURN sign, omnipresent at CIA headquarters offices, and surrounded by stacks of books, periodicals and reports on tankers and petroleum. His contact in Denmark, said Upchurch, was a man named Ned who would get in touch with him soon after he started the job in Copenhagen.

Mitch ended his mini-training that day by sitting through a dull sermon on security for business informants by an officer with bad breath who kept calling him Mr. Donahue and finally by receiving face-to-face thanks from the CIA director, Lowell Waterman.

Upchurch escorted him to the director's office just before an Agency car was scheduled to take him to Dulles Airport for a flight to Honolulu.

"A pleasure, Mr. Donahey." Lowell Waterman gripped firmly. A large hearty man, several inches taller than Mitch, he had a ruddy face that gleamed as if freshly shaven. "This is my lucky week. My son caught two touchdown passes for Princeton, the Senate armed services committee decided it didn't have to hear me after all on the trouble in Mali and now you agree to take on this important chore for us in Copenhagen."

The director stood beside one of the two flags that flanked his desk, the American and the Agency's banner—a sixteen-point compass rose and a yellow-beaked eagle set in a field of blue. His desk was bare save for a notepad, a clock and a color photograph of his son in a Princeton football uniform. The wall behind him held an autographed picture of the President patting his arm.

"Because of your reservations about the Agency," said Waterman, "there's all the more reason that we're in your debt for undertaking this assignment. While crime is a bit out of our line, this conceivably could surprise us all in the unfolding."

"I'll do my best." Mitch sensed that the shorter he kept this encounter, the better. Waterman had not invited him to sit.

"So our sincere thanks." The director took a step forward and Mitch backed up a step, easing toward the door, but Waterman grasped his arm. "A scene out of the past applies here. You know my father worked for the Eisenhower administration, an assistant over at State."

The director went into a familiar Washington stance, the-man-with-an-apt-political-anecdote. "At a White House meeting one day, Charlie Wilson, the former General Motors boss who was Secretary of Defense, reported on his trip to our forces in Korea. 'It's a scandal the way the Truman administration left those fighting men,' Wilson said. 'Do you know that I found one regiment with a two-year supply of toilet paper and not a single round of ammunition in reserve!' My father spoke up quickly: 'Well, Mr. Secretary, if you're in the front lines with no ammunition, you sure need lots of toilet paper.' Even Ike got a laugh out of that one.

"Just remember, Mr. Donahey, this won't be a toilet-paper job in

Copenhagen. We'll send you all the ammunition you'll need. Good luck."

As Mitch and Upchurch passed the rows of brightly painted doors on their way to the exit, Mitch said, "Cornball story from your director."

"He's a political appointee, you know." No executive up from the spy ranks, Upchurch implied, would be guilty of such scatology.

"Still I got a charge out of it."

"So did I." Upchurch sighed. "The first ten times I heard it."

The plane flying to Chicago en route to Honolulu was packed, smelled of feet and damp overcoats and spent an hour in heavy traffic circling in dense clouds above O'Hare Airport.

13

A week after arriving in Copenhagen to become Lorikeet Tankers' vice-president for chartering, Mitch Donahey felt almost at home. He settled quickly into his job and if it had not been for the separation from Mona, he would have relished his life in the Danish capital.

For the rootless, few cities offer the same illusion of stability, permanence and anchored family ties as Copenhagen. Its gestalt partakes of rooted institutions that blend common sense with compassion, democratic welfare politics, a homey royal family, massive public buildings that remind today of countless yesteryears, fine music, dance and art, a suspiciously rich diet coupled with an abundance of high-calorie restaurants, cozy well-furnished homes and a homogeneous population more congenial than most.

Mitch's boyhood had splattered over a number of American cities, thanks to a footloose salesman father who skipped from job to job. Mitch had lived in only two places long enough to think of them as home, Chicago, where he went to high school, and Honolulu, where he plied his craft of shipbroker.

Copenhagen seemed to fit him. Not having lived abroad enough to pick up the common maladies of resident foreigners—ennui, alienation and a kind of crabby dislike of customs hitherto deemed charming and picturesque—he resonated with goodwill. He arrived fresh from a glowing weekend with Mona in Montreal where they made love, pledged themselves as an exclusive twosome and laid plans to arrange their careers so they could live together. His initial contacts at the posh offices of Lorikeet Tankers were pleasant and thanks to the generous salary advance, he rented an airy loft apartment under the gabled roof of an eighteenth-century building on Nyhavn Canal. His new job went smoothly the first week.

In Montreal, Mona, by contrast, had sunk into a mild depression which their nightly trans-Atlantic phone calls failed to dispel. After long days meeting with Michaelson & Lygdamis executives, reporting on the sinking of the *Yandoon Princess,* she had been given a desk job while awaiting reassignment afloat. She complained to Mitch that the job, maintaining a large chart showing the location of M & L vessels, took only two hours a day. Any high school kid could do it, she said.

When she pressed for a master's berth afloat, Homer Richert, the operations officer, put her off with vague references to overstaffing and fewer tankers. From remarks dropped by other executives, Mona came to believe that the company had relegated her permanently to the tedious desk job in hopes she'd resign. "I'll be damned if I'll quit," she told Mitch in one call. But a few nights later she seemed less certain and by the end of the week, she talked about looking around at other fleets.

The press interview of Radio Officer Arno Joahannes caused more friction with company officials who were convinced that Mona had encouraged him to talk. From President Arthur Michaelson down, they thought Mona wanted to prejudice the public against them because of her strong opposition to M & L policy on drydocking and aging supertankers.

"In fact," Mona told Mitch in one of their phone conversations, "Michaelson told me straight out today that my attitude did not meet the standards of 'discretion and loyalty' expected of M & L masters."

To compound her difficulties in Montreal, Mona discovered that she harbored heavy guilt feelings deriving from the FBI instructions not to disclose the suspicions of sabotage on the *Yandoon Princess.* Special Agent Tom Jardine specifically had included M & L officers in the prohibition. Mona knew that her silence could cost the company heavily since a prime contention in many of the tangle of lawsuits was M & L's culpability in operating an aging supertanker without adequate drydocking.

The executives stewed, thinking themselves to blame for the sinking, while Mona reproved herself for withholding the truth—or what she believed to be the truth—of the sinking from them. Mitch, listening to her laments over several nights, learned that his woman had a New England conscience as well as a psychic machine that manufactured daily quotas of guilt.

"Hell, if it's bugging you that much," said Mitch, "call Jardine and tell him you've got to tell your bosses in confidence."

"But I couldn't do that," she protested. "The officers here would spread the news immediately to get themselves off the financial hook. It would ruin the investigation."

"Right. So quit worrying about it."

"But I feel so guilty, Mitch."

"At the risk of sounding macho, I'd say you need either a good lay or a good ship."

"Oh, both. Holy Jesus, yes, both. . . . But Mitch, think how you'd feel if you hadn't been able to tell me that I was on the CIA's suspect list."

"I know. That's why I refused to let them put me in that bind."

The condition of her public image also dismayed Mona. It lost more of its original luster the farther the oil pollution caused by her tanker spread on the Atlantic seacoast. That vast oil smear now extended more than 250 miles from Asbury Park, New Jersey, on the north to Virginia Beach, Virginia, on the south. Thousands of men toiled at the exacting job of scouring the heavy black taint from the beaches, wetlands, coves, rocks and wharves of four states.

Oil, glistening in the sun like green and purple water snakes, backed up into Delaware Bay and into Hampton Roads at the mouth of Chesapeake Bay farther south. A vile mousse bathed the beach at Atlantic City and clogged the cleansing machines employed to remove the pox from the casino city. Gamblers now took their breaks from the usual insurmountable odds by strolling along the boardwalk and leaning over the railing to watch the cleanup squads at work. Balls of grit, sand, salt and oil in sizes from marbles to basketballs washed ashore at Cape May, New Jersey. Countless shorebirds, particularly at Assateague Island National Seashore in Virginia, died grotesquely when petroleum soaked their feathers so badly they could not fly in search of food. Fishing along the coast came to a halt. Seaside resorts that usually did a passable autumn business shut down until the next summer.

Estimates of the cleanup costs rose to the vicinity of $100,000,000 as local, state and federal officials, together with the tanker fleet pool, quarreled over who paid what. Dozens of suits, involving seamen, owners, insurance companies and governments, were filed in the courts, insuring litigation for years to come.

Criticism of Captain Mona Harkinson grew apace. She had evoked considerable sympathy at the outset with her straightforward performance at the Philadelphia press conference. Feminist, union and youth organizations rallied to her side. But now editors and various marine experts reminded their audience that captains, whether male or female, were responsible for the condition as well as the handling of their ships.

After journalists dug into all aspects of the sinking, the age and drydocking cycle of the *Yandoon Princess* became widely known and those in the shipping industry who had decried the practice of employing elderly supertankers now aimed a barrage of criticism at Michaelson & Lygdamis for sailing a sixteen-year-old VLCC that went to drydock only once every thirty months. Much of this attack was leveled at Mona as well. In a speech to a shipping conference in New York, Marquis C. Framingham of a British tanker company, one of the most respected men in the industry, said, "We all know that the safe life of the supertanker of the VLCC or ULCC category is shorter than that of its smaller cousins. It can't be sailed as long or kept from drydock as long as the handy-size class. Certainly a company that insists on working a sixteen-year-old VLCC must bear responsibility for its maintenance in prime condition. And certainly a captain of whatever sex who accepts command of an elderly tanker must share responsibility for the vessel's being in good condition for safe ocean transit."

Editorial writers and talk-show experts frequently quoted Framingham and as time went on, fewer and fewer people stepped forward to defend the woman captain. When an official of NOW, the women's organization, said on one TV show that criticism of Mona Harkinson should be tempered by the fact that a novice woman captain was in no position to choose what ship she'd sail, hundreds of callers phoned in to say that did not excuse her for failing to refuse command of an overage tanker.

In light of the extensive pollution, the Coast Guard came under almost unanimous media attack for postponing the marine board of investigation. The Coast Guard's stated reasons for the delay—it took time to dive for evidence at the scene of the wreck and for technicians to prepare properly—were dismissed as insufficient. Some commentators hinted at darker motives, including political influence by the Lygdamis family. Curiously, not a single organ of the media mentioned the possibility of sabotage.

While much of this criticism rubbed off on Mona, what hurt her the most, crushing her morale and reducing her to tears, was the article in the *National Revealer* that Maggie Josephs, the newswoman, had foreseen in Philadelphia. Under a blazing front-page headline, GREEDY SEX LIFE OF CAPT. MONA, the tabloid carried a lurid story quoting two men and a woman who professed to know Mona's intimate desires and practices.

The woman, mess stewardess on a refrigerator ship, said that Mona "frequented a raunchy Lesbian pickup bar in Panama" where women of varied colors and nationalities put on live sex shows. One of the men, identified as a "close friend of Clay Floberg, Capt. Harkinson's former husband," said that she was unresponsive sexually as a wife and had to be "manipulated by a vibrator" to bring her to the threshold of passion. The other man, a tanker officer from the Dominican Republic named Arturo Domingo Flores, described an orgiastic weekend with Mona at a hotel in Port-au-Prince, Haiti. He said she got flaming drunk, performed fellatio on him, wept a great deal, snorted cocaine, sang obscene songs in French, danced nude in the hallways and paid for a Haitian call girl to share the bed with them while they took turns at "two-on-one" copulation and oral sex.

Mitch, who bought a copy in Copenhagen when he saw the *Revealer* headline, had read the story when Mona called that night from Montreal. Discussing it, she started out calmly, but soon broke down.

"I'm devastated, Mitch. I just can't face people." The sandy voice caught in a half sob. "Those horrible editors. I'm sure they paid thousands for those interviews."

"Sue the hell out of them!"

"Oh, that would only prolong the agony. And besides, there's just enough truth in the stories to make them libel-proof, I guess. For instance, I did go to a Panama Lesbian joint once with that woman who worked in the galley of the reefer I was on. Once! I didn't pick up anybody there and I never went back. Holy Jesus, it was just to see the place. Do you understand?"

"Sure. Look, Mona, none of it bothers me. I don't care if you worked in a Turkish harem. I love you."

"As for the vibrator bit, that was true too." Distraught, she could not drop the subject. "I was never with Clay the way you and I are. With Clay, I did need help. Then that frightful weekend in Haiti with Arturo whoever. I told you there was one time I'm ashamed of when I got sloppy and drunk and maudlin. Maybe I did all those things, I don't know. I do remember dancing in the hall and being in bed with two people, but not much else. It's mostly a blur of alcohol and bad sex."

"Forget it, babe. To your friends and your lover, newspaper smear jobs don't mean a thing. As for the rest of the world, who cares what they think?"

"I keep telling myself that, Mitch, but the fact is I don't want total strangers going around thinking of me as some kind of creepy slut. Also, I dread having Chrissy read it and of course she'll get hold of a copy over there. And how about tanker-fleet owners? They'll be damn slow to hire a dyke captain who picks up Haitian whores."

When Mitch switched the conversation back to the oil spill and the criticism of Michaelson & Lygdamis, Mona noted in her dispirited mood that much of the public outcry centered on her. "It's bad enough entering a popularity contest and losing." Her husky voice had none of its usual vibrancy. "But it's worse when somebody enters you against your will and you come out last."

As for his new job, Mitch conferred with Wasif Zabib almost daily and he paid close attention to the man's casual asides, demeanor and nuances of speech and gesture. At their first session Mitch persuaded Zabib to give Bert Takahara a try in the company's growing communications and electronics section. Mitch's former assistant flew in from Honolulu several days later for an interview. Impressed, Zabib sent him off to the *Zabibian* for training under the ship's radio officer. At another session Zabib decided that Mitch should make a familiarization swing through the tanker fleet and should hire a young Norwegian shipbroker as his chartering assistant.

Nothing in these talks with Zabib struck Mitch as unusual or suspicious. To the contrary, he found himself admiring the Jordanian's executive talent and liking him as a man. Zabib's essence became more rather than less appealing under the lens of close association. He showed sound business judgment and he dealt firmly, fairly and generously with some two dozen officers and employes at headquarters.

As promised, Zabib disclosed Lorikeet's ownership to Mitch. He showed him copies of papers filed with the Danish shipping authorities revealing that Lorikeet Tankers was owned fifteen percent by Wasif Zabib of Amman, Jordan, twenty-five percent by a venerable Swiss investment trust, Girard Maritime, and sixty percent by a formidable shipping pair, the Sung twins, Li and Chen, of Hong Kong. The Sungs, Zabib explained, preferred not to divulge their majority holdings, so he acted in all matters as though Lorikeet was primarily his property.

His curiosity aroused by the Danish media coverage of Captain Mona and the big oil spill in U.S. waters, Zabib wanted to know the usual things: where Mitch had met her, what kind of woman, whether friendship or love affair, her competence, the inside on the killing of Mario Didati. Zabib, like everyone else Mitch met, was fascinated by the woman tanker captain and never tired of hearing new fact or gossip from Philadelphia.

Mitch on first meeting had thought Zabib to be quite formal, but when he dined the first week with Zabib and Grethe Knudsen, he saw a lighter side, geniality, even playfulness at times. When Zabib invited him to play indoor singles with him at his tennis club, the *Kobenhavns Boldclub* in Frederiksberg, Zabib proved a good companion, fast with a quip, self-deprecating in manner and finally a gracious loser. In the locker room after the match Zabib asked Mitch to call him "Zab," his way of informing his chartering officer that he had been accepted in the inner circle of the president's friends and associates.

Despite this warming relationship, Mitch could not put his suspicions aside. The fact was that Zabib's good friend Alexandros Nicias still served as master of one of the Lorikeet tankers, the *King Misura*, and Nicias most certainly had joined the conspiracy that stole and sold the cargo of the *Gunnison Bay*, then sank the vessel, claiming an explosion had destroyed the tanker together with its 105,000 tons of crude oil. Was it possible that Zabib did not know of his friend's participation in the crime? Mitch probed gently in his last talk with Zabib before leaving on his familiarization swing around the Lorikeet fleet.

"Any message for your friend Nicias," he asked, "when I go aboard the *King Misura?* I'm due to watch her load in the Gulf."

"Just tell him he's expected here this winter as usual. You and Alex can compare notes on Hawaii. He's just been out there on a vacation."

Mitch heard nothing from "Ned," his assigned CIA contact, until the night before his departure. Returning home after dinner to pack for the trip, Mitch found a small unmarked envelope inside his loft door. In computer type, he read: "Call 395 7135 from a pay phone now. N."

He walked a few hundred yards to the hydrofoil terminal, where hourly boats plied between Copenhagen and Sweden across the Oresund, and dialed the number from the public phone booth.

"Hello." No name. American accent.

"This is Mitchell Donahey. Ned?"

"Why are you calling here?"

"I'm following instructions from a letter left under my door."

"Okay, fine. I'd like to meet there in the hydrofoil terminal tomorrow night in time to catch the nine o'clock boat to Malmö." A cool dry voice.

"Sorry. I can't make it." Mitch explained that he had to leave early in the morning, would not return to Copenhagen for almost two weeks. He told the purpose of the trip.

"Okay. Call this number at nine your first night back. . . . Will you be visiting the ship of Captain Nicias?"

"Yes. Off Kuwait, I believe."

"We hear he's been to Honolulu. See if you can find out where he stayed there, who he talked to. We understand it was not just pleasure he was there for."

"Will do."

"Have a good trip." The phone clicked.

Mitch flew out of Copenhagen on a breakfast flight the next morning. The survey journey was to be wide-ranging. Lorikeet owned nothing of consequence save the tankers that plowed the global sealanes or stood at anchor, when not under charter, in the Arabian

Gulf or other watery approaches to major oil fields. Since the ships shared no common home port, Mitch had to cover thousands of miles while tracking them.

The first leg was a short one. He flew over to Rotterdam to inspect the *Dwyer Ace,* a new handy-size tanker just acquired. The next day he traveled to West Germany and took a motor launch out from Bremerhaven to board a pair of middle-aged tankers, seven and nine years old respectively, that were earning a minimal keep while idle by serving as floating storage tanks for oil awaiting higher prices on the spot market.

Since two other Lorikeet tankers had just brought cargoes of crude to Europe from Saudi Arabia, Mitch flew to Spain and boarded the *Lawlor Chief,* a 70,000 tonner moored at a jetty in Tarragona at the mouth of the Rio Francoli on the Mediterranean.

Another flight took him to Bordeaux where he rented a car and drove to the big oil terminal at Le Verdun at the tip of France's Médoc peninsula. There he boarded the 267,000-ton *Zabibian,* largest of the Lorikeet fleet, and watched the discharge of oil into pipelines carrying the crude to refineries near Bordeaux. He dined with the *Zabibian*'s officers and master, a Frenchman named Jules Yvre, in the officers' mess and rated the food as comparable to that served in some of the Michelin-starred restaurants of France.

He also had a good after-dinner talk with Bert Takahara who as a cadet in training took his meals in the officers' mess. Bert had been aboard only a few days, but they were enough to convince him that he'd found his career.

Mitch's next flight took him to the Arabian Gulf. At Sea Island off Kuwait, he boarded the *King Misura* as oil was being pumped from an underwater pipeline into the long supertanker at 15,000 tons an hour. Captain Alexandros Nicias escorted him about the ship, then sat with him in the pump control room and watched the third mate guide the flow of oil into fourteen wing and center tanks by monitoring a series of buttons on the electronic console.

Later Nicias invited Mitch to his cabin for a talk. Located just below the bridge, the master's quarters had a large room that served as combination office and living area and an adjoining bedroom. The office section contained a desk-top computer and satellite marine telephone.

"Sorry I can't offer you a drink." Burly and dark-skinned, the tanker captain had long bushy sideburns that gave him a nineteenth-century aspect. "But that's one of Zabib's rules that you'll find strictly enforced throughout the fleet."

Mitch edged into the opening. "I understand you're a good friend of Zabib's. How long have you known him?"

"Longer than a whore's dream. Zab and I shipped out of Piraeus together on our first voyage thirty, no thirty-one years ago next month." His breath carried a high-octane smell of garlic. "I needed the work, but Zab, a rich-man's son, went for the adventure. We took to each other, been friends ever since."

They talked about the *King Misura,* the slow state of the tanker business, Nicias's problems with a relatively green crew and finally women, a subject that led Nicias to a subject that obviously had been on his mind. Mitch moved his chair backward, ostensibly to avoid the shaft of sunlight coming through a porthole, but actually to put more distance between himself and Nicias's megabreath.

"I saw you on television out of Philly with that woman captain." Merely stating the fact seemed to make him unhappy. "You been knowing her some time?"

"No, I met her in Honolulu not long before the *Yandoon Princess* went down."

"Are you . . . Well, you know, the TV people said you were going with her or something."

"Yes, Captain, we're a couple. Of course, she's in Montreal and I'm in Copenhagen, so I don't know how we'll manage."

Nicias was silent for a time, then blurted, "I don't hold with women aboard tankers. You won't find one even in the galley on my ship."

"I understand your feeling. But Mona knows the ropes at sea. You couldn't blame her for the steering's going out."

"Her ship."

"So she has to take the rap?"

Nicias nodded, his jaw set.

"Did you take the rap when the *Gunnison Bay* went down?" Mitch had hoped for a deft approach, but could not resist the temptation.

"You're damn right I did." Nicias came on with anger. "But not the same thing at all. We had no warning on that explosion. Nobody knows yet what caused it. Harkinson had twenty-four hours to figure what to do about her steering. If she's so damn good, how come she brought her ship so close to the coast in a gale-force blow with steering that could go out again any minute?"

"I can't answer that, Captain."

"Well, next time you see her, ask her." His anger had not cooled. "She could have ridden out that storm in deep water, you know, rudder or no rudder."

They lapsed into silence while Nicias, shifting about in his chair, tried to calm himself. "Coffee?" he asked at last.

"No, I'm fine."

"I apologize, Mr. Donahey. I know you must have a high regard for the woman. It's just, well, we all love women, but damn it, they ought to stay ashore. Anyway, that's my opinion." He took a new heading. "I must say Captain Harkinson is a good-looker, all right. You say you met in Honolulu?"

"Yeah, at the outdoor Mai Tai bar at the Royal Hawaiian. You know it?"

Nicias smiled assent. "Half a dozen times over the years, I guess. I always did like the pink palace. A lot better than hanging around those sleazy dives on Hotel Street."

"Zab says you were just out there for a vacation?"

"Yeah, not enough time though, only three days."

"Where did you stay?"

"Stay?" Nicias had not anticipated the question. "Oh . . . At a lady friend's. She's got a place up on one of those ridges."

"St. Louis Heights?"

"Could have been. I didn't pay much attention. Had a good view of the city. She had a pool. We didn't leave the place, if you know what I mean."

"I finished up my job there two weeks ago. What days were you there?"

"Shit, I'm lousy on dates. Maybe ten days ago, something like that."

"Good woman, huh?"

Nicias grinned. "The best."

"I lived out there five years, so I know a lot of the women."

But Nicias declined to take the lure and the talk turned back to tankers and the business of transporting oil. The *King Misura* had just finished loading when a sudden wild wind swept off the desert carrying a gritty bouillabaisse of sand, sea spray and oil. Back on the bridge with Mitch watching silently, Captain Nicias raised anchor and took his ship to deeper water along with a half dozen other tankers in the vicinity. The storm soon passed and Mitch rode ashore in a sea taxi while the *King Misura* got underway with her cargo of crude, bound for Rotterdam.

That evening Mitch flew down Saudi Arabia's Gulf Coast to Bahrain. His plane lowered over cross-hatched pipelines and jets of flaring gas that turned the bleak desert into a duplicate of New Jersey's acrid refinery belt. Out in the Gulf he boarded a fairly new Lorikeet tanker with automatic plotting table, integrated navigation system, a bridge that looked like the cockpit for a space odyssey and a master computer that did everything but cook dinner.

From the Gulf he flew across the head of the Arabian Sea to Pakistan. A fierce road warrior, who must have been blooded on the highways of Mexico, drove him from Karachi to Gadani Beach. There Mitch watched the beginning of the end of the *Tides of Fundy,* an old 40,000-ton Lorikeet tanker that Mitch had persuaded Zabib to sell for scrap. A horde of barefoot Pathans, galvanized by $3-a-day wages, assaulted the beached ship. Their loose garments ballooning in the wind like spinnakers, they swarmed over the rust-pocked hull and attacked any detachable object—rails, ladders, pipes, capstans—with sledge, crowbar and wrench. Grounded bow-first since it had been slammed ashore by the beachmaster, the vessel shrank visibly during the forenoon that Mitch watched the skillful dismantling. Later the deckhouse would be cut, slugged and torched away and the hull sliced up in plates, ready for steel mill recycling. That day Mitch counted no less than fifty-six ships lined up on the beach like a flotilla of rotting suicidal whales, all under attack by battalions of Muslim ship-smashers.

The next airliner took him to Singapore where the Sembawang Shipyard was modifying the *Monteporo,* the Lorikeet tanker that had lain for so long off Aden near the mouth of the Red Sea. The yard was reducing the *Monteporo*'s speed by several modifications, thus saving fifty tons of fuel or about $4,000 a day when under way. Once more Mitch absorbed a prime fact of the tanker business: with the enormous sums of money involved, even small adjustments could mean millions of dollars at year's end.

He languished for word of Mona. He had failed to reach her on the last two stops. She was not at work, her hotel in Montreal reported she had checked out and the Michaelson & Lygdamis operator refused to give the home numbers of any employes. Mitch assumed she had found new quarters and would call him in Copenhagen.

On the final leg of his trip, Mitch flew northward from Singapore over the South China Sea to Hong Kong. He occupied a window seat on the left side of the jetliner and for a few minutes in mid-flight he could see the coast of Viet Nam. Even though obscured by haze and as ill-defined as any other coastal terrain from five miles up, the land that claimed his youth still had the power to shake him emotionally. He stared down, memories pinned with pain, then abruptly turned away, beckoned the stewardess and ordered a Scotch.

He landed at Kai Tak Airport, the two-mile runway spiking into Kowloon Bay, then checked into his room at the Peninsula Hotel, elegant monument to the old Hong Kong, before taking a taxi to a Kowloon marine terminal where the last of the Lorikeet tankers he was to visit had arrived earlier that day.

A small tanker by modern standards, the 30,000-ton *Charles W. Bailey* was discharging residual fuel oil destined for heating plants and ships' bunkers. Captain Jake Tyson, known throughout the Lorikeet fleet for his disdainful independence, at first refused to let Mitch come aboard. Mitch had to show a letter of introduction from Zabib addressed to all Lorikeet masters before he was allowed to come up the gangplank. He found the captain to be a museum piece of a mariner, a crusty veteran of forty years at sea who wore a dark blue turtleneck sweater and dungarees, cursed with lurid ingenuity through clacking false teeth and viewed Mitchell Donahey as the emissary of a hostile power who could mean nothing but trouble for the master and crew of the *Bailey*.

Not until late afternoon did Captain Tyson become persuaded that "familiarization" was not a Lorikeet executive code word for spying on the company's mariners. When he finally did relax, abandoning his hunch that Mitch's mission held some sinister threat to his command, he turned into an engaging teller of tales who hailed from Baltimore and wanted anyone outside the crew to call him Jake.

After discharge of the oil and positioning of the tanker at another wharf, Tyson guided Mitch to a nearby waterfront bar for a day's-end drink. Hong Kong's B-girls already had begun their nightly hustle and the men had to turn down several Chinese, a Vietnamese and two seductive Eurasian women before they were allowed to drink by themselves. Even then the owner-bartender in the narrow smoky bistro kept trying to catch their eyes, motioning with his head toward one or another of his female lures.

"Nope, never got fuckin' word one about you on the circuit," said Tyson. "Hell, I'd have greeted you decent."

He upbraided the home office with appropriate obscenities, regaled Mitch with a story of his sole visit to Copenhagen headquarters when he told off the accounting department and threatened "to take the ass-hole who tried to cut my expense account and hang him out the window by his goddam ears." He seemed consumed with hatred of Lorikeet managers, but then reversed field without warning and began praising Wasif Zabib as the ideal owner.

"You know, I like that shrewd Arab bastard more than a whole lot. Let me tell you something, Donahey." He downed the gin from his shot glass and leveled a finger at Mitch. "I worked for a lot of owners in my time, most of them pricks you wouldn't wish on a Tangiers whore. Now Zabib, he's different. He shoots straight with you, pays good money, doesn't pull rank and never asks you to do those shitty jobs you didn't sign on for."

Mitch fattened Zabib's reputation with a few remarks of his own, then said, "All the masters I've talked to on this trip seem to like him, especially Alexandros Nicias on the *King Misura.*"

"Oh, Zabib and Alex are old friends. They shipped out together their first time at sea." Tyson paused, scratched at his grizzled jaw. "Matter of fact, that's about the only thing about Zabib I don't like —his staying friends with that smelly Greek."

"Why, what's wrong with Nicias?"

"You oughta know. You talked to him." He looked at Mitch as if expecting a comment. When Mitch said nothing, Tyson hunched forward on the table. "I don't trust the fucker, never did. I had a couple of run-ins with the guy fifteen, sixteen years ago when we used to both come in here. I had an Empress Orient bulker and he was master of an old reefer.

"He had a hard-on for this wealthy Chinese babe, well, mostly Chinese, some Portuguese, I guess. She was some slick looker, I'll tell you, back then when she was letting Alex lay her. But Christ, maybe you've met her. Zab tells me she's one of our owners. Sung Li? The Sung shipping twins?"

"Nicias had an affair with Sung Li? Are you sure?"

"Oh, yeah. It was big gossip here for a year or two. He used to take her around, the Jockey Club for the races, the Royal Yacht Club. I seen them once one summer at the Dragon Boat Festival where they race them long skinny boats that have a joker in the middle whanging on a big drum to give the beat to his paddlers. Oh sure, it wasn't no secret that Alex was balling the Sung twin."

"How about another?" Mitch pointed to Tyson's empty shot glass.

The captain shook his head. "No thanks. I go easy on the stuff during my tour. Tell you what though. How about dinner? I'll buy."

"Okay, you're on. I'd like that."

"I like the Broadway Ginza." Tyson's false teeth clicked as he talked. "Some of the best food in Hong Kong. But it's a yakuza hangout. That bother you?"

"You mean the Japanese Mafia?"

"Yeah. I think they own the place."

"No, if the food's good, that's all that matters. . . . Why don't you trust Nicias?"

"Twice he went back on his word on me. The son-of-a-bitch was lucky he got a second chance. He'll never get a third, believe me."

"Money? Women?"

Tyson shrugged. "Aw, it's all old crap years ago. But brother, I never forgot it."

Mitch finished off his gin and tonic. "I understand Nicias had the *Gunnison Bay* when she sank a few years ago. Engine room explosion, wasn't it?"

"So he and the crew claimed. Me, I never believed the story. You know two years after that he bought himself a million-dollar house on Naxos. Goddam castle. Sits on a high cliff overlooking the ocean. I hear he paid cash for it. Now I know he's made good money as a captain, but hell, he spends it as fast as he gets it. Big borrower, Alex."

They chatted more about the Greek master—Tyson thought it was Nicias who introduced the Sung twins to Zabib, thus leading to their investment in Lorikeet—before they left the bar. Tyson returned to the ship to change clothes while Mitch went back to the hotel to freshen up for dinner.

When Tyson, newly shaven and wearing a seersucker jacket, called for him at the Peninsula, they crossed the bay by the ten-cent ferry to Hong Kong Island and took a taxi to the restaurant. Located on the top floor of a Victoria waterfront building overlooking the harbor, the Broadway Ginza boasted a decor as hybrid as the restaurant's name. One side resembled a Manhattan eatery, linen-draped tables grouped near a long curving bar. The other offered bamboo alcoves with low Japanese tables and wall hangings of black-and-white *kanji* characters of the Japanese alphabet.

At Tyson's suggestion, they took one of the alcoves. "I can get out of this goddam coat," he said. They also kicked off their shoes. Mitch fell to studying the menu which featured hundreds of Chinese dishes as well as Japanese and American fare. "It may sound crazy," said Tyson, "but the Broadway Ginza is best known for Chinese food."

Taking the captain's advice, Mitch ordered *chang-cha ya,* duck smoked by the fire of camphor wood and tea leaves. When it arrived, he ate slowly, savoring each mouthful as he looked about the crowded restaurant.

"I'll be damned." At a table on the Manhattan side, perhaps sixty feet away, sat three white-suited Japanese men and his old sergeant, Bones Elger. Although Elger was half facing him, he apparently had not recognized Mitch or perhaps even seen him.

"Somebody you know?"

"Yeah, an old sergeant from Viet Nam. Listen, Jake, I don't want to have to say hello to the bastard. How about changing seats with me?" Tyson was situated where he could not be seen from that side of the room.

"Sure." Tyson, after the switch, looked where Mitch had pointed. "Is he the one with three Japanese?"

"Yeah. He's wearing a brown jacket, silk, I think. Skinny guy." Mitch frowned in concentration. The plump Japanese sitting across from Elger looked vaguely familiar.

"Your sergeant's in fancy company, Mitch. Those are yakuza."

"How do you know?"

"Wavy hair, white suits. That's yakuza style. But the giveaway is the left hands. They're all missing the end of the left little finger. Not all yakuza lack a fingertip, but any guy who's minus one, you know he's yakuza—and that he's been punished sometime during his career."

After a discussion of yakuza habits and the crime fraternity's operations in Hong Kong, Mitch gave Tyson some of Elger's background—collecting ears in Viet Nam, licensed tanker man who'd been second engineer on the *Gunnison Bay* and most recently had given him a hard time in Honolulu.

"Any chance of finding out the names and some other I.D. of those three yakuza?"

"Maybe. I'm friendly with one of the barmen, a Chinese guy who hasn't much use for his employers. Let me slip him fifty American and we'll see what he knows."

Mitch handed him $50 in U.S. currency and Tyson made his way to the bar. Mitch saw him take a stool at the end, beckon to one of the three bartenders, then lean forward and slide an arm across the bar. The bartender fetched him a drink of some kind and stood talking with the tanker captain. Tyson tarried for a quarter of an hour before returning.

"I told you your friend was in fancy company." The steady click of the captain's teeth had become a familiar sound. "You see that guy sitting across the table from Elger, the one with the paunch?"

"Yes." Had he seen him somewhere?

"The bartender says he's Takeo Kirihara, a big wheel from Kobe. The one nearest the bar is Toshuo Isobe, head man in Hong Kong. The third one is just in from Japan. The bartender doesn't know his name. All three are Yamaguchi-gumi, the biggest yakuza gang in Japan."

"Did he know anything else about them?"

"Not much. Elger and Kirihara ate here together last night. Isobe, the head man in Hong Kong, doesn't live here, but he's in and out from Japan."

"So old Bones is playing with yakuza now." Mitch finished the last delicate morsel of the smoked duck as he mused. "Doesn't surprise me at all. Not at all."

"You sound like you'd like to nail the guy."

"It would be a pleasure, Jake. The man's a menace." He continued to stare at Elger's table. Sure, he had seen the chunky Japanese, the one who smiled a lot. Where? And suddenly the scene flashed in mind. His own driveway in Honolulu, the night he and Bones talked while Mona and a Japanese man looked on from the cars.

When Mitch and Jake Tyson left the Broadway Ginza a half hour

later, Tyson to return to his tanker and Mitch to nap before checking
out of the hotel for a pre-dawn flight to Bombay en route to Europe,
Henry Elger was still deep in conversation with Japan's men of
crime.

"They're gone," said the Japanese to Elger. He was a slim handsome man who smoked almost constantly. "You can turn any way
you want now."

"You sure your man will follow the younger one, Toshuo?"

"Of course. I ordered him to."

"And you think Donahey didn't know I saw him?" Elger asked.

"He gave no indication of it."

Then Toshuo Isobe, the well-groomed chief of Yamaguchi-gumi's
Hong Kong branch, turned to the youngest man at the table and
spoke urgently in Japanese. The man immediately left the table, went
behind the bar and spoke several words to the Chinese bartender
who, with a look of surprise, put down a glass and dish towel and
followed the yakuza soldier into a back room.

"Now we'll find out what the older American wanted," said Isobe.

Five minutes later the Chinese reappeared behind the bar while
the Japanese emissary walked back to the table, sat down and slipped
an American $50 bill across the tablecloth to Isobe. He reported at
length in Japanese.

"The American was a tanker captain named Tyson," Isobe said to
Elger after the report. "He asked Yuen who we all were and about
our jobs in the brotherhood. So I was wrong. Your friend Donahey
must have seen you at our table."

"Fire that bartender when the place closes tonight," Takeo
Kirihara ordered. "Disloyalty cannot be tolerated."

Isobe inclined his head in agreement. "We will also leave him with
a few souvenirs."

"The vice-commander told us in Honolulu that Donahey should
be dealt with if it appeared he might expose us." Elger looked from
one Japanese to another as he talked. "When he gets a tanker captain
to come nosing into our business, he's already gone too far."

"Agreed." Kirihara turned to Isobe. "Deal with Donahey tonight."

"Hai!" The branch chief for Hong Kong palmed his wavy hair. "As soon as I find out where he is from our surveillance man."

Bones Elger clinked wine glasses with the three Yamaguchis.

Mitch walked slowly through the Kai Tak Airport toward the security installation where passengers were checked before fanning out to departure gates. He did not look forward to this 4:30 A.M. flight to Bombay, then on to Rome where he'd switch planes for the final leg to Copenhagen. A long weary haul and he'd had but a two-hour nap at the Peninsula after his dinner with Jake Tyson.

And that near-accident two blocks from the hotel still had his nerves on edge. Christ, he could have been killed. Some idiot gunned an old truck right through a stop sign at an intersection and if Mitch hadn't yelled at his taxi driver, they might have been mashed against a building. Luckily his driver had swift reflexes and he managed to yank the wheel sharply, turning the cab so that the truck missed it by inches and smashed against the same building. The truck driver, probably drunk at that hour of the morning, apparently fell or jumped from his vehicle just before the crash and took off in a crazy staggering run. The cabbie wanted to chase the guy, but yielded to Mitch's pleas that they continue on to the airport. It was enough to be trembling from shock. He didn't need to wind up missing his plane as well.

Of course, Hong Kong traffic was a horror on both sides of the bay and one had to stay alert. Still he had assumed, wrongly as it turned out, that a 3 A.M. drive to the airport could be made in relative peace.

He was fifty or sixty yards from the airport's security checkpoint when he heard his name called. Mitch turned to find a young Eurasian man at his side. Tall, wide shouldered, muscles bulging beneath a madras jacket, he had the affable demeanor of a tourist functionary of some kind.

"Mr. Donahey, I'm Wai Tam of immigration police." He snapped open a leather folder and flashed a plasticized identity card. "I dislike troubling you, but you're wanted at the immigration office."

"What for?" At this hour the last thing he needed, Mitch thought, was an encounter with Hong Kong bureaucrats.

"A routine matter, I believe." His courteous smile came touched with apology. "Something about your passport." He spoke flawless English.

"Why, what's wrong with my passport? Nobody bothered about it when I arrived."

"May I see it please?" The man held out his hand.

Mitch hesitated. Once in Guatemala, he had given up his passport to an official who didn't return it for six hours. "May I see your identification again, please, Mr. Tam? I didn't get a decent look at it."

"Now, Mr. Donahey, no delays, sir." He grasped Mitch's arm. "Just come along to the office with me."

Mitch wrenched free. "Hold it, man, I've got a plane to catch in less than an hour."

"This will only take a few minutes." Unsmiling now, Tam took his arm again, this time in a grip that hurt.

"Goddam it, I've got a right to see your I.D." His temper rising, Mitch tore away from the grasp and took several steps backward. "And don't try grabbing me again or I'll sock you." He pulled back his right arm in a punching gesture, though he knew he was no match for the hefty stranger.

Tam stepped forward. "Stop this, Donahey, or I'll have to put the cuffs on you." He reached for his back pocket.

Mitch continued to walk backward. Suddenly in the recesses of his mind, a warning sounded and he felt a wave of fright. This man was an imposter intent on harming him. Tam lunged at him. Mitch turned and ran to the security post, bolted in front of four or five startled persons waiting to pass through the electronic detection doorway, halted and then stepped through the detection framework. Only when he was on the other side did Mitch turn around.

Tam, a look of surprised confusion on his face, stood where Mitch had left him. He started toward the security queue, then stopped, obviously uncertain what to do. He was perhaps forty yards away.

"You come through security," Mitch called, "and I'll put the airport police on you."

Tam, standing as if rooted, glared at Mitch, glanced about him at the knots of people who were now watching the drama, then suddenly turned and ran toward the airport exit. He picked up speed as he went, the unbuttoned madras jacket flapping about him and his arms pumping like a sprinter. Soon he disappeared in the distant crowd.

"A thief. I guess he wanted my wallet," said Mitch to nearby passengers who were looking at him, anxious for an explanation.

But he felt certain now that the husky Eurasian posing as an immigration official wanted much more than his wallet. The encounter, coming on the heels of the near "accident" with the truck, had the shape of a larger danger. Had he accompanied the bogus Wai Tam, he might have wound up in a condition in which the driver of the truck apparently intended to place him. Somebody in Hong Kong wanted to kill him. Who? The only plausible answer involved Bones Elger and his yakuza friends. So Bones must have seen and recognized him after all.

Yet why did Bones consider him a threat? If Bones wanted to murder him—the mere phrasing of the question came as a shock—it must mean that Elger suspected and feared that Mitch knew a great deal more than he did. About what? Yes, the best evidence that Elger and the yakuza men were in a criminal conspiracy was the twin attempt here in Hong Kong to murder or kidnap Mitchell Donahey.

For the first time since this bizarre series of events started back in Honolulu, he experienced deep fear. Not since Viet Nam two decades ago had he been afraid of losing his life. And not until he was buckled into his seat on the jet airliner and wheels lifted from the runway to fold into the plane's belly did he feel sufficiently relaxed to close his eyes.

14

Once again Mitch stood at the door to Wasif Zabib's three-story town house on Copenhagen's fashionable Amaliegade not far from the palace of the Danish queen. Once again he rang the doorbell, one of several brass fittings that gleamed under the carriage lamp of the entryway. And once again Grethe Knudsen, wearing a modish outfit of soft brown wool, led him up the curving stairway with its rich burgundy carpeting.

Mitch noted his fatigue as he climbed the stairs with one hand on the carved wooden railing. He had arrived back from his survey trip only hours before, had intended to relax with a book and go to sleep early, but had been bidden to dinner at Zabib's home.

"Mitch, glad to have you back." A cordial Zabib welcomed him at the head of the stairway. A diamond stickpin glistened at his figured silk tie and he wore a dark blue suit of stylish cut. Behind him, as he shook hands, loomed the huge photograph of the supertanker that threw up a shower of spray as it bulled through heavy seas.

"What . . ."

Mitch halted at the top of the stairs. Could he trust his eyes? There, on a bright Mexican throw rug beside the long window overlooking the harbor and its scatter of ship lights, stood Mona Harkinson. Tall and radiant, she wore a black low-cut dinner dress and high heels and she looked more like a fashion model than a tanker captain.

"Mr. Donahey, I presume." Her gray eyes flickered with delight and her smile was at once playful and intimate.

Instead of taking her outstretched hand, he threw his arms around her, kissed her soundly on the lips and broke the embrace only when she whispered, "Mitch, please. Not now."

"How, when, what?" He was overwhelmed. "Where are you staying?"

"At the d'Angleterre, but I hoped you might rent me a room in your loft."

"You mean . . ."

"She means that she has come to stay," Zabib cut in. "Let's bring our little mystery drama to a climax." The tanker owner relished this. "Miss Harkinson has agreed to join the Lorikeet family. As of today, her name went on the roster of Lorikeet tanker masters. She will rotate with Jules Yvre as captain of our flagship, the *Zabibian.*"

Mitch stood mute, staring at Mona, trying to adjust. Grethe, in a gay mood, brought Mitch a drink. "Here's your favorite Scotch-on-the-rocks. Shock repellent." Her back to Mona, she whispered, "I like her, Mitch. She's stunning—and such presence."

"Okay, how did this all come about?" Mitch couldn't take his eyes off Mona. There was a luminescence about her, a kind of pulsing energy, so changed from the dispirited woman he had pictured beside her phone in Montreal. He felt a strong erotic current flowing between them.

Zabib waved them to the leather armchairs grouped about the long coffee table made from the deck planks of a ship. "Charge it to television, Mitch." The Jordanian went through his routine of tasting his martini only after pouring a drop on a finger and wiping the finger dry. "You know, in all the criticism of the tube, we tend to forget its beneficial impact. For instance, if one watches closely the behavior of someone on TV who's under intense pressure in a live news situation, you can get a pretty fair clue to the person's character. You can be fooled, of course, especially by skilled actors and politicians. But almost invariably a person suddenly thrust into a limelight he's not accustomed to will respond in natural ways that tell a great deal about his personality.

"So when I saw Captain Harkinson's televised press conference, I decided after the first few minutes that she was a woman of remarkable ability. She was cool, poised and in charge."

Though a faint blush hinted at her embarrassment, Mona obviously enjoyed the tributes that had been in short supply recently.

"She answered every question honestly," continued Zabib, "never tried to evade or fudge or make an impression. Also she knew what she was talking about ninety-five percent of the time and when she didn't, she turned to her chief engineer, that poor Didati fellow, for the particulars."

When he paused to take a sip of his drink, Grethe spoke up. "Tell them what we noticed about members of the crew, dear."

"Yes, yes," agreed Zabib. "Grethe and I were watching together and we noticed that almost all the deckhands and enginemen who spoke highly of Captain Harkinson were a cut above those who disparaged her."

"What do you mean by 'a cut above'?" asked Mona.

"They just seemed the more intelligent ones," said Grethe. "It was mostly the clods who ran you down."

"So, surmising what the general reaction in the industry would be," continued Zabib, "you know—what did you expect with an old lady in command?—I made a few inquiries around. A faculty member of the California Maritime Academy who had Captain Harkinson in several classes gave her a glowing report card as did an official of the Port Revel tanker training facility at Grenoble. I got the same reaction from some officers who sailed with her in the Med and on U.S.-to-Central-America runs."

"Don't forget Mitchell," prompted Grethe Knudsen.

"By no means. The fact that you showed up at her side in Philadelphia told me a lot, Mitch. I respect your judgment. Then when you came to work here, you'll remember I quizzed you about her."

"And I thought it was just curiosity," said Mitch. "How soon did you start asking about Mona? Right after the sinking?"

Zabib nodded. "Within a day or two. I guessed, correctly, that she was finished at Michaelson & Lygdamis. Frankly, the men who run that company are the plodding, unimaginative kind. Also I doubted if there'd be much call for her services elsewhere in the shipping world."

The Lorikeet president took a swallow of his martini. "So I knew I could land a first-class captain and at the same time get the kind of

publicity that Lorikeet otherwise couldn't get in a hundred years."
Zabib's grin had the cast of triumph. "Just wait until you see what
happens after we announce it tomorrow."

"And I'm bringing Bill Muldoon over as my chief mate and Arno
Joahannes as my communications officer, thanks to Mr. Zabib," said
Mona. "Bill and Arno are going to join me for the first tour on the
Zabibian."

She held a hand toward Mitch. "I fully intended to tell you, but
then I couldn't reach you on the phone during the last of your trip.
. . . So, I turned it into a surprise."

"Great." He hesitated. "But the *Zabibian?* She's 267,000 tons
deadweight. You told me you didn't trust any of the VLCCs."

"I do think they're too big and I wish the industry hadn't built
them." Her face hardened. "But I can handle them as well as any
man."

"I told her," said Zabib, "that it would look like quitting if she
backed down to a handy-size tanker. The super-weights are here to
stay, so best she get on with her career in the ships that will be
around as long as she will."

They finished their drinks and adjourned to the dining room with
its ambience of understated elegance, old silver, glinting crystal
chandelier, fine glassware, crisp linen and the apple-cheeked serving
maid in her gray uniform. They talked of art, music, politics—anything but business—during a savory meal of jellied consomme, filet
mignon, sweet potatoes, a salad and fresh fruits with French and
Danish cheeses. It was apparent that Grethe had taken to Mona
without reservation and that both she and Zabib were happy to have
the company of two lovers they liked.

After dinner Zabib and Mona spent a half hour in his library,
planning for the expected eruption of media attention after the next
day's announcement. They also arranged her work schedule. She
would fly to South Africa next week and take a helicopter out to join
the *Zabibian,* now in ballast en route to the Arabian Gulf after discharging her crude at Le Verdun in France. Mona would spend the
last leg of the voyage as a passenger, familiarizing herself with the
big tanker, before taking over command from Captain Jules Yvre,
with whom she would rotate three months on and three months off.

Her first voyage as captain of the flagship would take her to Japan.
Mitch's Norwegian assistant had obtained a year-long charter for the

Zabibian which would shuttle between the Gulf and Tokyo Bay, carrying Saudi-Arabian crude for the Tsuno Oil Co. of Yokohama.

Mitch and Grethe Knudsen chatted in the living room while the others conferred, then he and Mona said their good-nights and walked the few blocks to his apartment. It was a cold October night, stars pinned like steel studs to the black vault of sky, and they swung along briskly, Mitch in his sheepskin and Mona in a fur-trimmed winter coat.

"Isn't it incredible?" She laced her arm with his. "Two months ago I didn't know your name. Now I want to give up my apartment in London and move in with you."

"If you don't, I'll have you busted to third mate."

When they turned into the cobbled lane along Nyhavn Canal, she admired the nest of old sailing vessels with their high masts and at the doorway to his apartment, she ran her gloved hand over the carvings on the great oaken doors.

"Beautiful wood," she said. "They must be old."

"Seventeenth century, I'm told. They're twelve feet high and six inches thick. Around here, they build things to last."

But as they rode the elevator to his fifth-floor loft, he remembered. He glanced at his wristwatch. 10:20. "Damn it, I was supposed to call a guy at nine."

He threw open his apartment door for her, but backed away. "Make yourself at home. I'll be back in a few minutes."

He jogged to the hydrofoil terminal, pushed through a crowd of waiting passengers and placed his call in the public phone booth. It rang only once before the voice with an American accent said, "Hello."

"This is Mitch Donahey. Got back today. Sorry I'm late."

"Apologies won't help. Wrong times can be dangerous. What's my name?"

"Ned."

"Okay. Is tomorrow night all right to meet?"

"I'd rather make it this weekend." He was thinking of Mona.

"If it's just convenience, I insist on tomorrow night. Matters are on the front burner." The dry unemotional voice had a midwestern accent, Mitch thought.

"All right then. Tomorrow night."

"Take the nine o'clock hydrofoil to Malmö. I'll be aboard. I'll be wearing a dark blue cap, Greek sea-captain style, and carrying a plaid bag over my right shoulder. Don't speak to me. When we arrive, walk off the boat and take the first left street up the hill. I'll catch up to you."

"Got it. See you in Sweden."

In his apartment, after he tossed his sheepskin coat aside, he and Mona met in a wordless embrace. Hungry for each other, they hugged fiercely like lovers parting at an airport gate and when one sought to disengage, the other clutched anew.

When they did draw apart, words tumbled out. She loved his loft. He had a feeling of euphoria, like sailplane soaring. Holy Jesus, she said, they'd have a whole week together before she had to fly off to the *Zabibian*. Did she know, he asked, that she looked dazzling—the most gorgeous woman in Europe tonight? Did he know that she wanted to devour him?

"I still can't believe it," said Mitch. "It's a miracle."

"No miracle, sweet guy. Just a smart shrewd shipowner picking the best captain for his favorite tanker." She drew herself up, feigning haughty self-esteem.

"Yeah, I know. Still . . ."

"Still me no stills. Why did you have to go out to phone? Was she expecting you tonight?"

"The CIA chore I told you about on the phone. I'd forgotten to call at the appointed time. My contact insists I use a pay booth."

He mixed a nightcap while they bantered and laughed and nuzzled. Then he pointed out features of the large kitchen and the long living room with stone fireplace. The room overlooked Nyhavn Canal and swaying masts of the fishing schooners. The broad view also took in old gabled houses on the other side of the canal, moored hydrofoils near the terminal and the open harbor beyond.

From his cassette collection, he picked one featuring Nanna, a popular Danish singer, and soon her ballads of love poured from the stereo. When they walked hand-in-hand to the bedroom, she said that never in her life had she been so happy.

He turned up the heat and by the time they undressed, the room was toasty warm. Apparently the bedroom had been used once as an artist's studio. A skylight in the high ceiling gave them a view of the wide cloudless night, the heavens aglow with diamond lights born millennia ago on millions of suns in the far reaches of space.

They made love in celebration of their good fortune. Mona undid her upswept hair and let it flow across the pillows as she lay nude on the bed. Mitch buried his face in the wave of hair, inhaling its fragrance, feeling the softness as wispy as dreams. He kissed her shoulders, let his tongue wander down her arms and about her hands while her flesh quivered. "Heavenly," she murmured. He suckled her fingers, bathed her underarms in kisses, then tongued downward to her breasts. The nipples stood erect, sentinels of Eros, and he sucked each breast for long minutes, swirling his tongue about the soft mounds. On a surge of passion, Mona used her hands to bunch her breasts for him as if, blinded by desire, he could not find its object. He moved lower on the bed, stapled her flat belly with swift kisses and then at last, as she moaned with anticipation, he plunged his tongue deep into her vagina. As quickly he withdrew it, kissed her inner thighs, her pubic hair, her labia. He centered his tongue on her clitoris, prodded, sucked and bathed it. Minutes passed with his head burrowed in her crotch, his mouth welded to her wet sleeve of sex.

"That's enough," she said. "You're driving me crazy." But he ignored her pleas, thrust his hardened tongue against her and sucked until she squirmed to free herself.

When he mounted her, he began with slow languid strokes. She responded in a frenzy of passion, clawing at his back, thrusting up to meet him, rotating her buttocks, pulling his head down so that she could crush his mouth with hers. As they struck a quickened rhythm, she drove his mouth with her tongue in the same cadence. He felt a kind of delirium overcoming him. Now they increased the tempo, held fast to each other, felt a rising heat solder their bodies, heard the swamp-like sounds of sex and became drenched with sweat. Mona came with a great long shudder, flooding his penis and going so limp in his arms that he felt she had seeped into him through his pores.

But he did not stop and Mona, though she wanted to flee from this relentless pounding, could not bring herself to mount an escape. Instead she acquiesced in the attack, uttered little cries of anguished joy and let her mind float trance-like in the euphoria of sensual abandon. Gradually she moved back into a gentle rhythm that eventually persuaded Mitch to moderate his pace. It was as if a reckless night runner, hurling himself from shadow to shadow, had suddenly slowed to fall into step beside a woman strolling a moonlit path.

Their bodies tight together, his mouth fastened on hers, they rocked in slow sweet cadence, drawn as one person toward some invisible magnet of the senses. Like travelers along a dreamscape of velvet highways that stretched through satiny forests and meadows heavy with the fragrance of strange spices, they went on and on.

They seemed incapable of halting. Instead the beast of love accelerated bit by bit, minute by minute, until a kind of madness overtook them, mashing them together and sending them into a frenzy of mutual questing. Now indeed they had invaded each other, become a wild thrashing creature with four legs, four arms, two heads and countless apertures all screaming for surrender and release. For the first time ever Mitch lost himself completely in another person. For the first time ever Mona felt herself swept into the vortex of another human. Two beings became welded into one, and when they finally came, exquisitely together, they fell away exhausted, both marveling at the power of the tender demons that possessed them.

As if speech would have desecrated this fierce communion of love, they said nothing, merely held hands tightly and gazed with awe into each other's eyes. At last their breathing returned to normal, Mitch's eyes grew heavy and Mona kissed him softly on an eyelid. He napped a few minutes. When he awoke, he saw Mona leaning over him, fondly watching him.

"You are beautiful asleep," she said.

"But hornier awake." He gazed up at her. "You have storm-cloud eyes, Captain, and I love you."

"I love you, Mitch. Oh, holy Jesus, yes."

Later she said she was hungry, bounced out of bed, wrapped herself in his heavy wool bathrobe and went foraging in the tiled kitchen. Mitch tagged after her in a sweat shirt and jogging pants that slopped about his ankles. They settled on scrambled eggs, toast and decaffeinated coffee and Mona banged around the cabinets looking for a frying pan and utensils.

"Our first meal in our new home." She carried a tray to the table Mitch had set in the breakfast nook. Through a circular window they could see the lights on the old plaza of Kongens Nytorv.

"May there be thousands of them." He clinked his coffee cup against hers.

"Bring me up to date, lover." The deep voice enveloped him. "We haven't talked for seven, no eight nights."

"First of all, I stopped off in Zurich last evening and took Chrissy out to dinner. Fancy restaurant. Just what she wanted."

"You did!" Mona glowed. "You doll. What did you think of her?"

"T'riffic, to use her word. We took to each other right off. It was a lucky meeting. I found, during a plane delay in Rome, that I could make the stopover, so I called her and she said sure."

"What did she say about old mom?"

"Lots. She thinks you're great."

"And she liked you fine, huh?"

"Oh, yes. That, however, became a bit of a problem."

"Problem?" Mona frowned.

"Yeah." He hesitated. "Look, Mona, it was like this. Chrissy came on to me. I debated whether to tell you this, but decided I had to. I can't start out with you by keeping secrets."

"Tell me what happened." Her voice lost its warmth.

"Well, we had this candle-lit booth in one of Zurich's best restaurants. She wanted a fancy place and I obliged. She began batting her eyes, making flirty remarks, little gestures, you know, teenage come-hither stuff. Finally, I asked her straight out. Was she coming on to me? She said yes, she was, that she wasn't a virgin, knew how to handle herself and wanted to get laid."

"Chrissy asked you to make love to her?"

He nodded. "I said, 'Chrissy, I'm your mother's lover. We're going to live together if we can.' So, I told her, 'It would be impossible even if I wanted to, which I don't, so let's knock off the sex talk and enjoy a good dinner.' "

"And she said?" Mona tensed. Her food had remained untouched.

"She said it was time she learned about lovemaking and she knew I'd make a neat teacher."

"Christine said that?" The question came packed in disbelief.

"She did." But, Mitch recalled, her body said much more. He could see Chris sitting across the table in Zurich. A vivacious girl, built like her mother on thoroughbred lines, she filled the booth with the musky presence of sex. Neither coy nor coquettish, she had some of her mother's candid approach together with enormous teenage vitality. She was a bundle of raw energy demanding an outlet. Even at the close of the dinner, when she became persuaded that the night probably would end with a chaste friendly kiss on the cheek at the door of the dormitory, she laughed after a seductive pout. She flashed a high-heeled pump and part of a shapely leg at the side of the table. "You're mean. Look, I even wore my catch-me-fuck-me shoes." He had feared advances in the darkened cab riding back to Mlle. Jupon's school outside Zurich, but to his relief Christine sat apart from him and talked about school, studies and her roommate.

"How did all this end?" asked Mona.

"Hey, you sound like I'm on trial for something." He told her of the ride home. "Don't get me wrong, Mona. I like the girl a lot. She's got drive and she's smart. It's just that right now she's a steamy young woman—and probably in need of a long talk with mom."

"Did she ask you not to tell me about coming on to you?" Mona's voice had none of its customary intimacy.

"She did, but I made no promises. I said I'd see. I guess she thought I wouldn't tell you."

"So, in a sense you betrayed her."

"Betrayed her? Wait a big minute here, Mona. Are you suggesting that I shouldn't have told you?"

"I am. What happened, if it did happen as you describe it, was just the spontaneous combustion of a wholesome girl penned up in a girls' school. It was an incident, no more. By telling me, you put both Chrissy and me on the spot."

"Now you're making a small scene into a big deal. I told you I debated whether to tell you." He felt his frustration edging toward anger. "I came down on the side of telling you. I have to stay straight with you, Mona. I can't, goddam it, live with you as lovers and still keep secrets."

"You didn't know we were going to be living together right away." Her tone was dead cold now.

"That's picky. . . . Christ, we're into a fuckin' fight. Are you saying you'd rather not know that your daughter made a pass at your lover?"

"Yes, I am." It was a near shout. "You've put a thing between Chrissy and me. Please tell me, Mitchell, exactly what I'm supposed to do with this tacky piece of information."

"I thought that when Chris comes here for vacation, the three of us ought to sit down and talk about it."

"Oh, fine." She was indignant. "The inquisition. The grand inquisitors charge the young girl with the crime of lustful thoughts and indecent behavior and then flog her on the public plaza."

"No, no. I thought we could treat it lightly, no big deal, get her to laughing with us about it. Maybe suggest there's a good-looking young man out there who'd appreciate all that sexy zeal."

"Make like the whole thing was just a joke, is that it?" She said it as if Mitch had suggested they all get a good laugh out of the latest ax murder.

"In a way." He was angry now. "You're the one who said it was just an incident. Right, it was. So we talk it out, the three of us, and we forget it."

"The whole thing sounds to me like you're boasting." She was brittle in her own anger. "See what a big virile man we have here. Even sixteen-year-old girls make panting passes at him."

"Thanks a lot." He shoved his plate of scrambled eggs and toast aside. It slid down the table and collided with her untouched plate, the clink placing a period on their exchange—and marking the beginning of a long hot silence. Neither of them touched their food, but both drank the coffee and poured second cups.

"I apologize, Mona." They had been wordless so long, his own voice sounded strange. "In hindsight, I made a mistake."

"Let's just drop it. The damage is done." She was in no mood for instant reconciliation. "You started out telling me about your trip. So what happened?"

"You ask that with all the burning curiosity of the lifer wanting to know what day of the week it is." He resented her rejecting his truce offer. "Well, Lorikeet has a well-run tanker fleet. The ships are efficient, safe, not old rust buckets, good crews. He had one old tanker, the *Tides of Fundy,* but I persuaded Zabib to scrap her and I watched Arab shipwreckers tear her apart at Gadani Beach.

"I'm beginning to believe that our old ear collector, Bones Elger, is into tanker crime as a career. I saw him hanging out with yakuza —Japanese Mafia types—in Hong Kong." He described the scene at the Broadway Ginza when the Lorikeet captain, Jake Tyson, found out the names of the Yamaguchi gang members. "The top guy, Takeo Kirihara, was the one who was with Elger in Honolulu."

He told of his talk with Alexandros Nicias, the Greek captain's antipathy for women officers aboard ship, his friendship with Elger and his close friendship with Zabib. "Jake Tyson says he's convinced that Nicias got rich out of the *Gunnison Bay* scam. Says he owns a mansion on the Greek island of Naxos."

"I suppose I'll meet Nicias soon. He sounds like an unsavory character."

"He is and also resents you. He said when I saw you, I should ask . . ." He hesitated. After the dustup over Chrissy, this probably was not the time.

"Ask me what?"

"Oh, let's skip it. It's not important. Some other time."

Mona's gray eyes centered on his. "No, I want to hear it. I want to know what other captains are saying about me."

"Well, he said I should ask you why you brought the *Yandoon Princess* so close to the coast in a big blow with crippled steering that you knew might go out again."

"Nicias knows the answer to that very ugly question." Anger brought a flush to her face. "Do you?"

"No, I . . . But look, Mona, I know you did what you knew was best."

"The hell I did." Now she spoke with cold fury. "If I were a man, I never would have tried to make Delaware Bay in heavy seas with badly damaged steering. But I'm a woman, first to have a VLCC. Homer Richert and those other M & L officers count the dollars in every hour lost on scheduled delivery. If I'd kept the *Princess* out at sea and no further steering problems occurred, they'd have had my ass."

"Come on, Mona, you may be imagining reactions, you know."

"No." It was a half shout. "They'd have called me that timid female. 'One little breakdown and she panics. . . . The menopause mistress is afraid of bad weather. . . . Just like a woman. Can't take it when the barometer falls.' If a male captain held the ship out at sea until the dirty weather passed, Montreal might have grumbled, but they'd never have said a word to him. But me? They'd send me back to small tankers so fast, it would make your eyes blur."

"I understand, Mona. Believe me, I do."

"I'm not sure you do." She folded her arms. Emotional barricades? "And I'm damn sure a chauvinistic slug like Nicias knows perfectly well that he gets judged by a different standard than I do."

She fell silent, stared moodily down at the cold scrambled eggs and toast. When he asked if she wanted to hear about the rest of his trip, she merely nodded as she pulled his thick wool bathrobe closer about her.

So he continued. He talked for a half hour, pointing out the clues that appeared to link the sinking of the *Gunnison Bay* and the intentional crippling of the *Yandoon Princess*. Mona became interested and began asking questions. She followed closely, lost some of her edginess and appeared to be ready to put their first skirmishes behind them.

Concluding, Mitch described the suspected double attempt on his life as he was leaving Hong Kong. "I don't mind admitting it scared me. I'm sure it came from Bones and his Japanese buddies."

The story undid Mona. "Oh, sweetheart, I had no idea." She came around the table. He rose to her embrace and she buried her head against his shoulder. "I couldn't bear it if anything happened to you." They held each other tenderly for a time and when they parted, she drew her chair next to his.

"Add the Hong Kong tries to Didati's murder," said Mitch, "and you get an idea of what we're up against. Both of us should be awfully careful from now on."

"Are you going to tell all this to your CIA contact?"

"Sure. Everything."

"Maybe he'll have a suggestion on what we should do. I think you especially need some protection."

"Don't worry. I'm keeping my guard up." Mitch laid his hand on her arm. "Another thing, you and I have to face the fact that we may be working for a guy who either headed or agreed to go along with the *Gunnison Bay* scam."

"I was aware of that when I accepted his job offer." Mona, speaking softly, was subdued now. "I intend to watch and listen."

"There's even a chance now that Zabib, Nicias and Elger are working with the yakuza on some new scheme. In fact, we may both be setups."

"I don't get it."

"Zabib may have hired me as a blind for some operation. Same goes for you. He may be setting you up—easy to blame the next tanker accident on the woman captain who's already lost one ship."

"Thank you, Mr. Donahey." She said it with a touch of frost.

"Look, Mona. M & L didn't want you. Nobody else wanted to hire you either. The industry thinks you were responsible for the loss."

"For God's sake, Mitch, that was sabotage." She thumped the table. "You know it wasn't my fault."

"Babe, I'm not saying it was. You and I saw Mario's filed bolt. I'm talking about the perception in the industry. They think you're the goat. So Zabib may have hired you precisely because anything that happens can be blamed on you."

"Every source he checked told him that I was a competent captain. Zabib said I had 'remarkable ability.' You heard him." She loosened the bathrobe collar. She was growing hot. "He said he hired me because I was first-class and I believe him."

"I know what he said. But we have to be prepared to deal with what he actually thinks."

"What he thinks! Are you saying that I'm not a capable officer?" Mona stared at him.

"Christ, no. Don't twist what I say." His temper was rising again too. "I think you're able to handle any tanker. But the shipping world thinks you're not, and Zabib may be fixing to use you."

"It seems to me that you're very quick to pick up on what other people think."

"I am not, Mona. I think you're a fine officer."

"You certainly don't say that with any conviction." She brushed back the long tangled hair from her forehead with an impatient motion as if she were ashamed to be seen with this token of their love-making.

"You insist on confusing what I feel and believe with what people out there think?"

"Maybe because that's the way you put it, you know."

"Hell, Mona, I flew from Honolulu to Philadelphia because I believed in you." He had a boxed-in helpless feeling.

"I know you wanted me in bed. There's no dispute about that. I'm talking about your attitude toward my job. You sound like you agree with everybody who says I don't know my ass from a hawsepipe."

"I do not. Mona, that's ridiculous."

"You should listen to yourself sometime," she said hotly.

"Are you spoiling for a goddam fight or what?" He left his chair, walked over to a bar cart near the fireplace and poured himself a Scotch. "I can't believe this, Mona. I merely said we should be on the alert for a setup and you take it as a slap at your ability as a captain."

"My ears heard quite the opposite." Folding her arms, she continued to stare at him. "Zabib talked of his luck in landing a 'first-class captain' who'd bring the company lots of attention and you turn his upbeat move into a real downer."

"I refuse to carry this further." He felt like a suspect under her scrutiny. The gray eyes that had looked smoky with love were now hostile. He felt his stomach churning. "You won't listen to the logic of the situation. You want to fight."

"I do not. You do. And if I did want a fight, I wouldn't rush into it with booze as a crutch."

He resisted an urge to throw the Scotch in her face. "Mona, knock it off. I'm having one lousy little drink."

"You branded Zabib's hiring of me a 'miracle.' " She mimicked his midwestern accent when she added, "Only a miracle would land the poor old lady another ship."

"That was just an expression, for God's sake. It didn't mean a thing."

"For someone saying a lot of meaningless things, you pack quite an emotional wallop, my friend."

"Come on, let's go to bed." He felt cornered. Words were of no further use. "A night's sleep will give us a new look at all this, whatever the hell it is."

"No, I want to talk this out. Sleep is the last thing I need right now."

"Well, I need it. I'm tired out from the trip and I'm going to bed." He bolted the last of his drink and stalked from the living room. Over his shoulder, he added, "You can come when you're ready."

But she did not come. He lay in bed, trying without success to analyze what had happened to them and turning from side to side in a futile effort to fall asleep. Minutes passed. She came into the room, took her clothes off the chair without speaking and returned to the living room.

He made a pass at sleep by counting to a hundred. He got to forty-nine when he heard her talking, apparently on the telephone. He got up and padded to the living room. She had dressed and was putting on her fur-trimmed coat.

"Where are you going?"

"Back to the d'Angleterre. I called a cab."

"Mona, for Christ's sake, be sensible."

"I am sensible. But I must say you look silly standing there naked." And she went out, slamming the door. In a moment, he heard the grinding of the elevator as she descended.

Back in bed, an attempt at psychological dissection of their impasse itself came to an impasse. He spent the rest of the night in the half-drugged feverish state of the insomniac and when he did finally fall asleep at dawn, he was seized by a nightmare in which Bones Elger fired a blast from his M-16 at the huts of a Viet Nam village only to shoot down Mona Harkinson as she ran out in terror.

15

The hydrofoil slammed out of Copenhagen harbor and pointed toward Malmö on the west coast of Sweden's southern toe. Some twenty passengers sat on long wooden benches in the forward compartment of the stubby vessel. Mitch had selected an isolated spot on the starboard side that yielded, as it turned out when they reached full speed, the maximum of noise and vibration. Riding hard like a truck on a rough road, the ship slapped and pounded the waves on its thirty-mile dash across the Oresund.

Passengers bought coffee in plastic containers from the snack counter and sipped the hot beverage as protection from the cold autumn night they could not see. For the most part they huddled in silence, clumps on pew-like benches, but one elderly woman vomited into a carton and then stared glumly at the spray lashing the porthole beside her.

Mitch spent the trip alternating between bleak thoughts of Mona and guessing about the personality of his contact Ned who sat some twenty feet away several benches in front of him. Of the two, Ned proved easier to think about since he stirred far less emotion and no stomach spasms at all. As certified, the CIA man wore a dark blue cap, Greek sea-captain style, and carried a plaid shoulder bag. At first glance, he seemed vaguely familiar although there was nothing distinctive about him. Of medium height and build and marked by that kind of wary tension common to city people the world over, he could have been any of a hundred clerks, waiters, shopkeepers or cab drivers with whom Mitch had exchanged a few words around Copenhagen.

Yet that tug of familiarity bothered Mitch as they glanced at each other in the terminal while waiting for the ship to leave. Seated on board, he continued to call on his memory as he studied Ned's profile. And then, without warning, came the flash of recognition. Although he had noted the man three times previously, Mitch had seen the face at close range but once and then only through a cursory glance. Yet the sum total of the subtle shapes, gestures, forms, colors and perhaps even aura that permits one human being to recognize another from afar after a lapse of days or years enabled Mitch to identify this unremarkable stranger without the least doubt.

He had seen him, wearing the trench coat he wore tonight, on the bus from the airport back in September the day that Mitch arrived for his job interview with Zabib. He had seen him again that evening outside his hotel and then again the next morning at Kastrup Airport when he flew back to Honolulu. So the CIA had had Zabib's operation under surveillance before Mitch took his suspicions to the FBI and the Agency. How long before? Was the YANTANK file an old one at Langley headquarters and if so, what did that imply?

His annoyance at having been tailed by Ned was a bland dish compared to his bouillabaisse of feelings about Mona. The mere thought of her triggered disturbances that turned his body into a kind of chemical traffic jam and the image of her as she slammed the door of his apartment recurred repeatedly like bouts of fever. She had not answered in her room at the Hotel d'Angleterre nor had she returned calls he left for her at the office number assigned visiting tanker officers.

He had seen her when he stood at the rear of the company's conference room where she and Zabib met the media to announce her hiring as a Lorikeet supertanker captain. Several reporters of the international press flew in from London to join their Danish colleagues at the session. Her performance impressed Mitch. She was relaxed, confident and articulate, never weaseled out of a question nor lost her poise.

He was sure that she saw him when she looked about the room, but she gave no indication of it and their eyes did not meet. He thought she looked tired and drawn, but conceded that he could not tell accurately from a distance.

She stood sandwiched between Zabib and the company's finance officer, fitting companions, Mitch thought with an edge of malice, considering the fat salaries reaped by tanker captains for half a year's work. His feelings about her changed by the hour. He yearned for her, detested her ego, craved her, deplored her vacuum of logic, pitied her vulnerability, remembered her rich deep voice and guitar in the medley of ballads, thought that last night she showed about as much sensitivity as a clam, loved her and wanted to yank up her skirt and paddle her ass. He also wondered just what she was thinking today and where they went from here.

When the hydrofoil docked in Malmö, Mitch walked head down into a wind that bowled along the waterfront, rattling signs and hammering against storefronts. He took his first left as ordered, walking up the incline of a dark residential street. He heard steps behind him and soon Ned drew abreast of him.

"Slow your pace," said Ned, "and take your first left again. Enter the front door of the first house on your right. Don't take the time to knock. I'll go on ahead and open the door for you."

The agent quickened his step and by the time Mitch turned the corner, Ned was entering the side door of a modest frame one-story house. A minute later Mitch walked up the front steps and went in through the unlatched door. The room was dark and chilly. Ned, standing in a rear hallway, directed Mitch to follow him into an interior room that had but one small window near the ceiling. A glowing space heater rapidly warmed the air and the two men took off their hats and overcoats. Strong bulbs in a tasseled floor lamp cast a decent light. Sparsely furnished, the small room held an upholstered armchair, a worn sofa, several kitchen chairs, a frayed carpet and against faded striped wallpaper a framed photograph of Sweden's King Carl Gustav looking slightly apologetic above the rows of medals crowding his diplomatic sash.

Mitch and Ned sparred at first, feeling each other out as they traded biographical bits and groped about for mutual interests. Ned, it seemed, grew up in Cincinnati, schooled at Ohio State University and had been with the CIA ever since graduation. He had a son and daughter in college now, but was divorced. Intelligence work and family life didn't mix.

A man of about fifty, he used words sparingly, evinced little or no sense of humor and failed to respond to Mitch's efforts to lighten the mood. By the time they had shed their suit jackets, accommodating to the growing heat in the room, Mitch had concluded that he had drawn a tough one as his case officer. He hoped their success as a pair would not depend on the empathy between them or this venture would start off dead on its feet.

"Let's get clear on our communications first," said Ned. He sat on one of the hard wooden chairs, knees crossed, one leg swinging. "We have two safe places to meet indoors, this house and my apartment in Copenhagen. I'd be too exposed entering your place, but you can come in the front, back or side entrance of my apartment house. I'll brief you on that.

"Actually we could have met at my place tonight, but I wanted you to become familiar with this house—always our best spot when we need to be extra cautious."

Someone knocked on their door and Ned said, "Come in, Tage." A gray-haired man with spectacles brought steaming mugs of coffee, shook hands warmly during the brief introduction, then looked Mitch over carefully before leaving the room to the two Americans.

"Tage is our landlord. He has two sons in the United States. We rent this room and access to it from him. He has your name. You can trust him."

Ned sampled the coffee and set the mug on an end table near his chair. "We'll meet once a week, changing the day by one each time. This is a Thursday, so next week we'll meet Wednesday night. Never on weekends. Too many conflicting social events that would have to be ducked."

Sometimes in daylight, he said, weather permitting, they'd meet behind the hedges of a secluded rose garden in Kongens Have, a large park not far from the center of Copenhagen. When spring came, they'd best meet on one of the many trails of Dyrehaven, a deer forest near the Klampenborg S-train station. He handed Mitch a sheet of paper. "Instructions for contacting me in an emergency." They should be learned, then the paper burned.

His name, it turned out, was Rudolph Voth and his cover was as assistant political officer at the American embassy in Copenhagen. He should be called there only from a pay phone and only in a crisis. In that event, Mitch's name was Hal Norcross.

"On the substance of our job," he said, "I'm up-to-date on everything you told us in Philadelphia and Langley. Now I'd like to hear anything you've learned since joining Lorikeet here, your trip included."

"First," said Mitch, "you know I recognized you. You tailed me when I came here for a job interview in September. Does that mean Lorikeet has been under investigation for some time?"

"Not long." He was obviously miffed at being detected. "We were after another matter."

"What exactly? . . . To pick me up at the airport, you had to have had word from inside Lorikeet that I was coming."

"Oh?" A snide inflection. "That doesn't concern us now." The agent brushed the air with his hand. "Let's get on with your report."

Mitch told everything he'd learned that seemed relevant, from Captain Tyson's remark about Nicias's Naxos mansion to Bones Elger's huddle with yakuza chiefs at the Broadway Ginza in Hong Kong and Mitch's own narrow escapes a few hours later. "So naturally I'm worried," he said when he finished. "I'm not anxious to wind up full of holes. Neither is Mona. We thought we might rate some protection."

"That might be difficult. There are a lot of risks in this business." Ned swung his crossed leg briskly. "Providing you and Captain Harkinson with bodyguards would bust our budget here. You've heard of austerity in federal programs since the Reagan deficits, I'm sure."

"Are you saying flatly 'no can do'?"

"I'm saying it's doubtful for you and out of the question for Mona Harkinson. She's on Russell's suspect list."

"Oh Christ, are you guys still wasting time on that screwy theory?" It surprised him to see how quickly he rose to the defense of the woman who'd just walked out on him. "You might as well suspect Mother Teresa."

"We have cause," insisted Ned, unsmiling. He seemed bored or indisposed, perhaps both.

Mitch missed sardonic Russell Upchurch. The headquarters officer would have picked up on the Teresa remark and given it a wry twist of some kind.

"Captain Harkinson has gone to work for Wasif Zabib who is himself a prime suspect." Ned ticked off the fact in his flat midwestern accent. "That raises further doubts about her."

"Doesn't it occur to you that Zabib might be setting her up for something? For that matter, he might be setting me up too."

Ned nodded. "Yes, we know that's a possibility." The agent finished off his coffee, got up, hooked his thumbs in his belt and paced about for a few moments. "Mitch, your story of Elger and the Yamaguchi leaders corroborates what we get from other sources. The yakuza appear to be putting together an international syndicate for maritime crime. With their know-how, that could be formidable and very dangerous." Yet he seemed disinterested as he took a seat on the torn sofa where bits of stuffing protruded from the cheap fabric.

"Russell sent me a long message just before I came over here tonight," he said. "Langley, reacting to Harkinson's new job, has a specific task for you. As we understand it, the *Zabibian* is returning to the Persian Gulf . . ."

"Arabian. In the trade, we all call it the Arabian Gulf." He was annoyed by Ned's leg. It swung with the precision of a metronome.

"All right, to the Arabian Gulf, and then wherever the tanker goes, Harkinson will have charge of her?"

"Right. Mona is flying to South Africa next week and going aboard via helicopter. She'll have two weeks as a passenger to get the hang of the ship before she takes over in the Gulf."

"Mitch, Russell wants you to try to get a charter to Japan for the *Zabibian.*"

"Well, she's . . ." He was about to say that his assistant already had negotiated a year-long charter that would shuttle the flagship tanker between the Arabian Gulf and Tokyo Bay, but instead he decided to see where Ned was heading. "Why? What's the pitch?"

"We have it from a good source that the Yamaguchi had planned a scam of some kind for Captain Harkinson's next voyage—if she got one."

"That doesn't make much sense. Mona's first trip after the oil spill would be bound to attract media attention. Why pick a ship that'll get a lot of publicity?"

"Don't ask me. Frankly, as you know, this crime business is not my field." Ned sounded put upon. "We're just helping the sister service. My job involves the Soviets and the KGB." And that, his tone implied, was a task worthy of grown men. "Let's see, if I remember Russell's dispatch correctly, it has to do with prideful yakuza psychology. They're into the revenge bit. Having had a bust

aboard Harkinson's last tanker, they plan to get even and pull off
something big on her next one."

"I might buy that, but why Japan? What difference to the yakuza
where the ship goes?"

"More confidence heading into home waters." Ned's indifference,
Mitch thought, might fetch a yawn from the agent at any moment.
"That's conjecture on my part. As I say, on this operation I'm just
carrying out the wishes of Russell and whoever else at Langley."

Why this agent irritated him as much as he did, Mitch didn't
know, but he was of no mind to let him have an easy victory. "Much
as I want to help, no way can I guarantee a charter to Japan in this
bitch-awful market."

Ned folded his arms and stared at him. "Russell says the next
charter has to be to Japan. We have to throw out a solid lure for the
Elger-Yamaguchi combine."

"Listen, man, it doesn't work that way." Mitch felt the intolerance
of the professional for the uninformed. "I can't pick and choose, not
in this market. Let's say Mobil or Shell or Octagon wants to lift
265,000 tons of crude from Bahrain to the transshipment anchorage
south of Galveston. Suppose their charter man wants the *Zabibian*
for the job. I'm supposed to turn down a charter worth more than a
million? That's insanity and in the time it takes you to pronounce the
word, Zabib would fire my ass out of Lorikeet."

"You could find a good plausible excuse." Ned was unmoved. "I
do it all the time."

"Not in a free market, you don't. It would be suicide for any
charter guy who got caught."

"Don't get caught." At last Ned smiled thinly. "Russell says you
have tanker-chartering savvy and that you'll figure a way to do it. He
has great respect for your ability."

"Flattery's out of fashion. It went out with the puka shell necklace. . . . Listen, Ned, would you mind stopping that goddam leg.
It's bugging me."

"Sorry." Ned shrugged. "I'm going to have some rum in my next
cup of coffee. How about a drink?"

"Scotch and water, but that won't work either."

The agent went to the adjacent kitchen, spoke in Swedish to Tage
who soon brought in the beverages. Again the landlord scrutinized
Mitch as if to fix him in memory.

"Isn't it possible," asked Ned when Tage had left the room, "for you to let the shipbrokers know you want a charter to Japan?"

"Sure. But so do a hundred other tanker owners." Now, Mitch knew, he was continuing the game purely out of perversity. "If that's news, so is winning football at Penn State."

"What if you offered to charter out the *Zabibian* at a price considerably lower than the going market?" Ned sat down again on the aging sofa.

"I'd have some takers. I'd also be fired." Mitch took a swallow of the Scotch. It was a smooth brand.

"Not if a third party made up the difference." Ned's crossed leg was chopping air again. Boredom on a seesaw.

"No, but that would cost one or two hundred grand."

"We think we know a party who believes a *Zabibian* voyage to Japan right now would be worth two hundred thousand."

Mitch leaned back in the old armchair. "So much for your tight budget crap. I always heard you guys had lots of money to go with those phony I.D. cards." He savored the good Scotch again. "Okay, but it would take a lot of finagling to slip the money in without the charterer, the shipbroker and our finance department tracing it. Also to keep the broker and the tanker owners from blabbing about the huge bargain they got."

"We think that could be worked out. If you're agreeable, let me get back to Russell. Meet me at eight tomorrow night at my place and we'll lay out the scenario. Only take an hour."

Ned drilled Mitch on his apartment's address, phone number and means of access, coached him on how to approach the building. "So, agreed?"

"Not so fast. It sounds like you're sending my woman straight into big trouble." The phrase "my woman" sounded strange tonight. Perhaps he should have said "my once and possibly future woman." "Is she to be offered for target practice or what?"

"No, no. We would arrange for her protection." Ned yawned, quickly placed his hand at his mouth to mask the final exhalation.

"Boring, isn't it? All that life, death and survival stuff." Mitch was furious.

"Pardon me, please. It's just that . . ."

"I know. This is not your line." He took a swallow of the Scotch.

"The *Zabibian* only carries twenty-eight officers and crew. How are you going to put bodyguards aboard without their being spotted?"

"Did I say anything about bodyguards?" The leg was swinging again. "I said we would arrange for her protection."

"You do that with mirrors, I suppose?" Mitch wondered if he could appeal to Russell for a new case officer.

"We don't take protection lightly. There are ways and means. If we pledge to protect Captain Harkinson, the chances of her being harmed are minimal."

"Minimal," Mitch scoffed. "That's one of those bureaucratic words whose meaning is minimal."

"Not at all." The sarcasm left Ned undisturbed. He actually looked as if he might yawn again. "I mean that the captain would face little more than the average risks of any supertanker voyage. At any rate, my place at eight tomorrow night. . . . That's about it for the first night. You have twenty-five minutes to catch the last boat to Copenhagen." He looked at his watch as his leg continued to beat time. "I'm staying here for the night."

"Hey, you haven't told me a thing about what the Agency and the FBI have found out." Mitch felt cheated. "Don't I get some feedback?"

"I told you what we think the Elger-yakuza gang is up to. The evidence and where it comes from, you don't need to know. That's always Agency policy. Don't worry, any information you need, you'll get—if we have it."

He helped Mitch on with his jacket and sheepskin coat, escorted him to the door. Ten minutes later Mitch was aboard the last hydrofoil from Malmö and engaged in a hot inner debate over his refusal to tell Ned that the *Zabibian* already was chartered for a year of voyages from the Gulf to Japan. A crummily unfair way to start out helping the Agency, contended his upright-and-duty self. Just what that bored ass Ned deserved, argued his intolerant side. You want Ned to lie to you by omission? asked Mr. Upright. Don't think he doesn't, snapped Mr. Vexed. You should have given Ned all the facts. No operation can succeed on false information, lectured Mr. Upright. Aw, shit, said Mr. Vexed, we'll tell him tomorrow night that we just landed a long-term charter to Japan and thus get credit for a big fast coup.

The argument still echoed an hour later when he returned to his loft and began turning up the heat against the growing cold outside.

The phone rang as he stood before the open refrigerator, trying to decide between fried eggs, hot chocolate, peach pastry and cold roast chicken as his late snack.

"Hello."

The phone clicked dead. Just as he turned away, it rang once more.

"Hello."

"Mitch?" It was Mona.

"In only twenty-four hours you forget how I sound?"

"I've been calling you for two hours. Are you all right?"

"Yeah, I guess so, if you call feeling lonely, shitty and rejected all right. My woman walked out on me, in case you hadn't heard. . . . When was your last phone call to me?"

"Oh, about ten minutes ago. Why?"

"Somebody called a few seconds before you just did, but hung up when he or she heard my voice. . . . What's up, lady?"

"Mitch, I feel awful about last night." The low rich voice poured into his blood stream. "I want to apologize."

"Accepted."

"Not over the phone. I want to apologize in person. I'm at the hotel. May I come over and try to set things right?"

"Not unless you get here within eight minutes. That's when we pull up the drawbridge."

"I'm on my way." Now her voice had the lilt of music. "Hold the boiling oil."

It turned out that twelve minutes passed before she rang the door-bell and he punched the signal that permitted her to enter the elevator. When she came through his open door and into his open arms, she buried her head on his shoulder. Her cheek was cold and frosty air still clung to the fur collar of her coat. Before she drew away, she framed his face in her hands and kissed him slowly, gravely.

"Mitch, can I move in with you tomorrow?"

"Procrastinating lady. What's wrong with tonight?" A whistle blew merrily somewhere inside, at once dissolving the day-old chemical traffic jam.

"I'd like to stay with you tonight, but I'll bring my things over in the morning while you're at work."

He fixed two Irish coffees while she took off her coat and when he returned from the kitchen, Mona sat cross-legged on the long yellow corduroy sofa. She wore a gray turtleneck sweater and jeans and she looked at him with eyes brimming with love.

"I was a frightful bitch last night." She sipped at the mug of coffee, cream and whisky he handed her. "And to act that way with you when you've been more understanding than any man in my life, well, it was cruddy and shameful and inexcusable."

"All forgiven."

"Thanks." This was not easy for her. "You know, I spent all morning thinking, not about the upcoming press conference, but about why I acted like I did." She became pensive, staring at the mug in her hand. "And I decided, Mitch, that the whole thing had nothing to do with you. Nothing. It had ten percent to do with my own stinking ego and ninety percent to do with my hurt over Chrissy."

"I kind of figured that." He was tempted to go on, but checked himself. This, my friend, he told himself, is a time to shut up and listen.

"It just devastated me that Christine would do a thing like that." Her eyes moistened. "Such a terribly hostile act toward me. Imagine a girl throwing herself at her mother's lover. So dopey me, enraged at Chris, I take it out on you. Talk about misplaced anger!"

"Thanks, Mona. I hurt all day, but it's draining away like a—like a—oh I don't know. Suddenly it feels all springtime again."

"I feel like crying." Instead she blew softly on the mug of hot Irish coffee and looked at him with moist gray eyes. "I don't deserve you."

"That's your father talking, baby. You deserve it all."

"I feel I should apologize some more. It was such a hateful way to act."

"You've said it all already—and right to the point. We're back to square fourteen."

"What's fourteen?" She was holding back sobs now.

"That's the one where we decided I was your man and you were my woman."

"Yes, yes. Sweet square fourteen." She laughed and wept simultaneously. "Holy Jesus, I'm so happy. And right now the only way to tell you truly how I feel about you is with the guitar. Should I go back and get it from the hotel?"

"Save it for tomorrow night. It's cold out. We may get the first snow soon." He sank beside her on the corduroy sofa, took the coffee mug gently from her and folded her to his chest. Their kiss was long and sweet and then she nestled against him with her head on his shoulder. The fragrance of her hair filled the air around him.

"What should I do about Chrissy, Mitch? I just don't know how to handle it."

"Well, we both agreed it was no big deal, right? Hostile toward you, yeah, but you've got to realize she's at the age when she has to rebel. Her father's not handy, so she takes it out on you. Also you're a very, very successful woman and she wants to show you she can match you—in the only way she can right now."

"Yes, I've thought of that. But the question now is what to do."

"I favor the three of us talking about it when you get back." He caressed her forehead. "You could make some light cracks about it, but be firm too, so she gets the message. Then we take her to some shows, get her a date and by the time she goes back to school, it will be forgotten."

"I guess you're right. Much as I dislike facing her on it, going around carrying the secret, pretending you hadn't told me, would be worse." She kissed him and traced a finger about his face. "Can we go to bed now?"

"Not quite yet. I saw my CIA contact tonight and I've got some good news and some bad news. The good news is that they pretty much corroborate our suspicions—that Elger and some others have teamed up with Japanese yakuza for maritime crime. The bad news is that they want to set you up to draw fire." He told of his conversation with Ned.

"It's so ridiculous to keep suspecting me." Her glow faded. "Really, you know, it's discouraging."

"What bothers me more is the refusal to give us some protection. We'll just have to devise some of our own."

"Let's worry about that tomorrow. I have only five more nights with you and one of them is half gone. Now can we go to bed?"

For an answer, he stood up and pulled her to her feet. Leaving the drinks behind them, they walked toward the bedroom.

"I want to hear the wind sing around the big skylight," she said, "and I want all my knots to come untied and go away."

As they entered the bedroom hand in hand, he thought how

deeply he felt about this woman and how far they'd come in so short a time.

"I'm grateful," she said, "that nothing has changed between us."

But of course something had changed. A brilliant petal had fallen from the bloom of early love and the first memory had been laid away in that chest where lovers store old hurts, scars and grudges. Nothing was changeless, he thought, and that was all right too.

16

The long fat tanker eased through ocean swells under a black dome of sky that held endless empires of stars, some crowded like grains of sand on a phosphorescent beach, some pulsing in solitary brilliance, others gathered in geometric designs that had been known and named for centuries. Light from a cradle moon glimmered on a maze of pipes that crisscrossed the ship's otherwise bald deck and gave it the deceptive appearance of a traveling junkyard. The huge ship, stretching longer and wider than three football fields laid end to end, curled foam at its rounded bow as it drove through the water at fourteen knots.

The *Zabibian,* a sturdy ten-year-old very large crude carrier of 267,000 deadweight tons, rode low in the water. More than two million barrels of oil filled her great tanks to capacity. As she made the three-week haul from the Arabian Gulf to Japan's Tokyo Bay, the VLCC represented a tidy fortune. For what it cost to build her in a Korean shipyard, one could have endowed a small university. Tsuno Oil Co., owner of the liquid cargo in the tanker's belly, valued the crude at $25,000,000. It cost Lorikeet $13,000 a day just for the bunker fuel when *Zabibian* was under way and only a gaggle of millionaires could afford the total expenses of this single voyage.

But finances were far from the mind of Mona Harkinson this night as she paced about the covered bridge, leaned over the radar scopes with their sweeping beams of light, scanned distant seas with power-ful marine binoculars, chatted with the helmsman and chief mate or walked to the starboard wing to feel the warm night wind on her cheeks and gaze down at the dark waves slapping the hull far below her.

She was thinking of the voyage, her first in command of the Lori-keet flagship, and how smoothly it was going. The ship was nine nights out from the Saudi loading arms in the Arabian Gulf and was approaching the long Strait of Malacca between Sumatra and Malay-sia, about midway of the trip of 6,700 nautical miles. At the moment the *Zabibian* was pushing through the Great Channel separating the Nicobar Islands from the northern tip of Sumatra.

Several miles to her left, Mona could see the lights of another ship. This, she knew, would be the first of many she and the crew would see in the next few days as they cruised down the Strait of Malacca and through the narrow Singapore Strait into the South China Sea. The *Zabibian* plowed the main sealane traveled by tankers carrying Arab oil to the power plants and factories of Japan, the industrial wizard that had to import all but a fraction of its fuel. Every hour or so through the Malacca Strait and every few minutes through the Singapore Strait they could expect to encounter another ship, many of them tankers going to or coming from the island empire. The straits acted as funnels for vessels crossing the wide Indian Ocean on one side, as *Zabibian* had just done, and the South China Sea on the other.

Since this was the first ship Mona and her men had sighted in several days, it had stirred mild interest—anything to break the mo-notony of cruising untroubled tropic seas in fair weather. Mona and Bill Muldoon, the chief mate she had hired away from Michaelson and Lygdamis, had first spotted the ship as a blip on the radar be-yond the twenty-mile circle. When it came within visual range, they speculated, along with Manny Rodriguez, the Chilean helmsman, on the type. Muldoon thought container vessel, Mona opted for tanker and Rodriguez guessed refrigerator ship.

"Let's find out," said Mona. It was good to have company again after the vast torpid emptiness of the Indian Ocean. She picked up the bulkhead phone that connected directly with the radio room. Arno Joahannes was off duty, but Bert Takahara, his assistant, manned the post this eight-to-twelve night watch. "Bert, see if you can raise the ship that's off our port bow. We want to know what kind she is."

"Right, Captain." Bert, still enamored of life at sea despite several weeks of humdrum duty, courted responsibility on these night watches.

"It's the *Cape Lamwood*," he reported a few minutes later, "out of Southampton, Master Gregory Knowlton. He wants to talk to you, Captain."

Mona took up the voice radio microphone, an extension of the communications-room apparatus, which hung directly behind the helm. After a few stuttering misses, she connected with the *Lamwood*'s master.

"Good evening, Captain Knowlton. This is Captain M. S. Harkinson aboard the *Zabibian*. We're about three miles off your port bow."

"I've had you in sight. Tanker, aren't you?"

"Yes. We're lifting Saudi-Arabian crude to Tokyo Bay. And you?"

"Containers. Mostly textiles, Taiwan to Le Havre. . . . Harkinson? Lorikeet Tankers, Copenhagen?"

"That's right."

"Oh, you're that famous Yank woman captain then?"

Mona laughed. "Some say infamous, Captain."

"Not me. I lost steering once in a storm off Hatteras on your Carolina coast. Bloody night that was. If it wasn't for a wizard salvage tug, I'd of rammed the beach. . . . How's the weather in the Indian Ocean?"

"Like a pond. And the weather reports say more of the same for a week anyway. How about the Strait?"

"Some blowing at the other end. At this end you can fill your teacup to the rim and not spill a drop."

Unseen strangers in the night, marked only by running lights and the white pinpoints at portholes of their vessels, the captains soon ran out of chitchat and signed off with mutual wishes of good luck.

A few minutes later Takahara came up from the radio room on the deck below. "Message from Copenhagen, Captain." She was standing at a center window, watching the tanker's bow rise and dip in gentle rhythm and feeling the steady vibration of the great ship. Bert grinned as he handed her the slip of paper. It had become a nightly game, this delivery of the few masked words shortly before the home office closed for the day.

"Thanks, Bert." She spread the paper on the wide window ledge and snapped on a small flashlight she carried in a pocket of her jeans.

Capt. Harkinson, *Zabibian:*
ZPV MPPL TNBTIJOH UPOJHIU
NJUDI
1545 GMT

It was a simple cipher. A career cryptographer might take all of a minute to find the key and perhaps several more to transpose the note into plain text. Bert Takahara, who knew nothing of codes and ciphers, actually had spent a half hour searching for the key the first night. Now he unscrambled most messages on sight. The captain and the fledgling radio assistant played the game. She usually pretended that she didn't know that he knew the contents and he maintained the fiction of his ignorance. Actually, marking his respect for his captain, Bert Takahara never deciphered a message until after he had delivered a copy into her hands. She, after all, was entitled as the lover of the sender, while as a friend he rated a notch lower.

Mona, who had helped concoct the cipher her last night in Copenhagen, now transposed without bothering with a pencil, merely retreating one letter in the alphabet for each letter of the cipher, so that a Z became a Y and a P an O:

YOU LOOK SMASHING TONIGHT
MITCH

She walked through the open door where Takahara, waiting on the wing, breathed in the sultry tropic air of this latitude just a few degrees above the equator. This too had become part of their game. As the only two people aboard who knew Mitchell Donahey more than casually, Mona and Bert shared an interest in chatting about the man. Or more accurately, Mona liked to hear the sound of Mitch's name and Bert liked to see her face light up when she mentioned his friend and former boss.

They moved a few feet away from the bridge house, yet still distant from the ordinary seaman who stood watch at the end of the wing that extended out from the ship high above the water.

"Just a nice compliment tonight, Bert," she said. "Mitch is a thoughtful man. Of course, he's also a shrewdy who knows that women can't resist flattery."

"I figured since the message was short, it had to be sweet."

"I trust you're thoughtful with your woman. You do have one back in Honolulu, don't you?"

"Yeah, but she's the considerate one." He lifted a foot encased in a soiled worn running shoe. "She gave me these to wear in last year's Honolulu marathon. Good for shipboard too."

"Tell me about her." Mona leaned her bare arms on the high steel plate that served as a windbreak. She was wearing a short-sleeved olive-drab shirt with her dungarees.

"She's a local girl." He palmed his straight black hair as he considered. "You've seen those brown-skinned girls in the Hawaiian tourist ads? They swish along a beach with a plumeria bloom in the hair. That's Lee."

"Part Japanese like you?"

"No. She's got Chinese, Filipino, Portuguese and some Hawaiian in her. Mitch met her a couple of times. He says she should be the permanent Miss Hawaii. . . . But hey, Captain, don't think I won't check out those European women when I get my first time off."

They talked for a few more minutes and then Mona said in parting, "Bert, I appreciate your keeping Mitch's notes to yourself."

"No problem. Of course, I do have to log them for Sparks."

"Oh, I don't care about Arno. We're good friends." She laughed. "I'm sure he deciphers Mitch's messages the minute he comes on duty."

Back inside the bridge Mona found Bill Muldoon bent over the chart table, plotting the latest hourly position fix from LORAN and the satellite navigation system. She had a warm feeling about Muldoon who, she had sensed, did not approve of her when she first had come aboard the old *Yandoon Princess* in Nigeria. A traditionalist, he balked at the idea of females aboard a tanker, especially in the role of his superior officer. But she had earned Bill's respect during those hours when the *Princess* lost steering and wallowed out of control in wild weather off the Delaware coast. And like Mario Didati, Bill had let her know it. "You did your best, Captain," the chief mate had told her in Philadelphia that first night after the disaster, "and for my money, your best was better than most masters I've known."

A uniformly cheerful and accommodating man, though one not given to dishing out compliments, Muldoon had accepted quickly when Mona called him to relay Zabib's offer of a chief-mate's job with Lorikeet. Now he and Mona shared a loyalty of mutual respect and the easy kinship of shipmates who had gone through an ordeal together on another vessel.

"Bill, how did you know that was a container ship we passed?"

Muldoon laid down a pair of dividers and straightened up from the chart table. "Captain, when you've been at sea as long as I have, you get a sixth sense about ships at night." His seamed ruddy face crinkled in a smile. "That's what I tell them ashore. Out here, the honest answer is that I guessed."

"Good guess. What's your honest sense about our own ship? Do you like the *Zabibian?*"

Muldoon made a circle with thumb and forefinger. "Just right, this one. I like the way she rides, the way she acted in that dirty weather off the coast of Africa." Muldoon had come aboard with Mona by helicopter off Durban while Captain Jules Yvres still had charge of the tanker.

"You think the chief is happy with it?" The chief engineer, Risto Topelius, was a shy awkward Finn whose embarrassment in ordinary personal encounters often propelled his limbs into all manner of odd geometries.

"Who would know with Risto? The man gets so embarrassed, it's painful. But he knows that engine room, Captain. You don't have to worry about Risto."

"How about the brake on No. 2 lifeboat?" During lifeboat drill that afternoon, the starboard-covered boat had dropped some fifty feet into the water instead of stopping at deck level. The brake had failed.

"The second engineer and the bosun are working on it. We'll have it back in order by noon tomorrow. I'll guarantee that, Captain."

After another turn about the bridge, Mona went down to her cabin on the deck below, leaving Muldoon in charge. She was completing the day's paper work a half hour later when a knock came at her door and Bert Takahara entered with her permission.

"Big night." He laid another ciphered message on her desk. "I came right over." The radio room was located on the same deck as the captain's quarters. "This one's marked urgent."

"What does he say this time?" A wry smile played about her lips.

"I have no idea, Captain." Noting her skeptical, though not censorial, expression, he protested, "Honest. I didn't even try to guess at the cipher."

"That's okay, Bert." She was fond of Mitch's friend.

She turned her attention to the paper as soon as Takahara had left and closed the door behind him.

Capt. Harkinson, *Zabibian.* URGENT
CCZWSC QSPLNYQ DYUHPQ RSHXSYGW
NGWYICOH

1558 GMT

Since she knew that this time the simple subtraction of a letter would produce only gibberish, Mona used the more complicated scheme that she and Mitch had devised in Copenhagen for messages marked urgent. While even this arrangement would yield its secret to a professional cryptographer without undue sweat, it would baffle ordinary readers who did not care to spend a day at trial and error. Mona transposed it quickly by subtracting one letter of the alphabet from the first letter of each word, adding two to the second letter, subtracting three from the third, adding four to the fourth, then repeating the cycle for words of more than four letters. Worked out with the aid of a pencil, the message read:

BEWARE PUMPMAN CARLOS QUEBRADA
MITCHELL

Mona had made a point of talking with each crewman at some length as she made her rounds of the tanker and she'd had two get-acquainted conversations with Quebrada, a fat Mexican who managed to convey an impression of hearty corruption. She could imagine him as the owner of a squalid cathouse in a dusty Mexican City shantytown or perhaps as a motorcycle cop cheerfully extorting sheafs of peso notes from motorists unfortunate enough to drive through his sector. She guessed that Quebrada would pay bribes as willingly as he took them on the assumption that as the Mexican system worked, so worked the world. He had an easy disposition, joked a lot and could repair most any piece of machinery connected with the pumping of oil. Also beneath his sunny exterior, Mona thought she detected a streak of brutality.

This was the first note of caution from Mitch in the three weeks since she had flown out of Copenhagen to intercept the tanker off

South Africa. Wanting to explore the warning further with Mitch, she placed a call to his home in Copenhagen over the marine satellite radiophone. The number, said the operator, did not answer. Mona would try again the next day.

She called up Quebrada's record from the personnel file in her desk-top computer. He had sailed on tankers for twenty years, had a wife and five children at home in Vera Cruz and had once been jailed for a week in Rotterdam after a tavern brawl. No hint of criminal activity. She closed the file, turned off the computer and walked to the window overlooking the long deck and its interlocking network of pipes.

Below her a lone figure walked along the gunwale toward the bow. Arno Joahannes took his nightly constitutional with the regularity of the beat of the engine. At midnight, weather permitting, the Swedish communications officer made five circuits of the main deck or roughly two miles. Well, she thought as she watched him adjust his stride to the slight roll of the tanker, perhaps it was time to take Bert Takahara, Bill Muldoon and Arno into her confidence. She would talk that over with Mitch when she reached him tomorrow.

Mitch followed Ned's instructions for their second emergency meeting in as many nights. Wearing his sheepskin coat in the cold clear air, he walked from his apartment to the Kongens Nytorv plaza, took a cab to the somber old Carlsberg brewery on Ny Carlsbergvej, walked two blocks toward Sonder Boulevard, turned right to the first street crossing, circled the block, made sure he was not followed, then walked down a half-dozen cement steps to the side basement entry of a three-story brick-and-stone apartment house.

He entered the door that Ned had assured him he would unlock five minutes before Mitch's scheduled arrival. Sliding the bolt back in place, he walked beneath some heating pipes suspended from the ceiling, passed through a laundry area and paused at the foot of a flight of stairs leading to the vestibule of the apartments. Not hearing or seeing anyone, he walked up to the tiled lobby. The door of the first-floor unit stood ajar. Mitch entered, closing the door behind him.

"Right on time." Ned's first remark grated. He sounded like a teacher commending a normally tardy first-grader.

The agent took his coat, then led him into the sitting room that had the stilted fussy air of a nineteenth-century Sunday parlor. They drew up heavy lion-pawed chairs upholstered in faded cardinal velours beneath a chandelier of stained glass. An upright piano stood against one of the walls that seemed permeated by decades of cooking and tobacco odors.

Ned, apologizing for the dated appearance on Mitch's first visit, had said he rented the apartment furnished. By now, however, Mitch knew that in truth the agent cared little for his surroundings.

"Drink."

"No, thanks." He disliked this place.

"Did you get word to Harkinson about Quebrada?" Already Ned's crossed leg was swinging nervously.

"Yes. Bert Takahara receipted for the message to our communications man and I know Bert would take it to Mona right away."

"You're sure your Copenhagen operator can't decipher the messages?"

"As I told you, he doesn't have time." Mitch explained again. "I stand by while he sends it and then take the copy back from him. This is old stuff to him. He sends commercial codes every day and Zabib uses a cipher for some of his key people in the fleet."

"Good. I've already given you our congratulations for getting the charter to Japan, but Russell wants me to add his personal thanks." Ned sounded reluctant, almost as though he had tried to dissuade Upchurch from paying further compliments. "Russell says to tell you specifically that your Norwegian assistant couldn't have done better himself." Ned glanced sharply at Mitch. "Is that some kind of inside joke between you two?"

"Search me." So the wily Upchurch had discovered that the long-term charter to Tsuno Oil of Yokohama had been made a full week before the Agency asked Mitch to somehow wangle a charter to Japan for the *Zabibian?* And Russell was letting Mitch know he knew without letting Ned in on the news. Mitch was beginning to enjoy the spinning of these wheels within wheels. "Anyway, the charter saved the Agency a hundred grand or two, so you guys owe me."

"I have three things to tell you tonight." Ned leaned back in the old lion-pawed chair like a king on a throne. "The first is as we anticipated. We now have definite word from our sources that the

Elger-Yamaguchi group intends to use the *Zabibian* on this voyage for a venture of some kind."

"What kind of venture?"

"We don't know."

"Well, is Mona in any danger? How about the ship?"

"I can't help you on specifics." Ned's tone was remote, dry. "But, of course, there's danger any time the yakuza is involved."

Mitch waited, but Ned said nothing further. The silence angered Mitch. The agent tossed his little grenade, then sat back in insulated safety, letting others worry about lethal shards and maimed limbs.

"You must have some idea of what's cooking. Some little hint." Not trusting Ned, he began to imagine reasons why the agent would withhold helpful information.

"Except for the identity of our sources, you know absolutely everything we do." The crossed leg swung as if timed. "We want a safe and sound Captain Harkinson as much as you do."

"Come off it, Ned. The last I heard from you, she was still a suspect—idiocy of idiocies."

"That's the second thing I had to tell you." Ned put on one of his rare smiles, a thin little arrangement at the corners of his mouth. "Russell says you should know that Captain Harkinson has been dropped from the suspect list."

"Let's hear it for common sense, gang." Mitch clapped his hands. "Big victory, long awaited, over the drones of bureaucracy. To what beacon of enlightenment do we owe this discovery?"

"Your guess is as good as mine."

"Ned, if information were money, you'd be the world's wealthiest miser."

"Need-to-know, need-to-know." Ned sounded bored again. If the agent found his work so tedious, why, Mitch wondered, didn't he take up potting or stamp-collecting.

"And the third thing you had to tell me?" Mitch asked with some apprehension. Ned had a way of keeping his most toxic offerings until last.

"This is not certain, Mitch, but we have indications that you're in danger here." Ned paused. "We think Elger-Yamaguchi intends to do you harm here in Copenhagen. Whether they want to kill you or kidnap you, we're not sure."

Mitch felt a kind of quick tremor along his nervous system, but the news did not alarm him. He had been wary ever since the dual attempts on his life a month earlier in Hong Kong, had taken care entering stores, offices and homes, had noted escape routes from his apartment and had been cautious moving into new surroundings. Actually, he rather enjoyed the sharpened awareness and tension. It put an edge to life, spiced the routine of ordinary days and relegated the lazy yawn to memory.

"If they give me a choice," he said, "I'd prefer the kidnapping. The other route strikes me as a dead end."

"Spare me the puns, please." Ned shook his head. "I work with a man at the embassy who puns all day long."

"I take it I'm supposed to go it alone with no protection from the Agency. Just like Mona aboard ship."

"We have a deal with one of the officers on the *Zabibian* to look out for Captain Harkinson. As for you . . ."

"Christ, Ned, you could have let me know." His temper flared again. "I've spent some nights worrying about her."

"Frankly, I couldn't tell you earlier because I was just informed myself today that we'd made a deal."

Mitch was not sure he believed the CIA man. "What's the guy's name?"

"I was not told."

"Hell, man, if something happens aboard, I want to know who to contact." He drew back from the implication of what he was saying. "It makes no sense to leave me in the dark."

"I understand. I'll see what Russell says. . . . As for you, we are starting a watch on your place tomorrow from across the street. In case you need help in a hurry, we're working out of Apartment 2 directly across the canal on Nyhavn." He gave the street and phone number. "Since your building has no rear or side entry, we need cover the front only."

"But at the office or getting around town, I'm on my own. Is that it?"

"I'm afraid so, Mitch. With the budget cuts, we've had to curtail everywhere."

But Mitch surmised that men and women in a hundred cities around the world were getting twenty-four-hour Agency protection. It was a matter of priorities. The loss of a walk-in shipbroker with no clout would hardly make the intelligence digest which the CIA laid on the President's desk every morning.

"Do you have a gun?"

"Nope, don't own one."

"After your experience in Hong Kong, that's not very smart, Mitch." Ned got to his feet. "You can borrow one of mine." He left the room, returned a few moments later with a black pistol and a box of cartridges. "Colt .38. You want me to check you out on it?"

"No need." Mitch placed the gun and cartridges in his jacket pockets and at once felt encumbered and ill at ease. Not since Viet Nam days had he carried a weapon. "Anything else?"

Ned shook his head and to Mitch's relief did not offer him a drink again. Mitch had had enough for one night of this stuffy room with walls redolent of tobacco and cabbage fumes from decades past. Ned called a taxi but gave instructions to pick up the passenger several blocks away at the intersection of Ny Carlsbergvej and Enghavevej.

Mitch had the cab drop him at Kongens Nytorv, the circular plaza located two blocks from his apartment. Exercising caution after the new warning, he walked near the curbs away from dark doorways. The temperature had dropped to below freezing and his footsteps echoed sharply in the still air. It felt strange to be going armed along the tranquil streets of Copenhagen. He paused at the head of his block, but saw no one on the cobbled lanes that ran on either side of the canal with its line of moored sailing ships.

He put his key in the lock of the great oak doors that opened on the small elevator lobby and at that instant he heard the rush of feet behind him—and knew without turning that more than one person ran toward him. He had neglected, in approaching the apartment, to scan the deck of the fishing schooner berthed in the canal across the lane from his doorway. The boat lay perhaps thirty feet away. Obviously someone had hidden behind the vessel's wooden gunwale.

Mitch acted on pure instinct. Instead of turning to look behind him, he kept his eyes on the lock, twisted the key to the right and simultaneously kicked out his leg like a mule. As the door opened, he felt his foot hit bone, probably a shin. A hand snatched at his sheepskin collar, but he yanked himself free, threw himself into the lobby and slammed the door behind him. Mitch pushed his weight against the door and at the same time grabbed for the pistol in his jacket pocket.

But as his hand touched the gun, the door of the single first-floor apartment opened and an elderly man stepped out. He wore a heavy cardigan sweater and his look at Mitch was one of puzzled inquiry. He said something in Danish.

"Sorry, I only speak English." Taking his hand away from the gun, Mitch made motions to indicate that he'd been attacked. "I live in the loft."

The man nodded. Apparently he had understood. He hurried back into his apartment, but soon returned and again spoke rapidly in Danish, at the same time indicating by gesture that he had seen nothing from his window.

It was a half hour later in his own apartment, as Mitch prepared a hot tub, that he found himself trembling. It was one thing, he realized, to be confronted thousands of miles from home by apparent attempts to kill him, but quite another to be the target of assault just outside one's own door. For the second time since infantry days twenty years ago, he felt the chill of fear.

17

With a phone at each ear, he negotiated a charter almost by rote, for his mind was a third of a world away from Copenhagen, hovering above Mona and the *Zabibian* in the long Strait of Malacca. Was she in physical danger? Did she have protection arranged by the Agency? Only with difficulty did he wrench his thoughts back to the job at hand.

Clarkson, the London shipbroker, was dickering for the *Dwyer Ace,* Lorikeet's new handy-sized tanker, on a charter to Diamond Petroleum to shuttle between the Gulf of Mexico transshipment anchorage and U.S. Atlantic ports. Mitch neared a deal by late morning so when another charter opportunity opened, he turned the *Dwyer Ace* negotiations over to his assistant, Sigurd Eyde, while he tracked the new possibility.

Another London broker who specialized in charter deals involving the Russians asked whether the *Lawlor Chief* was open. The 70,000-ton tanker rode at anchor in the eastern Mediterranean awaiting work. Mitch, who had visited the ship when she was docked at Tarragona, Spain, stood ready to deal. The London broker's evasive approach, often a mark of Soviet interest, once again proved an accurate tip-off and Mitch eventually found himself negotiating through the broker with the Novorossiysk Shipping Co. of Novorossiysk, an oil port on the eastern shore of the Black Sea.

Novshipping sailed a fleet of more than a hundred medium-sized tankers and wanted the *Lawlor Chief* on time charter to augment its carrying capacity for oil exports. The Soviets owned a dozen large ocean fleets, chiefly general cargo and fishing vessels but including several hundred tankers. They chartered others from time to time, usually Greek carriers, adhered to western charter party rules and customs, met their bills promptly and had earned a name for tough bargaining.

Staying at his desk with a sandwich through the lunch hour, Mitch braced himself for prolonged haggling, but this time managed to near tentative agreement by mid-afternoon for a year's charter at a fair price. Before giving his final word, Mitch called Wasif Zabib.

"I thought we had covered everything in our discussions on policy," he said, "but here's an angle I overlooked. Do you have anything against chartering to the Russians?"

"On principle, no. But what's up specifically?"

"Novshipping wants the *Lawlor Chief* for a year."

"Come on up. Let's talk about it."

Zabib's bright office on the floor above offered a sweeping view of Copenhagen's harbor. A diagrammatic chart of the world, showing location of Lorikeet tankers by flagged pins, covered one wall. Against another wall stood a glass-enclosed model of the *Zabibian,* the Lorikeet president's favorite tanker. The model stretched a good twelve feet long and showed expert craftsmanship in the smallest detail. Zabib, sitting behind an oval-shaped desk of Danish design, was dressed as usual in the subdued expensive style of a London banker, tailored wool suit of midnight blue, figured silk tie, gold cuff links for his linen shirt.

"Let's have the details," he said.

Mitch described the overture from the London broker. "Novshipping apparently wants to work the *Lawlor Chief* out of Novorossiysk. They'll pay a bit more than the recent time charters in the West." The two men talked about the proposed deal for a few minutes; then Zabib said, "Okay, go ahead. No reason the Greeks should get all the Soviet business."

"We're doing pretty well for this slack market, Zab." An idea had formed and Mitch wanted to put his employer in a good mood before testing it. "Right now Eyde is closing a time charter of the *Dwyer Ace* to Diamond, so along with the *Lawlor Chief* and the *Zabibian,* that's a good chunk of our tonnage that we've put on annual charter recently."

"You've done a top job, Mitch, but then that's what I counted on when I hired you." Zabib, fussing with the sapphire ring on his left hand, basked in his own credit. "By the way, what do you hear from the *Zabibian?*"

Mitch drove into the opening. "Smooth going thus far into the Strait of Malacca. She ought to be off Singapore tomorrow night."

"I'm happy Mona had good weather for her first trip with us." Zabib's eyes dwelled on the model of the big tanker. He was never more content than when talking about his favorite ship and Mitch found it hard to believe that the Jordanian would ever entertain any kind of criminal scheme that would damage or reflect adversely on the prized flagship.

If there were an illicit enterprise slated for the *Zabibian* on her first voyage under Mona Harkinson, it would take place without the knowledge of Wasif Zabib. The Arab shipowner might or might not have been connected with the *Gunnison Bay* swindle. That, Mitch had yet to learn. But he was persuaded now that Zab's only link with the *Zabibian,* aside from ownership, was one of pride and affection. Mitch could see both in those dark eyes caressing the model of the supertanker.

"Did I ever tell you the history of the *Zabibian?*" asked the Lorikeet chief.

"No. She was Norwegian-owned, wasn't she?"

"That's right. She was built ten years ago in Korea by Hyundai in their big shipyard near Ulsan. The Oslo group sailed her for eight years under the name *Vestfjorden.* Two years ago the Oslo syndicate got into financial trouble and I bought her for $58,000,000, a bargain. I've sailed on a lot of ships, but never one as steady, as clean and as responsive as that one."

Mitch psyched himself up. "Zab," he said after a moment, "let me try something on you. It may sound off the wall, but I think it makes sense. You know, I rate pretty well with some of the top guys at Tsuno Oil. They've got *Zabibian* under a year's charter, but I'd like them to take our other VLCCs on time charter too. They place a lot of store on personal contact, so I'd like to go to Yokohama and spend a few days with them."

"You know I leave those details to you, Mitch." Zabib's gaze strayed to the harbor. It was a flawless autumn day and sunlight glinted on the brightwork of a dozen ships. "You do what you think best."

"But I'd also like to combine the Yokohama visit with a voyage on the *Zabibian*. Get to know that ship." Mitch talked faster now. His own gambit embarrassed him. "I could catch the tanker off Singapore tomorrow night and make the trip into Tokyo Bay."

Zabib smiled. "Of course, as you know, a half-dozen airlines can get you to Japan within a day." He shot his cuffs, twisted the ring again. "From Singapore to Tokyo Bay on the *Zabibian* takes about nine days, doesn't it?"

"Sure, the sea trip is a lot slower." Mitch nodded. "But it does accomplish two purposes."

"I'm not at all sure that Captain Harkinson would welcome a romantic interest during her business trip."

Mitch wished he could risk the truth, that it was his desire to protect Mona, not make love to her, that inspired his plan. Instead he merely said, "I think I can handle that."

Zabib thought for a time. "You're very anxious to make that trip, aren't you?" But with his gaze fixed on the sun-splashed harbor, he failed to see Mitch's nod of affirmation. "Well, that might have some pluses for us. Yes, I think . . ." Musing aloud, he suddenly slapped the desk. "Okay, done." He rose from his chair. "Just one amendment."

"Yes?" If this meant some kind of delay, Mitch quickly decided, he somehow must go now anyway. He just could not let Mona risk the rest of this voyage alone.

"We'll both go." Zabib beamed like a sun god.

"Both?" And at once his new belief that Zabib would never join or tolerate a conspiracy aboard his own flagship went into grinding reverse.

"Why not?" A buoyant Zabib strode from behind his desk and clapped Mitch on the shoulder. "Plenty of room. The *Zabibian* has two guest cabins. It'll be nine days of familiarization for both of us. Do you know I've sailed on her for only a single day out of Rotterdam. It's a fact."

The shipowner seemed as elated as a boy and Mitch now wondered if he were in the presence of an accomplished actor. This thought triggered another. With Zabib aboard, the danger to Mona would take on a new dimension.

"Of course, we both have to make it a point to stay out of Mona's way." Zabib bubbled along. "She's got her job to do and the last thing she needs is an owner looking over her shoulder or a lover crowding her for time." He rubbed his hands. "Actually, there are people I should see myself in Tokyo and Yokohama. Yes, this trip makes good sense." He took Mitch's elbow and walked him toward the door. "My secretary will handle the details. She'll notify Mona and get our plane tickets—also arrange just where we'll pick up the ship."

Mitch, walking slowly back to his office, was in a quandary. Was it possible, he wondered, that Zabib was no more than he appeared to be, a shipowner wanting an outing on his own treasured flagship? No, that taxed one's credence. Zabib had given no thought to a voyage on the ship that bore his name until Mitch had asked to go. Once again Mitch's mind began spinning in the old speculation, that Zabib somehow was linked to a conspiracy that embraced his old friend Alexandros Nicias.

The two shipping executives rode the launch that slapped through the oily and debris-strewn waters of Singapore harbor carrying them to the *Zabibian* as it prepared to negotiate Singapore Strait.

They had landed at Changi airport in mid-afternoon and taken a cab through teeming Singapore with its contrasting skyscrapers and sidewalk vendor stalls to the waterfront wharf where a water taxi service had its headquarters.

Now, sitting at the stern, they watched as the launch maneuvered through the world's second busiest harbor. Several hundred large vessels, bulk cargo carriers, container ships and tankers, rode at anchor while countless small boats scurried among them like ants at a picnic. Sampans, lighters, bumboats, junks, speedboats, sailboats, water taxis and launches drove about on their assorted missions in a scene of ordered chaos. Their launch headed toward the open waters to the west where a number of ships, including the *Zabibian,* moved slowly about. Like incoming jetliners banking in clouds above a congested airport, freighters and tankers circled until they got the word to proceed into heavily traveled Singapore Strait.

As the launch threaded through the roadstead, Mitch thought

once more of the extraordinary man sitting beside him. On their long flights from Copenhagen, Zabib had acted like a college boy heading for his first vacation abroad. In high spirits, he joked, told anecdotes from his days at sea, played several sets of gin rummy with Mitch, talked revealingly about women, both his wife and Grethe Knudsen, and to Mitch's consternation once again defended his friend, the Lorikeet captain Alexandros Nicias. The subject came up when Mitch mentioned that when he visited the *King Misura* off Kuwait, Nicias criticized Mona's handling of the *Yandoon Princess* and said he didn't approve of women aboard tankers in any capacity.

"Did he ever say anything to you about Mona's actions after the *Princess* lost steering?" asked Mitch.

"No. I knew he didn't like women at sea, so I didn't bother querying him before I hired her." After a moment of reflection, Zabib said, "You know, Alex is under investigation again."

"Oh?" Mitch feigned surprise.

"Yes. A Moses & Fabian investigator came to see me a few days ago." The shipowner spoke slowly as if the subject saddened him. "It seems they've reopened their old inquiry into the sinking of the *Gunnison Bay*. The investigator told me that they have good evidence now that the crew sold off the whole cargo of oil in South America and then scuttled the ship."

And, thought Mitch, Moses & Fabian owed him $750 for his bribe of Claude Bouchon to get the Frenchman from Tahiti to talk.

"If he's right," continued Zabib, "Alex would have to be guilty. No way could a master who was aboard his ship—and Alex was— not be a party to the double crime." Zabib looked like a man who wanted to deny what he had just said. "Unless, of course, the men mutinied and threatened to kill him if he ever told."

"What's your hunch, Zab? Do you think the tanker was scuttled?"

"No. I just can't believe that Alex would get involved in marine crime."

"One of your captains told me that Nicias built a mansion on the Greek island of Naxos two years after the *Gunnison Bay* went down." Now that Zabib had opened the subject, Mitch felt free to pursue it.

"That's true. Alex told me he inherited the money and I had no reason to doubt him."

"Do you still believe him?"

"I don't desert my friends." The dogged tone did not hide the fact that Zabib had evaded an answer.

Now in the water taxi Mitch watched the shipowner as the boat cut power and maneuvered in the shadow of the *Zabibian*. Still dressed like a conservative banker, Zabib had his arm resting on the stern gunwale and he had a look of eager anticipation as he watched tanker seamen prepare for the boarding. Having changed his mind about Zabib several times in the last twenty-four hours, Mitch still didn't know what to make of the man.

When a gangway was lowered from the tanker, a Chinese crewman of the water taxi carried up Mitch's and Zabib's bags and deposited them on the deck. Zabib and Mitch followed, Zabib in proper city suit and topcoat, and Mitch in his standard travel outfit, jeans, sneakers and light turtleneck sweater.

When they reached the deck, Mitch, looking up, saw Mona on the port wing. She waved briefly. The man who stepped forward and took their bags was Bert Takahara.

Mitch embraced his friend after Takahara and Zabib had exchanged greetings. "Communicators double as porters aboard this ship?"

"Only for VIPs," said Takahara. "Captain says I'm to take you gentlemen to your quarters and when you're settled, she'd like to see you up on the bridge."

In the house they took an elevator to the sixth or A deck, just below the bridge, where the captain's quarters, two guest cabins, the communications office and quarters of the chief engineer and chief mate were located. Mitch found himself in a plain but commodious room with a wide bed, dresser and easy chair for reading. The room had one closet for clothes and another that held shower, toilet and washstand. A single large window faced toward the bow and provided the room's sole touch of adornment: heavy beige drapes that could be drawn shut. Air conditioning, cooling this cabin as well as the rest of the tanker's house, was welcome after the heavy damp air of Singapore that threatened rain at any moment.

Actually a light tropical rain began to patter on the tanker as Mitch walked up an inner flight of stairs to the bridge. Dusk was gathering and the lights of Singapore as well as those of the ships in the roadstead and channel began winking on.

Mona stood looking out of a large front window toward the port side and holding a mug of coffee, a helmsman had his hands on the small wheel and a third man, probably an officer, shuttled between two radar scopes.

"Mitch!" Mona came toward him with a smile that he would not rate as the most cordial he had ever seen. She held out her hand, apparently to forestall a hug or other affectionate greeting.

"Greetings, Captain." He shook hands with her. "I imagine Zab will be up in a minute."

"Are your quarters okay?" She was not at ease.

"Fine, fine. Look, you go about your business. I don't want to interfere. I'll watch quietly from the back here."

She introduced him to Sven Ahlgren, the Swedish third mate, and to the helmsman, a bearded old seaman named Sandy Otis. The amenities concluded, she went back to her coffee at the window, but soon began making the rounds of the radar scopes, the depth indicator, the gyro compass, the heading indicator, the satellite navigation recorder, the LORAN readout and then outside on the port wing. Mitch noted that she paced a regular beat, covering some forty yards on each triangular lap like a caged animal on the prowl. The three mariners on the bridge did not speak.

Mitch stood to the rear, just in front of the chart table, and on one of her laps Mona stopped long enough to squeeze his hand and say, "I'm glad you're here."

"I can't be blamed for Zab. He insisted."

"I figured as much. We'll talk as soon as this traffic thins out. Why don't you go up to the flying bridge right above us? You get an excellent view of the Strait and the ship from there."

Ahlgren showed him the ladder outside at the rear of the wheelhouse and Mitch climbed up to the railing-enclosed platform that served as the *Zabibian*'s top deck. Actually it was the roof of the wheelhouse and it was bare save for several hooded instruments and the upper section of radar mast which abutted the aft railing.

The flying bridge, as Mona had said, commanded a view of the long tanker and the crowded waterway through which it moved so cautiously. The ship had entered the heavily traveled Singapore Strait now and the sun sinking into the sea to the rear painted the channel in rose and mauve. A light rain sprinkled the deck and a small rainbow arched over the twin lines of ships. A container vessel, stacked high with colored boxes, plowed the eastward channel about a half a mile ahead. When he turned around, Mitch saw another tanker in the *Zabibian*'s wake. In the westbound channel to port, a file of ships, spaced about a half-mile apart, moved slowly toward the setting sun. Traffic, Mitch noted, flowed at a modest pace. Six knots, someone had told him earlier.

After a few minutes he climbed down and reentered the wheel-house. Rain speckled the bridge's windows and five long wipers swept back and forth across the panes that looked out toward the distant bow. No one spoke for a long time. Talk on the bridge, Mitch was learning, shrank as traffic grew dense.

"I'd say we ought to bring her to zero five three about here." Mona broke the silence. "Check me on that, Sandy."

"Right on, Cap'n. . . . Zero five three," repeated Helmsman Otis. Coppery hair streaked his bushy white beard like rust.

Chief Mate Bill Muldoon, whom Mitch had seen briefly in Phila-delphia, came up to the bridge, made similar rounds to those of Mona, then stood for a moment beside Mitch.

"We're doubling up on the watch through the Strait," he said. "There have been collisions here. Heavy traffic. You've got to keep a sharp eye out."

"Been through here before?"

"Oh, sure. A dozen times. But Sandy's the man who knows the Strait. I'll bet he's made it on fifty, sixty trips. This is the old lady's first run through here, so we want to give her some support."

The city of Singapore was now full on the port beam and three islands of Indonesia, Lumba, Batam and Bintan, lay off the starboard side to the south. Small boats swarmed through the ship channels, seemingly daring the big freighters and tankers to run them down. A speedboat wheeled in a tight turn directly in front of the *Zabibian*, threw sheets of spray and left a boiling wake as it raced off to dart between a westbound refrigerator ship and a natural gas carrier. Helmsman Otis muttered profanely.

Behind a shield, Mona leaned over the lighted chart table where Third Mate Sven Ahlgren was plotting the ship's position as he did every quarter hour in crowded waters.

"Sandy," she asked when she resumed her pacing, "do you know whether that navigation light to starboard has a name?"

"Buffalo Rock."

"And the lighthouse up ahead?"

"It's on Berhanti Rock." Otis wasted no words when at the wheel.

Zabib came up to the bridge just as darkness dropped over the Strait, transforming the seascape of ships, islands, shores, city buildings and watery stretches into a black dome dotted with lights. Instead of a container ship laden with boxes ahead of them, they saw only a pattern of lights.

Zabib stood quietly beside Mitch just in front of the shielded compartment that held the charts and navigation aids. He had at last changed out of his business clothes and now, ever the fashion plate, he looked like a yachtsman at his club with his open-necked shirt and ascot, tan cashmere cardigan, tailored twill trousers and rubber-soled deck shoes. Well, he's welcome, thought Mitch, the ship's his sixty millions' worth.

Mona first saw Zabib when she raised her head after studying one of the radar screens. "My, you gave me a start." She came to him with outstretched hand. "You should have let me know you were here." In contrast to his yachtsman's costume, she wore her tropical working clothes, short-sleeved shirt and dungarees. Her hair was pulled back in a bun.

"I don't want to distract you," Zabib replied. "You've got work to do. I just want to stand and watch."

"Oh, we're in good hands with Sandy and Bill. Between them, they've been through this strait a hundred times."

"Still, it's your ship."

"Well, I'm committed here until we get out of the traffic." A crisp smile snapped on and off. "Tomorrow, out in the South China Sea, we'll have plenty of room and time to talk."

Excusing herself, Mona went back to her accustomed place at the large window on the port side of the bridge, but soon began pacing her triangular course from radar scopes to course compass to chart table to navigation aids to a bit of fresh air on the port wing. Aside from her occasional word to Ahlgren or Muldoon, her infrequent change-of-course directions to the helmsman and the hum of the ship's engines far below, silence wrapped the bridge as completely as did the night. Faces could not be distinguished in the gloom and the only light in the darkened wheelhouse came from the faint greenish glow of the radar scopes and from a crack in the shield around the lighted chart table.

The light rain had stopped and Mitch stepped outside for a breath of air. Sandy Otis, the bearded bosun, relieved at the wheel for a spell by another seaman, joined Mitch on the deck between the bridge and the port wing.

"You people seem plenty cool in there," said Mitch, angling for conversation. "Lots of traffic to handle."

"Not so cool. You have to pay attention in a crowd." Otis was a slow-mannered man with a whisky growl. "I don't mind admitting that all them native boats buzzing around give me fits."

"The chief mate says you've been through here a lot." Lights in the opposing westbound channel hinted at a parade of ships stretching for miles.

"Sixty-three trips, counting both ways." He leaned on the high steel plate that served as a windbreak. "Sure, the traffic's heavy passing Singapore. Still, if a man can learn to ignore the small stuff, it's pretty straight away. Not many changes in course. If you put into the harbor, they make you take a harbor pilot aboard. When I first come through here, a lot of the harbor pilots were British, veddy, veddy uppercrust ass-holes who talked like they were gargling marbles. They tried to make it appear especially difficult and like only one of their snob fraternity could handle it."

Otis yawned and stretched. "For my money, give me the Cajun pilots around Louisiana and Texas. Coon-ass, they call 'em. I've seen some old coon-ass pilots snake five or six empty barges through a twisting channel in a crosswind, the while dodging sandbars and heavy shipping, and make it look easy. When one of them ol' boys said a nice word about my helmsmanship, now, that was a real compliment."

Mitch sensed that Otis could yarn along for hours, but the bosun soon returned to his post at the wheel, leaving Mitch alone in the night's silence. Even the slap of water against the ship was too far away to be heard. The great supertanker slipped noiselessly through the sea, one of the long file of vessels gliding slowly eastward while the other long file, little more than a mile away, moved silently to the west. Standing in the dark on the bridge, high above the water, Mitch had a disembodied feeling as if the wheelhouse were floating through the night unconnected to sea or sky, a kind of lazy spaceship or airborne theater.

Soon after he rejoined Zabib inside the wheelhouse, Mona came over to them. "If you two want some dinner, you'd better go down to the officer's mess now. They'll quit serving in a few minutes."

But Mitch and Zabib both begged off. They'd had enough to eat and drink on the airplane. Instead Mitch stood watching the progress of the tanker and the lights of passing ships until his eyes grew heavy with the darkness and the steady pulse of the engines. Then he went to his room, undressed and fell sound asleep.

He awoke with a start, blinked in the dark, sensed someone leaning over the bed and instinctively lashed out with his arm.

"Easy." The voice came through warm, throaty and familiar just as a hand caught his arm.

"Mona." He sat up, shaking his head. "Next time phone ahead for reservations, will you?"

She sat down on the edge of the bed, framed his face in her hands and kissed him. The grainy after-blur of sleep came into clear focus. He reached out eagerly, clasping her to him, but she pulled away.

"No, not now, Mitch." She took his hands. "I only have a few minutes. We're still in the Strait. But I had a problem. I wanted to talk to you."

"You sure as hell had no problem with access. Walked right in."

"You didn't bother to lock your door."

"What time is it?"

"Just after twelve. Bill Muldoon has the watch now, so I can steal a few minutes."

He tried to pull Mona down on the bed with him, but she resisted and they wrestled a bit before she could free herself.

"Mitch, please!" Her tone sharpened. "Look, guy, I love you and you're my man, but on this trip to Japan, I can't make love with you."

"Why?" The rejection cut. He hadn't seen her in more than three weeks.

"You've understood me so well, sweetheart, so try once more. I just can't divide myself right now." She took his hands. "I have to pour all my concentration into this job. This is the big test of my life. I can't flunk it." He could see her but dimly in the dark room. He had closed the window drapes before going to bed. "And it's not just running this ship. It's the yakuza and Quebrada and the rest of that mess. I have to stay alert. I can't let down."

"Okay, babe. I hear you. It'll be an act of willpower to keep my hands off you, but I'll do it if I can pry a promise out of you?"

"A promise? Let me guess." She touched her forehead, mocking thought. "To make love all night as soon I get back to Copenhagen?"

"You're close. Actually it's all day and night and then a long vacation down in Madeira or the Canaries. Just us. Agreed?"

"Oh, holy Jesus, yes." She kissed him swiftly and he could feel the passion. "I want you so badly, Mitch." She said it with a touch of desperation, but then in the next breath switched back to Captain Harkinson. "Why did you come here?"

"Very simply because I'm afraid for you." Mitch leaned on an elbow as he told her briefly about Ned's warning. "I just couldn't sit still in Copenhagen while you were in danger out here."

"Mitch, I'm a big girl. I can take care of myself. And frankly . . ." She hesitated and he could sense that she had tensed. "I didn't want you here." She blurted it. "It complicates things to have you aboard and, of course, with Zabib here too it's almost too much to handle."

"I couldn't help it about Zab." He explained what happened.

She nodded. "I figured it was something like that when I got the message from headquarters." She bit her lip. "But now you're both here and we'll have to make the best of it. . . . So brief me on just where we stand with Zabib."

"I can't figure the guy. One minute I think he's come here in league with Elger and the yakuza and the next I'm convinced he's just a shipowner playing sailor on his flagship." He told her of his conversations with Zabib and they briefly discussed their employer but with no new insights to enlighten what they knew back in Denmark.

"As for Quebrada, I'm definitely suspicious of him." She described the Mexican and his aura of bluff venality. "You'll see him tomorrow. He's the one who goes around halfway between a waddle and a strut."

"He sounds like a Bones with a load of Latin lard on him. As somebody said of Elger back in Viet Nam, 'If he can't fuck it, bribe it, con it, steal it or extort money from it, okay, he'll shoot it.' "

Mona shifted uneasily on the bed. "After your message about Quebrada, I decided I needed some allies I could trust, so I had Bill Muldoon, Arno Joahannes and Bert Takahara come to my quarters.

I told them in confidence pretty much what happened in Philadelphia and since. Bill was sure we could also trust Sandy Otis, the bosun, and Risto Topelius, the chief engineer. I felt better having Arno and Bert. Honestly, you're helpless at sea if you don't have Sparks on your side. He's your voice to the rest of the world."

Mona got up, went to the window and peered out through the drapes. "Looks like good weather tomorrow." She came back and stood by the bed. "So the six of us had a talk. Without going into details, I just said we'd had word there might be trouble aboard and to keep an eye out for anything out of the ordinary."

"I liked Otis. I had a talk with him up above."

"Yes, a good man—and tough. Anyway, the six of us agreed to work together. And guess what?"

"Bert thinks it's all exciting as hell."

"He does, but the news is something else. Bill Muldoon is being paid by the CIA to look out for me."

"Oh, so he's the one." Mitch told her about the Agency's second thoughts on protection. "Well, I'll make one more on your side." He reached under the pillow. "And look, my Colt .38. First time I've carried a gun since I took off the uniform."

"Ugly-looking thing." When he tucked the handgun back, she said, "But I've got a revolver in my cabin too. Bill showed me how to use it." She leaned down and kissed him. "I've got to go back up now."

He pulled her down gently for an embrace and this time she did not resist. "Just one good long kiss," she murmured. She folded into his arms with a sigh. They lay together quietly for a few moments as tension dissolved and they felt the reassuring rhythm of each other's breathing and heartbeat. "I have to go now," she whispered as she moved from his arms. "Tomorrow. . . ."

Bells shrilled in the passageway, shattering the stillness of the night. To Mitch's ears, the clanging sounded like that of the old high school fire drills back in Chicago, loud and declamatory, an angry commanding noise.

While the bells clamored three distinct times, the ship's whistle above them emitted three long blasts.

Mona bolted from the bed and rushed to the door.

"Man overboard!" She ran from the room.

18

Pulling the sweater over his head, Mitch finished dressing just as he reached the door. When his hand hit the knob, he remembered. He turned back, pulled the loaded Colt from beneath his pillow and shoved it into a back pocket of his dungarees. Carrying it had not become automatic yet. He took the stairway to the bridge two steps at a time.

Doors stood open on either side of the wide wheelhouse, linking the covered bridge to the long narrow wings that stretched out from the ship. Two searchlights drilled downward through the muggy overcast night to the water on the port side. Mona stood far out on the port wing with an electrically amplified bullhorn. A half-dozen men occupied the bridge area, dark forms in purposeful movement.

"How about the current, Bill?" Mona called from the wing.

The chief mate leaned out the door. "One knot drift to the southwest."

Mona aimed her bullhorn toward the water. "Mind the shore side of the eastbound channel especially. Current running to the southwest."

Stepping out on the port deck, Mitch saw the covered lifeboat swing away from the *Zabibian* and head toward the tanker's sluggish wake. A powered thirty-footer that had been lowered from A deck, the boat was manned by two seamen. Moving quickly out of the bright shafts thrown by the searchlights, it soon became swallowed by the night.

Mona strode back into the wheelhouse, issuing orders as she went. "All right, Bill, let's hurry those musters. . . . I want to drop the hook first spot possible, Sven."

The seaman standing the port-wing watch gave Mitch a quick briefing on events that had been crammed into the three minutes that had elapsed since the alarm sounded. Man screamed. Apparently fell overboard from main deck, starboard side. Not sure, but think it was Sparks since he took midnight constitutional, weather permitting. Normally captain would put ship into standard Williamson turn, or a hard rudder single turn, bringing tanker back to spot of accident. But that's impossible in narrow channel and heavy traffic, so they dropped a boat instead. Cap'n taking ship to an emergency anchorage two miles ahead. "Sparks, Jr."—Bert Takahara—alerting ships behind to watch for man in water, according to the drill. A seaman had flashed the Morse code "O"—dash, dash, dash—to other ships via signal light. Chief Mate and Chief Engineer were mustering their men to make sure the missing man was Joahannes.

"Mitch!" Mona stood in the doorway of the wheelhouse. Spotting him, she hurried to the wing, drew him away from the seaman. "We're pretty sure it was Sparks. And worse, Muldoon thinks he saw the Mexican running across the deck near the spot of the fall."

"Quebrada?"

She nodded. "At least, I don't want to take a chance on him. Got your gun?"

"Right."

"Okay, I'm sending Sandy Otis, the big bosun, with you. Find Quebrada and bring him up here to the bridge. Tell him captain's orders. Keep hunting till you find him. . . . And Mitch, take care, huh?"

She summoned Otis, the veteran mariner with the full rusty beard, from the wheelhouse and together he and Mitch went down the stairs to the deck below where Mitch had his guest cabin. "Ten to one Sparks was pushed," said Otis. The big man had a lumbering gait. "No reason for him to fall over in this sea. She's flat as glass."

They conferred hurriedly on A deck. The house was about a hundred feet wide with no outside connection below A deck. Instead the interior gangway on the starboard side linked one deck with another.

It was decided that Otis would stand watch at the starboard end of the passageway, thus covering the stairs as well, while Mitch searched the cabins, working his way toward Otis.

He went through his own room first since it was located on the far port side. Gun in hand, he then stepped across the passageway to the quarters of the chief mate, was surprised to find that Muldoon had a shelved library of several hundred books.

The next room housed Wasif Zabib who had not yet put in an appearance since the alarm some five minutes ago. Mitch rapped on the door with his left hand while holding the pistol pointed upward beside his right shoulder.

"Just a moment!" When Zabib, still in his underclothes, opened the door several inches, he said, "I'll be out in a few minutes."

"I have to search your quarters, Zab."

"Search my . . ." The shipowner was astonished. "What's going on? Put that gun down."

Mitch continued to hold it against his shoulder, but at the ready. "Sorry. Captain's orders. We have to search every room." Mitch studied the face framed in the doorway. Zabib was still an unknown quantity.

"I insist on my privacy." Indignant, the tanker executive pushed the door to close it.

Mitch shoved his foot over the sill. The door slammed against his leg. Thrusting Zabib aside, he walked into the room, looked about. A wall-bracket light revealed a rumpled bed, a desk, chair and dresser, an open closet and a bathroom behind a half-opened door. He quickly searched the closet, then the bathroom. As he glanced about, he made a point of looking for firearms, but saw none.

He retreated as swiftly as he had come while Zabib, in undershorts and T-shirt, stood by with folded arms. "Just what's the explanation for this peculiar behavior?"

"Later, Zab." Mitch was curt. "We're searching the ship for a guy. Captain's orders."

Mitch heard the door slam as he reached the next cabin on the passageway, this one the communications office and the adjoining quarters of Arno Joahannes. Entering, Mitch saw Bert Takahara on his knees, half hidden behind a kind of electronic cockpit that held a large short-wave radio, radio telephone, buttons for interior signals and alarms and other gear.

"Somebody cut the power line." Takahara's usual exuberance had chilled.

"Cut the power?" Mitch wasn't sure he'd heard correctly.

"Right. Severed the cable. This baby's had it—for a while anyway."

"Isn't there an auxiliary generator for emergencies?"

"Yeah, but that's been cut too." Bert's dark eyes mirrored fear. "We can't send a word. . . . Mitch. . . ." He hesitated.

"What?"

"Somebody's after this ship."

"When did you discover this?"

"Just now. I had just turned in when the alarm sounded. The guy in the next foc'sle said it was probably Sparks, I busted up here to send the man-overboard signal and to raise the tanker behind us on voice. I wasted a couple of minutes before I found the cut lines."

Takahara crawled out, brushed himself off. "Was it Arno who went over?"

"We're not sure yet. You seen Quebrada?"

Takahara shook his head. "I gotta tell the captain." He hurried from the room and ran down the passageway.

At once the search for Quebrada escalated from a task of reasonable precaution to one of emergency. Somebody, it appeared, wanted both the radio officer and his communications equipment out of commission. And until this moment at least, Quebrada was the lone suspect.

After a fast search of Joahannes' adjoining room, Mitch went through the empty cabins of the two chiefs. He was just entering Mona's quarters when Otis called from the end of the passageway. Turning, he saw Otis walking toward him a pace behind a fat brown muffin of a man.

"This here's Carlos Quebrada," said Otis. "I found him between decks." He gripped the pumpman by both arms.

"Let go of me." Quebrada tried to wrench free.

Mitch stepped to meet them. He still carried the Colt, muzzle up, at the right shoulder. "Raise your hands, Quebrada. . . . Search him, Sandy."

Quebrada grinned as he lifted his arms. "Hey, what is this? You some kind of police? You know you violatin' my rights, *hombre*. You can't do this."

Otis patted the Mexican's torso, then down his denim trousers. "What the hell's this?" He pulled a handgun from Quebrada's hip pocket and turned it over in his hands for Mitch to see.

"It looks like a .22 automatic from here." Mitch leaned closer. "Ruger. . . . What's the idea, Quebrada?"

"I found it on the deck." His grin this time was one of cheerful innocence. "I was just taking it up to the captain."

"What deck did you find it on?"

"C deck." The Mexican frowned. "No, I guess it was B. I ain't sure."

Otis inspected the gun. "It's loaded."

"Just lying on the deck, was it?" asked Mitch. "A loaded .22."

"Yeah, I didn't see it until I kicked it with my foot and sent it skidding down the deck." Quebrada was enjoying his story. "So I thought I ought to bring it up to the captain, so nobody'd get hurt."

"We'll save you some trouble and bring the captain down to you." He turned to Otis. "I think it best that Captain Harkinson come down here. I'll hold him in my cabin. Better than a big scene on the bridge. Understand?"

"Got you." Otis put the handgun in his own hip pocket on his way to the bridge.

Mitch marched the Mexican pumpman down the passageway to his cabin. As Mona had said, Quebrada moved halfway between a waddle and a strut, the while shaking his head. "You got this all wrong, man. Shit, no guns allowed aboard this ship. That's why I was turning in the one I found."

In his room Mitch motioned Quebrada to a chair while he stood over him with the Colt still held at his shoulder. The Mexican, sweating, wiped his forehead with the skirt of his T-shirt, then slumped in the chair with his legs extended.

"Where were you when the alarm rang?" Mitch asked.

"When Sparks fell off?" Quebrada folded his hands on top of his belly.

"How do you know it was Joahannes?"

"That's what they say." He seemed completely at ease, in fact overly comfortable for a man sitting under a gun.

"Who said?"

"One of the enginemen, I guess it was."

"Who?" Mitch bored in. "What name?"

"I think it was Hutch. Aw, I don't know."

"Where were you when the alarm sounded?"

Quebrada bridled. *"Chingada,* who are you? Asking all these goddam questions?"

"I'm vice-president of this company. Now where were you?"

"I'm not talking except to the captain." Quebrada looked pleased with his decision. "He's—she's the only law on this ship."

Otis, returning from the bridge, reported that Captain Harkinson was too busy to leave. She ordered that Quebrada be placed in the cleaning locker where towels, detergents and cleansing supplies were kept. Located two decks below on C, the small inside room could be locked from the outside with a key that had been supplied by the officers'-mess boy who had charge of the locker.

"You can't do that." Quebrada said with a show of bravado. "What's the charge?"

"Carrying a weapon," said Otis. "Nobody allowed firearms except the captain. You know that."

They walked the pumpman down two flights to C deck and Mitch handed him into the cleaning-supply locker. The room, smelling of fresh paint, had a row of shelves filled with towels, cans and plastic bottles on one bulkhead. The remainder of the room, newly painted white, was bare. Mitch found a large empty can, told Quebrada he should use it in case he had to relieve himself. Otis fetched a pitcher full of water and a glass from the unlicensed men's mess on the deck below.

"What were you doing in Sparks' cabin?" Mitch asked Quebrada.

"I ain't been there in weeks." The Mexican looked around. "Where am I supposed to sit in this place?"

"Use a couple of towels."

"Come on, mister." Otis nudged Mitch with his elbow. "Skipper wants to see us up above right away."

Leaving, Otis locked the door behind them. They tried the elevator, found it in use and took the stairs. "Bad news," said Otis as they walked up. "Somebody cut power to the radio."

"Yeah, I heard."

"Captain thinks we may have a fight on our hands."

More people had crowded into the wheelhouse. In addition to Mona and Muldoon, there were Bert Takahara, Third Mate Sven Ahlgren, the Swede, and two men identified by Otis as Risto Topelius, the Finnish chief engineer, and the Chilean helmsman, Manny Rodriguez. In the background, alone and silent, stood Wasif Zabib. Even a man overboard and an armed intruder in his cabin had not disturbed the shipowner's commitment to fashion. He wore the tan cashmere cardigan and sported a striped foulard at the throat as if about to greet guests at a yachting party.

"The engine room's all accounted for, Captain," said Topelius. A shy man, he shifted about uneasily as he spoke his brief piece.

"Deck and galley accounted for, including the two men in the lifeboat," said Muldoon. "Sparks is the only man missing. Had to be him."

"Our radio's out," Mona announced to the group. "Bill, how many minutes to that anchorage?"

"Radio out?" Zabib was stunned.

"Yes, sir." Mona snapped it. "How many minutes to that anchorage?"

"Seventeen or eighteen, Captain."

"All right, Ahlgren, you've got the bridge," said Mona. "I want to see the following in my quarters at once: Muldoon, Topelius, Takahara, Otis and Donahey. . . . Sven, I'll be back up in a few minutes." She glanced at Zabib as she left the wheelhouse. "Make yourself at home, Mr. Zabib. This is urgent business."

Mona hurried down to the deck below trailed by the five men. Inside her office, she switched on a desk lamp beside her computer console, then stood with her back against the door to the passageway.

"This has to be fast," she said. "We may be in bad trouble. You all know the background from our talk yesterday. All right. There's a good chance that Sparks was pushed overboard. Bill here saw Quebrada running across the main deck near where Arno disappeared. Then Bert found that the power lines to the radio gear had been cut. We don't know who did it. Could have been Quebrada. Mitch and Sandy found Quebrada with a handgun. Quebrada's now locked in the cleaning locker. It looks like somebody means to act against this ship. Sandy has Quebrada's .22 pistol and Mitch has a Colt .38. Does anyone else have a gun?"

No one spoke.

"Quick, speak up. No disciplinary action for breaking the rules.

I've got the master's gun, a Colt .45 automatic. But we need more weapons."

"I . . ." Topelius, embarrassed, hesitated.

"What?" Mona snapped. "Say it."

"I have an automatic assault gun, an HK 91, that I was taking home for my collection," said the Finn. "I got it stashed down in the engine room."

"Any ammunition?"

"One box. That's about six hundred rounds."

"Know how to use it?"

"I fired it once when I bought it."

"Okay, Risto. As soon as we break," said Mona, "go get it and keep it on you. Report back up to the bridge with it. . . . Anybody else?"

Muldoon and Takahara shook their heads.

"So that's four people with arms," said Mona, "Mitch, Risto, Sandy and myself. My idea is to have the four of us on the bridge, ready for action. Anybody got a different idea?"

"Yeah." Muldoon spoke. "I think Risto, who's got the only real power weapon, ought to hide himself, but be close enough so he can hear a shouted command. How about in that spot behind the bridge in front of the stack? It's like a little fort in there."

"Good idea." Mona nodded toward Topelius. "Let the first handle the engine room, Risto. After you get the gun, station yourself behind the bridge. You know the place Bill means?"

"Check. I'll be there."

"I have no idea what the next move against us will be. Anybody have a guess? Speak up fast."

When no one spoke, she said, "One important thing. Keep an eye on the owner, Wasif Zabib. He's an unknown factor in this thing. Treat him courteously—he may be okay—but watch it."

Mona walked over and knelt by her small office safe. After twirling a combination, she opened the door, took out the .45 and shoved it into her dungarees at the waist. The protruding butt gave her the appearance of a female pirate. The men, watching silently, seemed fascinated by this operation.

"Okay," she said. "Sandy, you take the port wing. Risto will get his automatic and station himself behind the bridge. Bert's going to work on the radio. Mitch and Bill, you come back to the bridge with me. . . . Stay sharp, everyone. Anything can happen tonight."

As they filed out of the cabin, Mitch lingered a moment. Taking Mona's arm, he whispered, "Nice going, babe."

"Daddy finally would approve of me, huh?" Her twisted smile was one of irony. Then, opening like a camera's shutter for a fraction of a second, her glance revealed fear—and a poignant vulnerability. "Fact is, my knees are shaking. The only thing I ever fired was a cap pistol. Stay close to me, Mitch."

"Right with you." The adrenalin was pumping now and he felt that sudden elevation of mood, a high unlike any drug, that he had not experienced since the night patrols in Viet Nam. A strange amalgam of fear, wariness and highly sharpened perception, the chemistry bared his nerves, exposing them raw on his skin like thousands of tiny wounds. The world about him was new, vivid, hostile and invested with a powerful intensity. He dreaded it and yet he reveled in it.

Back on the dark bridge, lighted only by ghost-like rays from the green radar scopes, the tension had doubled. No one spoke, but everyone knew that some inimical element, alien to the routine of the tanker, threatened them far more than did a new distant rattle of thunder and an occasional flash of lightning in the far sky.

Zabib saw the gun at Mona's waist the moment she came back, turned for a surprised second look. Manny Rodriguez, the helmsman, kept his eyes straight ahead, did not acknowledge the return of his captain. Ahlgren, the third mate, retired to the chart table, leaving the run of the bridge to his superior, Bill Muldoon. Mitch's hand swung nervously at his side, close to the pistol in his hip pocket. Far out from the ship stood two silent lookouts, an unknown seaman on the starboard wing and Sandy Otis on the port.

Ahlgren had slowed the vessel as he neared the emergency anchorage. The speed indicator now registered between three knots and four knots, the minimum to maintain steerage, and the loaded tanker slid forward without a clear sense of movement. Like the night enfolding the east end of the Singapore Strait, the ship's vibration was muted.

"Radio?" Ahlgren directed the question at Mona.

"Still out," she said. "Takahara is working on it."

"One seventeen," Ahlgren called.

"One one seven," said Rodriguez as he turned the wheel.

After the tanker swerved into the new course, the third mate ordered the speed cut back to zero. The big vessel slid forward under its own momentum.

"We can drop anchor in about four minutes," he said.

"Prepare to drop the hook, Bill," said Mona.

Muldoon stepped out to the starboard wing with the bullhorn, relayed the orders for preparing to lower the anchor from the distant bow. The second mate and two seamen, waiting at the bow, released the chain falls, disengaged the windlass and took off the brake. The anchor chain ran out with a great rattle and clanking.

When halted at anchor, the *Zabibian* rode not far from the dark shore of Bintan, easternmost of the large Indonesian channel islands. No breeze stirred and the muggy air pressed in closely. An overcast shut out stars and moon. Thunder crackled in the distance and lightning winked across the eastern sky like fitful fireflies.

The tanker which had been following the *Zabibian* now drew near and was about to pass in the channel several hundred yards to the north. Mona put Sven Ahlgren on the blinker and the third mate signaled a Morse code message by flashing light: "Our radio down. Did you see the man overboard?" Back flashed the reply: "No. Regrets."

"All right then, Bill," said Mona to Muldoon, "we'll just hold here until the lifeboat returns."

Zabib, who had said nothing yet, stepped over to Mitch. "Now will you please explain what's been going on?"

"The radio power line was cut by somebody about the time Joahannes went overboard," Mitch replied. "Then we found a pumpman wandering around with a forbidden handgun." He hesitated to say more. "So it smells bad. We expect trouble."

"Why wasn't I told? I'm in good shape. I can handle a fight."

"Mona kept it to officers and crew." Mitch thought fast. "I guess just the people she was accustomed to working with in an emergency."

"But you're just a passenger like me?" Zabib said it with a bit of a whine, almost like a small boy who's been left out of the game.

"That's true, Zab." He felt sorry for the man. "I'm not clued in to everything. Maybe she doesn't want to bother you. If things ease up, I'll find out. . . . But I know how you feel."

"I think something's being withheld from me." Once again the firm, clear voice of authority.

A shout came from the port wing. "Small boat approaching to port off our stern!"

Mona strode out on the wing. "Put the lights on it," she ordered.

Ahlgren flipped a switch on the wheelhouse panel, then went outside to train the searchlights. Mitch also went out along with Zabib and others. The powerful beams walked across the water aft of the tanker, focused on a low craft with running lights.

"It's our Number One boat," Otis called.

The covered boat, roofed over to withstand heavy seas, drew alongside and headed along the flank of the tanker.

"We got Sparks!" It was a call from the seaman steering the powered lifeboat. "He's okay."

"Can he make it up a ladder?" asked Mona.

"He says he can," came the reply.

"Let's get the ladder over the side, Bill," Mona ordered.

Two seamen already were on their way across the tanker's network of pipes toward the spot amidships where rope ladders were lowered. Several commands later, the ladder was dropped some forty feet to the water. A lone figure, wet shirt clinging to the body, climbed slowly under the glare of the searchlights. When he reached the deck, the lifeboat veered off and swung back aft, preparatory to being hoisted aboard via the winch that had lowered it some thirty minutes earlier.

"Welcome home, Arno," Mona called down through the bullhorn. "Come up to the bridge and we'll pour some hot coffee into you."

Joahannes walked aft on the long deck. He was barefoot and had also lost his trousers. When he got close to the house, he cupped his hands and called upward: "I didn't fall, Captain. I was knocked overboard. I'm coming right up."

To the sound of the lifeboat's motor was now added the throb of another engine, this one stronger. The lookout on the port wing called: "Another boat coming alongside."

Once again the searchlights trained downward. A long narrow motor launch, perhaps fifty feet in length, headed toward the ladder. Flags flew at bow and stern. A half-dozen uniformed men carrying side arms stood in the cockpit. A marine siren whirred briefly.

"Who are you?" asked Mona through the bullhorn.

"Channel police," came the reply from below. "We're checking on the man overboard."

Mitch passed Mona on his way from the wheelhouse. "Careful," he said.

"I know. I'm going to have Sandy identify them before they come up."

Mona walked out on the long port wing to the end where Otis stood. He examined the uniformed men standing in the strong searchlight beams. They were all Asians.

"Yes, those are channel police uniforms," he said. "The Singapore Marine Police patrol the Strait."

"Please come aboard," Mona called down. The first man, she noted, already had his foot on the lowest rung.

"Well, I'm relieved," she said when she turned to Mitch. "We can use some police right now."

She turned her full attention to Arno Joahannes who had just arrived on the bridge. He was trembling from chill, he had a bloody gash on his forehead and his soggy shirt and undershorts were torn.

"I hear the marine police have come," he said. "Thank God, for that. I want them to arrest that son-of-a-bitch Quebrada, Captain. He swatted me with a club and knocked me overboard."

The lifeboat swung up to A deck and deckhands pulled it inboard to make it fast in its cradle.

Down on the main deck, the first of the marine policemen came over the side.

19

"Donahey!" The call came from the protected area behind the bridge.

Mitch walked aft on the bridge deck. Between the wheelhouse and the smokestack, a distance of ten feet, the broad base of the radar and radio mast provided a shelter for winds from starboard. A few feet to port, abutting the stack, stood a large locker for signal flags and other equipment. Thus a man standing directly in front of the stack had protection on all four sides.

Risto Topelius, the chief engineer, stood self-consciously in the center of the area with his assault rifle. He held it gingerly in both hands as he might an unfamiliar baby.

"How about . . . would you mind if we switch guns?" he asked. "I'm afraid I might shoot someone by mistake with this. I bought the HK 91 for my collection, not to fire it."

"Sure." Mitch took the weapon, inspected it, tried it for weight and shoulder fit. "Not too different from the M-16 I used in the service."

"Thirty rounds in the magazine. Here's some more." The engineer handed over the additional ammunition and took Mitch's .38 revolver in return. "I can handle this one all right."

"I guess you won't have to now that the police are here." Mitch placed the rifle on the deck beneath the flag locker. "Come on. Let's see what gives out there."

Five uniformed men filed on to the bridge from the stairs leading up from A deck. They wore blue uniforms with short-sleeved shirts, blue berets, blue cotton gloves and holsters and walkie-talkie sets attached at the belt. Down from the bridge Mitch could see two more policemen standing guard on the main deck near the rope ladder. Zabib, Ahlgren, Muldoon, Joahannes, Rodriguez and David, the officers' messman, were all on the bridge.

Now that the tanker stood at anchor, the wheelhouse was brightly lighted. A policeman stepped forward, set two large dispatch cases down on the deck. "Who is the captain here?" He was built like a neat rectangle, short, narrow and squared at the shoulders, and his epaulettes bore the insignia of an officer of some kind.

"I am." She came into the wheelhouse from the deck. "Mona Harkinson."

"Major Hung." He bowed, a movement so slight it could pass as a tremor. Apparently unsurprised to find a woman in charge, the major centered his gaze on the handgun butt protruding from the waistband of Mona's dungarees. "Do you carry that all the time?"

"No, but tonight we were looking at trouble." She told of the severed power line in communications and finding a crew member with a gun.

"And the radio still does not function?" Hung's speech had a guttural undertow and he tended to explode his th's. He was not easy to understand.

"Not yet," said Mona. "Our radio assistant is working on it."

"Where?"

"The radio room is on A deck, the one below us."

Mitch noted that the other four policemen had moved about the wheelhouse, so that there was now one at each door and two others standing back by the chart table. The man at the starboard door had a plump cheerful aspect, looked vaguely like someone Mitch knew.

Major Hung stepped to the chart table and spoke in a low voice to one of his men. The policeman left the bridge via the stairs to A deck.

"Would you and your men like some coffee?" Mona walked over to the coffee maker, which was being replenished by David, the messman. "This won't do tonight, Dave. Go down and brew us a couple of potfuls."

"Later, perhaps," said Hung. "The man who went overboard has been recovered. Am I correct?"

"Yes. Mr. Joahannes was picked up by our lifeboat." She nodded toward the radio officer who stood near the radar scopes. Some one had brought Joahannes a blanket and he stood with it wrapped about his shoulders despite the warm night. He sipped at a mug of coffee.

"Please tell me what happened, sir," said Hung.

"You bet I will." Joahannes put down the coffee and clutched the blanket. "I was taking my nightly walk around the main deck. Just forward of the house to starboard near the pipe going into Number Eight Tank, a guy says kinda low, 'Hey, Sparks.'" Joahannes' mouthful of tarnished teeth added a sinister touch to his tale. "I turn around—it's that Mexican, Quebrada—and he swings at my head with something that looked like a club. I ducked and the thing hit my shoulder and knocked me overboard. I yelled as I fell off.

"Lucky I wasn't hurt much—though where I got this cut on my forehead, I don't know. Anyway, I had the strength to swim hard to get away from the damn screw. Then I got my shoes off and later my pants. The water was warm, so I was floating, treading water and swimming around until the lifeboat spotted me, thank God. Smitty and Muhammad fished me out after maybe twenty-five, thirty minutes."

"Earlier, did you strike this man Quebrada or have an argument with him?" asked the major.

"No. Nothing. We never even talked or said hello or anything. I'm inside in the radio room all day."

Major Hung turned to Mona. "Where is Quebrada?"

"He's confined to the cleaning locker on C deck. He was found soon after the incident with a gun on him. That's a violation. I'm the only person permitted to have firearms aboard this vessel."

Hung glanced at Mona's waist again. "I see that you take full advantage of your rules. . . . Now I want to interrogate Mr. Quebrada."

"Mitch," said Mona, "please take Major Hung down to the C deck locker." She handed him the key.

"Change to dry clothes," Hung said to Joahannes. "Later I'll want to question you in detail." Turning to Mona again, he said, "Let me know when the radio is back in service. No messages are to be sent before checking with me. And the ship is not to leave this anchorage until I give the word."

"Don't worry," said Mona. "I'm not about to try lifting 250,000 tons of crude to Japan until this mess is cleared up."

Hung beckoned to a hard-eyed policeman by the chart table and the two men followed Mitch down from the bridge to the elevator on A deck. They descended two decks in the car and walked past the officers' mess and the galley to the small inside room where the cleaning supplies were kept. Mitch unlocked the door.

Carlos Quebrada was sitting on a nest of towels looking at an old comic book on derring-do in outer space. He rose to his feet with a rueful grin. When Mitch started to enter, Major Hung barred the way with his arm.

"I'll question this man in private," he said. Turning to the other policeman, a man of graven impassivity, Hung uttered a low guttural command of some kind. Then he stepped into the supply room and closed the door behind him.

It became immediately apparent that the policeman had been told to keep an eye on the American, for he stood by the door with one hand resting on his gun holster and his eyes trained on Mitch. Standing awkwardly in the passageway, looking at the uniformed Asian, Mitch wondered. The man looked more Japanese than Chinese. There were few Japanese in Singapore, a city populated overwhelmingly by Chinese with a minority of Malays and Indians. And Major Hung's growled command had sounded much like some of the snippets of conversation Mitch had heard from Japanese tourists in Honolulu. The thought of Japanese triggered a string of associations and into his mind came the luminous image of the Strait policeman standing by the starboard entry to the wheelhouse: a plump, middle-aged man with the cheerful look of an old friend bringing good news. Flash. Could it be? Hadn't he seen the man twice with Bones Elger, once at the Broadway Ginza in Hong Kong and earlier in Mitch's own driveway in Honolulu? No, too much imagination. That couldn't be Takeo Kirihara, the yakuza sub-chief. A close resemblance maybe, but that's all. Kirihara was older than the policeman, wasn't he?

Thoughts churned as he stood in the passageway. He was fairly sure that these uniformed men were legitimate policemen, yet he nevertheless felt strangely unsettled. What if they weren't? Curious that Major Hung had forbidden anyone to broadcast a message without clearing with him. Mitch reached into his hip pocket, feeling for the Colt. Damn. That's right. Chief Topelius had it now and the assault rifle Mitch got in trade lay three decks up behind the wheelhouse. How to nail down the identity of these Asian strangers?

An idea formed as Dave, the messman, came out of the galley with a large glass pot of coffee in one hand and a fistful of mugs in the other. A tall lanky young man, he wore a thin gold necklace.

"Dave," said Mitch, "I'm a vice-president of this company. Do me a favor, will you? On your way to the bridge, stop by Sparks' office on A deck and ask Bert Takahara to come down here, just for a second. Tell him it's urgent from Mitch."

"Okay, Mr. Mitch."

Takahara showed up a minute later. His face was smudged and his hands black with grime. "Another hour's work on the bastard. . . . What's up, Mitch?" He frowned as he glanced at the policeman.

Mitch drew Takahara aside and with his own back to the police guard, he spoke just above a whisper. "I got a crazy hunch these may not be cops."

"Oh? There's one watching me up in the radio room."

"So how did you get away?"

"I told him I had to get a tool."

"In English?"

"English, Japanese and some bad Chinese."

"Which one did he understand?"

Takahara shrugged. "Not sure."

"Bert, let's try this guy." He hooked a thumb toward the impassive policeman. "Walk over and say something casual to him in Japanese."

"Right."

Takahara bowed to the guard. *"Gokigen ikaga desu ka?"*

The policeman inclined his head. *"Okage sama de."*

"Nanji desu ka?"

The man glanced at his wristwatch. *"Ichiji desu."*

Takahara turned to Mitch. "He understands. He says he's fine, thanks, and the time is one o'clock."

Mitch again turned his back on the guard. "Bert, I think these guys could be fakes. They might be the yakuza-Elger gang. I'd feel better if we could send out an SOS."

"I'll try to get to the battery-powered radios in the lifeboats. I was about to break one out anyway."

"How you going to duck your guard?"

"I'll figure something." He hurried off along the passageway.

The uniformed man, as expressionless as pudding, growled something at Mitch. He gestured at his mouth, apparently notifying Mitch that he was forbidden to talk further.

The supply-room door opened. Quebrada, with his usual look of sunny malevolence, came out ahead of Major Hung who now had a drawn revolver. Hung barked a command at his subordinate—again it sounded like Japanese to Mitch—and motioned with his weapon.

"Follow him," he said, placing Mitch behind the guard. Quebrada walked behind Mitch and Major Hung, revolver in hand, brought up the rear. The four men trudged up three flights to the wheelhouse.

There was an air of impatience on the bridge. Joahannes had left, apparently for his shower and change of clothes, and so had several others, but Mona, Zabib, Muldoon and Topelius were standing about. The uniformed men were still there, one at each door.

Hung walked over to Mona. "I must ask you to hand over that handgun, Captain."

"Why?" Mona was stunned.

Hung snatched the Colt .45 from her waist and slipped the gun into his jacket pocket.

"How dare you?" Mona was furious.

"We have information that you and a passenger who is also your lover are carrying contraband." Hung spoke as if he had rehearsed the line. "We will search your quarters."

"You will do nothing of the kind." Mona spoke in cold anger.

Hung, not deigning to answer, merely shrugged. He gave a guttural command to his men, picked up his two dispatch cases and walked off the bridge several steps behind Carlos Quebrada.

"Everybody fold hands at chest," ordered the fleshy guard standing at a door. "Nobody leave. You leave, we shoot."

As he crossed his arms, Mitch stared at the man. Was this Takeo Kirihara? His hunch said yes, but he could not be certain. Although he'd seen the yakuza chief twice, he'd never seen him face to face.

"Do you have a warrant?" asked Mona. "You are violating the law of the sea."

"No talking!"

"I'll speak whenever I wish aboard this ship." Mona had not folded her arms.

In a flash the tubby guard whipped a pistol from his holster and fired at Mona's feet. The sharp report reverberated in the enclosed bridge like an explosion. A wooden latticework covered the steel deck and the shot penetrated an opening, ricocheted off the deck and hit the bulkhead near the gyrocompass with a strange little whine.

"No talk." He accompanied the reminder with a contradictory honeyed smile.

This time Mona, appalled but seemingly unfrightened, folded her arms like the rest of the *Zabibian* people. They stood stiffly, the silence broken only by an occasional cough and the clearing of throats. Mitch found himself near the port door between Zabib and Topelius, the only friendly person on the bridge with a concealed weapon. Mitch wondered why the invaders had failed to search everyone. The guard stood at the doorway at Zabib's elbow.

A shout came from below, apparently from one of the guards on the main deck near the rope ladder. Both Asians in uniform looked in that direction and in that instant Zabib whispered to Mitch, "These are not police. They're Japanese yakuza."

"How do you know?" Mitch whispered in reply.

"Look close. In those tight gloves, you can see the left little finger has been cut off."

The exchange buoyed Mitch despite their new predicament as prisoners. This was the first solid indication that Zabib was precisely what he seemed to be—a proud shipowner taking a trip from Singapore to Japan on his favored flagship. Mitch felt a surge of affection for the Jordanian. He had always liked and admired the man, but suspicions had dampened his feelings. Now, in a time of need, he had a comrade.

And it was true. If the yakuza had worn the gloves to conceal mutilated fingers, they had failed. Both guards on the bridge had drawn their gloves tight and in each case, a short left little finger could be seen clearly.

Major Hung, that neat rectangle in blue, strode back onto the bridge with Quebrada at his heels. Hung flourished the two dispatch cases over his head. "About ten pounds of pure heroin in each one," he proclaimed triumphantly. "We found some plastic sacks in Captain Harkinson's quarters and one concealed beneath clothing in a drawer of the man Donahey's cabin."

"I don't believe it," said Mona. "Open those and show me."

"I'll open them for the courts in Singapore," said Hung coldly, "and not before."

"This is a frame-up," said Mona. "I think you're imposters."

"You can tell that to the court." Contemptuous, Hung turned his back on her.

Mitch whispered out of the corner of his mouth to Zabib. "Zab, I'm going to shove you. Roll with it."

"We are taking Captain Harkinson and Mitchell Donahey into custody," continued Hung, "and conveying them to Singapore to await action of the courts." He spoke to the affable guard who had fired the shot. "Go get the radio officer, Joahannes. We are taking him to Singapore where a determination . . ."

Mitch shoved Zabib with all his strength, slamming the shipowner bodily against the young guard in the doorway. The man crumpled and fell to the deck with gun in hand. Mitch threw himself over the fallen man, rolled a few feet, scrambled to his feet and ran the few yards to the back of the wheelhouse. He snatched the assault rifle off the deck from beneath the flag locker and wheeled around to face anyone who might follow him.

He now stood directly behind the wheelhouse in the space that was protected on four sides, to the rear by the tanker's stack, to starboard by the broad base of the radar mast and to port by the flag locker. There were about three feet of open space between the rear of the wheelhouse and the locker on one side and the radar mast on the other. A ladder also provided the only access to the flying bridge atop the wheelhouse.

A shouted command—again it sounded Japanese to Mitch—preceded the thud of feet. Men were running nearby. Mitch braced himself reflexively in the stance that had once been second nature to him, feet planted, rifle at the ready extending from his waist. Although the night was even darker than earlier, rays of light from inside the wheelhouse fell outside the structure. A blue beret popped into sight from a corner of the wheelhouse, popped right back again. Mitch waited. A crouched uniformed figure slowly emerged, first the roll of the beret, then a handgun, then the head, then the arms, legs and torso. It was the fat one. Kirihara? The yakuza—Mitch was certain now—took a full step into view. The man was at a disadvantage. He was hunting in unfamiliar territory.

Mitch raised the rifle, aimed carefully at the legs—he had no desire to kill—and pressed the trigger. Brrrrrp. The burst of several shots from the semi-automatic tore into the man below the knees. He fell with a scream and the weapon in his hand clattered on the deck. It came to rest about ten feet away. Mitch ran out, rifle wheeling from the waist, and kicked the gun across the deck to the safety of his mini-fort. Back behind the flag locker, he picked up the gun and examined it: a .357 Smith & Wesson Magnum. Mitch jammed it behind his belt. The wounded guard rolled away, disappearing behind the corner of the wheelhouse.

Shouts came from within the bridge and from the main deck. The wounded yakuza cried again in pain. Somewhere in the interior of the house a shot was fired.

Mitch's body switched into a kind of overdrive, running cool on high power and tremendous energy. Once having fired the gun, he felt anxiety and fear evaporate, leaving him eager, wary, so finely tuned that he could have heard the approach of cat's feet. He felt none of the old lust to kill—and for that he was grateful—but rather an intense determination to protect himself and to rout the invaders. His thinking became nakedly clear, uncluttered by the usual ambivalences. Enough that he survive with Mona and keep the ship.

Crouched at the ready in his mini-fort, he assessed the situation. Besides himself of the tanker people, only Topelius, still in the wheelhouse, and Sandy Otis were armed. Who had fired that shot inside the house? . . . Bert Takahara needed to make his way to one of the lifeboats and an emergency radio. Two things, Mitch decided, had to be done: force the yakuza off the tanker and somehow bring the real channel police aboard in their stead.

As he stood rooted on the deck, his mind racing, he found himself directly facing the ladder to the flying bridge atop the wheelhouse. In fact, he was staring at the fifth rung of the ladder and if it had been daylight, he knew he would have seen the new coat of white paint which seamen had recently applied to the whole bridge area.

Of course. A natural. The flying bridge. Up there he could command lines of fire to the whole ship without being a ready target himself. He edged toward the ladder, looked to the right and left, saw no one, ran four quick steps, grabbed a rung and scrambled up. When he could see over the top, he slid the HK 91 ahead of him, then completed the climb.

He was now on the bare roof of the wheelhouse, a steel-plated area about thirty feet square. A railing extended around the perimeter and in the rear the narrowing radar mast thrust upward another twenty feet. The mast held a ladder that rose to a crow's nest near the top. Aside from this projection and several small hooded instruments, the flying bridge stood empty. No one on any of the decks below could shoot him as long as he stayed near the center of this square, whereas he could fire to almost any exposed part of the ship. On his belly near the edge he would be almost impossible to hit. In only two directions was he vulnerable. He could, of course, be shot from above, but he doubted that the yakuza, even with their sophisticated methods, had planned an attack by helicopter. Also he could be surprised by someone climbing the same ladder he had used. He determined to keep a close watch on the spot where the ladder was attached.

Kneeling now in the center of the flying bridge, he could see the place on the port gunwale of the main deck where two guards stood. They performed their sentry duty at the top of the rope ladder about midway between house and the tanker's bow or some 130 or 140 yards on a slant line from the spot where Mitch knelt. Dropping to his belly, he crawled forward until he reached the forward edge of the wheelhouse roof. He glanced behind several times to make sure that no one had ascended the ladder.

Despite the darkness, he could make out the forms of the two guards. In fact, thanks to light reflected from below, undoubtedly from the motor launch still tied alongside the tanker, he could see the cut of their uniforms and the shape of their berets. They stood several yards apart. Lining up his rifle, Mitch took a sight on one of the men who was speaking into his walkie-talkie. The man held the instrument in his left hand and a gun in his right. Mitch aimed at the knees. The man turned, took several steps while he talked. Mitch aimed again, held the sight for a moment, then squeezed.

The burst shattered the quiet night. Instantly came the screech of metal striking metal, a yelp of pain and the thud of a body on the deck. At least one of the cluster had struck the guard. His companion re-holstered his own gun, then grabbed the fallen guard by the shoulders and dragged him several yards down the deck to the shelter of a large power winch.

Complete silence ensued. Not a sound came from the crowded bridge. Nothing could be heard from the motor launch below. Mitch, alert to his own safety, glanced repeatedly toward the rear ladder to the flying bridge, then looked slowly about the ship. He saw rapid movement down on A deck. Some one was walking toward the Number One lifeboat. A man mounted a few steps to the block beside the roofed boat, swung himself aboard, opened one of the hatches and disappeared inside. Confident that the figure was Bert Takahara going for the emergency radio, Mitch swung his gun around to cover approaches to the craft. Shortly the hatch reopened and Takahara, if it were he, stood with an object in his hands. Mitch assumed that it was one of the marine safety radios that, when once triggered, sent out a constant series of SOS signals. Rescue vessels could then home in on the device.

"Donahey!" It was the voice of the man calling himself Hung as amplified by the electric bullhorn. The shout came from the bridge directly below Mitch.

"What do you want?"

"Listen carefully. If you shoot another one of my men, I will line up two people from the *Zabibian* and execute them." The warning was loud and the diction slow and measured. "I will start with the captain and the owner of this ship."

Mitch did not reply. He doubted that the yakuza officer would dare carry out his threat in patrolled, crowded waters, but he could not be certain. He had to admit that Hung had regained a decided advantage. His mind struggled to meet the challenge.

"Did you hear me?"

Again he remained silent. Better to keep Hung guessing.

"You have crippled two of my men," came the voice from the bullhorn. "If you do not reply within two minutes, I will shoot the foot off one of your people on this bridge."

"Okay, I hear you," Mitch replied at once with the knowledge that he had been outmaneuvered a second time.

After a pause, the electrically amplified voice boomed again. "Then hear this." Hung's words bounced about the tanker. "You have exactly two minutes in which to throw your gun down to this bridge deck and climb down and surrender. If you don't comply, I will shoot someone standing on this bridge."

Another ship moved eastward down the channel and Mitch guessed it would pass them several hundred yards to port in three or four minutes. Was the vessel, a large one, judging by the spacing of the lights, picking up Takahara's SOS from the lifeboat hatch? It seemed weird to be at the mercy of a criminal gang here with so many ships plowing the nearby channels and the lights of metropolitan Singapore still visible as a glow in the western sky. He must play for time. But how much time could he risk?

Suddenly, perhaps because of the simulation of battle conditions, he remembered the stock phrase of a hardened cynical regular Army sergeant in Viet Nam. "When cornered, counterattack. If it doesn't work, you'll never know it." Mitch decided to stall for time by threatening a counterattack.

"Hey, Hung!" he called.

"I'm here," came the prompt answer via bullhorn.

"Two of your men need medical attention. If you and your men leave this ship at once, taking your wounded with you, nobody will be fired on and your launch will be permitted to get away."

Hung shouted something—a Japanese expletive?—and then said, "I repeat. If you have not surrendered in two minutes, I will shoot one of your people. I am starting the count on my watch. One hundred twenty seconds . . . one hundred eighteen . . . one hundred sixteen . . ."

20

Mitch saw movement on A deck near the lifeboat. A figure that he assumed was Takahara ran from the boat to the narrow deck behind the house, used struts and a connecting pipe to pull himself up to the bridge deck and ducked into the protected enclosure behind the wheelhouse.

Mitch, bending at the waist, ran to the rear of the flying bridge and peered over the ladder. Yes, the figure was Bert Takahara. He was crouching beside the flag locker, apparently trying to decide what to do next.

"Bert." Mitch called in a low voice.

Takahara looked up, saw Mitch above him.

From inside the wheelhouse came the droning of numbers on the bullhorn. "Eighty-eight . . . eighty-six." The yakuza chief masquerading as a police major continued his surrealist countdown to murder.

Mitch swung down the ladder, pulled from his belt the .357 Smith & Wesson that he'd retrieved when the wounded yakuza fell. He pressed it into Bert's hand.

"You go around the port side," he said. "I'll take the starboard. We have to get the bastards before they kill somebody in there."

The bullhorn bleated its falling numbers on the muggy oppressive air: "Eighty . . . seventy-eight . . ."

A gun fired inside the wheelhouse. A single shot rang a prelude to shattering glass. The lights went out and the moonless night that shrouded the long tanker now blackened the bridge as well. Who shot out the lights? Topelius? No other friend on the bridge had a weapon. From inside came a babble of sound, shouted commands, a yelp of pain, heavy male voices freighted with fear. Nothing from Mona.

Mitch ran at a crouch around the side of the wheelhouse, saw a young uniformed man in the doorway. The yakuza was aiming his gun at someone within. Mitch jumped to his right to get a wider angle and fired a burst. The blast ripped into the fake policeman's arm, tore the gun from his hand and spun him about. He sank to the deck with a plaintive cry, a wavering bird-like lament. He slumped in the doorway.

The pistol lay at his feet for not more than a second before it was scooped up by someone bolting through the doorway. Mitch trained his rifle on the exit, but the man who came lunging out of the wheelhouse wore, not a uniform, but a cashmere sweater. A shot was fired after him, missed, ricocheted off the steel deck. Wasif Zabib threw himself away from the doorway, regained his balance and managed a wan smile as he turned to face the doorway with the gun in his hand.

Swiftly Mitch sought to assess the situation. Weren't the yakuza in the wheelhouse now reduced to but two men? Of the original five who came to the bridge, one fake policeman had been dispatched to guard the communications room and apparently had not returned even though Takahara had escaped by some stratagem. Two others lay wounded and disarmed, their guns now in the possession of Zabib and Takahara. That left the chief who called himself Hung and one other man.

Mitch was about to call Zabib when he heard the ping of metal on the bulkhead to his right. At the same time he felt a stinging sensation on his left arm. To his surprise a patch of red appeared on his shirt sleeve just below the shoulder. The shot, he surmised, could have come only from below. A portion of his body had extended above the steel windbreak which ran from the wheelhouse out to the wings. Looking down on the main deck, he saw a yakuza kneeling beside the power winch where he had dragged his wounded companion after Mitch's shot from the flying bridge. The man was aiming a gun, apparently an assault rifle, at Mitch for another shot. Mitch ducked down just as a burst splattered against the steel windbreak.

He heard a shot from somewhere around the house and when he rose above the windbreak for another look at the yakuza kneeling beside the power winch, he saw to his amazement that the man lay sprawled on the deck, his inert body half covering his rifle. Glancing quickly about, Mitch saw Zabib cautiously approaching the wheelhouse doorway with the newly acquired pistol in his hand. Obviously he had not fired. But someone had. The number of wounded or killed yakuza, out of the seven who came up from the motor launch, now totaled four. Mitch swiveled his eyes again and this time he saw the bearded bosun, Sandy Otis, standing where Mitch had recently crouched up on the flying bridge. Otis held a handgun, undoubtedly the .22 automatic pistol he had taken from Quebrada two hours earlier—hours that seemed like months. If Otis had indeed shot the yakuza, he qualified as an expert marksman, for the power winch on the main deck was located more than 130 yards from the flying bridge: a remarkable pistol shot by daylight and phenomenal—or phenomenally lucky—by night.

Mitch felt his arm again. It was sore now and the red spot on his shirt just below the shoulder had enlarged and become sticky with blood. Still, he had use of the arm and he did not regard the wound as critical. He had been grazed, he concluded, nothing worse.

Swiftly appraising the fight against the boarders of the tanker, Mitch saw that the odds heavily favored *Zabibian*'s defenders on the decks. On the other hand, the yakuza held the commanding wheelhouse.

While Hung's countdown chant stopped the moment the lights were shot out, Mitch could not take the chance that the bogus police officer had dropped his plan to shoot Mona, Muldoon or Topelius, the three tanker officers left inside the bridge, if Mitch did not surrender within two minutes—now perhaps down to thirty seconds.

With Takahara covering one of the two doors and Zabib the other, Mitch slipped by Zabib and placed himself at the corner of the wheelhouse. By craning his neck he could see into the nearest of the five large windows which stretched across the front of the wheelhouse, affording maximum visibility of the sea to officers on duty.

Although it was dark inside, the glow from the two radar scopes cast an eerie light, just enough so that people and movements could be distinguished. A strange scene was unfolding. The yakuza sent to the communications room must have returned, for Mitch saw three able-bodied men in the blue berets and uniforms. Major Hung was making himself a remarkable human sandwich. In the middle stood an armed yakuza supporting Kirihara whom Mitch had shot in the legs. Next to him Carlos Quebrada held the young yakuza whose arm had been shattered by Mitch's last burst. A second guard, using Bill Muldoon as a shield, had a grip on the back of the chief mate's belt. Major Hung had a similar grip on the back of Mona Harkinson's dungarees and he too was using the captain as a shield. On the deck lay Risto Topelius. The chief engineer was not moving and Mitch assumed he had been slugged and disarmed after shooting out the lights.

The bizarre people sandwich was lined up facing the rear doorway. Mona came first, then Hung, with drawn gun, then the largest yakuza and Quebrada supporting the two badly wounded men, then the young yakuza with readied gun and finally Muldoon who would have to walk backward while the young criminal soldier held his belt.

Abandoned on the deck, perhaps by design or perhaps forgotten in the turmoil lay the two large dispatch cases that Major Hung and a subordinate had brought aboard. So much for the purported evidence of smuggled drugs.

"We are coming out and going to the launch." Although Hung's shout arose from deep chords, Mitch thought he detected a sliver of panic. "If anyone fires or otherwise tries to stop us, your captain will be shot instantly. A second move against us will bring instant death to your chief mate."

With that, the five yakuza and Quebrada, sandwiched between their human shields, moved toward the stairway at the rear of the bridge. The shift in dominant fire power from the yakuza to the defenders of the tanker had forced Hung to abandon his plan to kidnap Mitch. The criminals, though still capable of murdering their hostages, were in retreat.

"We will take the elevator to the main deck," said Hung in a voice that sounded oddly sepulchral, "and then walk down the deck to the rope ladder above the patrol boat. We will shoot anyone who follows or interferes."

The minute the group disappeared, Mitch, Zabib and Takahara

moved into the wheelhouse. Takahara located a flashlight hanging in a bracket near the coffee maker and shone it about. Risto Topelius lay unconscious in front of the chart table. An ugly purpling lump on his forehead seemed to confirm that he had been slugged. Mitch called a lookout from one of the wings, instructed him to look after the chief engineer and give him what first aid he could.

"Okay," said Mitch to Zabib and Takahara. "How are we going to stop them leaving the ship?"

"I don't see how we can," said Zabib. "If we shoot, I have no doubt they'll kill Mona and Muldoon."

"They may leave the captain and chief mate behind, once they reach their launch," said Takahara. The man who once regarded the yakuza with schoolboy fascination now had a steely look.

"Yeah." Mitch stood with the assault rifle in hand. "I thought of that. Why take Mona and Bill with them? Just another headache. They have to make a fast getaway."

"Kidnap and ransom demand?" Zabib held the seized .357 Magnum awkwardly at his side.

Mitch shook his head. "Too risky—and not a yakuza thing."

Looking out the bridge windows, they saw the strange seven-person file marching toward the rope ladder amidships. Mona in the lead was being steered by Hung who still had a tight grip on the back of her dungarees. Muldoon, walking backward in a half stumble, was being steered by the youngest yakuza.

"Damn, I feel helpless." Mitch watched as the Japanese and their hostages detoured around a clutter of pipes. Helpless, he told himself, was such a mild word for what he felt. Actually, he was in a torment of frustration. But he knew, deep within him, that should harm come to Mona, he would track and kill Hung no matter how long or how far it took him.

From overhead came the sound of thudding feet. In a moment Sandy Otis burst through the doorway. "A police patrol boat coming on the port side." The bearded bosun was out of breath from rushing down from the flying bridge. He held the .22 pistol in his hand. "This time it looks like the real thing."

"Let's hope to Christ it is," said Mitch. "Where do you turn on that searchlight, Sandy?"

Otis flipped a switch on the port bulkhead and a powerful beam shone down on the water. Mitch spotted the bullhorn on a window

ledge, apparently where Hung had left it. Picking it up, he walked
out to the port wing in the van of the other men. Why he was
assuming leadership, Mitch wasn't sure. Perhaps because none of the
others, Zabib, Takahara, Otis, jumped into the vacuum left by the
seizure of the captain and chief mate. Perhaps because of his old
military training. All he knew was that there was no time in which to
choose leaders or flip coins. Somebody had to act fast.

Into the beam of the searchlight came a patrol boat of some forty-
plus feet with a high enclosed bridge, radar mast and mounted machine guns, one fore and one aft. The aluminum craft had POLICE
lettered on the side of the bridge and flew the red-and-white Singapore flag with five white stars and a crescent in its red upper half. On
board stood a half-dozen armed men in blue uniforms, identical to
those worn by the yakuza, including short-sleeved shirts and berets.
They all wore yellow life vests with "PT 7" stenciled on the breast.

The boat slowed down preparatory to pulling alongside the spurious police craft and at once the difference in the two vessels became
obvious. The yakuza launch had a covered cockpit rather than a
bridge, no radar mast, no POLICE legend and no mounted machine
guns. Also none of the intruders who had boarded the *Zabibian* wore
life-preserver vests bearing the stenciled number of the boat. In contrast to the first arrival, this PT boat smacked of official marine
police.

"Responding to your distress signal." The voice, with its clearly
articulated English, came amplified from the patrol boat via a bullhorn.

Mitch thought fast. What to say that would not endanger the lives
of Mona and the chief mate? But time raced. He had to risk.

"We have been boarded by pirates," Mitch called through the
electric megaphone. "Approach us with caution. And watch that
launch. We think there are armed men aboard her."

"Are you the master?" The patrol boat reversed engine, backed off
from the other craft.

"No. Our captain, a woman, is held hostage by the boarders. They
also hold the chief mate. They are now approaching the rope ladder
with intent to leave this ship. There has been gun fighting and we
have wounded four of the pirates. Only one of us has been hurt. We
think the boarders are Japanese yakuza. You can identify them because all of them are wearing copies of your police uniforms."

"This is Captain Lum of the Singapore Marine Police," boomed the bullhorn on the patrol boat. "I order everyone in the power launch and everyone aboard the tanker to lay down your firearms. You are to stand exactly where you are now with raised hands. Anyone who refuses will be shot. This order applies to everyone. I repeat. Everyone."

"I guess that means us, too," said Mitch. He placed his assault rifle on the deck. "Let's hope these are real police this time—and not some of those pirates we've heard about."

"The pirates came from the Indonesian side," said Otis. "Not much question that these are Singapore marine police." He put his pistol on the deck. Takahara and Zabib followed suit. "I was wrong the first time, but I'll bet a month's pay on this bunch."

Standing on the port wing, enclosed by the chest-high steel plate, the men all raised their empty hands above the gunwale. They had a gallery view of the action down below. Major Hung and his little parade of wounded and hostages had halted on the main deck a few yards from the rope ladder. He still held his handgun as did two of his men. Hung looked down toward the patrol boat's mounted machine guns, apparently calculating the odds.

He glanced up at the bridge, looked around the main deck and then back at the patrol boat and its firepower. Silence wrapped the long tanker and the two boats. Out in the channels, the lights of two ships passed one another, one headed toward Singapore, the other toward the South China Sea. Mitch put himself in Hung's place, considered the options. Threaten to kill the hostages. Fight it out. Pump oil over the side, polluting the Strait—unless he and his men were allowed to leave the tanker unharmed and unfollowed. And yet, of course, whatever Hung did, the launch eventually would be captured in this crowded waterway. In the end, the yakuza had not a chance in a thousand of escaping.

Marine police waited with drawn weapons and manned machine guns. Mitch could see Mona standing upright, her shoulders thrown back, the stance of a proud woman awaiting her fate.

At last after seconds that seemed like hours, the invader who called himself Hung stooped over and laid his gun on the deck. No *kamikaze* blood flowed in his veins. He had surrendered.

As Hung straightened up, raising his arms, he shouted something in Japanese, a hoarse, guttural command. The two other yakuza in the group dropped their pistols on the deck. One raised his hands as did Mona and Muldoon. Quebrada and the other gang member had their hands full supporting Kirihara and the other wounded man.

Below, bathed by the searchlight, three men on the yakuza launch came out in the open with raised hands. When one of them glanced upward to the bridge, Mitch was astonished to see the thin face and scrawny neck of Bones Elger. So he wanted to be in on the kidnapping, did he? And was that the point of this whole operation—to get Mona and himself? Somehow revenge seemed a waste of time and energy for the reputedly cost-efficient yakuza.

Now the police PT boat pulled alongside the launch. Three men carrying rifles stepped aboard, escorted Elger and two Asians over to the PT boat where they were placed under guard at the stern of the boat.

Five men, led by Captain Lum, a short, squat but exceedingly active officer, scrambled up the rope ladder. After a short conversation with Mona and Major Hung, which Mitch up on the wing could not hear, Lum gave orders and the three able-bodied yakuza were led to the rope ladder while a man aboard the PT boat trained the bow machine gun on them. They went down the ladder, walked across the launch and gave themselves into custody on the patrol craft. Since all the men from the PT boat wore the yellow life vests and no gloves, it was easy to distinguish them from the yakuza despite the counterfeit Singapore marine police uniforms worn by the Japanese and Elger.

Captain Lum conferred further with Mona and Muldoon and a policeman took Quebrada by the arm and led him aside. The chief mate called for several seamen to come down from the house. In a few minutes a boom was swung out over the port side and a line dropped to the patrol boat. There marine policemen attached a hammock-like net which was raised to the main deck. One of the wounded yakuza was placed in the hammock and then lowered to the police boat. The operation was repeated for the other three casualties while Mona and the Singapore marine police captain made their way to the bridge of the *Zabibian.*

Meanwhile Risto Topelius had been revived by a seaman and had walked unsteadily out to the port wing. The lump on his forehead still looked forbidding and he said that he had a throbbing headache and felt nauseated. Mitch, Zabib, Otis and Takahara decided among them that the chief engineer should be taken back to Singapore for examination. There was a chance he was suffering from concussion. The seaman helped Topelius to the elevator and escorted him down to the main deck where his shipmates used the boom and hammock to lower him to the PT boat.

Mona appeared her normal self when she and Captain Lum appeared on the bridge, now lighted by the large flashlight that Otis had propped on the window ledge. Carlos Quebrada stood in the shadows under guard.

"How you doing, Mona?" Mitch was amazed that she showed no signs of aftershock.

"Okay, now." She smiled thinly. "But on that long march down to the rope ladder, I thought I'd had it." Then she saw Mitch's arm and her eyes immediately reflected her concern. "Oh, Mitch. You've been shot."

"Nothing serious. Although, I guess along about now I could use a dressing on it."

Manny Rodriguez, who had just entered the wheelhouse, was sent below for a first-aid kit.

Captain Lum, who appeared to be Chinese, placed his pistol in his holster, then undid his life vest and laid it aside. He took a stance of authority with folded arms in the center of the bridge.

"Now I want to hear just what happened." His clipped English had a British accent. "All the men wearing blue police-type uniforms have been placed under arrest on our boat. The wearing of our uniforms is evidence, at least on the surface, of criminal intent—unless they were attending a masquerade party." Lum smiled at his own joke. "But that does not exonerate the rest of you. First, where are the guns you fired?"

"Out there on the port wing." Zabib indicated with a nod of his head.

Lum gave an order, apparently in Chinese, and one of his men went out and came back with the firearms. He deposited them on the window ledge beside Lum.

"Now I want everybody connected with the tanker identified and brought up here to the bridge," said Lum. "Unless someone is needed in the engine room. He can stay there."

Mona ordered one of the seamen to round up all officers and crew and bring them to the bridge.

"Now then, I want your story. Captain Harkinson?"

Mona took a good ten minutes sketching not only the arrival of the yakuza after Joahannes had been pushed overboard, but some of the background that prompted an official investigation in Philadelphia after the sinking of the *Yandoon Princess.* While she talked, Rodriguez returned with first-aid supplies and the second mate, doubling as the ship's paramedic, cleaned and bandaged Mitch's arm.

"And why do you think the alleged yakuza boarded . . ."

"More than alleged," Mitch cut in. "Look at their left hands. Little fingers all cut off at the upper knuckle. And look under their shirts. I'll bet they're all heavily tattooed."

"Thank you. And why," Lum repeated, "do you think they boarded your tanker tonight?"

"I'm mystified." Mona, showing the strain now, leaned against the long ledge beneath the windows that served as the eyes of the tanker. "The phony heroin charge was just an excuse to get Mitch and me to come along with them. So I suppose they were here to kidnap us and perhaps kill us later, I just don't know."

"That's it," said Mitch. "An act of vengeance. That's all I can come up with. Ten to one those dispatch cases are empty."

One of Lum's men, responding to a gesture from the captain, brought him the discarded leather cases. Mitch was right. There was nothing inside. The captain set the cases down near the firearms, then asked, "Does anyone care to add to or make corrections in the captain's story?"

"I'm the guy who went overboard." Arno Joahannes had changed into dry clothes. "I just want to say that I'm the one that that man over there, Quebrada, walloped with a club and knocked overboard. For no reason. I hadn't said a word to the guy."

Lum turned to Quebrada. "What's your name?"

"Carlos Quebrada, a citizen of Mexico."

"Did you knock this man off the ship?"

"No."

"Where were you when he went overboard?"

"I got nothin' more to say."

"Did you have a handgun in your possession as the captain has told us?"

"I ain't talkin'. *Nada.*"

"All right," said Lum to the marine policeman standing beside

Quebrada. "Take him down to the boat. We'll let the magistrate question him." Lum turned to Mona. He was a crisply efficient officer. Having already filled his apparent quota of one joke per episode, he intended to waste no further time. "Now, Captain, I'll have to trouble you to come along with us to Singapore to place charges. Also Officer Joahannes. And I think it would be advisable if the owner you mentioned—a Mr. Zabib?—came along as well. And Mr. Donahey too since he can identify the American you said was working with the Japanese."

"How long will all this take?" asked Mona. "We're behind schedule now."

"The preliminary charging can be done as soon as the courts open this morning. Of course, in case of a trial, you'll be wanted later as witnesses—a month or so from now perhaps."

"Well, good. I have to have the radio power line repaired anyway." Mona fussed at her hair as if readying for departure. "Just so we're under way by tomorrow evening. More than a day late in Tokyo Bay we can't afford. Beginning the second day, it costs us $50,000 a day in penalties."

"I understand the problems of the rich," said the captain drily. "We'll have you back to your tanker by tomorrow afternoon."

Mona, Mitch, Zabib and Joahannes went to their cabins to ready themselves for the trip to Singapore and ten minutes later they were seated in the patrol boat and bouncing over the dark waters toward the glow of Singapore some thirty miles to the west. Mona wore a simple pantsuit, Mitch and Joahannes wore sport shirts, but Zabib, to Mitch's amusement, was dressed as though for a garden party, pin-striped suit, monogrammed shirt, silk tie and the usual sapphire ring. They sat in a row under cover of the bridgehouse.

Behind them on mats under the covered forward section of the boat lay the four wounded yakuza and Chief Engineer Topelius. A marine policeman was doing his best with elementary first aid.

Mitch sat next to Mona. He could feel the fatigue in the warm body pressing against him, but he could also see the pride in those gray eyes and in the set of her jaw. "We licked them," she whispered, fiercely triumphant. And he knew that having come through it together, they had forged another bond between them.

Seated in the open stern facing the tanker group were the invaders and Quebrada. In their blue berets and uniforms, the unwounded invaders numbered six in all, Bones Elger and five Asians, most of whom looked quite Japanese. Under the muzzle of a machine gun, they sat silently and glumly, splashed now and then by spray, their eyes downcast save for an occasional glance at their captors.

On one of these glances, the eyes of Elger and Mitch met for an instant. Elger rammed a finger skyward in the familiar obscene gesture of defiance.

Mitch smiled. He didn't mind a bit. This was one battle where Sergeant Bones wouldn't cut a single ear.

21

The *Zabibian* slid through long swells under a quarter moon and a sky ablaze with stars. The tanker had emerged from the Singapore Strait an hour ago, now rolled gently in the open ocean. With Sandy Otis of the rusty beard at the helm, the ship headed northeast across the South China Sea toward the Luzon Strait between Taiwan and the top of the Philippines.

Freed of the trauma of fighting off the yakuza boarders and the tensions of navigating the crowded, long and often narrow channel, officers and men had relaxed to the point of torpor. Most of the men were asleep as was the owner and chief passenger, Wasif Zabib, now affectionately dubbed "the gunslinger" by the crew, an appellation he obviously relished. Third Mate Sven Ahlgren had the bridge watch.

Captain Mona and Mitch stood on the starboard wing for a breath of sea breeze and a quiet chat before turning in for the night. Both were drooping with fatigue, neither having slept in more than thirty hours. They had not returned to the channel anchorage from Singapore until mid-afternoon and then Mona had to get the vessel underway and cleared of the Strait before she felt free to go to bed.

"This is the first chance I've had to tell you how great you were," she said. "Without you aboard, sweetheart—and you know I didn't want you here at first—God knows what would have happened to us."

"I guess I'm okay in certain kinds of emergencies. It's the emotional ones—you know, people-to-people stuff—where I flunk out."

"Not true. You did just right in our one big fight." She slid her arm inside his and in the dark of the wing snuggled against his shoulder for a moment. "What do you guess will happen to Elger and his yakuza buddies?" she asked when she raised her head again.

"I think they'll get put away for a few years. Singapore is tough on pirates."

All nine yakuza, together with Bones Elger, had been held for trial without bail by a Singapore district judge that morning on charges of illegal boarding of a ship, shooting with intent to kill, attempted armed robbery, impersonating Singapore marine policemen, carrying weapons without a permit and assault and battery on the person of Risto Topelius. In addition, Carlos Quebrada was held for trial for clubbing and attempting to drown Arno Joahannes, the radio officer.

While the financial power of the yakuza was reflected in their ability on short notice to retain one of the leading and most expensive defense lawyers in Singapore, the attorney had failed to gain the reduction or dismissal of any of the charges. Trial date was set two months hence when Captain Harkinson would be in her vacation cycle and available to testify. Mitch, Zabib, Takahara, Otis, Topelius and Joahannes all were slated to return for testimony.

Mitch had used some of his time to visit a hospital near the courts and have his wound properly cleaned and dressed. The Chinese doctor predicted the muscle would heal fully within a week. Topelius, it turned out, did not have a concussion. The Singapore doctors pronounced him fit to continue the trip to Japan provided he did not work overtime. While the tanker people were in Singapore, a marine electrical crew from the city went aboard the *Zabibian* and repaired both the regular and auxiliary power lines in the communications room. The tanker's crew repaired the electric fixtures on the bullet-scarred bridge.

"I can't understand," said Mona, "why that fancy defense lawyer didn't raise the point of jurisdiction. Actually, you know, the eastbound channel in the Strait is part of Indonesia's territory. The Singapore marine police are supposed to confine themselves to their waters, which means the westbound channel."

"Maybe the lawyer will spring it later," Mitch leaned his arms on the windbreak. The night was fresh and warm and he felt pleasantly drowsy now. "But can't you go anywhere to answer an SOS?"

"You can and should, which Captain Lum, thank God, did. We owe a lot to Bert Takahara for getting the lifeboat's radio out. I never heard how he got away from his guard."

"Oh yeah, I forgot to tell you." Mitch laughed. "Bert began talking to the guy in Japanese. Turned out the man came from the island of Shikoku where Bert's grandparents lived before they emigrated to Hawaii. So Bert gets swapping folksy bits of chitchat with the guy and when he pleaded he had to go to the toilet, the guard let him go alone into the john in the radio room. So once in, Bert merely wriggles out through the side porthole and sneaks up to the lifeboat."

"Well, we owe him a lot." Mona stretched and yawned. "If I don't get to bed soon, I'm going to collapse."

"One thing still bugs me. Why did Elger, Kirihara and the gang ever invade us in the first place?"

Mona nodded. "I've gone over and over what happened and I can't figure out what their goal was. To grab you and me and then knock us off later? Was that what it was all about?"

"Maybe, but that's not yakuza style from what I've heard. They'll go in for vengeance all right, but usually at small risk to themselves. Not like the Mafia. And this operation! Special-made uniforms, motor launch, the precise timing, hitting us on cue when Quebrada got rid of Arno, that's all major-league stuff. I can't believe it was just to get rid of us."

"And the two dispatch cases," Mona added. "That was all part of some big plan. But what?"

"Yeah, bringing aboard two empty cases and . . ." Mitch smacked his forehead. "Hey, I just had a wild thought. What if those cases weren't empty when they brought them aboard? Suppose they *were* filled with drugs of some kind and suppose . . ."

"They did plant them in my cabin and in yours," Mona finished. She took his arm. "Come on. Let's go down and have a look."

They first searched Mona's quarters, starting with the bedroom. They looked in the large closet, tried panels, went through the bathroom thoroughly, looked on and under the bed. In the adjoining captain's office, they began with the computer and typewriter center, searched drawers of the desk, looked behind the upholstery of chairs, peered under the table and took books off the shelves of the bookcase. Finally Mona opened and closed the drawers of two file cabinets.

"Holy Jesus! Look at this."

The bottom drawer of one file cabinet held a number of Lorikeet forms for marine record-keeping. They were used so rarely that a film of dust covered the papers. A steel divider separated the front from the back half of the drawer. From the space behind the divider Mona pulled out a plastic container, then another and then a third.

Opening a container, Mona found a tightly taped plastic sack covering a second sack that was filled with a white substance that looked not unlike salt or sugar. Each of the three containers had similar contents.

Mona balanced a plastic box in her hand. "That must weigh a good two or three pounds." She looked at Mitch. "Cocaine maybe?"

"No, that's heroin—a fortune's worth of it."

They sat in silence for a moment, then Mona replaced the boxes in the drawer and closed it. "Okay, now let's go look in your cabin."

It took only a few minutes to find two more rectangular plastic boxes with similar contents in Mitch's room. They were hidden under the mattress near the headboard.

"A safe enough place," said Mona. "Quebrada knows that the mattresses are beaten and reversed only after the switch in crews. Every three months, in other words."

"And who ever looks in the captain's quarters?"

"Right. Nobody."

Mitch sat down on the bed. "So how do we figure this? Is it a frame? They plant the heroin and then tip off the police when the ship arrives in Tokyo Bay? And we spend the rest of our lives in a Japanese prison?"

"Hey, you are groggy." Mona sat down beside him. "We weren't even supposed to be here, remember? We were kidnapped, taken off in that launch, maybe killed. So then two other people travel to Japan in my quarters and yours—maybe the chief mate in mine. And when the ship docks, a yakuza comes aboard under some guise or other and takes the stuff ashore where they sell it."

"That's more like the scenario." Mitch looked at the two containers lying on the bed. "God, the whole batch is worth millions at retail street prices. The Yamaguchi-gumi could get fat off this one trip."

He sat staring at the boxed heroin, struck by the enormous disparity between the modest size of the packages and the huge amount of money they would fetch. Men would kill for them, addicts would rifle their own mothers' pocketbooks to buy a few grains of them. The narcotic had generated a grubby circle of addiction-suppression-crime-law enforcement-hypocrisy. And within that squalid circle, multitudes prospered—transporters, dealers, pushers, lawmen, psychologists, prosecutors, attorneys, social workers, politicians, preachers, writers and healers. The white powder, as deceptively pure and unsoiled as a wedding gown, had spawned the ultimate in human corruption and idiocy.

"Let's see now," he said, reconstructing events. "Old Hung, that fake Chinese, comes aboard with his two dispatch cases loaded with about fifteen pounds of pure heroin. He and Quebrada go down to our rooms for their phony 'search,' taking along the cases. Quebrada shows Hung where to hide the heroin. They come back to the bridge with empty cases, wave them around—but don't open them—claiming they found heroin. And . . ."

"And that's the excuse for hauling us away on fake charges." Mona took up the speculative replay. "So the ruse helps them do away with us and at the same time enables them to ship millions of dollars worth of heroin to Japan. Very neat."

"I think that's it," said Mitch, "which means the yakuza probably have someone else aboard—officers or crew—who'll smuggle the stuff off when we tie up."

"So what do we do?" Mona looked haggard. "I can hardly think straight any longer."

"Legally, I guess, we should call Captain Lum and tell him what the yakuza planted on us—or else call ahead to the Japanese port authorities and tell them what we're bringing."

"No, that'll just make me more notorious than I am right now." She slapped her hands on her dungarees. "I want to get rid of that damn stuff, Mitch. One more controversy involving me and nobody will believe a thing I say—ever."

"We can dump it overboard."

"Right. Nobody knows it's here except the yakuza and Quebrada —and whoever their other man in our crew might be."

"And they're not about to tell anyone." Mitch reached out for the containers. "All right, Mona. The quicker we get rid of this, the safer I'll feel too."

"Okay, let's do it right now."

"Got a knife?"

"A pocketknife in my desk."

Mitch wrapped the containers in newspapers, took the package and followed Mona down the passageway to her office. There he removed all the plastic bags from the containers, made small slits in the sacks with Mona's knife, rewrapped the sacks in a large newspaper bundle.

"Easiest off the starboard side near the lifeboat," she said. "Let me look first to make sure no one's around. Then we'll carry it out."

"Hell, I can manage it."

"With a wounded arm? Don't play it macho now."

She walked to the end of the passageway and out on A deck, then came back and helped Mitch lift the package and the five empty containers. Walking fast, they carried them out and then, under the hanging lifeboat, threw bundle and containers overboard.

"With those sacks slit, the heroin will dissolve fast," he said.

They could neither see nor hear the splash. The big ship, running at fourteen knots, filled the night with its own medley of sound, from the throb of the engine to the wind peeling off the stack.

"Never thought we'd go through our first ten million that fast," he said.

They stood for a moment looking back toward Singapore Strait and the winking lights of vessels plying one of the world's most congested waterways.

"My first time through," Mona said, "and do you think Chrissy would believe I was boarded by pirates? Some baptism. Holy Jesus."

"We survived. For tonight, that's enough."

"Not quite," she said. "I'm too beat for lovemaking, but I'd adore to fall asleep in your arms." She took his hand. "I need it so."

"Who doesn't?"

And as they walked across the deck, he could feel the vibration of the great tanker, hear the wind whistling softly past the struts and see the brilliant tapestry of stars overhead. He felt the warm pressure of his woman's hand and he was content.

Epilogue

Bones Elger, Carlos Quebrada, Takeo Kirihara and eight other yakuza, facing a variety of marine felony charges, were tried by a Singapore high court in the old Supreme Court building on St. Andrew's Road. The high point of the trial came when Kirihara denied that he and the other Japanese were members of Yamaguchi-gumi. With permission of the bewigged justice, the prosecutor made the defendants show their truncated left little fingers, then strip to the waist so the court and spectators might admire the lush tattooing that entwined them like jungle vines. Elger, Quebrada, Kirihara and the others all were sentenced to prison for eleven years.

Bones Elger appeared on the first day of trial minus his left ear. Rumor had it that a yakuza sliced off the ear with a knife on orders from Vice-Commander Toru Higashiyama in Kobe. It was said that Higashiyama ruled that Elger must be punished "in a manner suitable to his personality and career" for his part in the *Zabibian* and *Yandoon Princess* fiascos.

Third Mate Sven Ahlgren was discharged from the *Zabibian* officer complement in Tokyo after Captain Harkinson found him pawing through the bottom drawer of one of her file cabinets. He denied all knowledge of any narcotics hidden there, but raised no complaint when the captain dismissed him with pay, plus a plane ticket home to Sweden.

In Philadelphia a long-delayed Coast Guard Marine Board of Investigation found after an exhaustive hearing that an act of sabotage caused the sinking of the *Yandoon Princess* off the Delaware capes with the resultant flow of oil that smeared 250 miles of the mid-Atlantic shoreline in America's worst pollution disaster.

In later criminal action, thanks to a CIA-assisted investigation by the FBI, Nikos Miaoulis, extradited from Greece, and Jerry Artwick, extradited from England, were convicted of sabotage on the high seas and sent to prison for seventeen years. Prosecutors failed in their effort to link the two men with the Yamaguchi-gumi and Henry Elger. Yukio Osagawa, second engineer on the *Yandoon Princess*, disappeared and Elger, interviewed in Singapore, refused to talk. Nevertheless both American and Asian prosecutors believed that the Singapore and Philadelphia trials destroyed an infant alliance between the yakuza and American marine gangsters aimed at control of crime on the high seas.

An indictment of Jerry Artwick for the murder of Mario Didati was dismissed by a Pennsylvania court for lack of evidence. No one was ever convicted of killing the chief engineer of the *Yandoon Princess*.

Wasif Zabib, with more sorrow than malice, fired his old friend Alexandros Nicias as a Lorikeet captain after he became convinced that Nicias had indeed participated in the conspiracy that sold off the *Gunnison Bay*'s cargo of oil and sank the tanker in the deep Pacific. While Moses & Fabian, the marine investigators, accumulated abundant evidence of the conspiracy, the many nationalities involved, the lapse of time and the failure of any single nation to press the case resulted in no formal charges being brought anywhere. Another obstacle was the refusal of Claude Bouchon of Tahiti and other key persons to testify in public on the allegations they made to Moses & Fabian in private.

Mona Harkinson, now the world's best-known tanker captain, continued her profitable association with Wasif Zabib's Lorikeet Tankers and soon began taking her guitar on voyages. She made the Arabian Gulf-Japan trip through Singapore Strait so often that it became known as her milk run. She also made miscellaneous voyages, carrying crude oil around the world, but always on her favorite ship, the *Zabibian*.

Mitchell Donahey continued as vice-president for chartering of Lorikeet for many years.

He married Mona in Honolulu after their joint court appearance in Singapore. They bought two homes, one a stone mansion in Copenhagen with a view of the Danish capital's harbor and the other in Honolulu on the shore beneath Diamond Head only a few steps away from the apartment where Mitch had lived as a shipbroker. Mona's daughter, Christine, moved in with a French movie actor a year after graduating from Mlle. Jupon's school in Switzerland.

Interviewed on their fifth wedding anniversary, Mona and Mitch told a European television program that they had the best of all possible marriages. "We're apart just long enough to begin pining desperately for each other," she said in her husky voice. "And then," said Mitch, "we're together just long enough to avoid picking at each other."

Thanks

Many people, generous with their time, eased my way into the unfamiliar but quickly engrossing world of tankers, oil and shipbrokers. Of these, I especially want to thank:

Richard H. Innis and former President Randolph Harrison of Poten & Partners, shipbrokers, New York City.

Drew Finley and Captain C. M. Lynch (now retired) of Arco Marine, the tanker arm of Atlantic Richfield Co. Also Captain Robert Lawlor and the officers and crew of the *Arco California,* a tanker on which I traveled from Long Beach, California, to Valdez, Alaska, terminus of the Alaska pipeline, in June 1985.

Ernest Dunbar, Janice Carter and others of Exxon's public affairs department.

Parenthetically, it should be stated that the efficient, well-run tanker fleets of Exxon Shipping Co. and Arco Marine bear no resemblance to that aging marine invalid, *Yandoon Princess,* as described in this book.

Jack G. Knebel, my son, a San Francisco attorney who does considerable work in maritime law.

Ewa E. Wallace, R. S. Platou, shipbrokers, Oslo, Norway.

John H. Bowen and Roy Essoyan of Honolulu, Annette Götzsche of Copenhagen, Denmark, and Stu Glauberman of Singapore.

Officers of the U.S. Coast Guard and of the nation's maritime academies.